THE BREAKING OF LIAM GLASS

Charles Harris is a best-selling non-fiction author and a writer-director who has won international awards for his work in cinema and TV. He lives in Hampstead with his wife. They have two cats, who currently live with them, and two sons who currently don't.

Also by Charles Harris

Police Slang

Teach Yourself: Complete Screenwriting Course

Jaws in Space

CHARLES HARRIS

The Breaking
of
Liam Glass

MARBLE CITY PUBLISHING

Print Edition 2017

Licensed by Marble City Publishing

Copyright © 2017 Charles Harris

ISBN 10 1-908943-82-3

ISBN 13 978-1-908943-82-8

To Elaine

1

Tuesday 8 pm

'Every day's newspaper starts empty of ideas – and some of them stay that way.'

Gareth Whelpower, 'Off-Stone – Memories of a Newspaper Man'

1

The Canyons

It was like they weren't there. Millions of Londoners streamed past the Gordon Road Estates every twenty-four hours, in their cars, buses and trains, but they didn't see them; as if they were invisible, easily ignored. A mixed-up part of town, full of mixed-up people, where nothing much ever happened. Squeezed between the rich glamour of Regent's Park, the neon buzz of central London and the squat seriousness of Euston. High-rise blocks towered over low ones; pensioners scratched along next to smart-casual media consultants; bankers in Reiss suits lived beside teenage gangsters in shades. If you parked your car next to one of the little squares, you didn't know if you were going to come back and find a glossy leaflet for Hatha Yoga under the wipers, or the wheels gone and the car up on bricks.

But something was about to happen tonight.

Liam Glass was waiting angrily in the dark outside his front door on one of the first-floor walkways – shuffling from one foot to another, hunched into his hoodie, waiting, waiting, waiting; waiting for his mum, who was inside, searching endlessly through drawers and bags. He shivered as a dankness rose from the concrete and the road below glistened like fire under the street lights. A Tory election leaflet had been shoved half through their letterbox. He pulled it out and scanned it, frowning in concentration.

Katrina finally arrived with her debit card and a bustle of urgency.

'So as you remember the PIN number,' she said, holding out a scrap of paper. She thought he was still a kid.

He took the card, but not the note with the PIN, and turned away, grumpily.

'You'll forget!' she called. But he was already stomping off down the steps.

Of course, he was just a kid, but not to himself. Tall for his age. Hormones rising. Ready to fight for his place in the world. Down he went, into Gordon Road, down the hard-lit electric canyons like he was in the Wild West. And full of his own thoughts: football matches played and unplayed, Xbox games waiting, friends, Shay Begum and Zen Methercroft, Facebook, Instagram, real girls from school, naked women on websites he thought Katrina didn't know he knew...

He passed Royland Pinkersleigh, who was rhythmically flailing around with a rag and soap suds, swabbing down the wall outside his little gym, All Roads Lead to Royland. Royland flailed faster, trying not to think of all his problems, trying not to think of his partner Sadé in the tiny gym office, wrestling with the accounts. Sadé, who would be only too pleased to remind him about their debts as soon as he went back inside. Royland half glanced at Liam, thought he'd seen him before but couldn't remember where, then applied himself to the rag and bucket once more.

Liam stepped into the road, right in front of Jamila Hasan's green Mini Cooper...

Jamila was distracted, thinking about the art-gallery opening she was already late for – and she the guest of honour as the local councillor. At the last moment, she swerved and missed him. She hooted, but Liam hardly heard above the tick-tick-oomp-oomp of the music playing out of his earphones. She hooted again as she sped away from him, desperately composing the speech she was supposed to be making to the assembled art lovers and local journalists in fifteen minutes' time.

Liam trotted past Jason Crowthorne, chief reporter of the Camden Herald, who hardly noticed him in the dark, saw him and didn't see him, just another hoodie, shoulders hunched, round-faced, ear buds in his ears, staring at the phone in his hand.

An hour before, Jason had turned twenty-nine, but he'd kept it to himself and had merely stolen a Twix from the vending machine in the newsroom. He didn't like sharing personal grief.

Now he locked his car and shivered in the cold April breeze. He turned away from Liam, who was ambling down the road in the other direction.

Didn't see either, as the others hadn't, the two dark shapes following.

Jason took out his own phone to tell his ex he'd be late, then put it away again, unused. He walked fast down a narrow side street, checking the names on the ugly square buildings. It was April 2010 and there was an election going on out there. The whole country was fighting for its future, but the deputy editor had sent him down Gordon Road on the Death Knock. He was supposed to be seeing his ex and his daughter tonight. Bea was the most important person in his life and his most fervent fan, but at ten years old how much longer would she be impressed by his stories of basement disputes and endangered trees?

He hated the Death Knock, still found it upsetting getting stories from the recently bereaved, and should have told Tam, the deputy editor, where to stuff it, an experienced journo like him. The Death Knock was for juniors (and him nominated once for Young Journalist of the Year, though longer ago than he cared to remember). But Tam had no experience, had been promoted above her competence. She wouldn't even have understood. And anyway there was what he'd read in the editor's office earlier in the day – and was trying hard to forget.

He found what he was looking for, a half-glazed door on the ground floor, and gathered his courage to ring the bell.

'You must be Danielle,' he said to the pale face that answered it. The girl was probably in her early teens, with black lipstick and eye make-up and that typical goth softness pretending to be hard. He introduced himself as Jason Crowthorne, senior journalist on the Camden Herald. She grunted and he took a step back. It was a personal technique of his. It took people by surprise and made them feel they were in control. Beyond he could see a dark hallway. Coats were piled up on chairs or folded on the floor and a sad mumble of polite voices came from inside.

'I was sorry to hear about your dad,' he said in his most sympathetic voice. 'I just want to check we have all the facts correct.' In truth what he wanted was a picture and a heart-warming quote. 'I feel for you, Dani. And your poor mum too. Your dad... ripped from both your hearts. By a truck laden with frozen foods.'

She stepped to one side. It never ceased to amaze him how keen people were to share their most personal moments with a strange journalist. Twenty minutes later he found himself back on the damp pavement holding the family's favourite photo of the deceased and a number of unusable quotes about what a drunk, thieving bastard the man had been. He slipped the photo into his pocket and decided to make up some quotes of his own. The Herald's readers didn't want bad news about the departed. Not unless they were celebrities. As he walked back to his car, he opted for 'Overcame personal obstacles' and 'An original approach to business'. These pleased him. Just the right amount of truth without depressing the readers.

Liam Glass walked on through the Estates, their silent walkways and covered passageways glittering with night-time drizzle, and just a few teenagers still mooching in holding patterns in the dark, smoking and selling spliffs, keeping an eye out for members of the wrong crew.

The first cash machine the boy came to was jammed. He stood there, taken aback. Then he bent down and inspected it, as if that would help. It looked scratched; someone had been trying to jemmy into it like a fruit machine perhaps, hoping to hit the jackpot. He'd have liked to have given up and gone home, but his mum would have walloped him. He was hungry and it was a pizza-shaped hunger.

After a few minutes of staring and wondering how to make the machine work he remembered there was another cash machine not far off. It was a few hundred metres down the road, stuck in the side of a newsagent's – or used to be. He hadn't seen it for a few months. He moved on, pleased with himself for remembering, hoping it was still there. He flipped the card to and fro between his fingers like a magician and recited the PIN under his breath, but he didn't spot the shadows still following...

...while, at the other end of Gordon Road, Katrina waited, standing in a yellow square of window on the first floor, looking down into the street for her son. Stubbing out another cigarette. Brushing the hair from her face with anxious hands.

2

Covert Intelligence

Jason sat heavily at his workstation and cast a baleful eye over the lines of deserted computers that stretched across the newsroom, their twirling screen-savers dancing merry patterns for nobody. Through the narrow, dark windows of the Camden Herald flickered the evening lights of Chalk Farm. Two remaining juniors huddled over their keyboards at the far end, their faces pale under the flat light of the fluorescents. None of them should have been working so late on a non-deadline night, but he supposed they were as worried about their jobs as he was.

He dragged his attention back to the computer and tapped out a two-par story about the death-by-frozen-food-truck, but he couldn't stop thinking about what he'd read in the editor's office. He'd been standing by Whelpower's desk, waiting to talk about a campaign he wanted to run on cuts in mental-health care, when he saw a memo from Tam, printed out and sitting on a pile of papers. It was facing the other way, but reading upside-down was one of Jason's most essential journalistic skills. The deputy editor was writing about how to save money on staff, it seemed. One line stood out: experienced journos cost more than juniors. Jason had been re-running the sentence in his head all afternoon, trying and failing to recast its meaning in some positive way.

He glanced at his watch. It was late and he still had to compose captions for some heart-warming photos Tam had fallen in love with. A group of schoolchildren who'd dressed up as hippopotamuses to raise money for a local retirement home. He tried to boost his enthusiasm by doodling with puns. Hippo-hippo hooray. Pachyderm pick-me-up.

He grew distracted by a dim orange glow that filtered out from the editor's office. Gareth Whelpower was also still working – working, but not on the Herald. His shape could be seen in the gloom through the internal window, sifting through piles of desiccated cuttings for his memoirs.

There was no-one who'd taught Jason more when he joined the paper. A lizard-like man from Antrim, Gareth Whelpower was surprisingly tough. He'd exposed councillors and bishops. MPs and royals trembled before him. Working his way up to the Observer from the Belfast Telegraph, his greatest successes included Combustion-gate, tracking a celebrity businessman whose company made cars that caught fire. And Syringe-gate, publicising the suicide of a doctor hounded by the government for exposing misinformation in a dossier on the war on drugs.

Jason knew a mentor when he saw one and he loved the man's passion for the newspaper industry. He insisted on being taught, even when Whelpower told him to piss off, calling him a creep and a sycophant. Jason offered the editor his first carefully crafted articles. Whelpower tore his prose apart. He forced Jason to rewrite. And every time he rewrote, his style grew stronger and Whelpower would tear it apart again.

'What's the story, man?' he'd say. 'Why should I care?'

Jason made sure that Whelpower cared.

'More details,' Whelpower said. 'More precision.

More passion.'

Jason added details, precision, passion.

But local journalism was changing. The Camden Herald was fighting for readers, competing against the Hampstead and Highgate Express and the Camden New Journal. The Herald's owners asked for heart-warming stories about adopted kittens, not difficult issues that might put off advertisers and divide their readership. Whelpower delegated more and more. He shrank visibly and started to look backwards rather than forwards. He set out to write the story of his life. His desk began to fill with piles of old cuttings and trays of congealing Asian takeaway.

Jason wanted to run important campaigns like Whelpower had, on issues such as cuts to disability benefits and fraudulent landlords. He'd gone to him a year before with a list of the number of young men stabbed to death in recent years. 'This is a big story,' he'd said. 'Damian Ross in Tufnell Park last year. Keith Berman in Camden Road. Ahmed Siddiqi after a water-pistol fight at a party. And the councils do nothing. Just close down the police stations and gyms.'

'Old news, isn't it?' said Whelpower, nodding slowly over his cuttings.

'Kids dying.'

'Front page for one day and then forgotten. Go do whatever Tam's told you to do.' And the editor had turned back to his computer screen with a sigh.

Now, as Jason watched from the other side of the newsroom, Whelpower's red-rimmed eyes scanned the stacked papers in his office and then lifted towards him. Jason nodded uncertainly in greeting, wondering if he should ask about the memo. Would Whelpower save his job? But the editor's eyes wavered and dropped to his desk again. Is he deliberately avoiding looking at me? Jason asked himself. Does he know if I'm on the list to be downsized? If I'm going to be dumped, I need to make plans.

He snatched up his mobile.

The first number he tried went straight to voicemail. A bright voice told him his call mattered. He agreed and left a message for them to ignore. The second call also went to voicemail. This one didn't bother to lie.

A narrow shadow fell across his desk.

'Tyronne,' Jason said, without looking. 'What are you still doing here? It's Tam you have to impress, not me.'

Tyronne Brewer stood over him, shifting his balance. He was one of the young journos who'd been recruited by the deputy editor to bring fresh blood and think outside the box. Her head had been colonised by an alien being who'd papered the inside with clichés.

'Tam's gone and handed me the Primrose School arson.'

Jason tossed the phone down. 'The Friday Fire Freak!' The woman was playing games now. This had to be a sign he was on the way out.

'She says I'm ready to rock,' Tyronne said with a quaver of nerves. He was keen, thin as a biro and exuded a permanent air of concern. Which in his case was wholly deserved. Despite this, Jason had a soft spot for him. The kid was likeable and tried hard.

'Does she? Good for you.' Jason spun round twice in his chair. 'A big one,' he said finally. 'A good byline at your age. More grist for the CV. If you don't screw it up.'

'You guess?' Tyronne sucked his teeth. 'Is it true that Tam's making an announcement about downsizing tomorrow? I heard from Yusuf. You didn't know?'

'Of course I knew.' Jason picked up his mobile and jabbed the touch-screen with more force than before. 'Was that all?'

'Totally.' Tyronne ran a hand over his cornrows. Jason waited and Tyronne cracked first. 'She wants more vox pops, doesn't she?'

Jason stared out of the distant windows where cars flickered past like commuting fireflies. He wondered what ordinary people did for emotional torture. 'How many have you found so far?'

'None.'

'That's a starting point.'

'I can't get anyone to say a single word on the record.'

'Sorry, I'm too busy.'

'I didn't ask you for anything.'

'We're agreed, then. Now, if you'll kindly step out of the light.'

'Look...' Tyronne frowned at him, then folded bravely. 'OK, that's OK. I'll manage.'

But now Jason was feeling sorry for him. 'Who are you going to try?'

'I don't know.'

'Give me a few minutes. Then I'll see what I can do,' he said with a sigh, dialling again. The third number answered. Many times, in the next twenty-four hours, he'd wish it hadn't.

3

No Pizza

How long? Ho-o-ow lo-o-o-o-ong can it take you, Liam?
How long, Lia-a-a-a-am? I'm going out of my mind. Out.
Of. My. Mind. How long, Liam-baby?

He'd been gone an hour already and his homework
book on the kitchen table not even touched, and
sometimes Katrina wished she had a man around, but
not that man, not that man for sure, and the pizza man
had been and gone and would have accepted the debit
card himself. She hadn't known. She went out and leant
over the parapet, looked up and down in both directions.

Going out of my mind.

The cashpoint was right there – she could almost see
it. But there was no-one below on Gordon Road under
the street lights, just two Bengali teenagers, one tall, one
short, kicking something small and dark on the ground.
One more time she took her phone from her handbag.

'Yo!' His voice answered bright as ever and she said
'Liam' just in case, but of course it went on, 'Leave that
message, bro!' Like he was black or something. He
always refused to change it. She said, 'Liam, Liam-baby,
this is Mum again. Waiting. Like, the pizza came and
went back, and where the fuck are you?'

Katrina went back to the walkway. The Bengali
teenagers were jumping in and out of the shadows now,
hoods up, larking about, and she called out, 'Hey!' One
of them looked at her and then they both ran off. The
street was silent without them.

She thought about strangling Liam when he got back,

good kid and all. He was mush-brain, except when it came to kicking a ball. Not the brightest shop sign in the High Street.

Liam-baby, where are you? She looked up and down and then stopped in her open doorway and thought of phoning his friends. She'd start with Shay and Zen, she decided, though they'd just had a fight with him about football. But she didn't want to be a stupid mother, making a fuss about nothing. He'd be back in two minutes and asking for his dinner and getting on Facebook. But there was no-one and she felt a chill coming off the walkway. This was mad. She'd rented a DVD of *Avatar* to watch, and she had to iron her blouse for the morning and this wasn't even doing any of it.

She went inside to grab her denim jacket and car keys to go look for him, and then she stopped. Perhaps she should wait in case he came back.

Her stomach felt sour with fear, but she drove to the cashpoint by the bank anyway and he wasn't there. She looked around for those two Paki teenagers too – there was something about them, but they'd disappeared.

So she sat in the car and phoned Liam's mates, all she could think of, Shay and Zen and Kyle that she was sure was into drugs, and Chardonnay who got him to dye his hair purple for a month. When she didn't have the numbers for his friends she phoned their parents, even Mo Patterson, who was a pig and made sarky comments about people who worked in Tesco. But they all said no, shit, no, fuck, no, Shay, Zen, Kyle, Chardonnay, Mo, they hadn't seen Liam at all. Not on a school night. They'd talked to him on Facebook – but that was well over an hour ago.

She came home and when she opened the door she called his name in case he'd come back, but the flat was silent and dark. So she lit a Lambert and Butler and turned on the light in his bedroom, which felt weird, too bright. And she sat at his computer, with all his clothes on the floor and his smell, sticky and male. She felt ill. She posted a message on his Facebook page, for what that was worth, and even tried some girl called Jules who he'd been messaging, but didn't get a reply. Then she thought of phoning 999, but again she didn't want to make a fuss.

She phoned 999.

'I know this is like stupid,' she said, 'but have you arrested a kid called Liam Glass?'

The woman on the 999 asked why she was calling. Katrina said, 'I don't know where my son is.'

The other woman asked how old he was and when she last saw him, and said, 'Most come back in the next twenty-four hours – two hours isn't long at all, Mrs Glass, not for a kid of fourteen, they get up to all kinds of things.'

'I'm sorry,' Katrina said. 'I didn't know who else to call.'

'You should phone the local hospitals. It's worth it. For peace of mind.'

'You think he's in hospital?' Katrina could hardly breathe. The phone, the woman's voice, Liam's clothes on the floor, his unmade bed, it wasn't real. It was like she was in *EastEnders*.

'He's probably fine. But for peace of mind.'

So Katrina went onto Google and wrote down the numbers of the local hospitals and there were six. She didn't want to do this but forced herself to be brave and started with the one that was closest. Her heart was in her mouth, just like in the stories in the magazines. She tried to breathe slower the way the writers always told you in articles about stress. She asked each operator if there was a Liam Glass, fourteen, and each operator told her they didn't have anyone called Liam Glass. She double-checked they'd heard his name right, and they all said they didn't have any fourteen-year-old kids at all, not tonight. And each time she asked if they were sure, and they were sure. Some were friendly, some not.

Then she ran out of hospitals and she didn't usually like taking Valium, but she took one all the same.

4

The Find

It lay glinting in the darkness beside a patch of street dandelions by George III House, one of the larger blocks on the Estates. He was on his way home with Sadé and picked it up without thinking, wondering why someone should have dropped a small knife. It had a muddy handle and the blade looked slightly rusted. When he peered closer, he decided it wasn't rust, or at least it wasn't totally rust. It was blood.

'What have you got there?' said Sadé and Royland showed her. 'What did you pick that up for?'

'It was lying there, innit.'

'So? You just pick up every thing you find? You stand there with a knife in your hand so everyone can see you? Have you got half a brain?'

'No, I don't,' he said. 'I mean—'

'No, you're right first time. You don't have half a brain. Look up.'

Two couples were heading towards them, past the shuttered shops; middle-aged and white and talking nervously. They didn't look like they would react calmly to meeting a man with a knife. He thought quickly and hid it in his pocket.

'What are you doing now!' shrieked Sadé, forgetting herself. She took it down a few decibels. 'Are you mad? Just drop it back where you found it.'

'It's too late,' said Royland. 'They'll see me.'

'It's too late now for sure, boy.'

'What they going to think? They see some big thirty-year-old black man throwing away a great big knife.'

'Which is why you should never have picked it up in the first place. And now you got fingerprints on the thing and blood and everything in your pocket. What you going to do now? Burn your jacket?'

'I don't know,' he said. 'I should take it to the police.'

'You joking, boy? Some big thirty-year-old black man walk into a police station with a knife dripping blood? They'll have you flat on the floor with cuffs on before you can shout Rodney King.'

'OK, OK. Let me think. And it's just a little blood.'

'I see, and that makes a difference.'

He thought of dropping the knife when the street was empty again, but right now it was growing busier. Six noisy twenty-somethings were charging out of a pub, joshing each other. He looked even more suspicious standing doing nothing. He resumed walking.

'Come with me,' he said. 'We'll find somewhere to put it down. Walk normally.'

Royland tried his best to step out as innocently as possible and to ignore Sadé as she marched ahead. He hissed, 'I said, normally.'

Sadé had been in a bad mood since Monday morning when she showed him the gym's draft annual accounts. Nor was her mood improved by the email they'd received sixty minutes later from the council, cancelling a vital youth-group contract in three short lines. She'd hardly said a word for two days. It was unusual and worrying.

The middle-aged foursome had stopped speaking and were stealing sideways looks at him and Sadé as they passed. Royland nodded warmly in greeting and Sadé stared straight ahead. The two white women clutched their handbags more firmly and the two white men gripped their phones.

Sadé muttered, 'You planning to get rid of that thing before Christmas?'

Royland kept his hand in his jacket pocket, holding the knife like he was glued to it, and felt an idiot. But he'd made his play. He turned left down an alleyway between two council buildings. Here he could drop the knife, but at the other end he could see two youngsters hanging around, Bengali kids with hoodies and attitude. They were watching him, doubtless wondering what he was doing, strolling with his girlfriend between the stinking bins and split bags. He put his arm round her and walked past with a bright attempt to whistle a tune that turned into a thin squeak. They turned right. In front of them was Attlee Gardens, closed for the night – and at last the street was empty.

He told Sadé to stand guard while he dumped the knife and she said, 'Go, go, go!'

Heavy music beat out from Scott House, one of the blocks of flats that towered over the little park. Rather good dub on quality bass speakers, Royland was thinking, when Sadé elbowed him in the triceps. He rubbed his upper arm and told her to keep watching out. He gave the hilt a quick clean with a handful of weeds like he'd seen on TV and tossed it over the railings. It fell into a display of tulips a foot beyond. He bent down, wiped his hands and said, 'Shit.'

'What's the problem?' said Sadé.

'They'll never see it there.'

The tulips were close together and the knife was invisible among them.

'Who cares, Denzel?' she said. 'Who needs to see it ever?'

'There may be clues on it that the police will need.'

'What are you now? CSI? It's in the wrong place anyway. And most clues will be from you, most likely.'

'I wiped those off.' Royland poked a stick through the iron railings, but the knife lay too far away for him to reach. He felt sick. This was surely vital evidence in a crime and he, Royland Pinkersleigh, might have ruined any chance of a prosecution. How could he face himself in the morning?

'Sure you did, Denzel.'

'What's this with the Denzel?'

'You're like Denzel Washington in that movie, all heart and bad acting and ready to sacrifice yourself and care nothing about your woman.'

'I care.'

'Sure you do.'

'What movie?'

'I can't remember. It was crap, though. I'm going home. You do that any longer and someone's going to spot you, for sure.'

Sadé gave a snort and stalked off towards home. With a sigh, Royland decided that facing himself was less stressful than facing Sadé, gave up trying to uncover the knife and turned to follow.

5

Good for the CV

All around Jason's workstation lay the last week's newspapers, like piles of autumn leaves. He loved everything about them, from their jumble of pictures and words to their sweet, papery smell. He couldn't bear the thought of never again being a part of this unstoppable flow of news and opinion. The country was going bust and bankers were being rewarded with bonuses. MPs and councillors were nicking the remaining money and being rewarded with reselection. Real reporters were out finding real stories, not bigging up schoolchildren dressed as animals, for a pitiful salary and a hope of future glory.

He waved Tyronne away and watched him bounce across the newsroom as if he'd just won the Pulitzer Prize. Whelpower was still hunched over his unfinished memoir in the slanted orange light of his anglepoise, oblivious to everything in the main office, but then he looked through the internal window and favoured Jason with the slightest of thin smiles. Jason half smiled in return, but his mentor's expression didn't change. Jason suddenly felt something was being demanded of him, but he didn't know what. Instead, he broke eye-contact and turned to his phone.

'What's going down, Andy?' he said. An array of pink and green hippopotamuses danced onto his computer screen. Earlier in the day, he'd found this online game, Angry Hippos, while googling for inspiration for his photo captions. His current nemesis was Iris, a ten-year-old competitor from Dagenham, whose skill in exploding mammals rivalled the big-game hunters of old.

'Hi, Jason. I'm fine. Cheryl's fine. Duane's fine. Thank you for asking.'

'How are you, Andy? How's the family, Andy? Are you at the police station? It sounds very weird in there.' Jason could hear an erratic electronic bleep and a radio playing Bengali hip-hop.

'I'm buying emergency nappies, aren't I? And I'm late into work. The duty inspector will kill me and then Cheryl will kill me more. You're not still working, are you?'

Jason liked Andy. Andy Rockham was a friend. And solid. And his third best contact in the police. 'Not at all. You sound like you need a drink. Friend to friend.'

'And you want a story.'

Jason felt hurt. This was not fair, even if it was right. Friendship demanded a certain degree of dishonesty. 'All the more reason to book in that drink. Call me a covert human intelligence source.'

'I have nothing for you. And do you even still have a job? I heard rumours the Herald is downsizing.'

'I'm fine. No problem.'

'Pleased to hear it. I was worried.'

Jason could hear two people arguing over the sell-by date on a prune yogurt. Meanwhile, a third of his hippos blew up in a myriad of coloured blobs. Iris ratcheted another thousand points on the scoreboard and messaged a suspiciously mature 'Suck on that.'

'Listen, buddy,' he said finally. 'Sling me something I can take to the nationals. My journalistic skills are turning to McFlurry. Tam's asked me to write captions for schoolchildren dressing up as zoo animals to help deprived geriatrics. Do you suppose there are actually people in Camden who like reading that kind of thing, or are we just adding to the suicide rate?'

'It sounds heart-warming.'

'It's this kind of story that gives high-school massacres a good name.' Jason anxiously twirled a rubber band between his fingers. 'What about this big raid I keep hearing about?'

Andy said nothing for a long moment. 'I'm not on any raid, am I? I'm buying nappies. And once I clock in, I'm straight out again.'

'To the raid?'

'No, Jason, to A&E. It's a bollocks job. No interest for you there.'

'Which hospital? What's happening?'

'Down, boy. Wait for the press release.'

'I'm down already, Andy. I'm down so far, I can see the sheep in New Zealand. Give me a hint. A postcode. I can work out the rest for myself.' Jason tried desperately to keep the desperation out of his voice. On the far side of the newsroom, one of the juniors pulled on a brown puffa jacket, ready to leave for the night. 'If you're off to A&E then there's someone in trouble and the nation deserves to hear.'

But DC Rockham just grunted and asked what would happen if he bought nappies that were two sizes too large.

'It doesn't bear imagining. I'll ring you in half an hour.'

'Don't.'

'Then I'll—'

'Listen, Jason. I can't talk to you.'

'Me or any other intelligent, insightful, investigative journalist?'

There was another significant pause.

'Andy?'

'I like you, Jason. You're a good friend, but just now you're off-limits.'

'What?'

'No direct communication. An order from the top.'

'What have I done wrong?'

'Your campaign against the closing of Hampstead police station.'

'Which many other people are also saying—'

'Your piece on a rise in the fear of crime, just as we're cutting the number of coppers out on the streets.'

'My readers have a right to be scared.'

'Articles on unsolved burglaries and car thefts.'

'Come on! What do you want me to do? Cover up the truth? Lie to the readers of the Camden Herald? Pretend your bosses didn't screw up?' Jason sat bolt upright. 'Come on, Andy. You're hiding something!'

But Andy had cut him off. He'd never done that before and Jason stared at the Nokia's display, trying to convince himself that it was an accident or a lost signal. In front of him, five more of his hippopotamuses met their maker.

He picked up his office phone and dialled a number from memory. As he waited, he scribbled a Post-it to himself to ask his ex what she needed for Bea this month. Then he added a reminder to extend his credit limit. He had his dignity. If he was going, he was going to jump, not be pushed. And to jump he needed a good story.

Then he spotted Gareth Whelpower's eyes on him again. The Herald's editor was staring at him, from his office, clutching two pieces of yellowing paper and opening and closing his mouth like a large, pale guppy on the floor of a dimly lit fish-tank. Jason wondered anxiously if these might be his redundancy notices. But they looked too old. Slowly, Whelpower raised a hand.

Before he could respond, an operator came on the line.

'This is Detective Constable Andy Rockham,' said Jason briskly. He explained that he'd sadly been delayed on his way to A&E and wished to confirm the condition of the victim.

The hospital operator passed him on to A&E and A&E checked their trolleys thoroughly. They were sorry to disappoint DC Rockham, but they had no appropriate victims in stock. Jason expressed surprise, but they remained adamant.

He dialled a second hospital. They took an age to answer.

'Hello, this is DC Rockham phoning from Kentish Town police station,' he said when they finally bothered to pick up.

An email pinged. Where's my hippo story?

Jason regarded it with disdain. Tam must be logged on at home. He refused to be impressed by this display of night-time commitment from the deputy editor, but no doubt it warmed the hearts of the Herald's owners.

A second email arrived. From a Mrs Weston about a journalist who'd harassed her family this evening at her husband's wake. He deleted it. Next to his elbow, his Nokia gave a plaintive bleep. Tam had also received the complaint.

It soon transpired that the second and third hospitals were not expecting the police either.

Whelpower seemed to have given up waiting for him and was resting his head on his desk between the trays of Thai green curry. He looked unnervingly motionless, but Jason didn't have time to deal with this. He rang a fourth hospital.

'This is DC Rockham,' he began.

6

Moon-Face

She almost didn't notice the police tape in the darkness – donotcross donotcross donotcross – fluttering blue and white, like pennants belonging to an invading army. It was late and Jamila was tired after the art gallery opening; too many drinks, too many people who thought she could solve their problems. They seemed to believe that every councillor had the leader of the council on speed-dial. Her speech had gone well, though, she thought. Her support for Gordon Brown's help for the arts got applause. Her impromptu joke about David Cameron's Eton schooldays got a small laugh (she'd better check it actually was Eton he went to, not the other one). She'd managed a subtle reminder to vote for her in May. Problem was, as everyone in the room knew, the polls were down another three per cent this week. The whole country hated politicians in 2010, and it seemed they hated Labour most of all, though it wasn't Jamila's fault. Here in Camden her local party were in opposition to a Con-Lib coalition, but the voters didn't care. They still blamed her for what the government did. Any councillor with a majority as small as Jamila's was in danger.

She pulled her Mini Cooper over to the side of the road and stopped. Two policemen were guarding the space, a small square with a stone seat and a little tree and not much else. She checked her phone. There'd been no email from the council or police, and councillors were normally told if something important had happened in their ward.

She started to open the car door to go and speak to the policemen, who'd been studiously ignoring her. Then she remembered the alcohol on her breath and rapidly closed the door again. The nearest policeman looked over suspiciously now – he was short and almost as dark as her. She avoided his eye and scanned her phone messages, as if that was what she'd wanted to do all along.

Whatever had happened here probably wasn't very urgent or significant. A car accident or a fight. It could wait till the morning. Jamila glanced quickly across. The policeman seemed to have found something else to watch, so she started her car again and drove off with considerable care.

During daylight hours, Camden General's grim concrete cladding had all the allure of an abandoned gun emplacement. By night, the concrete disappeared into shadow and its bright windows shone enticingly. They said: here people get cured.

Jason sped past urgently in his tiny Renault and wrenched the car into a half-space on a nearby corner, two wheels on the pavement. He contemplated his available options. Hospital staff had grown all too cynical where the press was concerned. It was a dreadful reflection on modern life that medical professionals wouldn't divulge private details of their patients' lives without significant reimbursement. He reached under the passenger seat and tugged out a bottle of Laphroaig, then scavenged the car for a bag to put it in. There was only one: bright lilac with pink and yellow flowers, but it would have to do. Drinkers couldn't be choosers.

Jogging towards the hospital, he texted Tyronne with

the numbers of a teacher and a fireman. These will solve your problem, he wrote. They'll give you good, anonymous quotes. But don't, on any account, let anyone know their names, especially Tam. Then he phoned Josette.

'I'm sorry,' he said. 'I know I promised. One more thing and I'll be there.'

But his ex sounded surprisingly understanding. 'Happy birthday. Almost to the minute, in fact.'

'Two hours ago. But, really, I hardly think about such things.' He ran across the main road, avoiding a 168 bus as it reared up out of the night.

'Twenty-nine, eh! Hold on, Bea's dragging the phone out of my hand.'

Bea came on the line and the moment he heard her voice he felt happier.

'I baked you a special cake. Chocolate with extra icing, and raspberry jam inside.' When she did something, she didn't hold back. He loved her for it.

'All by yourself?'

'Arthur was supposed to be supervising. But he went to bed early.' Arthur was Josette's new partner and tired easily. 'When will you be here?'

'Very soon. I need to find out about a story, sweetheart.'

'Important.'

'Very. Top secret.'

'What do you have to find out?'

'Whether it's a story.' He turned into the hospital forecourt and walked briskly into A&E. His daughter was silent for a moment.

'I don't know if I'll be allowed to stay up longer,' she said, and Jason felt dreadful.

'I will be there when I can,' he said. 'Promise.' The

A&E receptionist glanced up and immediately reached for a phone to call security. He reversed out of sight and selected another corridor. 'Let me speak to Mum.'

Josette returned and insisted it was all right, they all understood the constraints of his job.

'Can she stay up a bit more? Till I get there.'

'It's a school day tomorrow.'

'Just this once.'

'Just this once.' Her voice grew huskier. 'And we need to talk. But it's not urgent. Any time.'

Jason promised to be there within the hour. For a moment, after ringing off, he felt strangely empty. He should be with his little girl. But then his spirits rose again. They always did when he was following a story. A story took his mind off all his other problems.

It always surprised Jason that some people hated hospitals. He thrived in them, striding the wards in search of victims and perpetrators. Sometimes he wore a white coat to smooth his way. And even when patients realised he was a journalist, they still often wanted to speak out, believing that three column inches on page nine might well inspire a hospital to spend more on their treatment. He was press power made flesh.

So it was with confidence that Jason now worked his way through a succession of lonely basement corridors to reach the far side of Radiology. Here he was spotted by two security guards talking over cups of coffee. Doubling back, he veered round the morgue and slalomed past Medical Records – where there were no guards. A minute later, he entered A&E from the rear, through Resuscitation.

There was a gentle, dislocated feel to the A&E ward – isolated from the world outside yet crammed with its broken people, sitting or lying in cubicles. Outside one cubicle sat a uniformed policeman, straight-backed, surreptitiously reading from a neatly folded copy of Heat ('Katie Price: She Never Thinks about Peter'). But beyond him stood Andy. And his friend was not looking pleased with life.

This was not good news. Jason stepped rapidly into the nearest cubicle and closed the curtain. A woman lay on a bed, clutching her arm, and gazed at him in surprise. He nodded to her and she whimpered something half audible.

'You'll be fine,' Jason said with a warm smile and pulled the curtain open an inch. Andy was attempting to pacify a blood-stained Chinese chef and his angry wife. Jason's journalistic nose twitched. He decided to take a chance and strode back out again, brandishing the lilac and yellow bag. 'For Detective Constable Rockham,' he said to the uniformed policeman with a confident nod. A confident nod, he'd found, deflected many an awkward question. He took a step past.

At this point things started to go awry. First, his arm found itself folding back in an unusual manner. Next, the hospital revolved in a way that hospitals normally didn't.

'Nice to be welcomed,' said Jason, his voice muffled by a grey partition that now pressed against his face. He'd encountered PC Throwbart before – one of the older constables and an amateur martial artist. He could have gained, Jason felt, from working on his social skills.

Andy came over. 'What the fuck are you doing here, Jason?'

'You said you'd be in A&E.'

'I didn't say which one.'

'OK, you got me bang to rights. I've planted a GPS tracker in your boxer shorts. I thought I might pick up some scandal. You know, this partition is rather hard.'

'Not a good choice of boxer shorts if it's scandal you're looking for.' Andy inspected the contents of the lilac bag thoughtfully and suggested that PC Throwbart might leave off the ju-jitsu.

'Are you sure, sir?' Throwbart released his grip with reluctance and sat down again, slowly taking up his magazine once more ('Paris Hilton: I Am Really a Shy Person').

Andy Rockham reassured the hospital staff that the ward was not under terrorist attack. Jason waggled his jaw and attempted to straighten his neck.

'Maybe you need more adventure, Andy. I could fix you up. I know some randy nurses. I could give your undergarments an introduction.'

'My undergarments are spoken for, thank you. As is my drinking time.' Andy handed back the bottle and pushed his hands deep into his pockets – rather a defensive posture, Jason felt, with which to greet an old friend. 'You can't stay here.'

'Hey, Andy. This is me. Not some rookie. You remember the Buckfast Road front-page air-gun appeal? That was a great campaign, wasn't it? And the mugger with the mullet! We work well together. We're a team.'

'Yes. Well, that's over now, isn't it?'

'For writing about a couple of bungled burglary investigations and some cutbacks? The borough commander isn't against free speech, is he?' Andy's silence suggested this might indeed be the case. 'Andy, don't make me beg. I'm on the down escalator to journalism hell. Is this it?' He pointed the Laphroaig towards the chef and his wife. They'd stopped arguing and were now hugging each other in tears.

'This is nothing. I told you. A minor domestic. He

drinks. She hits him with a wok. They're in here once a month.' Andy gestured towards the exit.

Maybe he's right, Jason thought, subsiding. Sometimes the universe is not on your side. He turned to walk away. As he did, a doctor came out of the next cubicle. He shot a wary look towards them and departed at speed, but not before informing Andy he was ordering fresh tests for the unknown male.

Jason stopped. 'Unknown male?'

'We're sorting it out.'

A quiet bleeping came from the second cubicle and Jason squinted in. A young man lay unconscious, hooked up to a web of oxygen tubes, drips and monitors. He didn't look in a happy state. 'Who got it this time?'

'We don't know. That's why we call him an unknown male, Jason. The clue is in the name.'

There was something poignant about the motionless shape. Something Jason couldn't quite pull into focus. 'How old?'

'Try cutting him in half and counting the rings.'

'You must have had a guess.'

'We're estimating eighteen to twenty-two.'

Jason twisted his head for a better view. 'Does he look familiar to you?'

'No.'

'The young bloke in the gold lamé dress who couldn't sing.'

Andy was quite certain that he wasn't the *Britain's Got No Talent* finalist Jason was thinking of. And since the unknown male had presented with no credit cards, no driving licence and no mobile phone, they were unlikely to find out any more at the current time.

'Shame. So what happened? Where?'

'Forget it. There's nothing you can use till we've

talked to his next-of-kin.'

'How do you talk to his next-of-kin if you don't know who he is?'

Andy was clenching and unclenching his fists, which Jason did not feel was a good sign.

'Trust me, Andy. I'm a journalist.'

'That's what worries me.'

Jason considered defending his profession, but instead he peered again at the body. Flat, pale moon-shaped face. Oxygen pumping into him through a mask. Fluids trickling down from a cluster of drip-bags. He was hardly more than a mass of medical despair. With a shudder, Jason briefly considered what it must be like to have everything stolen from you. Your name, your past, your future. He couldn't imagine how he'd feel if that was Bea lying there, unconscious and hardly alive.

'Poor bugger,' he said, with a stirring of compassion. He pushed it away and tugged out his pocket camera. 'Let's sling his picture up on the website,' he suggested. 'A reader might recognise him.'

'No hope.'

Andy and Throwbart were watching him, arms crossed. He looked again at the motionless body. Still, there was something about the young man. Something Jason couldn't quite grasp. 'Run over? Heart attack?'

Andy shook his head.

'Come on, I'm not going to post it on WikiLeaks.'

'Stabbed and probably mugged.'

'Another one.'

'Just another local mugging. And you're to write nothing about it till we say.'

Jason felt depressed – and angry at himself. Andy was right. There was no big national story here. He'd have been better off eating birthday cake with his daughter and waiting for tomorrow's press release. Again he started to move away. But a half-formed thought pulled him back. 'OK. But I think you're wrong,' he said.

'Fuck off, Jason. You don't publish until I say.'

'No, I mean his age.' A new nurse entered the cubicle and inspected the monitors and Jason quickly took a close-up of the victim while Andy was distracted. 'He looks younger. More early teens.'

'Just leave it,' Andy said.

'Andy, I've seen kids today. Some of them are massive. There was this piece I did...'

He stopped. It took a moment for him to realise what he was realising and then his pulse began to speed up.

'Go on,' said Andy.

'Go on, what?' He adjusted the sleeve of his jacket. That blonde hair. That face. Though of course it wasn't so pale before.

'You were saying.'

'Oh, nothing,' said Jason. He turned to the nurse. 'How do you normally work out their ages?'

'Normally we ask them.' She wrote down a reading and left.

'You were talking about a story you wrote.' Andy was staring at him suspiciously now. As was Throwbart.

'I'm not allowed to talk to you. That's what you told me. We're not supposed to communicate. I'm no longer your confidential human intelligence source.'

Andy flushed red with anger. 'Sir?' said Throwbart, standing up and flexing his arms hopefully.

Jason looked again at the face under the oxygen mask. He was probably wrong. Kids changed so fast. He turned before Andy could reply and walked rapidly towards the exit. Behind him, he heard the blood-spattered Chinese chef emerge from the other cubicle, complaining loudly, while his wife followed, eagerly listing his moral flaws.

7

Fact Checking

Jason lived in Gospel Oak, only a short distance away. He was an aggressive driver at the best of times and he was pumped up. As a result, he reached his home rather quickly.

Home was a small studio flat in an old conversion; four very basic rooms reached by a fire escape. Jason ran up the steps, slammed the front door shut behind him. Then he pulled out his camera and looked again at the picture of the kid under the oxygen mask. He had a nose for stories, a good one. Maybe it hadn't been twitching much recently, but he knew what worked and what didn't.

Two years ago Jason had written a piece about a young kid of about twelve, called Ryan or Leon or Leo, he couldn't remember exactly. He wasn't the brightest pixel on the monitor, but he had one thing that the world wanted: he could kick a ball. And he was tall for his age. So he'd been spotted playing for his school and talent scouted by Chelsea. It was a nice story to write on a quiet week. The kid provided a few predictable quotes he must have learnt off *Match of the Day*. The mother dug out pictures of her boy breaking records scoring goals for his school and standing in a Chelsea kit looking uncertain yet proud.

There'd been just one slightly frustrating aspect to the story. Jason had struck up a decent rapport with the mother, who had a bit of zest, pretty if a bit plump. And at one point, between slagging off her fellow workers at

Tesco's, she let slip something about the boy's father. It seemed she used to go clubbing when she was younger and got friendly with a few local Premiership footballers. More than friendly. She never quite said, but the implication was clear.

Jason had immediately tried to follow this up. A Premiership dad would have lifted the story to a new level, but the woman refused to say any more. He tried every trick he knew, but she was immovable. He dug out a few of her friends, but nobody seemed to know much about her past. One fellow cashier at Tesco's seemed to think she might have lived in Stepney once or possibly Charlton. But then the leads dried up.

And that was it. Jason had too many other articles to write to spend any longer on a vague hunch. He succeeded in filling a half-page with blather and thought no more of it. Until now.

Because the face under the oxygen mask looked remarkably like the kid, and – this was the key point – while your average comatose teenager would go nowhere, a comatose teenager with a grieving Premiership footballer father was tabloid news.

Jason felt hot. He threw off his jacket and turned on the laptop that sat on his dining table. Next to it lay a folder stuffed with cuttings and notes on all the stabbings he'd covered. Too many innocent kids in the wrong place at the wrong time. One teenager knifed to death after an argument on Facebook. Another, because he'd hidden a friend's scooter seat as a joke. A scooter seat! The most recent was Keith Berman. The kid's photo stared out from the centre of the page, a snap taken by his mother in the family garden just two weeks before he was killed. Keith had been in a bar celebrating the end of his mock GCSEs with his friend Matt when a twenty-

year-old, Alan Wilmington, decided Matt had been
looking at him oddly. The two of them got into an
argument, but Keith kept out of it. When Wilmington
drew a knife, Matt ran away, but Keith thought he was
safe, because he hadn't got involved. Two witnesses told
Jason how Keith was cornered by Wilmington and three
other men outside the bar and stabbed eleven times in
five seconds. For being a friend of someone who'd
looked at another person the wrong way.

You couldn't make it up. Gareth Whelpower was
right about details. 'A good detail is the match that lights
the story,' he'd said, buying Jason a pint after he covered
the court case. It was the details in Keith Berman's death
that made Jason want to cry with anger. But he wasn't
going to change the world from the soggy platform of
the middle pages of the Camden Herald. 'Front page for
a day, then forgotten,' Whelpower had said. It had been
true of Keith Berman, true of all of them. He needed to
get more than five column inches in the nationals and
the only way to make the nationals take notice was if
there was a celebrity involved.

He had that dizzy feeling he rarely experienced and
often dreamt of. He might have the makings of a splash.
He tried to control his emotions. He didn't want to get
over-excited. He tried not to visualise a double-page
spread under his name on pages eight to nine of the
Mirror, the Mail or the Post. His photos of the boy in
Intensive Care ('a talent cut down before his prime'). His
personal interview with the father ('talented, charismatic,
grieving') and mother ('attractive, devoted, distraught').
His byline: 'An exclusive by Jason Crowthorne.'
'Tragedy of a Future Footballing Star.' 'The Talent of
England Laid Waste.' Most of all, his campaign: Fight the
Knife. A campaign that would take Fleet Street by

storm, change the face of the nation, change the law, even.

But he was getting ahead of himself. Maybe it wasn't the same boy at all. He was torn. Part of him wanted it to be, and another part was horrified at the thought. He needed to be quick. He had to find the article to check his memory wasn't fooling him and then his notebook, with the mother's phone number and address. The laptop was taking an age to start. Finally it settled down. He composed himself and logged onto the Herald's staff intranet. There was his work screen again, as smug as a second-rate deputy editor, with his awful attempts at hippo puns as he'd left them. He clicked to move on, but the site froze.

The article he wanted was somewhere inside the newspaper's stupid archive and right now it was refusing to give anything up, holding onto its secrets like a bad-tempered child. He picked up the laptop and shook it. But the little laptop didn't like that at all and came up with some kind of blue screen and a peeved error message, which at least was a reaction of sorts. But now he couldn't get any of the keys to respond.

Jason screamed in frustration and flung himself into a chair. He took a deep breath and went back to the laptop which had decided to take its revenge by checking its hard disk, counting its millions of sectors, like a pedantic bureaucrat, immovable and self-satisfied.

Jason decided life was too short. He could try googling on his phone, but the Herald's site was obviously down and anyway he couldn't remember the kid's name or the mother's. He left the computer to enjoy its technological huff and half walked, half ran into Bea's tiny bedroom, which doubled as his storeroom and archive.

He could smell the residual aroma of his daughter's talcum powder, that reminder of the childish innocence that he loved about her. He'd taken the flat after the divorce (although he could hardly afford the rent) mainly because it had a room just big enough for a visiting four-year-old to stay in. Bea was the most important thing in his life. He had brought her here when he first saw the place, for her approval, and she'd sat on a little wooden stool, very seriously, looked around her and pronounced it good. In the six years that followed, he'd played and read to her here – on alternate weekends. They'd progressed from Snap to PlayStation and from Cinderella to Aung San Suu Kyi. He shared his plans to write important stories that would change the world, and she put her arms round him and said he was her best hero. He'd nursed her through a twenty-four-hour tummy bug, hugging her and giving her hourly sips of hot lemon water. He could still see her pale face looking up at him from the pillow, asking if this was what Joan of Arc had had to go through. And when she finally fell asleep, he'd checked hourly to make sure she was still alive. Now she was approaching her teens and he wasn't sure how to do it anymore. How to be the best father.

He knelt down by the bed, feeling strangely as if he was saying his prayers, and started pulling out the boxes of cuttings he kept underneath it. His filing system was thorough if idiosyncratic. The first box contained all the stories by journalists he prized and tried to emulate. Harold Evans and Phillip Knightley on thalidomide, Murray Sayle on Kim Philby, Gareth Whelpower on Thatcher, Blair and the City of London. He particularly loved the series of articles in which his mentor had hunted down Sir Max Robertson, tracking how he'd stolen from the pension funds of companies he owned, condemning many of their former workers to a miserable retirement. Step by step, over the months, Whelpower had closed the net, facing down libel writs until Sir Max was left blustering in court but exposed.

In the next box were stored those of his own articles that he felt most angry about: recent attempts at campaigns that he'd started with enthusiasm, only to have them stopped by the deputy editor for not being heart-warming enough. Finally, at the back were two A4 cardboard boxes where he'd stored his earlier pieces. Not all of them. Josette loved recycling and one awful winter had persuaded him to throw armfuls of cuttings into the recycling bag. That was shortly before she went the whole distance and recycled herself into the arms of the redoubtable Arthur.

Jason pulled out the nearest. It was full of dusty Christmas decorations, twisted tinsel, torn paper chains, a string of tree lights without a plug. What on earth were they doing there? He was sweating now. His panic turned into doubt. It was getting late. Maybe he was wrong to even consider waking the mother, who he hadn't spoken to for two years and who was probably asleep by now. Did he have the right contacts to push this story forwards in any case? And was this a story after all? He'd got it wrong so many times in the past, was he just getting it wrong again? He doubted everything: his instincts for a good story, his ability to write it and sell it to a busy news editor. Now his mood slipped into a deep sense of futility.

He tossed the decorations to one side, only to uncover student writings and clippings from early jobs that he could barely recall. Work he'd been so enthusiastic about, fresh and innocent as he was, and so sure that Fleet Street was just waiting for him to reveal his supreme talent. It was painful to look at them.

He tore the sellotape off the last box with no great hope. And then there it was, the first cutting. Filed totally in the wrong place. There was the boy standing petrified, in all blue. Liam Glass. Just as he'd looked an hour ago in A&E.

A feeling of triumph swept over him. He felt like punching the air. His doubts were forgotten. And still there was a part of him that didn't want it to be. Jason had got on well with the kid. The boy had done what he was asked with a certain lumpish patience: posed for the pictures, shown off his Cruyff Turns, answered Jason's questions with dogged resignation and no expectation of a reward.

At the bottom of the box lay a dozen of his spiral-bound notebooks, carefully dated, and the date of the cutting led him to the right page. Here he'd written a phone number, an address – a flat on the Gordon Road Estates – and the mother's name, Katrina. He checked his watch again. It was long past eleven, but this had to be done now. He felt the excitement rising. The story was on.

8

Night Desk

Some time in the cruel hour around midnight, when husbands murdered wives and armies secretly prepared for dawn invasions, the night news editor on the Post was scrolling down the PA feeds with a satisfying sense of despair. The world was doomed, but there was nothing he urgently had to do about it. The government was heading rapidly down the pan, but nobody much cared about that, unless it involved money or sex. Local elections were drivelling on, but nobody much cared about them either – even when they did involve money or sex. A nuclear power station was leaking, but the owners had slapped on an injunction to stop the papers telling the public. Meanwhile, a minor royal had been YouTubed doing bondage with a no-talent from The X Factor. All very depressing.

Through the windows of the vast open-plan office he could see the darkness of London, splashed with brilliant lights where abandoned City offices teemed with Romanian cleaners – and above: black nothingness. Not exactly black of course, as no sky was ever fully black in London, but a curry-like yellow-brown.

It was fully six hours since he'd taken over from Lyle Marchmont, the daytime news editor, and at least another two and a half until he could go home to bed. The night news editor yawned and decided that now was probably a good time to hit the cappuccino machine, thus ensuring he was away from his desk for at least twelve minutes. He stood up. And immediately his desk phone rang. He looked down his nose at the handset as if it had personally insulted him and he let it ring six times, willing it to stop. On the seventh he snatched it up and said, 'Aye. Dalgleish.'

'Tom,' said a voice enthusiastically. 'It's Jason Crowthorne.'

Dalgleish vaguely remembered Crowthorne doing work for the Post from time to time but wasn't going to admit it too readily. He gave a non-committal grunt.

'From the Camden Herald, chief reporter and senior crime correspondent. Sorry I haven't been in touch recently, but I've been ridiculously busy on some great stories.'

'Camden Herald, aye? I'd heard talk they were downsizing...'

'Not a problem. Everything under control.'

'Good. Youse no supposed to be in shifting with us tonight?' said Dalgleish, knowing he wasn't.

'Not tonight...' There was a pause at the other end. 'I was just wondering if you'd filled that job yet.'

'What job would that be, then?'

'I heard about Charlie. Sad way to go. Flashing that old lady. He was always so good at doorstepping. And friendly. He used to advise me about—'

'You've phoned me tonight about Charlie's old job?' Dalgleish glanced at his watch incredulously.

'No... Yes... Kind of. I've got a story you'll love.'

The night news editor didn't reply.

'Fourteen-year-old kid stabbed.'

Still Tom Dalgleish didn't speak but looked wistfully towards the kitchens in the hope of reaching the cappuccino machine before a shifter could come over and interrupt him.

'Promising footballer. He was on trial with Chelsea

and now he's in a coma at the Camden General. I've got photos.'

'Of him being sliced up?'

'Of him two years ago, wearing Chelsea kit. I did a piece about him here.'

'It's no quite the same thing.'

At the other end, Jason was locking his front door. He infused his voice with an urgent tone of professional confidence. 'He might die.'

'Soon?'

'I don't know.' Jason paused on the fire escape and contemplated ways he could find that out.

'Get back to us when he has.'

Jason scoured his brain as he ran downstairs and crossed the road. 'He's a good kid...'

'Good kid? Doing well at school? A great career ahead of him, everybody loves him, could be playing for England, nae bad word said about the lad?'

'Well...'

'The victims always are. It doesnae help. We went off-stone at ten. The paper's locked and I'm nae changing it just for a stabbing.'

'I'm not asking you to change the paper,' said Jason, speedily refining his angle of attack. 'This is for tomorrow. And the day after tomorrow. And next week. Exclusive with the family. A big campaign against stabbings,' he continued with passion. 'Like Charlie used to run. "The Post Against the Terror Of the Knife". "How Much More Young Blood Will It Take?" "Chopped Children". "Sliced Youth".'

'"Sliced Youth"?'

'Well, something like that. I could have taken it to the Mirror, Sun or Express, but I wanted to come to you first.'

'Go to them. Nae hard feelings. Though you'll hae a tough job.' Dalgleish sounded as if he was about to put the phone down. Jason tasted the sour tang of failure once more. Was it him? Maybe success was the bullet that didn't have his name on it. But tonight he refused to give in. Not on the night of his birthday.

'There could be something else.'

There was a long pause at the other end. Dalgleish counted to five and was about to begin a less than polite sign-off.

'I can get you the mother. Exclusive,' said Jason, playing for time in the hope that the truth might catch up with his mouth.

'What about her?'

'She's a single mother.'

'I'm shocked. I—'

'The tragedy of her life. Broken Britain. Singles fun to grieving mum in two decades.' Jason was machine-gunning wildly now but he couldn't stop himself.

'Very sad. Our readers have got their own problems. They don't give a fuck. A stabbed boy might do for your local, but this is the national press here. We need more than this to break a story. Ye understand. Like if the father's a footballer too...'

There was a long pause.

'Is he?' said Dalgleish, sounding more perky than he had the whole conversation.

Jason waved a hand at the empty air. He'd hoped to avoid committing himself before he'd spoken to Katrina Glass. 'I couldn't exactly say that.'

'What could you say?'

He reached his car, parked in a disabled parking bay.

'The father is a well-known player or no?'

'I'm saying...' What was he saying? 'I wrote the piece

two years ago...'

'Go on.'

He searched his memory. What had the mother actually said? Jason found he was trembling. 'She used to go clubbing with high-profile players.'

'Used to?'

'Fifteen years ago. Before the boy was born.'

'I may be interested,' said Tom Dalgleish now. He thought of saying more but decided it would only encourage the man. There was still a clear route to the coffee machine, but he could see stirring – one young sub-editor was about to come over and speak to him, so he needed to move fast.

Jason felt his excitement grow in parallel with a sharp sense that he was projecting himself off the edge of a rather steep cliff. The night news editor had shown interest. But Jason didn't have the boy's father or a hint of him. He didn't even have the mother yet. He was flushing hot and cold. He started the car – it juddered, stalled and then started again.

'The exclusive's not about the father, exactly, Tom.'

'You're saying his father was a big star footballing cunt.'

'Kind of... Not really... But let's reframe that thought...' A police siren wailed in the distance. He needed to speak to the mother fast. 'But, Tom, the real story is surely the boy, isn't it?' He dropped his voice to a whisper. 'Lying in a coma. A glittering career cut short in its prime. A major campaign to save young lives. I mean, absent fathers are two-a-penny. But this poor kid...'

Dalgleish returned, his voice equally low. 'You know, you're right. This could be a big splash, Jason. This could be the making of you as a journalist. Child in a coma, grieving mother, the terror of knives—'

'Exactly. And—'

Dalgleish's voice suddenly rose. '— and the bastard's fucking father. I thought you were a professional. Or do you never fucking want to work with the Post again?'

The line went dead.

9

The Mother

The entryphone rang in the night and she thought hazily, that's all I need. She picked it up and said, 'For fuck's sake, what the fuck? Did you leave your fucking keys behind? That's all I needed. I'll give you fucking keys.' And pressed the button. Then she went back to the bedroom, grabbed herself a blanket and made her way back to the door, wrapping it round her nightie for warmth, feeling like she'd been smashed on the head, her brain thick and slow. There was someone outside, but it wasn't Liam. He was crouched down, peering through the letterbox; she could see his misshape through the bobble-glass.

'Mrs Glass?' called the blob.

'Ms Glass,' she said. Sharply.

'It's Jason Crowthorne,' he shouted from the other side. 'From the Camden Herald. I'm sorry to come round so late.'

Her throat tightened. She didn't want to answer.

He poked some old piece of newspaper through the flap. 'I wrote about Liam. Two years ago, when he had a trial at Stamford Bridge. Bottom of the page with pull-quotes and photos of him in Chelsea kit and shaking hands with John Terry. You remember?'

She tugged open the door and found his face at the level of her groin. He gave an embarrassed grin and jumped up, but before he could speak, her stomach clenched and her arms and legs felt like they were paper. They could hardly hold her.

*

The hospital reception had that hard-lit depression of the middle of the night. The few people around needed to be there for serious reasons: a wan teenager on crutches, a thin old woman, rigid in a dressing gown, staring through the blank windows.

The reporter fiddled with a crumpled black notebook as they waited. 'Do you want me to contact anyone?'

'No-one.'

'His father?'

'He doesn't have a father,' she said firmly.

He didn't seem to like this. He tapped his biro on a page. 'I thought... Two years ago, you said something...'

'What business is it of yours, then?' A bit louder than she'd meant.

Then there was this other one who came out of the lift. He introduced himself as Detective Constable Rockham and was about her age, maybe a bit younger. He frowned a lot and kept his voice low, as if he didn't want to frighten her, and there was a policewoman with him who kept trying to smile to keep her calm. Katrina was doing her best to stay calm. What was freaking her out was all of them trying to keep her calm.

'This is Katrina Glass,' said the reporter. 'The boy's mother.'

'That's yet to be ascertained, Jason.' The detective glared at him and then said sorry to Katrina, this was not the usual way they did things.

'Maybe not, Andy,' said Jason, 'when journalists and police trust each other to do their jobs.'

The detective bit his lip, looked like he wanted to say something different and then asked Katrina again if she was all right.

'Just show me my son.'

He apologised again for any confusion and asked if she could show him any proof of identity.

'For fuck's sake,' said Jason. 'She's the kid's mother.' He waved the cutting at him, but Andy hardly glanced at it.

Katrina had been poking around inside her handbag. 'I don't know,' she said. She jerked her head towards Jason. 'He just came and told me to come to the hospital as quickly as possible. I don't have my debit card. Liam had it.' She bit her lip and brought out her Tesco staff ID and asked if that would do. 'Just show me my son,' she said again, her voice sounding odd, hoarse, out of her control.

'I can vouch for her,' said Jason.

But Andy can't have heard, because he didn't answer him. 'We're not sure if it is your son, Miss Glass,' he said, indicating the lift with a shake of his head. 'Dana?'

The policewoman held the doors open for her. Jason tried to follow, but Andy blocked him with a hand. 'Just Miss Glass.'

'This is my story, Andy,' Jason said. 'I've found your unknown male's mother for you.'

'If it's him,' said Andy. He sounded angry.

'Listen.' Jason put his arm round the policeman's shoulders in a warm and friendly way and dropped his voice so Katrina, waiting in the lift, could hardly hear it. 'If it's him, I'll tell her story, exclusive. The start of a big campaign to stop bloodshed in the streets. I'll make you the hero.'

'I don't want to be a hero. I want to be employed.'

The journalist took his arm back. 'You're making a big mistake.' But, mistake or not, the lift doors were already closing and he was left firmly behind.

They opened again on the fifth floor and the

policewoman led Katrina into a room, where there was a nurse, standing next to this body in a bed with drips and monitors. Her heart jumped and she knew, even before she saw his hair and his face through the see-through part of the oxygen mask.

She couldn't speak at first. She nodded and then she started crying and dug for a Kleenex in her handbag.

'Is he going to be OK?' she said finally.

'He's asleep,' the nurse said. 'He's not in pain.'

'When will he wake up?'

'I'll get the doctor. He can tell you more.'

'Just tell me what's going to happen with my son,' Katrina said.

The nurse handed her a tissue and Katrina wiped her eyes and blew her nose and a second nurse arrived and repeated that the doctor would tell her more. The doctor came just a few minutes later. He was an African, short and stocky, not a West Indian. Katrina knew the accent from Dadir who worked in the deli section at Tesco's.

'He's been stabbed,' the doctor said. 'He's lost a lot of blood. We'll know a lot more when he wakes up.'

Katrina felt like she was dying. 'When will that be? Soon?'

'We don't know. When he's ready. Sleep is good for him right now.' He looked like he was going to say something more, but instead he said he'd be checking on Liam frequently and he left.

After the doctor had gone, the detective called Andy said, 'I have to ask you some questions. I'm sorry I have to do this now, Katrina, but we want to find out what happened.'

She tried to be strong, for Liam. 'He's a good kid,' she went. 'He had a few fights when he was younger, but he's better now. He's been getting better marks at school and everything.'

The policewoman led her to one of the grey plastic chairs and they both sat next to her. Andy wrote down her full name and details in his black notebook and then Liam's. He said that when they found Liam he had no identification, no card, no mobile phone. Katrina started to cry again and stopped herself and said, 'I bet he fought back. He's stupid like that. I always told him, just give them what they want.'

He made a note and told her where Liam had been found. She said as how he never went to that cash machine, he went to the nearest one, the one at the bank. But Andy said it seemed the bank cash machine wasn't working tonight.

'It's all my fault,' she said helplessly. 'If I'd known the pizza took debit cards...'

'Does Liam have any enemies that you know of?' the policewoman asked. 'Has anyone made any threats of any kind?'

'No,' she said. 'He never has fights with people, not really.' But then she told him about the two kids she'd seen in the street while he was gone. 'In hoodies. Paki kids. One tall one, one short. And the way they looked at me...' As she spoke, she became more certain. 'I knew. I saw it in them. It was in their eyes.'

Andy asked more questions and wrote down her answers in his neat printing, but afterwards she couldn't remember anything else she'd said.

II

Wednesday 1 am

'The two most powerful forces in journalism: a deadline, and a cheque.'

Gareth Whelpower, 'Off-Stone – Memories of a Newspaper Man'

The Night Watch

There'd been a shout. Not far from the centre of the Estates, just by George III House. Then a scuffle, and maybe a scream.

The first texts had started soon afterwards. Shapes had been seen running. A cry half heard. Police cars came. An ambulance arrived and left.

Little was known and when little is known everyone feels free to know more. One of the Paki crews knifed a Japanese tourist, people told Andy as he went door to door with the three uniformed police who could be spared. An Asian had been stabbed by white vigilantes while kissing his girlfriend... Five of the Euston Go-Go Girls had fought off ten from the Barbie-Doll Gang from Holborn...

The more exotic the story, the more enticing. Add a few things. Pass it on. The text screens glowed in the streets and in the flats.

There was little warmth in the air, this night, but there was heat in the messages.

In his flat on the edge of the Gordon Road Estates, overlooking Euston station, Royland Pinkersleigh gave up trying to sleep. He slipped quietly out of bed, leaving Sadé huddled into the duvet, a solid weight that belied her slimness. She'd fallen asleep in seconds, while Royland lay recycling his favourite worries. The night was not long enough for all of them. The current Top Ten included the gym, the VAT, the rent, the falling number of gym members, the council's cancelled youth club contract and the money he needed to refurbish the ladies' changing rooms following the bursting of a pipe at the very moment when Beyoncé Phillips had been straightening her hair – not a pretty sight.

But tonight, straight to Number One: the knife.

He padded across the floor with ninja-like care, aware of his weight on floorboards that murmured sneakily under him. He'd have preferred carpet. Royland liked comfort, but Sadé was adamant that only bare wood was acceptable for people who aspired. He told her, his grandmother grew up in a shack in the back streets of Kingston, Jamaica. She dreamt all her life of having a floor with a fitted carpet. But there was no point. If Sadé said you didn't have carpet, you didn't have carpet.

The door squeaked as he opened it. Sadé shifted, muttered something and went back to sleep. Royland slipped into the small kitchen-diner-breakfast-entertaining room and closed the door quietly after him. He rolled out the one rubber exercise mat he insisted on being allowed, upwardly mobile floorboards or no, and started in on his first ab crunches of the day.

He should have left the knife where he first saw it. Or phoned someone. Made a report. There could have been blood. DNA. Valuable evidence.

He turned to lie on his back, under the cornflakes and jars of herbs, and tried to think of his hip flexors, then rotated onto his front and tried to focus on his glutes, but it was no good. He leapt up in frustration and switched on the radio by the cooker, soft as he could. He'd just missed the main news. He'd have checked Google, but he'd left his phone by the bedside and didn't want to risk disturbing Sadé. Didn't they do some kind of late-night local bulletin? Maybe they'd mention if there'd been an attack. Maybe they'd say if they'd found the weapon.

But what if they found the knife but in the wrong place: that would screw up the investigation, wouldn't it? Hundreds of police officers investigating in the wrong place, all because of this knife he'd dropped in a park when it should have been in a street a hundred metres away. He told himself he was being stupid. What difference would a hundred metres make, or a park instead of a street?

He started one-arm press-ups. He could feel the sweat on his biceps and he liked that. But he was just too big. He had to be careful not to rock the dining table at one end or jiggle the glass ornaments on Sadé's little bookshelf at the other.

The radio played a hip-hop song. He must have missed the local news too.

11

ICU B

'I don' believe this, man.'

'What's wrong wit' that?'

Manuelo gestured with horror towards the four lines of cards Tariq had laid down under the overhead lights of the hospital morgue.

'What did I open? Did you even hear what I said, man? Two hearts. Two hearts, man. We could have had a slam here.'

The other two porters chuckled. They perched on NHS wheelchairs around a scrubbed-down autopsy table which Slovan had thoughtfully covered with an empty black body bag. Behind them ranged lines of numbered steel fridges, each humming with its cargo of bodies.

'All that money you could have won,' said Wole happily.

'We'll get you down anyway,' added Slovan.

'Tariq, you never heard of Blackwood, man?' Manuelo glared at the dummy. 'Listen good. Isaacs in '92—'

'Oh, shit,' said Tariq. 'Not wit' the history lessons now.'

'A man without history is a man without a soul. You should read the Bridge columns for once in your life instead of festering here with all these dead people. Make something of yourself.'

'Like you.'

'I saw a hand like this once in the Lagos Open—' started Wole.

Manuelo's Nokia went off. It was the same person who'd been trying to phone for the past thirty minutes. He decided he had probably let him sweat enough already.

'Play the damn lead, Wole,' said Slovan.

'I'll have to take this,' said Manuelo.

'What's so urgent?' Wole slapped down the jack of clubs. 'The bodies will wait.'

'It's not hospital business. It's important business. Play the fucking hand for me, Tariq. And don't you throw it, to prove me wrong. I need the money just as much as you.'

Jason was sitting anxiously scanning a discarded copy of the Mail in the hospital canteen when Manuelo wove his way round the empty tables towards him. There wasn't any news in the paper Jason hadn't already known, but he liked to torment himself by inspecting the bylines to see whose careers were taking off instead of his. A few night-shift workers huddled in distant corners pretending they didn't mind still being awake. Without looking up from the paper, Jason jabbed his hand towards a seat in an attempt to appear calm and dominant. He took a sip of black coffee from a paper cup. Manuelo stayed on his feet.

'You said it was urgent.'

'Sit. Have a coffee. On me.'

Manuelo sat. He tapped the table meaningfully. 'I just bidding a slam.'

Jason tore his eyes from the leader column. 'Right, NHS work. I should have realised.'

He liked Manuelo and his approach to life. He was his own man. The Health Service demanded total confidentiality, but the porters were hired by independent contractors, so Manuelo had reasoned he was not legally bound.

'Information wants to be free,' he'd said when they first met, around the time that he showed Jason his certification as LLB, LLM and PhD in International Law from the University of West Manila. 'I signed a contract with 24/7 Human Resource Services of Luton. I sign no damn contract with the Camden General Hospital. You can't enforce no third-party agreements,' he'd said, slamming a heavy hand down on the vinyl canteen tabletop and checking no-one was watching him pocket the pack of cigarettes that Jason had slipped him.

'How's the family?' Jason asked now, tossing the Mail away from him with vigour.

'Which family?' said Manuelo affably.

Jason decided to let the question slide. 'I need to find a patient. He was in A&E before and he's been moved.'

Manuelo took a deep breath. It was his standard negotiating ploy. Everything was deemed dangerous to his future career... but in this case it seemed it actually might be.

'They get very protective about patients here.'

'It's a kid, just been stabbed. The police are hushing it up.'

'A conspiracy!' Manuelo slapped his forehead with joy. He loved getting one over on The Man.

Jason poked an urgent finger at him. 'One of the worst. Habeas corpus. False imprisonment. You know what the Feds are like.' He knew he was pushing the boundaries a bit, but he didn't have time to be too precise about the truth. 'This could be big. Tabloid.'

'Man, I know the Feds.' Manuelo pulled out his Blackberry, then grew serious. 'It will cost you. My contacts. They got jobs to look to. I'll have to pull some favours. This is not cheap work.'

Jason was expecting this, but he felt depressed even so. Why were people so greedy? Wasn't there more to life than personal gain? 'This is all I have,' he said, sliding across a colourful Camden General Trust brochure that he'd lifted from reception.

Manuelo opened it and gazed at the six complimentary directors-box tickets to Spurs that Jason had intercepted on their way to the Herald's sports desk. Jason could see him rapidly calculating their resale value.

'Shit, I'll need more than that.'

'That's really all, Manuelo. The freebies are drying up.' Jason was telling the truth. A local paper like the Herald hardly paid enough to cover his everyday bills plus Bea's maintenance. All his cards were rapidly cruising towards their limits. A few sports or opera tickets, or review copies of books, helped ease the pain, but even they came in less frequently than they used to. However, if he was going to save his career, he would have to take a risk. He suggested Manuelo might share said risk and consider the tickets a down-payment for when the story was sold. As friends. 'You know I'm good for it.'

'I'm a Christian, Jason. Neither a borrower nor a lender be. It's against my ethical code.'

'You have an ethical code?'

Manuelo stood up. 'Now you offend me.'

'Wait,' said Jason. He couldn't afford to lose him tonight and he was sure there was a place for ethics in journalist–porter relationships, even if for the moment he couldn't see quite where. 'Think of the good you'll be doing. Information needs to be free. You said that.'

'Not that free.'

'You'll be playing an important role in saving lives.

And helping us stick it to The Man.'

'Money. Tariq got real money from the Sun last month – none of your tickets or review DVDs. Two hundred.'

Jason knew this was at least five times what the Sun would have coughed up. He himself had never actually paid real money for access to anywhere before. It wasn't something you did working on a local paper. But now he was trying to become a tabloid journalist. He agonised for a moment, then tried not to think of his growing overdraft and offered twenty. Manuelo came down to a hundred. Jason tried reducing the price further, but the little porter wouldn't budge.

He considered the issue as he drained his coffee. By the time it came to pay, he'd either have cash from the Post or he'd be able to dump Manuelo and find another mole. You had to be tough to succeed in Fleet Street. Or at least that's what he kept telling himself. 'It's a deal,' he said.

'He's on the fifth floor. ICU B.'

'You knew all along!'

'Tariq saw him up there twenty-five minutes ago. Man, he said he looked in a bad way. Mother crying and everything.'

Jason stood up and gripped the muscular little porter's arm.

'Haven't too many people gone already?' he said with passion. 'Too many of every race, shot, stabbed and beaten in our cold, hard streets. Don't you want to help stop the tide of blood? This could be big. "Cut Out the Knife". "Ban the Blade". And on the front page.' He created the front-page splash in the air with a wave of his hand. '"The Innocent Victim". Like the Unknown Soldier, but with intravenous tubes attached.'

'I don't like it when you talk in headlines,' said Manuelo. He shifted a little on the spot. 'When you talk in headlines, you're trying to get me to stick my neck on the line.'

'I need to get into that ward.'

'See what I mean?'

Jason was still gripping his arm. 'I've got a sale. But only if I can talk to the mother.'

Manuelo glanced around the canteen. 'This will take serious money.'

'You mean, like a minute ago? Finding out where he is? All those contacts you had to ask?'

'OK, just double it.'

Jason sighed despondently. 'Put it on the tab,' he said.

Manuelo smiled. 'I always like doing business with you, Jason. You teach me so much about negotiation. You drive such a hard bargain.'

Jason looked at him quickly to see if he could detect any irony, but Manuelo was already turning away, beckoning him to follow.

Manuelo planned their journey to the fifth floor with the focused concentration of an SAS patrol in the jungle. Jason must maintain radio silence. If they were intercepted by hospital management, he was to let Manuelo do all the talking.

'Just name, rank and serial number,' said Jason.

'What, man?'

Jason just smiled. 'No sweat.'

Manuelo directed Jason to the lifts, while he himself paused at an internal phone – laying a false trail to confuse management about his current work-schedule. On the fifth floor, they re-formed in front of a plain door with a heavily scratched plastic protector. Here, the stubby porter tapped a code into a keypad, looked both ways and ushered Jason inside.

Jason found himself in a narrow, twisting corridor. Manuelo pointed the way forward, past shadowy pathology labs filled with unguessable machines, whose wires and protuberances grew like sinister tendrils. Finally, they reached another unmarked door. Here Manuelo brought out a bundle of swipe cards and flipped one nonchalantly against the reader. The door clicked softly open. Within lay the ICU ward, oddly silent but for the hum and bleep of life-saving machinery.

'From now, you're on your own,' he said in a whisper.

'Where do I find him?'

'Seventh unit from the nurses' desk.'

Jason stepped through. 'I owe you,' he said.

'Damn right,' said Manuelo and the door clicked shut.

Jason was indeed on his own in Intensive Care.

12

Exclusive

Jason passed by the shapes of patients on either side, entangled in skeins of tubes and wires like alien cocoons, machines flickering and twittering softly in the night. In the seventh room from the nurses' desk, as Manuelo had promised, he found Katrina bowed over Liam's bed. He stood a moment and watched her from the doorway. After all his efforts, had he the right to interrupt? He thought what a wreck he'd be if it were Bea lying in Intensive Care. He remembered the moment she'd been born, surrounded by all the equipment of the maternity suite, her face red and angry – and he'd felt so proud. This was a real person, full of noise and yet fragile and vulnerable. And it had hit him suddenly that she depended totally on him and Josette – they were the ones who had to protect that tiny being from a dangerous world.

But this was no good. Dalgleish was waiting. He cleared his throat and prepared his most sympathetic voice.

'Who the hell are you?'

A stout black nurse stood behind him holding a serious clipboard. Jason fumbled in his pocket and flashed his press pass, holding his thumb over the bit that said Press.

'DC Rockham sent me.' He dropped his voice confidentially. 'I led the team who identified this boy.'

The nurse frowned. Jason glanced for the briefest moment at her name-tag. 'Esmerelda,' he said, escorting her a short distance from the room. 'Detective Constable Rockham is most keen that Liam's mother is fully supported. Are you up for that?'

'DC Rockham can say what he want. Me, I'm following what the doctor telling me.'

'Good. And I'm glad you're on the ball.'

Esmerelda clutched her clipboard to her chest as a shield.

Jason's voice grew yet lower and more serious. 'It's vital that no journalists get into the ward. This could be a big story. Massive. We wouldn't want Ms Glass harassed because of a leak from here.'

'Maybe, but is ICU you're in. You can' stay here unless you're a parent.'

'I appreciate that and respect it. But I have to stay on guard with the boy for when he wakes. Any delay now could be disastrous to catching the person or people who did this. I wouldn't want you to feel guilty about that. I know you want us to arrest the bastards and bring them to justice, Esmerelda, don't you?'

The nurse stared at him and then called, 'Ms Glass, is this man OK to be here with you?'

Katrina didn't look round. 'Whatever.'

Esmerelda shook her head in resignation and trotted off with her clipboard still held protectively to her frontage. Jason entered the room. The boy looked so flat and lifeless. He tried to ignore the knowledge that Fleet Street would much prefer it if the kid died, preferably with a famous father and ideally well before the deadline for the next edition so that appropriate tributes could be assembled to maximum poignant effect.

'Liam's looking good,' he said, wishing he did.

'Like you see him.'

He remembered warming greatly to the kid when he

wrote about him two years before. Liam had been much like any other innocent twelve-year-old who could kick a ball a few yards and demonstrate Cruyff stepovers until you lost the will to live. Chelsea's Academy staff peered and poked at him for six weeks, then an assistant coach lined half the intake up on the training pitch and simply told them all to piss off. They weren't up to scratch. Liam Glass took it without malice, like he'd taken most things in his short life, with a shrug and a vague feeling that things could be better, but not for the likes of him. Jason had been angrier. He hated the smugness of the dismissal. But he also hated the total bovine acceptance in the pale teenager's face. He wanted to hug him and then shake him. Where was the ranting? Where was the rage against the bastards who ran the system? Where was the demand that life should be better, that people shouldn't shit on you, that fate could be kinder than this? They gave him hope and they snatched it away, without warning. Liam had simply said, 'I weren't like good enough.'

Katrina was sitting by the head of the bed. 'I read it in the Express,' she solemnly informed her comatose son. 'People get better if you talk to them. It stimulates the brain. You'll need that for when you wake up. They say one cut just missed a lung, so you're lucky there, Liam-baby. The liver isn't as bad as it could be. The spleen...' She relayed to him every detail of his condition as the Intensive Care team had explained it to her, then she ran out of medical material and started in on the latest gossip off *EastEnders*. Liam's eyes remained closed.

There was a chair next to her. After a decent minute, Jason gave up waiting to be invited to sit and sat. He was all too aware of the passing of time. All journalism ultimately runs by the clock. The more he saw Liam's body, air pumping into him through the oxygen mask, tubes of essential fluids hooked into his veins, the angrier he got. He thought of all the teenage knife-deaths he'd covered. None of them got more than a few lines in the national press. Here at last was a chance to get knife crime onto the front pages. Nothing sold tabloids more than sex, crime and Premiership footballers. Preferably all three in the same story. But for Jason to break the story nationally he needed two things. He needed Katrina's words – exclusive to him. And he urgently needed the father's name.

So he did what all normal human beings do at such urgent times: he delayed.

He took out a pen and laid it on one leg. He took out a notebook and laid it on the other. He ensured they were perfectly straight. Then he changed his mind and put them away again. Instead he tugged out a little black voice recorder and turned it on.

'What are you doing there?' Katrina said.

'Nothing.' He turned it off again.

He eyed the complex tangle of wires and tubes that were keeping Liam Glass alive. He checked his watch once more – it was later than he thought but not as late as it might have been. The moment he looked away, he found he'd totally forgotten what time it was and so he checked again. Then he ran out of things to do that weren't what he was trying not to do.

'I'm here for you,' he said. 'I can tell people your side of the story. How you feel. What Liam is really like. His future.'

She turned her attention from the bed and stared at him blankly but didn't speak. Her hands fluttered uncertainly like startled birds and then settled to await further developments. Her eyes were red from crying.

She was smaller than he'd remembered from two years before, with a more angular face and an air of wary confusion. He had the sense that for her everything was a puzzle set by experts – doctors, policemen, journalists – who somehow knew this game better than she did. Esmerelda came in, adjusted a monitor briskly, wrote something down and left. Katrina's hands fluttered and settled again. Jason drew himself up in his seat.

'I've never forgotten your son,' he said. 'I remember having good fun with Liam showing me how to kick a football and me doing OK. I think we got on well, yes? We had a laugh. Me, him, you. He looked good in my article, didn't he? You liked it, yes? Many journalists would have just banged it off in a few minutes, but I felt your son deserved to have the words crafted with care. By someone who cared.'

'That copper, he didn't want you here.'

'He wouldn't. Look, I can go if you want me to. Just say the word. Just one word. I'll leave you totally alone. On your own. Solitary.' Jason waited a second and then, before she could answer, he gesticulated importantly towards the bed, the whole scary medical apparatus that was bleeping and winking around it. 'So many cases, so little time to be noticed,' he added, widening his gesture to include the ward and then the world beyond. 'The police are overwhelmed. How do they decide whether to pursue an easy parking offence or a difficult stabbing with no witnesses?'

'I thought...' She picked anxiously at some fluff on her jeans.

'Hospitals, too. How do they decide where to put their efforts? Who are they going to keep alive?'

Katrina looked over at her son. 'But...'

'Look, I'm totally sure he's getting the best possible

care.' Jason placed a hand on hers. She looked at it and he rapidly took it away again. 'Just like I'm sure that the police are going to devote all their resources to finding who did this. And the fact that the police aren't here now bears no relation whatsoever to their commitment. There's nothing to worry about at all.'

'How do they decide then?'

'They have their ways.' Jason pulled his notebook out again and flipped through the pages with an air of mystery. 'Ah!' he said. And then, 'Of course.'

'What's that?'

'Nothing.' He slipped the notebook away once more. 'But then...' He interrupted himself. 'No, nothing.'

'For fuck's sake, tell me.'

'Well, it's a total coincidence, I'm sure.' Jason bent towards her. 'There were these two stories I covered recently. One of them was about this middle-aged woman who was attacked in the street by a gang of thugs. Vicious, it was. Broken this, bruised that...' He shuddered at the memory. 'The victim's husband wouldn't talk to us. So the editor spiked it. Instead we ran a story about a prize pumpkin. You know what happened?'

Katrina shook her head. He tapped her leg, his voice sibilant with distress. 'The police dropped the case. The hospital sent her home with a bottle of aspirins... Dreadful mistake.' He sat back again. 'Probably a complete coincidence. Like the other one.'

'What other one?'

'You don't want to know.' But when she didn't reply, he told her anyway. This was the story of a young man who was mugged in a situation remarkably similar to Liam's, and whose parents did agree to speak to the newspaper. In depth. He jabbed a finger into her knee to emphasise the difference that this had made. 'The police started doing their job. Every uniformed officer was brought in to conduct house-to-house interviews. The hospital allocated the best equipment and the top specialists to curing the kid. The muggers were arrested, the young man's life saved.'

He hesitated as if concerned he'd worried her again. Katrina became rather thoughtful. A different nurse strode in, stared at a drip-bag and left.

'The power of the press,' Jason mused aloud and then stood up. 'Time to go and leave you alone.'

'Wait a minute,' she said.

'You need peace and quiet.' He stepped towards the door.

'I know who did it.'

'You do?' He returned at speed.

She twisted her fingers uncertainly.

'Go on.'

'You must put it in the paper. When he didn't come home, I like phoned his friends, but he wasn't with any of them, so I went out and drove around looking for him. There was nobody, except people going home. Ordinary people—'

'I've got the picture, yes.'

'And then I saw them.'

'Them?' Jason tugged out his notebook again.

'Two Paki kids,' she said, eyes open wide. 'In hoodies. It's like they're here now, right in front of me, isn't it? I saw them and immediately I could tell. I'd seen them before. They were jumping in and out of the gutter and laughing.'

'Jumping and laughing?'

'Exactly.' She sat back, case proven. 'Jumping and laughing. Without like conscience or nothing. And when they saw me, they ran.'

'They ran? Any other reason to think it was them who attacked Liam? Blood? A knife? His possessions?'

'It was in their eyes.'

Jason closed his notebook without writing anything. 'That's very useful. I'll make sure it's headline news.'

'I told the copper. Do you think he went to look for them? Did he, fuck! I gave him an exact description.' She shook her head. 'If it was a black kid knifed by whites, they'd be banged up already.'

'Well, I don't know...'

'So, what do you want in exchange?'

He hesitated. 'What?'

She looked up at him. 'What's the deal?' Her hands were still now. Her jaw resolute. 'Get the police to fucking do their job. Get the doctors to cure my son. The power of the press. That's what you said.'

Jason drew breath and tried to hide his nervous anticipation. Mulled over the possibilities. He sat down again and took both her hands. They felt surprisingly hot. 'Katrina, you'd have to agree that you'd only talk to me and nobody else. No other newspapers or television.'

'And if I did, it would help get the police and the doctors to do their best, like you said?'

'I can't promise, of course...'

'But with that other young man, the one you wrote about before...?'

'Things went well,' he said modestly. He reached into his inside jacket pocket and took out two small bundles of stapled A4 paper.

'What's that?'

'An exclusivity agreement.' Jason was always prepared. You never knew when you might need a contract. He smoothed out the crumpled sheets. 'You just sign here.'

She stared at the papers.

'You don't want to read it all. Trust me. Legal talk. Life's too short.' It was perhaps not the best choice of phrase, but thankfully she didn't seem to notice. She took the biro he held out and signed. His pulse leapt. This was the first step.

'And here,' he said. She signed. 'And here.'

In the back of his mind, his national campaign against the tyranny of the knife was already taking shape. Under his byline.

'I have to sign all these times?'

'Lawyers. Can't live with them, can't live without them. And here. And here.' He hovered above her and slid the completed contract away with great excitement. He handed her a pound coin; she stared at it.

'That's a token advance,' he said importantly. He jammed the signed agreement back into his jacket pocket. His chest swelled with the feeling of growing success.

'And,' he added in a throwaway manner, 'I'll just speak to Liam's father.'

There was a long pause. Longer than Jason would have liked. As pauses went, this was not a good one and it filled him with unwanted doubt. He avoided her eye and hoped nonetheless.

'He doesn't have a father.'

Jason's chest stopped swelling. 'Doesn't have a father, as in... Is his father dead?'

Katrina pulled her hand from his and let him understand in no uncertain manner that she didn't know or care if the man was still on this earth. And in the unhappy event that he was, she had no desire ever to see or hear of him again. 'No way in hell,' she added, in case she hadn't made her point strongly enough.

This was not good. No father, no national press. Jason found himself sweating again.

'I want to help you, Katrina.' He groped his way forward, sentence by sentence. 'You have values and you stick to them. That's good. I'll make it clear you didn't want to involve Liam's father but that for the boy's emotional good—'

'His father doesn't get involved.' She turned back to her son. She looked so alone.

'Absolutely. And I support that position entirely and completely.' He scoured the situation for wriggle-room. Why couldn't life be easy, just for once? 'Is there perhaps a way we can use his name without him getting involved precisely? I mean, he doesn't need to be "involved".' To his horror he found himself making air-quotes with his hands. He sat down on them quickly. 'Not as such. How about I say it wasn't you who put us on to him. An anonymous source. A well-wisher.'

She was shaking slightly. He grew afraid she was having a fit. Her mouth moved without making a sound. When she finally spoke, it was with anger and finality.

'Let me make this clear, Jason. How about, "over my dead body"?'

She put her hand on Liam's arm. The boy breathed in and out with the machine. Not a flicker of consciousness.

'OK. No problem. No father. I just wanted to be clear.'

Jason pulled out his mobile. 'I'll just tell the front desk about the two Asians you saw.' He tapped it briefly and then stared in disbelief at the screen. 'Shit,' he said. 'My battery's gone. Can I borrow yours?'

Katrina gave him a suspicious look.

'There's no time to waste, Katrina. We ought to circulate their descriptions immediately, warn all my colleagues to keep an eye out, before the attackers are able to go into hiding.'

She dug into her handbag with some reluctance and handed him her phone, extricating it from a tangle of keys and Kleenex. He stood up nonchalantly and offered to leave her in peace.

13

The Collects

The nurses had settled into their late-night routine of frowning at monitors and waiting for flatliners. They appeared innocent and well-meaning, but Jason knew better. Hospital staff were not to be trusted. Carefully avoiding all contact, he locked himself in a toilet on the far side of the ward.

The toilet proved to be reassuringly clean, with grey plastic-clad walls, but remarkably cramped, even for a toilet. He squeezed in, perched on the toilet-seat lid with Katrina's phone and opened its address book. He felt bad doing this. He told himself it was necessary, but somehow he still felt sullied.

He flicked through Katrina's contacts, avoiding those with surnames on the charitable assumption that she'd probably be on first-name terms with men she slept with. That left him with four male names, aside from Liam. But on their own they didn't help much. There were too many Garys, Mikes, Toms and Matts in football.

He started by phoning Gary, but it went straight to voicemail. He left a guarded message and tried Matt. After ten rings, a voice asked huskily if he was aware what time it was. Jason didn't consider one in the morning to be a problem, given that he had urgent business, but the man at the other end did, putting the phone down before Jason could mention Katrina or a possible son. After this, he gave up phone calls and sent carefully worded texts. He also placed a couple of veiled questions on Twitter to see if that might yield something, but it didn't. He concluded that the Internet was an overrated medium. Great for finding porn but not much more. For a brief moment he considered googling to see if Katrina had been involved in porn but dismissed the idea. Any clues as to who Liam's father was clearly weren't to be found online. They were going to be in Katrina's flat.

Katrina was still sitting where he'd left her, eyes closed.

'Katrina,' he whispered softly, touching her on the shoulder. 'The best way you can help your boy is to get some proper sleep. I'll take you home.'

'Liam?' Katrina opened her eyes.

'He's fine. I want you to rest.'

'What the fuck does it matter what you want?'

A good journalist makes his subject feel she is the most important thing in his life, but at the same time he mustn't betray how much power she has. Jason performed his own verbal Cruyff stepover: he was only thinking of her, he said – a nap, a change of clothes... But he thought it politic not to mention that he needed to get inside her flat. He pressed gently under her arm and eased her up to standing.

'I can't leave him,' she said, once upright.

Again Jason explained why she had to let him take her home. He put his arm round her waist... and felt the warmth of her body.

'No.' She stopped again and he wondered why people constantly acted in ways that were not in their best interests. He felt desperate. Dalgleish and the Post were waiting, and they were waiting, specifically, for a grieving Premiership love-rat dad. He had little time to produce one, if he ever wanted to be taken seriously by the paper again.

'You're sure you want to stay here?'

She nodded blearily.

'Can I go back to your flat and get you something? A toothbrush? Something personal of Liam's to help jog his memory with? His laptop maybe?'

'No.'

Oblivious to his pain, Katrina folded herself back into the plastic chair and Jason was left standing over her, contemplating matters. And, in particular, contemplating her open handbag and her keys, glinting. A new thought occurred. He'd never actually stolen anything before. But this was an extreme situation. It was, he told himself, for the good of everyone. He started to move before his better instincts could have a chance to interfere.

'Let me just slip your mobile back in your bag,' he said. 'And then I won't be long. I have a few things to take care of.'

So saying, Jason placed the mobile carefully back where it had come from, and when his hand came out again there were fewer objects glinting in the bag than there had been before.

The streets were empty by this time. On his way back to Katrina's flat, Jason passed a small square just off Gordon Road, cordoned off with donotcross tape. It gave him a jolt. This was where Liam had been attacked just a few hours earlier. A scuffle, a glint of metal, a pool of blood.

Katrina's downstairs entryphone was operated by keypad. He slipped her keys out of his pocket. A code was taped to the back of the fob. He keyed it in and the lock clicked open. Was he doing the right thing? As he walked up the dank concrete stairs and along the first-floor walkway, Jason interrogated his conscience. His conscience told him he was about to enter a flat without permission, to invade someone's privacy, and, with luck, to obtain personal possessions and information that he had no right to. What's more, she might well notice the keys had gone before he had a chance to bring them back.

His conscience was too active, he replied. After all, Katrina was too preoccupied with Liam to start looking for her keys. Further, she'd agreed that he could tell her story to the world. She had agreed to give up her privacy. Further still, the exclusivity contract contained many useful permissions, including allowing him to obtain her family photographs and personal details (for example). It just didn't specify precisely how he should obtain them.

He found her door, looked up and down the walkway to check it was empty, but something still made him hesitate. The flats were silent, though metal shrieked nearby – a night train approaching Euston station. Did he feel guilty? He didn't feel guilty, came the resounding answer. So resounding that it entirely drowned out any small doubts he may indeed have had. Jason Crowthorne was not heartless. He couldn't begin to imagine what it would be like for him if his own daughter were hurt in any way. And yet he was also a professional, he told himself. Jason had read and admired all the great war correspondents. This too was a war zone, a war against crime. If his daughter were lying in a coma, he hoped some journalist would have the courage to tell her story.

Take a war photographer, he argued to himself. Suppose he came across a dramatically injured child in need of urgent help. While lining up the photograph, the child might die, but the world would see and be moved – and other children might be saved. Saving the child, he might lose the photograph and thousands of children could die. Some things just had to be done.

So, brave war reporter that he was, Jason unlocked Katrina's front door and dived in, slamming it behind him.

It was dark inside and cold, with a sweet-sour tang of nicotine and forgotten cooking. He tried to push aside his nerves and opened the door to the front room. All around lay the odd details of Glass family life. Muddy trainers under the coffee table. Diamanté cushions on the frayed sofa, gleaming dimly in the orange light from outside the window. He walked rapidly over to a line of photos on the polished mantelpiece, trying to make as little noise as possible. Some framed, some loose, they showed Liam at a variety of ages and sizes, from lying in a cot to kicking a ball on a beach. The Post would want them all. To Katrina, these pictures were her memories. To the newspaper industry, they were part of the story, the collects. And his job was to collect them. He'd make sure to tell the Post to return them after everything was over.

He slipped his rucksack off his shoulder and swept the photos into the front pocket. Sadly, not one of them contained an eligible man.

It was approaching two in the morning and he felt his nerve failing along with his energy. In the kitchen, he boiled himself the strongest black coffee he could, out of the sticky remains of a jar of granules, and then stopped again to listen for any sounds outside before opening cupboards and drawers, delving into souvenirs of Greek holidays and ancient weekend-breaks. But there were no potential fathers here either.

He advanced courageously into Katrina's bedroom. The bed was a mess, a grey, torn duvet thrown to one side, and the embarrassingly personal left-over smell of her perfume. For a moment the intimacy of the room gave Jason pause, but he bravely fought off his moral qualms. He pushed aside half-used mascara and half-empty packets of Durex. Now Jason opened a drawer and discovered it was filled with flimsy knickers. Here he did indeed hold back... but then he reminded himself he was a war reporter making moral sacrifices for the larger good... and unshirkingly plunged his hands through Katrina's undergarments. No diary. No photos. No letters tied in ribbon. He began to hate Katrina for her selfishness. Refusing to store records of her personal life. What right had she to withhold private information from posterity?

There was one room left, a brightly coloured plastic sign blu-tacked to its door, with rockets, soldiers and cricket bats, like boys' room signs have had since the 1950s. So original. Jason turned the handle slowly, as if Liam's spirit might still be hovering inside. The door stuck. For a nervous moment, he thought someone was stopping him on the other side. But there was no sound, so he pushed harder.

Even in the semi-darkness, the room was as predictable as the sign outside. The football and music posters taped to the walls. The Argos computer that perched unwatched on Liam's desk. The clumps of dirty T-shirts, socks and pants dropped in front of his open cupboard. He rifled through Liam's few drawers and single cupboard. But if the boy had any inkling of who his father was, he hadn't kept any mementos.

The computer was still logged onto Liam's Facebook page, showing pictures of the boy hunched into his hoodie next to a range of sallow-faced youths. He'd need these pictures too, but he had nothing to put them on. Urgently, he searched around. There was nothing useful in any of the drawers. Then, peering under Liam's bed, he found a small plastic bag with a small stash of weed. Jason contemplated it a moment, then slipped it into his pocket. Next to it lay a pair of old boxer shorts hiding a memory stick. He extricated it with distaste, plugged it in and scanned the contents. Mostly cheap porn. He deleted the porn and downloaded the photos.

The problem was, the photos were still up on Facebook in public view, for the whole world to copy. There was no knowing what rival journalists might do – rivals who didn't have the boy's interests at heart as Jason did. So, after a further tussle with his conscience, he tried to remove them. Unfortunately, Facebook asked him for Liam's password. The site seemed to have a problem with strange people messing with Liam's account. It was most unfair.

Jason took a deep breath. Time was passing. He informed Facebook that he, Liam, had forgotten his password and waited for the replace password email to arrive in Liam's inbox. It was all too simple. He made a mental note to write an article about Facebook needing to update its security checks. When the email arrived, he hid, deleted and deactivated everything he could find. Just in case. Nobody would be able to find Liam on Facebook until he reactivated it. He contemplated the final confirmation screen with only a slight feeling of moral unease...

... and heard a key rattle in the front door.

Jason jumped to his feet in fright. He looked desperately around. There was no other way out and it was too late to hide anywhere else, so he squeezed himself into the tiny gap between the cupboard and the wall, jabbing his elbow painfully on a mini snooker table that had been abandoned there. He clenched his jaw to stop himself swearing, nose jammed against the cupboard back.

Two male voices could be heard. Friends of Katrina's? Police? Rival journalists? Jason forced himself to breathe more slowly and tried to think of a reasonable explanation for being discovered in Liam's bedroom, surrounded by rifled underwear.

The two voices exchanged a few indistinct comments.

Then one of them laughed and a door opened and closed on the walkway further down. Jason exhaled. It wasn't Katrina's door he'd heard after all.

It was getting late. He topped up his coffee, took it back into Liam's room and drank thoughtfully as he inspected Liam's choice of wall art – a girl off a vampire movie and a mildly attractive runner-up from *Big Brother*, whose talent was to open her blouse three buttons lower than the competition.

He took out his phone and sent out a few more tweets about the stabbing to follow up on those he'd sent from the hospital – not too many, just enough to stir the pot. He had four Twitter accounts under different names, names like @newsshouldbefree and @bestukjournalist, which he often used to boost his articles, and now he turned to all of them.

To his surprise, his tweets started a larger number of chirpings than usual in the virtual forest. Some insisted a Paki or Somali kid had been attacked by a white gang. Others that a white kid was attacked by Pakis or Somalis.

Jason grew anxious and rattled off an urgent message confirming that the victim was white and that he was sure there was nothing racist in it.

Hardly had he finished when a new tweet arrived.

SOMMALI THUGS I TOL U SO.

Jason started to reassure @whitesupremassy that there was no reason to finger African migrants and manfully resisted suggesting a correction to @whitesupremassy's spelling. But before he could send it, @topworldnation had re-tweeted @whitesupremassy's message and to his horror a hailstorm of similarly considered opinions spattered his screen.

No. Pakis, without a doubt, said @stgeorgeforever.

The bludbath is comming, added @funnyguy666.

Time to fight back, enthused @nopeaceinourtime.

Aghast, Jason closed his Twitter app before he could receive any more. He should really leave, but now exhaustion hit him.

He sat on the narrow bed, felt his muscles relax and tried to imagine what it would be like to be Liam, school results drooping, professional football a half-forgotten dream, wandering into a vaguely imagined adulthood stimulated only by posters of the gormless and semi-dressed. He laid his head on the World of Warcraft pillow and stared unhappily at the ceiling, white and featureless as fog. He would give himself a minute to collect himself and then he must slip the keys back into Katrina's bag before she missed them.

As he lay there, he found his thoughts drifting to his daughter. Bright and sassy, one day she would dazzle the world. He considered the possibilities: lawyer, doctor, even journalist. Lawyer would be best. He should discuss this with her next time. She was only ten, but you couldn't plan too early.

In January, her class had been told to write a letter in their exercise books as if to someone in the public eye, telling them what they wanted for the future. Bea had not only written a three-page letter to the prime minister, she'd actually posted it. She'd told him precisely what he should have done after the 2008 banking crisis, and how to stop it happening again. Jason had never felt so proud. But then she asked what articles he'd written about Britain's future and he had to explain that it didn't quite work like that on the Camden Herald.

'It's all right,' she'd said, putting her arms round him. 'Human interest is just as important.' Patronised by his own ten-year-old daughter! How would she feel about him in twenty years' time if he was still writing about school charity projects and prematurely felled trees? When she had become a high-rising MP or international lawyer and Tam, the talentless deputy editor, would have no doubt risen to become editor of the Daily Sport.

No, he needed to file this story. And he needed to do it fast. He was no nearer to finding Liam's father, let alone establishing if he was a footballer and famous, yet, still, he found himself composing words, strong words, about a stabbed boy, a tragedy unfolding, a mother in pain...

If you have good words, Gareth Whelpower always said, don't wait. Write them down. Jason grabbed one of Liam's football fanzines and a biro. Many nights in the past, Josette had woken up to find him jotting notes to himself in the margins of a convenient library book. Many nights. Her admiration, their huskily whispered plans for his career success. He'd held her close in the dark, the soft touch and sweet smell of her skin, and then after a few minutes... But this wasn't helping at all.

He dashed off a lead paragraph in the space beneath an advert for an irresistible deodorant. Then added two

more pars up the side of the page next to a profile of
Ronaldo. They were good. He lay back again and cursed
the night news editor for not seeing a great story when it
was thrust at him, even without the missing dad.

14

The Call

With two bars of Bach, Jason's phone jubilantly announced a call. He jerked awake. He'd been dreaming anxiously of hippopotamuses, cleavages and footballers dressed as doctors. He couldn't remember where he was, and then he could. In a panic, he checked the time on Liam's football-shaped clock. It was after half past three. He'd been asleep for over an hour and Katrina might discover her keys gone at any moment.

He sat up and urgently swallowed a gulp of caffeine, in the hope of restoring his neurones to partial function. It was cold and scummy. He squinted at his phone, which showed a missed call. He didn't recognise the number, but at three in the morning it could only be the night desk on the Post, chasing their celebrity stab-victim story. On Liam's bedside table lay a fanzine covered in a strange semi-legible scrawl. He urgently pushed the fanzine into his bag. He needed to go. He picked up the mug.

His phone rang again, its electronic merriness echoing loud in the dark, empty flat. Maybe it wouldn't be so bad. He'd simply tell Dalgleish the father didn't exist after all. Or at least he wasn't a celebrity, which for Fleet Street amounted to the same thing. What would be the worst that could happen? What could they do to him? He decided not to think about the worst that the Post could inflict on his career.

He took a deep breath and answered the call.

'Mr Crowthorne?' It was a man's voice, but not one

he recognised.

'Who wants him?' He attempted to move out of Liam's room, but as he stood up, his legs stung with pins and needles.

'You were looking for the possible father of a lad who got attacked last night.'

The voice at the other end was soft and trustworthy, melodious with a northern edge, perfect for selling insurance or payday loans. But Jason was not in the mood to be trusting. 'Who is this?'

'Were you?'

'I can't say.'

'That's a shame. A friend of my client received a text from you. You were asking about people who knew Katrina Glass fifteen years ago.'

'Your client?' Jason took a final medicinal dose of cold coffee and dumped the rest in the bathroom sink.

'I'm sorry, I should have introduced myself. I'm Tony Potts of Potts Sports and Media PR.' The man paused, as if waiting for a sign of admiration or at least recognition, but Jason was sadly unable to help. Not because he hadn't heard of Tony Potts. The man was probably the second or third biggest name in PR. Only the last week, Potts had been all over the television news explaining why his newest singer, Getta L. Yffe, had been painfully maligned by pictures that showed her crouched over, her head in a toilet. Contrary to first impressions, he told all channels, she was simply searching for a nose-stud that had accidentally fallen into the bowl. No, the reason Jason didn't respond was because his brain was filling up with too many questions. He walked painfully towards the front door and tried to regain his focus.

'I'm sorry to phone you in the middle of the night

like this,' Potts was saying, 'But my client believes he may be the father of this poor lad you mentioned. Liam Glass. He is of course distraught at what's happened, which we picked up from a text message you sent to one of my other players earlier. He can't wait to see Katrina and comfort her, and see what he can do to help his son. He is, of course, a man of means, given his record in the Premiership.'

'Of course.' Jason leant on the front door for support.

'We hope that won't be a problem. Coming to see his son, that is.'

'No, no. No problem.' The hallway, lit by the street lamps outside, had brightened attractively. The air acquired a fragrant softness as if from spring meadows and flowering fields. Even the screeching of the night trains leaving Euston sounded as musical as nocturnal birds. After many years' doubt, Jason found himself believing again in a just universe. 'Mr Potts, I'll be delighted for your client to visit immediately.'

'I'll be in attendance too. Of course.'

Jason nodded, then realised that Tony Potts needed a more audible response and agreed vocally. He was regaining his composure and his circulation. He asked for the client's name.

'That information is confidential, until we reach an agreement on appropriate publicity.'

'I have to have the father's name.' Jason tried to calm himself. It was vital that he had a name to tell the Post.

'I see,' said Potts, and after a brief moment for reflection he gave Jason the name of Benicio Paulino, one of the most prestigious footballers of the current generation. A maestro with a scoring record that surpassed the sports-writers' superlatives and hitherto considered to be a man of solid moral probity. This revelation would rock the football world to its foundations. There was only one sticking point.

'The child's white?' said Potts.

'Totally. Blonde, blue eyed, the lot.' Jason hoped desperately that he'd somehow misheard the name, but Potts' silence put paid to that. The shadows dimmed again, the air in the flat regained its foetid odour of old pizza and the night trains were reduced once more to soullessness. Jason felt sick. There was a long, long pause at the other end of the phone.

'Oh, that's a shame. It would have been remarkably helpful to him.'

Jason could picture the footballer only too clearly. He was perhaps one of the most photographed sportsmen of recent years and the one thing he most definitely wasn't was white.

'I'm sorry,' he said.

'That's life,' said the agent. 'It's always worth having a pop.'

Jason had wandered too close to one of the front windows and was dangerously visible from the walkway outside. He turned back rapidly and was about to end the conversation when a question occurred to him.

'What did you mean, helpful?'

'Helpful? Did I say that?'

'You said it was a shame because it would have been helpful to him.'

There was another of Potts' long silences. Clearly he didn't have to worry about his phone bill.

'Well, you have to be aware of Benicio's image problem. He does nothing aside from stick balls in the net every game. Nowt. No vices, no drink or girls. No childhood skeletons. The man's a walking sedative. Even the sponsors run away. He couldn't sell cat food. We've tried planting compromising stories, the lot. A ghosted bio? I had one poor lad trying to write one for three months. Ended up on Valium. You've seen the headlines: "Boring Benicio". "Predicta-Ball Beni". "Beni We Go Again". Even his fucking goals are boring. He makes it all look too easy. Beni's the nicest guy you'll ever meet and nothing interesting has ever happened to him outside the six-yard box.'

There was a deep reflective sadness in Potts' voice. 'He'd have made a great love-rat.' He gave a sigh. 'Oh, well. It were a nice idea.'

He hung up and Jason gave a quiet howl of anguish. And then he stopped, his heart still beating fast. He went over what Potts had said, trying to remember the precise words. He wanted to make sure he hadn't misunderstood.

Then, with great trepidation, he found Potts' number on his calls received list and dialled him back.

15

The Deal

Jason had interviewed many second-rate celebrities, third-rate local dignitaries, fourth-rate authors and One Direction – and in doing so had discovered a fundamental rule of life: they were all as unimpressive in person as on TV. Tony Potts, however, broke the rule. Potts was more. More impressive, more frightening, more monumental. Dyed chestnut hair floated imperiously in the breeze. Deep contours ran like seismic fault-lines across his face. As he lifted his glass, he examined Jason with a powerful yet shifty gaze that made Jason think obscurely of a Yorkshire Salvador Dali without the moustache.

'This may be stupid,' Jason said, attempting to gather his courage.

'Try me, lad. I'm here.'

Indeed, here he was in the all-night Polo Bar in Liverpool Street, facing Jason across a chicken Caesar sandwich and bright-green detox smoothie. Jason didn't even know you could order such things at four in the morning.

'Everything I say is off the record.'

'You're the reporter, not me.'

Jason had sketched it all out in his head... and now none of the words he'd planned made sense. He felt awkward, stupid and in awe of this man who mixed with the most powerful people in the world.

'I hope this is worth my while, lad,' Potts said, delicately cutting his sandwich into pieces, while Jason remembered how long it had been since he'd last eaten. He wished he'd had the courage to order some food, but he'd not wanted the distraction.

'I cancelled a conference call to Kuala Lumpur because you told me this would be important.'

'And it is,' said Jason, growing less certain by the nanosecond. A waiter delivered a pile of pancakes to a taxi driver at a table nearby. 'You remember you phoned me earlier about Benicio, who you thought might be a love-rat but isn't.' Potts didn't seem to feel this undeniable fact was worth a reply. He sipped his detox drink and waited. 'But on your books... you have other footballers...'

Potts stopped in mid-sip.

'I wondered...'

'I get what you wondered.'

'I wondered...' Jason continued nonetheless, unsure he could ever restart if he stopped now. 'Whether you had other players who might feel their careers would be aided in the same way.'

'Is this a trick?'

'What?'

'Are you wired for sound? Are you trying to set me up?'

'What? NO. No, no, no, no.' Jason recoiled as Potts rose, his large hands outstretched, ready to rip open Jason's jacket and shirt and search for a microphone. 'You gave me the idea yourself, from your call. I'm looking for a father. For my story. You can provide a celebrity father. Not just you, of course. I was going to phone some of the other agents around. I just thought I'd give you first shout. I'm sorry. Forget I said anything.'

Potts stood glaring at him across the table.

'Who said owt about forgetting it?'

'What?'

'You know, for a bright, up-and-coming reporter, you say "What?" too much. It makes you sound like you're out of your depth, and you're not out of your depth, are you?'

'No. No, not at all.'

Potts sat down again and drummed his thick fingers on a plate.

'It's an interesting idea. What have you got so far? The mother? The boy in a coma? A lovely lad, good student, nowt bad ever said about him? Took trials for Chelsea?'

'How did you know about Chelsea?'

'I can use Google too. It all helps. But it's not enough, is it? So a famous dad would seal the deal. Have you got a paper lined up?'

'The Post.' Jason attempted to regain some of the initiative. 'And they're very keen. But, listen, if we move on this, everything goes through me.'

'I see. They don't know what you're up to.'

'I didn't say that.'

'No problem. Who are you talking to there? You'll have phoned the night news desk and got Tom Dalgleish. Who no doubt told you to come back when you've got the goods. But in the morning you'll need to deal with his daytime news editor. That'll be Lyle Marchmont. He's no pushover, and be careful, he is one of the few who still have a couple of ethical principles. Though you'd have to dig hard to find them. So, everything goes through you.'

Jason felt a growing and decidedly frightening sense that this could really happen. Potts was treating him seriously. 'Yes. Everything.'

Potts waved a waiter over and ordered a slice of

strawberry cheesecake and this time Jason took the plunge and asked for an egg bap.

'Hungry?'

'I've been up all night on this.'

'A hungry reporter's the best reporter. What about the mother?'

'Ah, well...'

'How do you read her? Would money make a difference? Would she sue? Would she insist on a paternity test?'

'I don't know, exactly. She's very insistent on not telling Liam anything about his father. This is her.' He scrabbled urgently through the pocket of his rucksack. He could hardly believe this conversation was really taking place.

Tony Potts inspected the snapshots thoughtfully and handed them back.

'I don't remember seeing her with any of my lads. No matter. Most of the women take the money. Couldn't afford to sue, any road. Not unless one of the other papers puts her up to it. Mind you, I wouldn't bank against it. But, no matter, if she comes out and says he's lying, that's another headline. If she asks for a test, it keeps it in the papers for weeks. And when the test fails, it don't prove they didn't sleep together. We run stories about how he begged her to have his love child. Maybe she even lied and told him the boy was his.' He was growing lyrical in his passion. 'Aye, "Knife-Crime Mother Hid True Father From Her Own Son". She'll deserve all she gets. She can't prove otherwise. We could sling a fair bit of mud in her direction.'

Jason felt extremely uneasy. 'She hasn't said no yet.'

Potts looked almost regretful at the thought.

'Look, she's a nice person.'

'They all are. Don't worry. She won't be a problem. We'll see she's all right. She'll be rich. Think of all the medical bills it would pay for. Which reminds me, are you happy with the treatment he's getting? We can organise better. Would she turn her back on saving her kid's life? I know just who to talk to.' Potts drained his smoothie, told the waiter to put the cheesecake in a box to take away and started tapping notes on his iPhone.

Jason contemplated his bap as he tried to convince himself that no-one was going to get hurt by this. Indeed, that Katrina and Liam could only gain from a little judicious wealth distribution.

'If you're having second thoughts, Jason,' Potts said, without raising his eyes from his touch-screen, 'I could do this on my own.'

There's nothing makes a person so sure of an idea than the fear someone else might steal it. 'This was my idea, Tony. I came to you first.'

'That's what I thought. Eat up. I'll get Sharon to email you CVs and photos when she gets in. Marty, Nuno and Razza for starters. You decide which fits best. It'd be nice if there was some family resemblance. Not black at any rate.' He chuckled softly. 'It would be good if we could cast it by lunchtime.' He snapped a gold credit card towards the waiter and shrugged away Jason's slow attempts to take out his own.

'But first we need to talk money,' Potts continued.

Jason's heart slowed and he lost his appetite for his breakfast. He should have known there'd be a catch.

'I can't afford—' he started.

'Don't get any fancy notions. This could make a front-page splash on a no-news day, but more likely pages four five or six seven. Depends on who we pick.'

Jason waited to hear the worst. Maybe Potts would

take payment in stages.

The agent was making calculations in his head. 'A hundred and fifty thou', max,' Potts said slowly. 'That's all I can give you. You take out of that for expenses. And some of that will have to go to the mother.'

He waited for Jason to reply, which was always going to be an unlikely outcome. Jason pretended to be fully occupied with his bap. Everything seemed to have gone very quiet.

'Two hundred thousand would be tops, Jason. I mean it. That seems only fair. Don't get greedy. Remember the Post will be paying you summat too.'

'Of course,' Jason managed.

And they shook hands on it.

III

Wednesday 5 am

'A free press would be a great idea – we should try it one day.'
Gareth Whelpower, 'Off-Stone – Memories of a Newspaper Man'

16

Conquering Heroes

The first hint of daylight began to brighten the curry-coloured sky over the Estates. Those who'd been awake all night watched it blearily and started to head for their beds in the high- and low-rise blocks that clustered like army encampments around the little blood-stained square. And those who'd been sleeping slowly reappeared, made themselves a builder's tea or instant coffee, stretched, scratched, showered or didn't. The messages that had come in during the night were read and returned. Things were worryingly unclear. People needed to know more. They demanded to know more. They spread their electronic tentacles.

The older residents of the Estates, like Mrs Chowdhury and Mr Baines, preferred to get their information face-to-face, but while they were awake early, as usual, it was too soon to drop in on Mr Patel or Mrs Leach, or pass an offhand word to the health visitor. Twice, Mrs Chowdhury lifted the phone to call DC Andy Rockham and twice she let it fall back. She had his card from when he called three months ago asking questions about a spate of car thefts. But suppose he was busy on something more important. Or even at home asleep. Who was she to disturb him? Standing by her eighteenth-floor window, watching the approaching dawn, she continued to muse on the sounds she'd heard below in the night. They grew all the more horrible in the rehearsing. She decided to leave it one more hour, and then she'd phone. For sure.

*

'Did you see the tits on that one?'

'Did I see you staring at them?'

'Throw me another bottle.'

'Did you see the face of the trustafarian I nicked?'

'I'd give her one for a reduction in charges.'

'Stuck half out the khazi window.'

'Drop some H on him, that'll sort his rights out.'

'His face or his rear end?'

'What?'

'What could you see stuck out the window? His face or his rear?'

'Fucking tried to tell me his legal rights.'

'His rear. Then his face.'

The beers and the whiskies flashed across the desks. A bottle of Beck's was waved in Andy's direction, but he sent it away. The buzz from the returning heroes filled the main office, but he wasn't a part of it. He was attempting to finish the paperwork from the night and not watch PC Dana Bookman. She was one of the group sitting gazing adoringly at the detective sergeant who'd led the charge into the club in front of a dozen TV cameras, for the benefit of the mayor of London's new policy towards getting himself re-elected. The night's foray was going to be on breakfast TV and they'd been taking bets on who'd be left in and who'd end up on the cutting-room floor.

Dana appeared far too aroused by what she was hearing. Her blue eyes gleamed and she leant in close. Andy shouted across at her: Katrina Glass had phoned 999 when her son didn't come home and he wanted to know why no-one had told him. When Dana was slow to answer, he lost his rag and snapped at her to call Integrated Borough Operations (Disintegrated Borough

Operations) and she snapped back that it wasn't her who guessed the boy's age wrong. He wanted to apologise for his strop but couldn't and went round the main office banging things down and generally acting like the kind of officer he hated.

He'd not yet checked to see if there was CCTV footage at the cashpoint. He scribbled himself a large note on the back of a memo and jammed it under a Met Police souvenir mug.

While he'd been away from his desk, someone had stuck a yellow Post-it on his keyboard. It read: DB – Station Bike. He looked around, but none of the others seemed to be close enough and all were busy with their own chatter.

He knew what people said about Dana Bookman. The station bike: always up for a ride. He'd heard it when he'd first transferred in to the borough. PC Bookman had the problem of being unfairly attractive – unfair to her. She'd learnt to deal with the unfunny jokes, to fight off the grabs for her rear end and to deliver severe dents to male egos and other soft parts. Dana was not the most beautiful woman Andy had ever seen, but she had fire in her eyes, an attractive curve to her lips and a dry wit. He focused his thoughts on Cheryl and Duane and his commitment to family life and buying disposable nappies, but, since the birth, Cheryl had been unavailable and his treacherous unconscious had begun to incite civil unrest. Twice recently he'd had dreams about seducing Dana. Once as she lay in a squad car wearing delicately expensive lingerie... and once on a mountain-top, egged-on, for some obscure reason, by the Dalai Lama and Gordon Brown.

He was fed up with watching the rest of CID trying

to get into Dana Bookman's knickers, so he tracked down the scenes-of-crime officer on the other side of the room. She was sharing a white wine with a PC who was generously outlining his expertise in using a Rammit to break down doors. A woman in her mid-forties, the SOCO reluctantly dragged her attention away from the young man's penetrative skills to describe how she'd searched the square where the Glass kid was stabbed and found sweet fuck-all. No mobile, no credit or debit card, no house keys, definitely no knife. Squat, she said, apart from drying blood and the usual urban flora of crisp packets and empty beer cans. Andy was welcome to investigate further. He went to the duty inspector.

'We've not found the knife, sir. Give me some people to search the area, look for the weapon, talk to the locals.'

The inspector was a young kid on the fast-track promotion scheme. Like the others in the office, he thought of Andy as just Andy – working off the rest of his years and avoiding the hard graft. 'Stay in the office,' he said, his feet on the desk, a Glenfiddich in his hand, as he read the latest minutes from the Police Liaison Unit and laughed at selected passages. 'There's not long to the end of the shift. If the kid dies, the case goes to the MIT team. If he doesn't, there isn't the money anyway.'

There was nothing like death to focus the budget.

Andy returned to his desk. The reminder to pick up the CCTV still sat under his mug. Twice he picked up the phone and twice he was interrupted with trivial bits of business that the heroes couldn't be buggered to deal with. The DS from the raid was now enacting a choice moment when the TV cameras had caught him rugby-tackling a crackhead on the stairs. Dana was drinking it in. Andy tried to ignore them and focus on the attractions of his computer screen, but he kept checking back to see her sitting on the desk, sipping Beck's, smiling and laughing. She caught his eye and winked and he quickly returned to the report he was supposed to be finishing.

Was he being stupid? Was PC Bookman just another opportunity in life that he was letting slip?

The heroes were splitting up and talking of going home, possibly via one of the few late-drinking establishments they hadn't recently raided.

Dana came over. 'Anything I can do?' she asked.

He said no quickly and tried to think of her voice not as the sighing of a summer breeze but as that of a professional police officer with the power to arrest, handcuff and use appropriate force. Strangely, these thoughts didn't help. He thanked her brusquely and said he needed to clear his mind and type up his night report. So he was grateful when Dog Henderson bounced in, with all the energy of a man too dim to be depressed at having arrived early for the new shift. Dog read through Andy's handover report with much excitement at having a nice juicy stabbing to deal with and clapped his hands in glee. His real name was Keith. Nobody could remember why he was called Dog and he wouldn't say.

Andy took Dog to one side and said it would help him out a lot with Cheryl if he could get home early.

Dog slapped Andy genially on the side of the head. 'Lots of gossip to catch up on. Sleep well.' Then he bounced off to share the latest football news with the rest of Early Turn.

As Andy drove home with his bags of disposable nappies, he was sure there was something he'd forgotten, but he couldn't quite recall what.

17

Crime Scene

Jason found himself driving past the crime scene again on the way back after meeting Potts. He pulled over next to a small newsagent's tucked into the corner of the square, shutters pulled down tight. He needed time to think. He'd shaken hands with Potts on a deal that would mean lying to the public and, worse, lying to the news editor on the Post. He could hardly believe the money that he was being offered, but that made him even more scared. Money like that came with strings attached. No, rewrite that... massive great hawsers and anchor cables. Nooses, even. Was he already in too far to pull back? Could he simply phone Potts and say he'd changed his mind? But Potts was the only hope he had. Nobody else had replied to his texts. The photos he'd taken from Katrina's were leading him nowhere.

He drummed his hands on the steering wheel. The scene hadn't changed since he'd noticed it earlier on the way to Katrina's flat. Police donotcross tape rustled romantically in the pre-dawn breeze, and there was an aroma of spring in the slowly brightening darkness: the deceiving, manipulative scent of cherry blossoms that could betray you into believing anything, into believing that life could become better, that there might be a story to sell, that your ex-wife might take you back. It made him feel eager, scared and cynical at the same time.

Pictures make stories, Whelpower always said. Despite everything, Jason's journalistic instincts were still alive and they told him to take some now. But two coppers stood on the cordon, eyeing him warily. One rubbed his arms to keep warm while the other, taller, leant against the wall of the newsagent's, their gaze somehow combining mournfulness with disdain in a way that only policemen seemed to manage.

Jason tugged out his pocket camera, turned off the flash and waited patiently till the coppers were distracted by an urgent need for nicotine. Then he snapped the scene from his side window.

A good journalist knew there was rarely anything useful to see at a crime scene, otherwise the police would never have let you in. But still you had to have a look. He climbed out of his car and walked over, holding out his press card. The shorter policeman held it under a street light and examined it slowly. Jason liked being with coppers, it made him feel as if he was in contact with the grit of real life. The policemen didn't seem so enthusiastic about their current experience of grit, but Jason offered his most personable face and asked what was up. They shrugged with different degrees of intense gloom and confirmed this was where something had happened.

'And?'

And the scenes-of-crime officer had been and gone.

'And?'

And nobody never told cordon coppers nothing.

Jason's own bonhomie was beginning to wane, but he felt it would be too ignominious to retreat so soon. So he stayed a moment and contemplated the area in the hope there was something to notice while the two PCs, satisfied with their contribution to police–press collaboration, went back to flapping their arms in the shadows on the far side. Blocks of council flats peered down onto the tiny square with its concrete bench and single brave but scraggy tree. Inserted into the side of the newsagent's Jason could make out a cash machine. On the dark ground beneath spread something that might have been blood.

The coppers were still watching him, so Jason strode meaningfully round the perimeter of the tape. He nodded to himself with an air of concern, wrote random words in his notebook and returned. Then, above the cashpoint, he saw a security camera, a cheap old model bolted to the newsagent's wall.

At that precise moment, a small van appeared, Naik News printed in bold letters on the side, driving jerkily, headlamps wavering, as if it was annoyed at having to be up at five-fifteen in the morning. It approached, swung a U-turn, bumped half up onto the pavement and stopped. The driver climbed out and peered suspiciously at the blue and white tape.

'What is this doing here?' He addressed Jason, holding his head stiffly braced, as people did who felt that they should be taller than the universe had allowed. 'This must not be outside my shop.'

Jason felt he should defend his two New Best Friends and informed Mr Naik that a young person was in hospital, stabbed, and this was a story of major national importance. Mr Naik puffed out his chest and pointed a finger. He was very sorry indeed for the damaged individual but failed to understand how scaring away his customers would assist matters. He shook his head with considerable passion and was about to continue, but he was interrupted by a delivery truck that roared up and slowed just long enough for two heavy bales to be tossed with a thud onto the pavement.

With the first of the day's newspapers, Mr Naik's concern was now divided between his oppressors and his morning's work. The work won. He jabbed his finger towards the three of them, as representatives of all that ruined the life of the small trader, searched for the right words to caption the gesture, failed to find them, then stalked off to raise the metal shutter with an angry rattle and disappeared inside.

Jason left it five minutes before presenting himself at the open door. He sniffed an opportunity. If the security camera had been working during the attack, he might blag a quick snapshot of the monitor before the police released the footage to the general press. Pictures made stories. He might have the chance to get a few hours ahead of the competition.

Naik had set up a trestle table in the body of the shop and was stooped over it, noisily splitting the stacks of the morning's papers, which were now being thrown down from passing vans in quick succession. He shuttled between them and his orders file, scrawling figures on each masthead as he muttered a mantra of streets and numbers: 'Clive Terrace 5, Melbourne Gate 7, Churchill House...' The narrow space was filled with the sweet smell of fresh newsprint. A true journalist, Jason glanced first at the bylines. A Telegraph stringer was breaking a story about West African oil bribes and an obscure duke. The Mail led with a new report on falling house prices: shared byline, a staffer and a freelance. The Post was split between the financial incompetence of all the political parties and a half-famous batsman who'd been two-timing his wife (single front-page byline by a young shifter who Jason knew. Lucky bastard). He tore his attention from the front pages and took one step closer.

'No,' said Mr Naik, flipping a page of his order file and not missing a beat of his mantra.

'I just wondered...' Jason brought out his card and an

affable smile, but both were wasted.

'No,' said the newsagent, not looking.

'The cashpoint outside...'

'13, 21c Albany...'

Jason grew more than a little annoyed. Did the man not realise that here was news in the making? The very headlines that might be on these papers tomorrow. He tried greater volume.

'The security camera...' Somehow Naik's resolute resistance turned what should have been the strong tones of a future national correspondent into a rather plaintive croak. As Jason cleared his throat to try again at a more manly pitch, the other man suddenly bounced up.

'All right. All right. You fucking police.' And Jason knew he should most definitely tell him that he wasn't police.

'Mr Naik...' he ventured. But before he could continue, the newsagent tossed a bundle of Independents angrily to one side and rushed to the back of his shop. He slammed up a counter flap sending Twixes and Hello! Magazine returns flying like an explosion of coloured shrapnel, then dived disconcertingly under the till.

'I have work to do.' His voice emerged from beneath.

'I have to tell you, I'm not—' began Jason, earnestly addressing the counter.

'The time you people waste is my time,' continued the muffled voice. 'I am the one who will get angry phone calls if the Express is one minute late. Or if the Post fails to contain its celebrity supplement. Me, not you. They all tell me they can buy instead from the supermarket now. Or read it free on the Net. This is what it is today.'

He shot up abruptly, an inch from Jason's nose. He

must have tunnelled right under. 'Here you are, Officer.' And he pushed a VHS cassette into Jason's hand. 'Take it.'

Jason found himself holding the master tape. His brain froze. He searched for the words. He struggled with the desire to be honest. He hadn't asked to be given the master. He just wanted to see a few screenshots of the attack.

'This tape—' he started, but could get no further.

'I know. The machine is not a new one,' said the newsagent. 'I'm sorry. Blame me. Arrest me for it. Or give me the money for a big computer and I am very happy.'

'Mr Naik,' said Jason slowly, finding it difficult to reboot his brain.

'You want it in a gift box now?' Naik waved his arms impatiently. 'You want a fucking carrier bag? This is what you get. I don't tie it in ribbon. Now I must work. You can interview me later. I saw nothing. I was at home in bed. If there is anything, it is on there.' He thrust his way back through the waiting papers and magazines to the trestle table.

Jason was fully aware of the fine line between letting people accidentally fall into the belief that you were a member of the forces of law and order and deliberately impersonating a police officer. No. Delete that. There was a rather thick line: with freedom on one side of it and jail on the other. He could have refused the tape. He could have handed back his chance to gain exclusive access to what might prove to be the only visual evidence of Liam's attack. Instead, his pulse accelerating, he pulled out one of his exclusivity agreements.

'You'll need to sign this,' he said in his most authoritative voice. He didn't truly expect to get away with it, but Naik didn't read the words. He saw six places that said Signature and he snatched up a biro and scrawled his name six times.

Of course it was still not too late to tell the truth. But Jason's journalistic heart drummed fast at the thought of the shots that might be on that cassette and how much they might be worth. Pictures made stories. He deliberated over his duty to be honest to one person and his duty to bring the truth to the nation. He saw visions of front-page exclusives and individual bylines and more than that: he saw money being poured into his empty bank account and (of course) into treatment for Liam Glass. And he saw his national campaign against knife crime become a very real possibility. Maybe without needing Potts after all.

'Are you still here?' said Naik, angrily throwing copies of the Guardian and Mail in all directions.

'No,' said Jason. 'I mean, thank you. I'm going.'

'Go,' said Naik, scrawling new numbers. 'Go earn the money we working people give you. Go and stop crime.'

Jason nodded enthusiastically and left the newsagent's. The two policemen were just visible in the half-light, their cigarette ends glowing on the far side of the square. He held the cassette nonchalantly in his left hand, which happened to be masked from view by his body.

'Caught On Camera: Thugs Who Cut Down Chelsea Hopeful'.

So was this what it felt like to be on the brink of a national story? Jason crossed the road under the eye of the two coppers and the ten metres felt like fifty. He climbed into his car and slid the black plastic cassette into the glove compartment.

'Tragic Felling Of Future England Star'.

'End the Carnage On Our Streets'.

It was Andy's fault. He had cocked up twice now. First he got the boy's age wrong. Now he should have been here to collect the CCTV himself.

'A Special Report by Jason Crowthorne'.

But now Jason noticed the taller policeman was making a phone call. The man looked towards him.

Jason fumbled urgently with his keys and started the engine with more of a roar than he intended.

The policemen stubbed out their cigarettes and began to move towards him. He wiped a nervous crescent from his misted windscreen and pulled away at speed.

18

Balls on the Line

Jason sprinted up the fire escape to his flat, pulled out the cassette and placed it proudly on the single table in his kitchen-living-dining room. It seemed to be a standard VHS. He stood it on end, then laid it flat, and the squat black plastic looked wonderful and mysterious from all angles. What treasures did it hold?

His laptop had finished checking its hard drive and sat grumpily waiting for a password. He typed it in, then dived urgently into a cupboard in the kitchen and tugged his old video player from under two saucepans and a skillet. It didn't look happy. There was a dent in the top, a dead spider in the slot and it hadn't been used for a year and a half. Still, he wiped it encouragingly with a kitchen cloth, plugged it in, gently inserted the tape and pressed play with the trepidation of a bomb-disposal officer probing an unexploded mine.

Nothing happened. He pressed again and now the mechanism leapt into action with a horrible whine. He panicked: the machine was fucked. Worse, it was chewing the tape. He quickly pressed pause and the whining stopped. Sweat ran down the back of his neck. Nervously, he tried again. This time the noise was worse. He hit the front eject button at speed and grabbed the cassette before it could change its mind and return.

He'd need to find somewhere with the necessary technology, but he didn't have any friends who still had VHS. Not enough time for everything – he was starting to feel severely stressed.

To make things worse, he paused on his way out to look at his emails. In his inbox sat five urgent messages sent by Tam during the night. He admired the deputy editor's tenacity if not her editorial skills. He deleted the first three unread. The fourth started: Are you taking the piss? At a time like this. I thought you'd have more respect. It's deadline day too and no hippo article. The police say they won't talk to you anymore and I've received an official complaint from the widow of the man who was killed by a truck. I want to see you in the morning and...

He didn't know what she meant about respect – strangely over-the-top, even for her – and he trashed it. The fifth read: You're fired. You've already had two official written warnings in the last six months. I'm emailing HR and making Tyronne crime correspondent. Deal with it.

Jason stared at the words. She couldn't mean them. Could she do that? Didn't she have to go through the editor? He couldn't not have a job. After all the agonising, he couldn't believe it had actually happened. He'd go to HR and fight her in the courts. Illegal dismissal. She was just trying to get out of paying redundancy. Then again, this was probably what she'd been planning all along. She was devious enough. He was starting to regret not having talked to Whelpower last night when he'd had the opportunity.

He started to type an urgent reply, copied in to his mentor, then stopped himself. It was too late.

Fine, he said to himself, the Herald was the past. He was free. He felt the old electric surge – a feeling he hadn't enjoyed for many months. He had a big story. He just needed to sell it.

19

Lady in Red

It was outside that it first happened. She'd desperately needed a Lambert's and she'd not in fact had one since she came in. Katrina dug into her bag, checking she'd brought a packet with her. She found the cigarettes and her lighter lying loose, not in the inside pocket where she normally kept them, which slightly surprised her. Her hands trembled as she put the handbag over her shoulder and opened the door to the Intensive Care room, and her legs felt wobbly. She looked back at Liam, still unmoving. She felt awful leaving him there, but she needed time to herself.

Downstairs, hospital reception was empty except for a security man standing staring at nothing. She gave him a little wave and tried a smile, even though she didn't feel it – because she knew what it was to have a shit-awful job and be bored out of your mind. This one might have been Somali. There were a lot of new Somalis came to work at Tesco's and they didn't know anything at all about how to do things until you explained it to them.

Once through the main doors, Katrina lit up as soon as she could. The sky was turning grey and the air was sharp in her face. Liam would get better, wouldn't he? And she had to have faith. *Liam-baby, I've got faith.* When he was small and he'd spent a month in the incubator, she'd had faith then. He was so tiny and he fought so hard.

She went over to a corner away from the entrance and cried and then got herself sorted.

There were three other people also sucking urgently on their fags. Two wore pyjamas and dressing gowns. The third was a young girl in black bike leathers who pointed at her and said, 'I saw you before. You didn't see me.' She flicked ash. 'Ruby Treb.'

'Ruby?' said Katrina. 'You know, I made sure to call my son Ruby if he'd been a girl.'

'Wow!' said Ruby with a smoky wave. 'That's real. Katrina, there's a reason for everything. We could have even been sisters in a previous life.'

Katrina looked at her and the other girl was taller and too thin, and she herself was short-arsed and two sizes too big on the hips. But who the fuck knew the strange ways of reincarnation and how they worked? She had a friend who worked in Lidl who'd once fought under Boadicea and married an Iceni prince. Katrina had looked up the names on Wikipedia and they were there.

The motorcycle girl was going on about how she'd seen her in A&E. She'd been in one of the curtained-off spaces with her boyfriend and he was in a coma too after he went under a bus right in front of her.

'It was mental,' she said, taking a last drag on her stub, 'because Callum's even good on bikes. And he was literally talking to me all the way in the ambulance and we were making jokes about public transport. And then he fell asleep and wouldn't budge and they had to cut his leathers off. He'll be pissed about that.'

And she trod out her fag and lit another like automatically. So Katrina had to tell her about Liam, and Ruby said he might know her kid brother Marko, with a k. They were the same age.

Katrina said she didn't know about any kind of Marko with or without a k, but she'd ask Liam when he, well, when he...

She stopped and Ruby said she was sorry and she was even stupid and she shouldn't have upset her. Katrina went like she wasn't upset. Not by her. And she turned her face away and said she was sure Ruby's boyfriend would be fine.

There was this hissing from the automatic doors as they opened and closed once. But there was no-one there. Just the early breeze blowing. She could hear it banging against the window frames above, like it was pissed off. Then the doors opened again and Liam walked out.

He was wearing his tight jeans and white hoodie, though still with his tubes, mind you.

'You woke up?' she said and she took two steps towards him. Liam sucked his lip and stood there silent, his hands jammed into his jeans. 'They let you come down?'

And Ruby was going, 'You're right. I should be upstairs with him. Holding his hand. Not smoking away down here.'

'I'm here,' Katrina said. Liam didn't take his eyes off her. The breeze ruffled his hair and then died away. His face was grey as the concrete walls. She wanted to hold him, hold her Liam-baby, make it right, but she was scared.

She said, 'I'm here, baby. Baby, I'm here for you. It's all right.'

Ruby was staring at her. 'I'm watching the doctors,' she said. 'You got to push them. I'm not even exaggerating. You got to fight for what you want.'

Katrina turned round. Ruby wasn't looking at Liam at all, and when Katrina looked back, Liam had gone.

At the entrance to Intensive Care, Jason was greeted by a

square-shouldered Irish nurse, who scrutinised him with the welcoming manner of a North Korean border guard. Jason tried dropping Esmerelda's name, which had no effect. Similarly with DC Rockham's. In a faint voice, he offered the nurse a specific amount of financial inducement. There was a pause. A part of him hoped she hadn't heard him, but she had. The door opened.

The Irish nurse pocketed the twenty-pound note he'd produced with less ceremony than he'd have liked, given the pain of handing it over, and stalked off to the far end of the ward. The ward seemed more or less as Jason had left it. The early-morning shift moved from room to room displaying a mechanical optimism that Jason recognised to be fifty per cent front. This was what professionals became good at – looking like they were in control. Like Yogi Bear running off the edge of a cliff, paddling blindly, held up by thin air. The nurses were paddling fast.

Liam lay motionless, just as he had all night: eyes closed, machines flickering and bleeping. However, Katrina was nowhere to be seen. Worse, nor was her handbag. Jason hadn't planned for this. He slipped Katrina's keys out of his pocket, stared at them, as if they could give him the answer, then quickly stuffed them away again. He checked no-one had been watching him through the door. What if Katrina had called security? Or the police?

He took the keys out once more. He needed a cover story. Imagine she'd accidentally dropped them earlier and failed to notice. Where would they have fallen? He stood where her handbag had been left and mimed picking it up. Saw, in his mind, the keys falling out.

Then he heard footsteps approaching the room and froze with anxiety, but they stopped nearby. Nobody appeared. There was only Liam, chest rising and falling, oxygen hissing.

Jason couldn't look away. The boy seemed, if anything, worse than before; greyer, flatter. Jason felt anguished and impotent. He was a journalist – surely he could do something to help this child. He'd worshipped the great journalists, from Hugh Cudlipp to James Cameron. Devoured Private Eye. He remembered again how Gareth Whelpower had built his case against Sir Max Robertson, painstakingly, lovingly, fact by fact, spending days poring over the minute details of company accounts, digging out disgruntled bookkeepers and unhappy ex-secretaries, fighting everyone who'd tried to stop him. And yet it seemed Jason could do nothing to save Liam's life. Nothing to stop the rising tide of teenage victims.

He found he was still holding Katrina's keys. He let them drop quietly to the ground next to one of the drip-stands. He looked down. No. They were too obvious. Katrina would have spotted them there. He reached out with his foot and carefully pushed the keys under Liam's bed.

At that precise moment, a voice cut in and he jumped.

'If you're a doctor,' the voice said, 'it's about bloody time.'

A figure stood in the doorway dabbing her eyes, a woman in her fifties with tightly curled red hair and a dress and face to match.

'Who are you?' he managed to ask, trying to adjust to this vision of redness.

'Christine Glass. His grandmother. You've given up, haven't you?'

'I'm not a doctor, I'm a journalist.'

She looked him up and down without moving from the door. 'Yes, Kat told me about you on the phone. Well, that only proves it, doesn't it?' Jason didn't understand. 'When did you ever see three people allowed in to see a kid in Intensive Care? I watch *Holby City*. I know how things are done. But they've decided it's all over. It don't matter how many they let in now. Doesn't say much for you, does it? Kat said you promised better medical help. The power of the press. The best equipment, the best doctors. That worked well, didn't it?'

Jason tried to think of some words to string together. He was usually so good with words. Instead he turned round and left the room. He found the Irish nurse, bent over a box of used needles.

'When was Liam Glass last seen by a consultant?'

'I can only discuss the boy's medical condition with his family. For Christ's sake, I shouldn't even have let you in.'

'Well, you did. You want me to explain his lack of care to my readers? Go look at him. The kid's the colour of a week-old piece of cod. You want to see tomorrow's headlines? "Camden General Kills Stabbed Boy".'

The nurse hesitated.

'Well?' Jason asked. 'Your choice.'

He returned to the room a minute later. 'A doctor's on the way. The power of the press.'

'Maybe.' The Red Queen sat and surveyed him dourly. 'I sometimes read newspapers. I don't know I ever read anything in them that tells the truth.'

'Where's Katrina?'

'Search me, I just arrived. Probably outside having a fag.'

'Of course.' He thought for a moment. He had so

little he could do and even that was slipping away from him. Perhaps, though, the grandmother might be his salvation. She must know something about who the father might be. However, no sooner had he begun to search for an opening than the Irish nurse walked in to inspect the monitors.

'The consultant has one more patient to see first,' she said with a hard look at Jason.

'Thank you,' he said.

She gave him another glare as she left.

Moments passed in silence as Jason considered his options. Liam's oxygen pump hissed and Katrina's mother gave a series of deep sighs. On closer observation, he could see strong resemblances between Christine Glass and her daughter. The sharp nose, slightly edgy manner and dramatic dress sense. Right now she seemed to be ruminating on Liam's medical state, her eyes flickering, her tongue running round her mouth, thinning out the bright lipstick.

'The consultant will be here soon.' He wished he could say something more encouraging.

'Liam didn't deserve this.'

'Popular, worked hard at school...?'

'You're joking. None of us Glasses are ever going to win prizes. But he didn't deserve this. He's never done anyone any harm. He's one of the softest kids I know. Rescues spiders from the bath. Always asks you how you are. Always has something nice to say about people.' Christine dabbed warmly at an eye and left a row of eyelashes sticking to the tissue like a little black centipede. 'Shit.'

She was crying and she stopped herself with sheer force of will. 'You know Kat said she saw the kids who did it.'

'She told me. She doesn't actually know, though, does she?'

'She knows. The police don't care. She gave you their descriptions? You'll put it on the front page?'

'Totally. Big headlines.'

Christine glared angrily at her grandson. 'Why didn't he just hand over the money? A few quid and a card, it's not worth fighting over.'

Liam's chest rose and fell with a regular beat.

'Maybe he takes after his father,' Jason said carefully, not even looking at her.

'Who's his father, then?'

This was a question he wasn't expecting.

'I thought you might know. I mean, Katrina as good as told me.' He paused. He'd found pausing one of the most useful skills for a journalist. People had an instinctive need to fill silence with information. Normally.

'Did she? She never told me a bloody thing.' Christine dug into her handbag for something with which to glue the little line of false eyelashes back on again. 'And I never asked her. Who gives a fuck? He's not here. Makes no odds.' She located a plastic tube and a mirror and dispassionately started the complicated operation of repair.

Jason despaired of these people. Had they no idea about what was important?

'It makes a difference to me,' he said with more intensity than he intended. She looked over to him in surprise. 'I want to help stop this.'

Christine was poised, the centipede balanced on the end of a finger.

'I'm fed up with writing stories about kids getting stabbed. You get a few lines in the local paper, a councillor says something should be done, maybe some idiot gets caught, maybe not, and everyone forgets about it till next time. But if we want people to take notice, if we want the front page, we need a story. Which means I need to know who Liam's father is.'

'I thought you already had the front page.'

This was going badly. Jason was reduced to the frightening prospect of telling her the truth. Even though it went against his deepest journalistic instincts.

'I'm doing a deal with a national paper,' he said quickly. 'And I've told them that Liam's father was a Premiership footballer.'

'You told them what?'

'I kind of said I knew who he was... Well, there were things your daughter said two years ago. She dropped some pretty heavy hints.'

She gave him a thin smile. 'She never really told you anything, did she?'

Jason shook his head abjectly. 'The father's what interests them. If I don't get the name, there's no story, and I'm in the shit.'

'Then you're in the shit.'

'You think you can get Katrina to tell me who he was? I mean, you're her mother.'

His phone announced a new text. He glanced down. It was from Josette, reminding him to collect Bea from school in the afternoon. For a moment he felt a warm surge of connection. His ex was awake right now, just a few miles away, and thinking of their child. Then he remembered he'd promised to drive over last night after the hospital; the surge of connection changed into a wave of guilt. He tapped out a rapid apology for the night before and promised to pick Bea up later.

'My daughter's never listened to me in her life

before,' Christine was saying, as he sent his reply. 'I don't see why she's going to start now. She always said she don't want anything more to do with the man.' The centipede resumed its ascent.

'You'd have thought she'd want to have her revenge. Why should men get away with it all the time and women have to suffer? Let him pay what he owes.'

Christine glued the false eyelashes back into place and admired the restoration in her pocket mirror.

'I tried that one fifteen years ago, Jason.'

Her restored perfection seemed to please her. She flipped her mirror closed.

He was about to renew his attack, but as he was regathering his forces, the consultant arrived, trailing clouds of calm assurance, followed by the registrar. And at the same moment, Jason's mobile rang.

'That should be turned off,' said the registrar, a short, angry man. 'And you're not family, are you? Out.' He glared at the Irish nurse until she nodded firmly and escorted Jason from the ward.

Jason watched the door close behind him with resignation and answered his phone.

'Jason?' Somehow Josette managed to sound uncertain and warmly enticing at the same time. 'I thought, since you were obviously awake...'

'I'm sorry about last night.' He attempted to move rapidly down the corridor, but his legs felt heavy. 'This story...'

'It's OK. We never really expected you. It's not that. Arthur's going down with the most horrible flu, and I've got a breakfast meeting...'

Jason paused by the lifts. It hurt that she hadn't expected him to honour his promise. Was that so normal?

'So, Jason, do you think you could?'

'Could what?'

She had that annoying habit of assuming you knew exactly what she was talking about. But she also had the ability to sound remarkably sexy at six in the morning.

'Take Bea to school,' she breathed in his ear. 'I'll make it up to you.'

'Don't worry about making it up to me,' Jason said nobly, knowing he was being used. No matter. He loved spending time with his daughter, whatever the reason.

'I mean it.'

Sometimes, Jason mused to himself as he slipped the phone back into his pocket and stepped into the lift, even war reporters had family business to deal with.

20

Social Media

Royland jogged through the cool early-morning mist that veiled the tower blocks. He always hoped to catch some keen clients waiting outside the gym, eager to get their muscles juiced before they clocked in for work. Usually he was disappointed.

'Of course you are,' Sadé would tell him at predictably frequent intervals. 'This is a place filled with disappointment. Look in the street – everyone is shaped like a jam doughnut. You couldn't have found a worse postcode in the entire world to start up a gym, boy. The City bankers leave their flats early and go to their City gyms. The rest spend all their money on booze or burgers.'

This was her way of supporting him. She didn't want her man to be unhappy. If he knew he was going to fail from the start, then surely he'd aim low and not be hurt. Unfortunately, Royland was one of those cheery types who was always aiming high and so was always getting hurt. But, being a cheery type, that didn't stop him.

'Read the books, woman,' he said. 'The race goes to the swift. Thomas Edison failed nine hundred and ninety-nine times before he made the light bulb. The Beatles played for ten thousand hours before they got good.'

'You have to fail for ten thousand hours before the gym gets to break even?'

'If necessary, yes,' said Royland happily. 'You should really study these books. Negatives are for wimps.'

'I should be burning those books, boy. They give you mush for brains. Not that this was difficult to do.'

Nevertheless, Royland bounced out of bed most mornings and usually jogged off with unreasonable hope in his heart. This morning, though, his heart was heavy and his mind preoccupied and he found himself running a detour. Before he quite realised where he was going, he'd trotted to Attlee Gardens, where he'd dropped the knife the night before.

Surreptitiously, he peered through the iron railings at the tulips beneath. No knife. For a moment, his chest flooded with relief – someone else had taken it. It was their problem now, not his. But then he spotted the dark hint of a hilt and felt desperately guilty.

It wasn't too late. He could run round and get it from under the flowers and go drop it back where he'd found it in Gordon Road. No-one would know.

But the streets were starting to fill up – people walking to work, cycling, climbing into their cars. He told himself Sadé was right, the knife was nothing. That stain on the blade was rust. No-one had been attacked at all.

When Royland reached the gym, it was five to seven and for once there were customers waiting on the pavement – three of them, flapping their arms in the cold. He unlocked the two padlocks as quickly as he could. It was a message from the universe. Everything was a message if you knew how to read it. He tugged up the shutter, with its tasteful red and green Arabic graffiti. The graffiti was a message too. He'd once asked an Iraqi friend what the writing meant. The friend contemplated the airbrushed curlicues and said, 'I don't think you want to know.' But the man was an atheist. To Royland, such elegant calligraphy could only be a sign of spiritual blessing. His friend shrugged and said, 'If that's what you wish to believe.'

So far, believing what he wished had taken Royland a long way – as far as his own gym, with its name over the door: All Roads Lead to Royland. But not as far as being in credit. Maybe he wasn't believing enough. Sadé, never a ray of sunshine, was right: unless he made something happen soon, they'd be lucky to survive the month. This morning even the presence of three punters failed to raise his cheerfulness meter more than half a notch.

He clicked the switch in the main studio. The lights flickered on and four treadmills bleeped their greetings. He was followed in by a pair of young professionals who lived together and never stopped talking. Royland strode resolutely past a cross-trainer towards the TV with an expression that brooked no interruption... only to find an interruption being brooked. Neville was a retired travel agent with a perpetually anxious expression, who regularly puffed his way through a fitness plan Royland had carefully prepared for him, without ever getting noticeably fitter. Today he stood in front of Royland asking for advice about push-ups. Royland curtly sent Neville to the other side of the room to lift weights.

Neville went, unhappily, and Royland switched on the TV, high on the wall. A cheap flat-screen he'd picked up from a rather suspect shop that disappeared a week later, the picture was always a little unusual. People would unexpectedly develop green heads or break into blobs. He started to work up a sweat on a stair-climber while he watched it. This morning the monitor had settled on tastefully rainbow-coloured zigzags through which Royland could just detect a newscaster. A plane might have crashed in Fiji, more birds and insects might be dying than anyone thought... a mauve and yellow man said that climate change wasn't to blame, a blue-faced woman said it was... and someone had won a football match. No knives.

He picked up the remote as he worked out and flipped through the channels, trying to find the breaking news. Neville struggled manfully with a pair of five-kilo dumbbells. The slim young couple shouted merrily to each other as they pounded away on adjacent treadmills, making it difficult for Royland to hear. It always annoyed him when people gossiped noisily over the piped drum'n'bass that had been carefully designed to maintain clients' momentum and levels of monthly payment (*The Designer Businessman Handbook: Create Your World for Financial Success*). But then he began to catch snippets of their conversation.

'Kid... gang... knife...'

Royland froze. Of course, now that he wanted to listen, they dropped their voices to a murmur, drowned out by their thumping feet. Why didn't people speak more clearly? He found a sudden compelling reason to move closer and adjust something important on a resistance machine.

'It was only Twitter,' the man was saying.

'Only Twitter? What do you mean?' The woman panted heavily as she ran. 'OMG. Don't you read the papers? Like, hello, whole political campaigns are being started by Twitter!'

'It doesn't mean it's true.'

'We saw the police tape, Martin.'

'Well, that proves everything, doesn't it!'

A serious group of three men had arrived, coming off night shift, and were now gathered around the free weights. One picked up a kettle bell and shouted over. 'We heard some white gang attacked some other black gang, eh.'

'Nah,' his friend broke in from the chest press. 'A black gang even cut up a young Asian kid, innit.'

'I heard a kid fought off a whole gang,' called the third. 'Almost got away but was caught by a ninja throwing-knife, eh!' He mimed the trajectory with admiration. 'Boom.'

'No way, fuckwit,' said the first. 'They said there was blood and brain everywhere. Body parts and the lot.'

'A young kid, bro. Seven years old. Top in his school.'

Royland felt weak. The woman looked down from her treadmill.

'You see anything, Royland? You're often around at night.'

'Not a thing,' he said, staring hard at a particularly stiff nut that he was trying to twist for no good reason. 'Totally quiet. No. Nothing.'

'What did I tell you?' said her man, pressing the cool-down button. 'Just gossip. If anything had happened, Royland would know. He hears everything.'

'He just heard it,' she said striding angrily on. 'From us.'

'Yes, but he didn't hear it before.'

Royland moved heavily to a rowing machine. But the stupid knife stayed in his mind like it was jammed there and he couldn't get it out. Every glint in the cardiovascular room was the glint of sharp metal. Every clink from the weights became the vicious scrape of an edged weapon.

21

AltEn

It was eight-twenty-five when Jason's Renault lurched to a halt outside the small red terraced house in Brondesbury. Almost not late. Urgently he checked his Nokia. No responses from anyone who might have really known about Liam's father. Still nothing at all from Potts. The man hadn't been in contact since they'd met at four. Maybe he was thinking of backing out. This was worrying. He had seemed so definite. But then, Jason thought to himself, that was the job of the celebrity PR agent. To sound entirely convincing while talking bullshit.

The talk with Potts kept going round in his mind. For one brief moment, he had believed... With a certain amount of resignation, even relief, he tried to forget it. The plan was just too dangerous. However, the prospect of trying to sell the Post the unseen CCTV footage instead of a philandering footballing father wasn't going to be easy. He could put off phoning them a bit longer, but only for half an hour at the most.

Josette answered the bell. She was wrapped in a short white towelling dressing gown and announced that they'd been waiting. He followed her in, picking his way past musty raincoats, damp boots and three bikes of different sizes.

'Sorry I'm late. I've been trying to find this woman's son's unknown father.'

'Girlfriend problems?'

'No. A story.'

'Right,' said Josette over her shoulder.

'It's a big one.' He felt the need to make the point and his ex rewarded him by looking a fraction more interested. He wondered for a second why he cared what she thought.

'Have a coffee at least.'

'I thought we had to rush.'

'Jason, chill for once. Relax. Enjoy life.' Josette tapped him flirtatiously on the chest. To his surprise, memories of years of intimacy came flooding back. 'She'll be ready in two nanoseconds.'

He didn't feel he needed lessons from Josette in time management, but she seemed to be wearing very little under her dressing gown, which he found momentarily distracting. She ushered him into the kitchen, where his daughter beamed up at him from a bowl of Coco Pops. Immediately he felt better about life. When Bea smiled, everything seemed soluble.

'Happy birthday,' she said as they kissed and hugged warmly. 'You're late. And you didn't come last night.'

'I'm sorry,' he said.

'It's OK,' said Bea. 'It's normal.'

'Shouldn't we be going?' said Jason, mentally running through all the things he had to do in the next two hours. He felt mortified that she took his unreliability so easily. He turned to Josette. 'I thought you had an urgent breakfast meeting.'

'I do.'

'She does,' said Bea, decimating the last of her chocolate-flavoured bowl of fun. 'And I've caught Arthur's flu. I've got symptoms.'

Bea's symptoms were examined and disbelieved, and their owner sent bouncing upstairs to brush her teeth.

Jason sat in her place. The kitchen was not his style.

Furnished in stripped pine that went out in the seventies, it was hot and steamy from a pan of boiling water. Josette liked to make coffee in what she called the traditional French way. He glanced pointedly at his watch as she tipped rich ground coffee into the saucepan and chattered passionately about how Arthur's new project was going to change the world of alternative energy.

Jason had seen Arthur's new world of alternative energy: a large hole in the ground in the vicinity of Queen's Park, where he had paced out the ground-plan for a community solar generator, next to a pile of rubble. The hole was not yet his, but he had great hopes of making it his. He'd asked if Jason could help by slipping thinly veiled adverts into the Herald disguised as editorial. Jason had at first refused to lower his standards and then, not wanting to appear mean, had filed three different articles on the solar potential of areas near Kilburn until Tam had cottoned on. Despite this media onslaught, the hole remained a hole.

Josette turned back to the coffee but then paused.

'What's the problem?' he asked. 'Do you need more money for Bea?' He hoped that wasn't the case, not today of all days.

'No,' she said quickly. They weren't asking for handouts. The only problem was that the Cherryfield AltEn Project, as the hole was now known, needed to move on to the next stage. 'It's nothing but minor cash-flow problems. And you had promised in a rash moment... But, no, it's fine. We'll look into adding to our overdraft facility. You've been so generous already with Bea's support. It's a shame she won't be able to get the 3D Blu-ray disc of *Disgusting Monsters* that all her friends have got, but that's life, isn't it? And we'll have to refuse the invite from her best friend to go on an outing to London Murderers Alley. There's also next month's Wii Smarty-Pants game party. That's out. She can't turn up without a present. But she's a resourceful kid, she'll cope, like she always does.' Josette placed a large steaming French-style bowl of bitter French-style coffee in front of him.

'How much?'

Before she could answer, his phone buzzed with an email. He hesitated before looking.

'Go on,' said Josette.

'No, it's only work.'

'You always used to put work before family. I'm OK with that now.'

The message was from Potts: On the case. Send full details of boy – height, weight, age, hair colour, ethnic type.

A second message arrived a second later: And shoe size.

Jason took a deep breath and relayed the information to Potts such as he knew it. He made a guess at Liam's height and weight. He wondered what the point of the shoe size was, but took a stab at that too. Maybe Potts was already thinking about sponsorship. The man was amazing – every possibility covered. This was the secret of his success. It didn't matter what exactly you did, as long as you did it with total thoroughness. Jason made a mental note. No half-measures. He felt better about life. Potts was going to save his career. He turned back to Josette.

'How much?' he said again and logged into his online bank account.

'No, Bea can do without,' Josette said. 'Even if you did promise last month... Kids get too much thrown at

them, don't they? That's what we always said.
Simplicity. Self-reliance. It doesn't matter that the TV
doesn't work at the moment.'

'How much?'

Josette allowed herself to be forced into naming a
figure suitable for a minor Russian oligarch. He smiled as
if nothing was wrong.

'You're a good father.'

'I try to be.'

'You should have more children. You deserve to.
You're good at it.'

He made the transfer. If he could, Bea would have all
the Wii parties and 3D Blu-ray discs and Filthy
Murderers trips she desired in her little innocent heart.

A minute later, Bea came sauntering down equipped
with shiny yellow raincoat and plastic yellow shoulder
bag. She said goodbye to Josette, ran back to shout
goodbye to Arthur and informed Jason they were now
very late indeed and she was going to be in deep trouble
at school.

Jason started the engine and rammed the Renault into
gear. She asked what the story was that he was writing.
Arthur discussed important stories from the news every
evening.

'Good for Arthur,' Jason said as he accelerated and
looked across to check she had her seatbelt on.

'He always has interesting things to say about them.
Like the election and MPs expenses and—'

Then she looked up and gasped. A Morrison's lorry
was lurching towards them. Jason swerved to the left.
The lorry missed them, horn blaring.

'Different people find different things important,
don't they?'

But Bea was prattling on beside him regardless. 'Tell me your story. Is it important? Where will I be able to read it? Will it be in the Camden Herald as usual? Go right here.'

Jason swerved down an avenue on the right. 'Why?'

'There's roadworks by the station and this is a good shortcut.'

Jason loved her and everything she said. It wasn't because he was her father: he recognised intelligence when he saw it. He wondered how much he'd have to pay for a degree at Oxbridge or the Sorbonne.

'I'm writing about a boy who got badly hurt. You know, a knife attack. For a Fleet Street newspaper. But the newspaper wants to know about his father and some fathers are very unhelpful and try to stay anonymous. But I'm also going to be running a campaign. It's going to be big. To keep kids safe from knife attacks. Where next?'

'Left by the park and we're almost there.'

Jason took a rapid left, hooted a slow van and overtook at speed, narrowly missing a refuse truck coming the other way.

'How hurt is he?'

'He's in a coma. That means—'

'I know what a coma is. That's horrible. You must write about it. Turn right here and then left again. Poor boy. You've got to run that campaign, Dad. I'll be so proud. Zeb keeps talking about his father, who filmed the Haiti earthquake for the BBC. He says he's his hero.'

'Zeb should show more modesty.' He became aware that he was gripping the steering wheel rather hard.

A light turned red and he accelerated through it. Jason wondered what to say next. His little girl was getting older and he wasn't sure what to talk to her about anymore. Other people seemed to manage the job of being a father so easily. However, apparently having covered journalism sufficiently for the moment, Bea started describing a game called Warzone BludShed she'd played on a friend's computer. It seemed to involve dismemberment and torture. She said Josette let her play it, though Arthur wasn't so keen.

Jason took a fast right across the front of a bus and pulled up. They'd stopped thirty metres downwind of Buckingham Grange, the expensive little Montessori-lite prep school that Josette and Arthur and Jason had chosen. Jason had been politely insistent that Arthur should have his say as second daddy, although he'd expected Arthur to refuse out of tact and politeness. He had not yet learnt that Arthur refused nothing.

Cars jammed the street, creating a cloud of exhaust to rival the carbon footprint of Poland. Children of various ages were being offloaded, kissed and furnished with bags, scarves and good advice. Jason leant over and unclipped Bea's seatbelt.

'Do Mummy and Arthur argue about much?' he asked.

'What a silly question.'

'I just wondered. If you ever heard... No, you're right, it is a silly question.'

'They argue all the time,' Bea said, nonchalantly climbing out.

'They do?' Jason tried hard to look uninterested.

'Sometimes they even shout. And Mummy threw a book at Arthur and told him to sleep in the living room. That was funny.'

'Grown-ups can be very funny,' he agreed wholeheartedly as she leant back in to give him a hug. 'Do they do any other funny things?' He knew he shouldn't ask more, that this was a dangerous line he shouldn't cross, but what was the point of having lines if you never crossed them.

'All the time,' she said with great seriousness.

Jason told her warmly that he loved her and that she must have a good day and to be ready for him to pick her up after school and only him.

'No, not after school,' she said. 'We have Brain Building clubs in after-school on Wednesdays. And then Body-Mind after after-school. Don't you remember?'

'Gotcha.' And he gave his little girl another hug and a kiss. She accepted all this with an offhand grace and a small sneeze, which he wiped with a tissue. She wanted again to know about the boy in the coma and Jason said he'd tell her more after after-after-school. Then he watched thoughtfully as she sprinted up the road, his future international lawyer, and disappeared into the pullulating crowd of varied shapes, sizes and ethnic types, all of them unaware of how their futures paled against hers.

22

Bengali Rasta

'No way, no way, no way, no way, no way, no way!' The voice came from the shadows over on her left. 'No way,' it added for extra emphasis. 'You talking out of the back o' your manifesto, innit.'

'I'm telling you—' she said.

'Yo' no believe dat ting. Yo' jus' wan' our votes, man.'

'No, I—' This was horrible. And unfair. It was her breakfast meeting. She had to force it back onto the issues. She had so much to say.

'Thassit. Jus' like dem others.' The voice was harsh and pushy and the man who belonged to it wore baggy combat trousers and a wispy goatee beard and despite the Caribbean street talk was as Bengali as Jamila. Which was to say he was a Londoni – born right here.

'Let me explain—'

This was only supposed to be a meet-and-greet, one of the regular breakfast meetings that Jamila was proud of, giving her insight into issues on the Estates and cementing the love of her ward constituents. There were only fourteen of them in front of her right now – white, black, Bengali, Chinese and of indeterminate mixes – scattered around the meeting room at the Evelyn Street Sylheti Social Centre, clutching coffee, croissants and deep-fried luchi. They all looked to Jamila Hasan to save their businesses, their jobs, their streets or just their rubbish-collection schedules. But Mr Rasta-Bengali-Londoni was in full flow.

'Yo' no gwan answer my question. Yo lot never answer no questions. Yo lot jus' wan' de power and de money and de celebrity, innit. Yo lot—'

Worse, the others were starting to grunt in agreement. Jamila might not have been large and imposing – in fact she was rather short and slightly plump and nobody had ever believed she would amount to anything – but she had an abundance of energy and determination. When she wasn't working as a councillor, she was doing her day job as a presentation coach, teaching advertising executives, company directors and freelance writers to look their best in speeches and interviews. She was good at it too. On her day she could be Winston Churchill crossed with Mother Theresa. Right now, short of sleep and hung-over in a very un-Muslim way, she was falling short of Richard and Judy.

'As local councillor in this ward—'

'Local what? You no gwan be local anyting come four weeks' time. We got your number—'

Mustering all the energy and determination that was musterable, she pointed her finger at her heckler without fear or favour and tried to think of something to say. But all she could think of was the polls in that morning's papers, which were even worse than the day before. Her chances of re-election were sliding by the hour, it seemed. It was very unfair. She tried her best. It didn't even help that nobody in the room much liked the Tories – they were against politicians of any sort. Just one person seemed to be on her side. A smart young white woman sitting over to the right who smiled and nodded at every word she said. Jamila had hardly noticed her at the start, but clearly the woman was of above average intelligence.

'Look at de high-speed link! Wha' this one doing to

stop that?'

'And I pay fortune on the Tube!' said an older Korean woman.

The room's occupants were now debating among themselves, ignoring Jamila, who was perched at the front of the semi-circle of plastic seats, for maximum interpersonal feeling. She had to finish this and get out somehow.

'And de local rents. And all dose flat that got sold off and raise de prices so none of us can afford?'

'Yeah, yeah!'

'And de migrants—'

'Yeah, yeah!'

'Hey, man, we all migrants—'

'I talk about dem *new* migrants—'

'Believe it!' came from all sides.

'The truth—' she cut in.

'If I wantin' de trut, I don' ax no politician.'

That got a laugh from everyone except the young white woman, who rose further in Jamila's esteem. It was the fault of the media. How could her voters think straight when their heads were filled with Page Three and *Celebrity Big Brother*.

'Read my local crime manifesto.' From the table behind her Jamila snatched a handful of leaflets and thrust them into their hands. Newly printed, waiting for her when she'd arrived there that morning, full of her wise thoughts. She could smell the fresh ink, the fragrance of hope.

'Crime, yeah? You got some planned?' More laughter.

'An' what about de stabbing?'

'What stabbing?' She looked at Mr Rasta-Londoni in surprise.

'De stabbing dat took place last night, innit. You

don't even know about it. Jus' three streets away. What kind of finger is dat on the pulse, woman? Dey saying all kinds of things. Dey saying our gangs did it. What you say about dat? You gonna defend us or jus' ax for our votes, Ms Local Crime Manifesto?'

Dimly, now, she remembered the police tape from the night before. 'I've been to the scene,' she said. 'The police are keeping me briefed at all times.'

'You no know,' interrupted the Chinese woman, waving Jamila's manifesto at her as if it counted for nothing. 'You just ask, "What stabbing?"'

Jamila's phone buzzed with an email from Orange advertising two-for-one cinema seats. 'That's the police now,' she announced loudly. 'I have to go. This has been great. Thank you for sharing your views. And if you want to support the party, there are always many ways you can help.'

'You finished?' said the Bengali Rasta as the small assembly of citizens stood up, draining their coffees and swallowing last mouthfuls of dhal. 'We not. We got all de other issues—'

'There's another group coming in.' Jamila swept up the remaining leaflets.

She nodded to an elderly Bengali caretaker, who had been day-dreaming in the corner. He gazed at her in some surprise as the sewing circle didn't start for another hour, but she ushered her constituents warmly out of the door. The white woman hung back. She must have been about Jamila's age, maybe slightly younger. Jamila felt a connection with her, and she sensed the other woman felt it too. Something she'd not had since Melissa left. Maybe, if the woman was keen, she could join the campaign team Jamila didn't yet have. She gathered up her three boxes of manifestos with difficulty and said, 'I hope I can count on your vote.'

The woman smiled apologetically. 'I can't vote for you. I live in Crouch End.'

'I'm sorry?' Jamila felt foolish and confused. The caretaker started to bang the plastic chairs together.

The woman handed her a dispatch note to sign. 'I'm Suzen. I'm from the printer's, round the corner. I just delivered the handouts.'

The Evelyn Street Sylheti Social Centre was an old labyrinth of a building, rooms of assorted shapes and sizes crammed together with the haphazard glee of a Bengali street market and filled daily with workshops on teenage drug abuse and courses in repairing microwaves. Already women were arriving, chattering busily, to prepare one of the smaller rooms for a crèche. But the person Jamila urgently needed to see was not among them. It took an exhaustive search to track Golam Kamal to a tiny photocopying room at the back. Here he stood pondering a very new and extremely complicated machine which towered over him like an intergalactic spaceship.

'What is this stabbing?' Jamila launched at him without preamble.

'I don't believe it.' Golam jabbed a touch-screen control panel without visible effect. 'I ask for a simple copying machine, don't I? What do they give me? This – thing – that makes books, prints pictures, washes my laundry and does everything except copy.' He leant dangerously far into the machinery and peered at its various arms and flaps. The Sylheti Centre administrator was an angular bearded man of middle age who seemed himself to be made up largely of unruly parts and whose life was dedicated to ensuring that local Bengali politicians put as few of their ridiculous ideas into practice as was feasibly possible.

He hopefully opened and closed a beige drawer.

'The stabbing?' repeated Jamila, finding her nose worryingly close to the administrator's elbow.

The elbow jerked sideways. Jamila ducked just in time.

'Horrible. Dreadful. I sent you an email. Look at the email.'

Precisely as he spoke, her phone buzzed. She extricated it from her handbag and examined the screen. The email wasn't from Golam, in fact, but from the police. The Rasta-Londoni was right. A white teenager had been stabbed. There was no press release yet, and the police and council did not want to discuss the question of local racial involvement.

'I bet they don't,' said Jamila.

Then the email from Golam arrived. It simply said: Stabbing rumours. Tragic. No alarm.

'No alarm?' she said as he bent double over the paper tray.

'Very sad, but no reason to panic,' he replied, over a bony shoulder. Then he said 'Aha!' and straightened. But nothing happened.

'People are saying it may be Bengalis who did it.'

'Rubbish.' Golam was frowning now. 'Just a lot of Twitter and stuff. Hot air. I always say: remain silent and no pigeons will fly. If only people listened. Look at all this.' He indicated a stack of copying waiting to be fed into the machine. 'Statistical reports on tandoori house wages, statistical research papers on arranged marriages in Hendon, statistical meta-studies on everything else. Pah!'

'My voters need me, in their hour of need.'

'Your voters hardly know you exist. Anyway, a tall asparagus ends up in the pot,' opined Golam, with a thump on the side of the copier to emphasise his point. The machine gave an apologetic bleep, grunted three times and jerked into action. Golam gave a wide grin of satisfaction.

'So does the short one,' said Jamila. 'Thank you. Now I know what I must do.'

'Patience.' Golam stepped back to admire the whirring fruits of his mechanical prowess. 'If only more people were like me.' He tugged his beard proudly. 'What must you do?'

But she'd gone and he was speaking to an empty room. He shook his head sadly. The ward councillors rarely listened to traditional wisdom.

23

The Father

Jason had travelled just half a mile in the past twenty minutes, jammed in the aftermath of the school run that clogged the sclerotic arteries of West Hampstead. He really ought to get back to the hospital as soon as possible. It was time to speak to the Post, but no suggested fathers had yet arrived from Potts. Jason was growing increasingly anxious. He felt as if he was diving off a high bridge into very deep water.

He didn't have the father, but he had a CCTV tape. That alone could give the paper a great visual story. Maybe. It was a risk. It wasn't what they'd asked for. It was also the truth, which made it even riskier. Nobody really ever wanted to hear the truth. Lies were much safer.

The traffic lurched one metre and stopped. The street was solid with some of the most expensive road vehicles on the planet, yet none of them were capable of moving at more than four miles per hour. Jason prided himself on his knowledge of shortcuts. A true journalist, he liked to say, was never stopped by mere traffic. He swung the car left and discovered an empty street, which he raced along in triumph, only to enter a one-way system that directed him magisterially in a circle back to the street he'd started on. He re-joined the same queue of cars he'd left, two hundred metres further back.

After a short pause, he turned on the hands-free and dialled.

'Has he still got a heartbeat?'

Jason could hear the morning hum of the Post's newsroom in the background. He cleared his throat. 'The boy? Yes, Lyle. As far as I know he's still alive.'

Lyle Marchmont was the daytime news editor. He'd joined the Post at the same time as the night news editor but could hardly be more different: tall, laid-back and Home Counties, where Dalgleish was short and hard, from the tough side of East Kilbride. So of course the two of them were immediately known as the Twins. Unlike many tabloid editors, Lyle, a foppish man who wore striped shirts like a banker, had never bothered to pretend he was working class. He was at ease with his embarrassingly good education and inconvenient intelligence and saw no reason why these should stop him slumming for money. Jason liked his honesty, yet soon learnt that – as with Dalgleish – the smallest mistakes were greeted with a sulphuric stream of sarcasm. Either was capable of making a young reporter on shifts feel as if he'd let down the entire country.

'How much alive?' Lyle was saying. 'Of course, we all hope the kid lives, but if he's going to die today, I don't want him dying just after the deadline. It'll screw up the editions something rotten.'

Jason couldn't confirm whether Liam's struggle for life would fit in with the Post's schedules.

'How are things on the Herald? I heard they were dumping staff. You're not for the chop, are you?'

'Absolutely not,' said Jason, revving the throttle nervously. 'Just looking for new challenges. Fresh fields.'

'I've sold your coma kid to Paddy,' Lyle continued after a moment's pause. 'She's just back from breakfast with the leader of the opposition. She loves the story.' Jason's pulse started to race. The editor of the Post loved his story. 'Well done. This could be the making of you, Jason. So, who's the famous father, then?'

Jason checked his messages. Still no fake fathers from Potts. He felt partially relieved. Now was his chance to come clean. He hadn't actually lied. Despite his excitement, he hadn't told Dalgleish he knew who the father was. Or had he? He tried to remember the precise words he'd used during the night. Behind him a driver had decided that pressing the horn twenty times would improve his life.

'I've got CCTV of the attack,' Jason said, deciding that lateral thinking was his best ploy. He avoided saying whether he'd actually viewed the shots. To his enormous relief, Lyle swallowed the bait and asked for more details.

'Newsagent's security camera. Pointing straight at the scene.'

'You can see it all happening? Clearly?'

'That's what CCTV generally does.'

There was hesitation at the other end. Jason accelerated three metres and then impatiently jammed on the brakes as the traffic halted again.

'And you came by this legally, I take it.'

'I've got the tape, Lyle. Right here. I was handed it by the owner. Confidentiality agreement signed, nothing to worry about.' He patted the bulge in his jacket pocket to reassure himself as much as anything.

'We'll have to look at it.'

Jason took a deep breath. He'd managed to steer the story away from the father.

'So, tell me about the father,' said Lyle.

Ahead, a shiny 4x4 Volvo had managed to collide with a BMW sports car at three miles an hour. Both drivers climbed out, gesticulating. Jason gripped his phone tightly. 'Lyle, it's all under control. I'm working it.'

'Working it?'

'About to tie up the negotiations.'

'You told Tom Dalgleish that you had the father.'

'Ah. Well, I said I was getting him.'

'Good. I trust that Tom and I haven't been made to look like twin idiots.'

Jason felt hot. 'No, no, no, of course not.'

'You do have the father, don't you?'

'Have I got the father! There's a laugh!' In front, the first driver threw a useful punch at the second, who replied with a jab into the ribs.

'Good.'

'Absolutely.'

'Because if you've made me and Tom lie to the editor, you do realise you'll never work here again.'

'It's all totally under control,' Jason said again. The second driver followed with a right-left uppercut combo. Four pedestrians started to shout encouragement.

'And you can tell me who he is.'

'Lyle, these negotiations are at a delicate stage... The man needs reassurances before he gives me his name.' To his relief, Lyle sounded convinced by this. Jason leant his head limply against the steering wheel.

'He is Premiership, isn't he, Jason? England star? Defender? Striker? Give me something to work with here.'

'I'll have it all for you very soon, Lyle. I promise.'

'You certainly fucking will. Paddy's very into Premiership footballers right now. Flawed role models. Heroes and villains. Plus, the owners have just taken a stake in a new sports web portal. Yesterday, she played snooker with the minister.' In the background, Jason could hear Lyle's name being called. Lyle grunted something indistinct as he waited for Jason's reaction.

'Of course,' said Jason.

And now, to his dismay, Lyle was listing what he wanted delivered within two hours: the CCTV pictures, photos of Liam and family, the exclusive with the mother, the name of the footballer with proof of paternity. 'Paddy's not sure yet about a full-on national anti-knife campaign, but if you can deliver the goods, I'm pretty sure I can swing it for you. With your name in large, glittering letters all over it. Or is there a problem?'

'No problem.' Jason sat up again. For the first time in his life, he was being let into the game. All he had to do was deliver a father who was a fake.

'Good. Because you know the Premiership balls-for-brains father is absolutely key to this story, Jason. Without him, this is just two pars buried somewhere nobody will read.'

'I totally understand, Lyle.'

'You'd better be sure. No father, no splash. No splash, no byline. End of contract. Goodbye, Jason.'

In front, the first driver had the second in a headlock and was busy introducing his opponent's face to the side of his SUV.

IV

Wednesday 9.30 am

'It's a simple job. Find the truth, take the pix and file the
words on time.'

Gareth Whelpower, 'Off-Stone – Memories of a Newspaper Man'

24

Carluccio's

On Gordon Road, people were afraid and angry. Rumours twisted into gossip, gossip tangled itself into beliefs and beliefs knotted into certainties. The police searched the Estates for a knife and gave up. They continued knocking on doors for information but without much hope.

By now, most of the residents knew that a white kid had been stabbed. Greta Leach and Toklis Chowdhury had been busy retweeting it. Dulé Pascal and Mamun Reza were among the first to put it on Facebook. Followed shortly by Will Unthank, tousled and now on his way to bed after over-celebrating a friend's birthday.

The Rhodes Street Boys were among the suspects. They were a Bengali gang and controlled the Estates and people were saying it was Bengalis that had gone for the kid, though nobody could say why. The Rhodes Street Boys went onto Facebook to say: Not us, it weren't us. This didn't help anyone a great deal. On the one hand, the Boys rarely denied it if they really had stabbed someone, but on the other hand, they often told lies.

Of course, both police and residents knew how the gangs worked: most of the graft was done by kids of eleven or twelve, short-arsed foot-soldiers for the older leaders. By 9 am, however, the majority of said foot-soldiers were unwillingly installed in their classes at Euston Comprehensive (an 'outstanding centre of learning excellence'), unable for the next few hours to pursue their primary life-goals of selling drugs and knifing each other.

Not that getting to school was ever easy for the Rhodes Street Boys. Their white rivals, the Up Town Youths, ran the territory between them and the school, patrolling the narrow streets that the Rhodes Street Bengalis needed to cross. Each morning, young Rhodes Street soldiers had to choose: they could take the direct route and gain face but risk a beating, or they could slink round the back, taking the long, cowardly way, filtering discreetly through estates that were more difficult for the Up Town Youths to police. This morning, they'd played safe and taken the detour.

So everyone breathed a temporary sigh of relief. The younger members of both gangs found themselves being taught about gravity, democracy and sonnets, while texts buzzed round the school, stories circulated, challenges were issued and the foot-soldiers gazed longingly out of their classroom windows at the adult world of beckoning violence. Lunch was going to be the next big moment. Then they'd decide whether to stay in relative safety or move out into the streets and follow their insatiable desire to shorten their young lives.

Jason drove on as the morning traffic began to clear. He accelerated through a red light and turned on his car radio, in case there was a mention of the knifing, but there was nothing but phone-in vacuity. Radio was so bloody slow, filled with no-brains wittering about their honeymoon disasters and favourite Take That songs.

The phone rang.

'Yes!' he barked at it.

There was a short, surprised pause. Then a woman gave her name, Zoe Sharpleside – crisply, like she was announcing her byline. 'Lyle Marchmont has put me on your love-rat story. Where can we meet?'

Jason had been worried about Lyle. The news editor would be watching him like a drone, following him from on high with a merciless gaze, ready to destroy him if he so much as suspected a lie. But now the drone was forgotten. Here came a stealth bomber. How could Jason arrange a fake father with Potts while a staff reporter stood next to him watching his every move? He braked hard for an irritatingly slow cyclist hidden in a black cagoule and told the staffer how delighted he was by her offer of help. 'However,' he continued, 'I'm really sorry, I'm rushing around following leads, not sure where I'll be next. And in any case, there really isn't anything for you to do, everything's under control.'

The voice was implacable. 'It's wonderful that you're chasing angles. I can come and chase them with you.'

'I—'

'Actually,' she added softly, 'Lyle says this is non-negotiable.'

'OK,' Jason said, capitulating. 'I know a good coffee place.' And he gave Zoe Sharpleside the address of Carluccio's in King's Cross. Somehow he forgot to mention that Gray's Inn Road was being dug up and that there was a demo scheduled against the war in Iraq. But doubtless she'd find this out for herself. If she was that good a journalist, she'd already know.

Patience, he told himself, as he slipstreamed a 98 bus up Willesden Lane towards the hospital – on the other side of the borough.

'He's so pale, Kat,' said Christine with a sigh. 'Like a sheet, he is. And flat with it.'

Kat said not a thing but contemplated her son. Christine's heart felt swollen and her stomach kept turning with fear. She would sell her soul for her grandson to sit up again. She would give her life to hear him laugh at her watching *Britain's Got Talent*, or complain to her that Kat had grounded him from playing *Grand Theft Auto*. At the same time, she found herself thinking more and more about what Jason had said earlier, and the possible advantages to Liam of serious newspaper interest.

'They keep coming in and fussing and fiddling with things, but I don't see nothing changing,' she said, blowing her nose. 'If you don't have money, they don't care. That's the world today.'

'They do their best,' said Kat.

'Do they? I'm not so sure. I've seen things in hospitals.'

'What have you ever seen, Mum?'

'I've seen things, believe it. Remember when I almost cut my thumb off peeling a tomato?'

'Why the fuck were you peeling a tomato?'

'That's not important. It was a recipe. Look, I was in Casualty five hours, I could have bled to death, Kat.'

'But you didn't, did you?'

Christine stood and stroked an anxious hand over the nearest of the tubes that led down to Liam's arm and tried a different tack. 'I know I know nothing. I'm only your old mum and have just wanted the best for you and little Liam. My age, you expect to get ignored.'

'Your age? You're still out clubbing weekends and your skirts are shorter than mine.'

Christine dismissed this as irrelevant. 'Do you see any improvement in him?'

Kat had to concede that she didn't.

'I'm just saying.'

And for a while she stopped saying. Which made a deeper impression on her daughter than the most persuasive words could have done. Instead she sighed again and opened a copy of the Post, which she happened to have bought five minutes earlier at the Hospital Friends shop.

Kat announced she was going for another smoke. But she didn't. Instead, she went and walked up and down the ward, outside the room, muttering to herself. Watching from the doorway, Christine couldn't hear more than the odd word. Then she saw her daughter stop and stare into a shadowy corner inhabited by a scuffed fire extinguisher.

'Liam-baby,' she heard Kat say. 'Tell me what you want me to do?'

But it seems she didn't receive an answer from the fire extinguisher, or at least not a very useful one, because after a period of time she broke eye contact and went on with her walk.

As she did so, Jason was parking his car in the grim, concrete hospital car park. The lifts were busy with out-patients so he ran up the stairs towards Intensive Care. He still hadn't heard anything from Potts. What was to stop Potts going direct to the Post and cutting him out altogether? He was simultaneously excited and seriously scared. He'd started to make a phone call, then changed his mind and started another and then changed it back. And so he was approaching the door to ICU B when it opened and the consultant and registrar came out.

They saw him and turned in the opposite direction, but Jason was too quick. He caught them up by the lifts and asked how Liam was doing.

'You're not a relative, are you?' said the consultant. A tall man with glasses and an unreasonably suspicious nature.

As he spoke, Jason's mobile buzzed. To his relief, the face of a footballer appeared – Tony Potts had been as good as his word after all. This one looked a bit small and Spanish, but definitely white. A step in the right direction.

'A close friend.'

A second photo arrived – red-haired, Russian this time, and bearing even less resemblance to Liam than the one before.

'Journalist,' said the registrar and told him again to stay out of the ward.

'I have the mother's permission. The public deserve reassurance that Liam Glass is in good hands. Ms Glass has agreed to waive her privacy rights in the interest of her son's future health.'

Far from reassuring Jason or his public, the two doctors asked him now to leave the hospital and when Jason protested they phoned security. Jason didn't wait to be escorted out but headed back towards the stairs. After the first two footballers, the supply had stopped. Jason was so distracted by this and by the unfairness of the senior medical staff that when his mobile rang he answered it.

'What's going on?' said Jamila Hasan.

'What's going on where?' he said, stopping in the corridor for a moment.

'You know where. You know everything. You have contacts. I get an email about a stabbing, I see texts and tweets. I try the Herald and rival local papers, who know nothing, and the police, who tell me even less, so I turn to the one person who has his finger on the pulse. They don't seem to like you much in the Herald office, by the way. There was a mood.'

'I can imagine. I've been busy.'

'Aha! Busy at what? At this stabbing? Who is it, who did it? I'm going round and round in circles here at the town hall. Why are the police not telling me anything?' Her voice rose in outrage.

Jason liked Jamila. The little Bengali councillor never did very much, but she loved being in the news. He'd first met her five years ago, leading a march of local shopkeepers against the repainting of a double yellow line in Cabot Place. She'd given him some advice on presentation, drawing on her expertise as a coach, and he'd placed a steady stream of local stories featuring her in return. Jamila Hasan would argue for the abolition of rain if it got her a picture in the Herald with a quote.

'I've spoken to the BBC's *Lunch for London*. They want me live at midday...'

Jason almost collided with a passing trolley of coffee and buns. 'What do the BBC know about this?'

'Only what I've told them. We must have more police. More youth clubs. More CCTV—'

'CCTV?' Jason felt the weight of the tape in his jacket pocket. He still hadn't had the chance to view it. And he didn't need Jamila making waves about it either.

'Yes, the police are saying nothing about CCTV. The borough is filled with security cameras, on poles, on walls, on rooftops, and yet when it comes to this terrible attack we are shown nothing. You know why? They are all in the wrong place. The council has them filming the parking bays. This is all they care about: parking bays. I am going to make a big fuss about CCTV today. I'm adding it to my Local Crime Manifesto.'

'I wouldn't. Really, I wouldn't.'

'Why not?'

Jason searched for a reason that would make sense. He needed her to stay quiet and not ruin his story, but he'd never known Jamila Hasan to stay quiet about anything in the four years since she'd been elected. 'You don't want to go off half-cocked.'

'Let the police explain themselves to me, to the voters.'

He needed time to think. 'We should meet and compare notes first. Attack from a position of strength. That kind of thing.'

'Is there something I should know?'

'Just don't talk to anyone before I've seen you.'

'Shit. OK, the town hall at eleven.'

'That soon?'

But she was gone. He jogged urgently towards the stairs again. He felt sure he could manage Jamila. She rarely held on to an idea for long. Again his phone rang. Again he made the mistake of answering it.

'Where the fuck are you?' It was Tam. Behind her he could hear the stuffy rattle and bleep of the Herald's offices.

'Hi, Tam. I thought I was fired...'

'Screw being fired. Everything's upside-down here today, as you can imagine. And I'm hearing about some yob who got stabbed and I need two hundred words.'

He ran down to the ground floor. 'If things are upside-down, maybe you should think more carefully about who you sack. Put one of the others onto it. Tyronne. Isn't he the new crime correspondent?'

'Tyronne wouldn't know where to start. At a time like this, I need you in the office, doing your job.'

'Sorry, I can't hear you,' Jason said, reaching reception.

'Yes, you can. I need you.'

'You're breaking up. Repeat that.'

'Don't play fucking games with me,' Tam yelled. 'Today of all days.'

'The signal's going...'

'You're fired again.'

His mobile rang again as he strode out of the front doors.

'Where the hell are you?' Zoe Sharpleside sounded remarkably like Tam, only even more unnerved. No doubt Lyle had been phoning her every five minutes for an update.

'Zoe,' he said, trying hard to sound caring. 'Where are you?'

'King's Cross. Don't you pick up your messages?'

'King's Cross! What are you doing there?'

'That's where you told me to be.'

'No,' he said coolly. He spotted Katrina smoking outside with a young woman in leathers and turned rapidly in the opposite direction. 'I said Brent Cross. *Brent* Cross not King's Cross. Maybe we had a bad connection.'

'I heard you clearly. If you're trying to blow me out...'

'Seriously, I'm sitting right now in Carluccio's at Brent Cross. You should be able to get there in forty minutes if you move fast.'

A slight drizzle was starting. Jason decided to leave his car in the car park this time. Instead, he flagged down a taxi, leapt in and asked for the town hall – in King's Cross.

25

Conspiracy Theory

Jason trotted briskly up the marble town-hall stairs, feeling slightly better about life. Potts had texted to say that more footballers were on the way, and the Post's nosey staffer should be heading for the other side of the borough. What he had to do now was keep Jamila Hasan in line and stop her screwing things up. She meant well, always voted precisely as her party told her to, and rarely had an original thought. In normal times, she would have been safe in her ward for decades. But these weren't normal times.

The councillor sat waiting for him alone in Meeting Room 2, checking emails on her Blackberry.

'The party doesn't want to know,' she said, settling herself urgently on a high-backed chair. 'Mine is not, it seems, a priority seat.' Licensing Panel A had just finished processing an appeal from a kebab shop that wanted to offer lap-dancing as a natural addition to Camden's rich cultural heritage. Jamila had put her lack of beliefs on the line and abstained.

Jason sat opposite her at the elegant inlaid walnut table that filled the room, half listening while in his mind he began dividing up the large sum of money Potts had offered him. Half would go to Katrina and Liam. Maybe a little less, as he'd be doing all the work. He'd put a chunk aside for a special holiday with Bea, even better than the week they'd spent last year in Rome. She'd loved the crumbling majesty of the Roman Forum, the fountains from *La Dolce Vita* and the house where Keats had died. They'd marched up the Spanish Steps together, hand in hand, with him chanting 'Truth is beauty. Beauty truth.' He'd even spare some cash for Josette and Arthur, out of goodwill. He was feeling an inordinate amount of goodwill at that moment. He forced himself to pay attention to Jamila's words.

'I'm strengthening my Local Crime Manifesto.' She pushed a draft across the table.

Jason examined the glossy leaflet and Jamila's scribbled additions. He felt decidedly anxious about the frequent mention of security cameras. He didn't want Jamila stirring up a search for the tape. He leant towards her and adopted a confidential tone.

'I'd lighten up on the CCTV angle.'

Jamila gazed at him with a degree of suspicion. 'Why?'

'Privacy issues. Big Brother. We already have more cameras than Communist China. Bad for votes.'

'But the voters want them.'

'I'm just saying. Friendly advice. I'm hearing stuff on the street.'

She raised a stubby finger. 'Jason, there's something going on. Nobody's returning my calls. Ha! Doesn't that tell you something? The Safer Neighbourhoods team, the press office, the borough commander, the council. They're all avoiding me.'

'Don't they usually?'

'Yes, but this is different. Doesn't your nose tell you? There are goings on here.'

She was like a dumpy, unfit basset hound who'd managed for once to catch a squirrel and was damned if she was going to let go. He needed urgently to give her something else to chew on, some titbit to keep her quiet.

'There are goings-on,' he said, stalling. 'But not these.'

'Tell me. What? What's going on?'

'If you were talking to me exclusively, then we could share info.'

But Jamila shook her head. 'I'm booked on lunchtime TV, don't you see? I'll be speaking to the people. At the very spot where it happened. Just three quarters of a mile from here.' She threw out an arm and pointed in approximately the right direction.

'OK. What I'm going to tell you is totally confidential.' Jason cast around for something to distract her with. Jamila froze, waiting eagerly, her arm still thrust out in statesmanlike mode. 'There are dangerous rumours going around,' he continued.

'Rumours?'

'Racism. For example. Among other things. You could make things worse. It's not true, but—'

'I understand.' Jamila nodded knowingly. 'I've read the tweets. There were a couple of particularly revealing ones, from @newsshouldbefree and @bestukjournalist.'

Jason winced. 'Oh, I wouldn't necessarily listen to—'

'You should follow them. They're horrible.'

He searched his memory for anything he might have accidentally let slip via his four anonymous Twitter accounts.

Jamila, meanwhile, was deep in thought. 'Inflammatory situation,' she said. 'Two communities at war.'

'A true statesman, or woman, always knows when to calm things down.'

'Least said, soonest mended?'

'Precisely.'

'Silence is only golden for the oppressors,' Jamila said, exploring her newly discovered principles. She tapped the side of her nose. 'Trust me, Jason. *Lunch for London* will be my platform. I will speak only of peace and conciliation. Binding together two angry communities in their time of strife, yes? This is what I do. If only my few rhetorical powers were halfway adequate to the task. Sometimes great demands are thrust on the shoulders of those who feel so, so small. Indira Gandhi, Mother Theresa... Bono. And now me – although you could say I am so lacking.'

Jason could only agree.

26

The Walking Byline

He could do no more. Jamila Hasan would say what Jamila Hasan wanted to say, and Jason's one consoling thought, as he trotted down the damp town-hall steps to Judd Street, was that nobody would take much notice of her. They never had before.

There'd been a brief shower while they were talking, but fresh sunshine now gleamed off the puddles in the road like scattered diamonds. His phone rang.

'It's Zoe Sharpleside,' she announced angrily.

He was surprised it had taken her that long. 'Ah,' he said, trying hard to sound as if he cared. 'I'm really sorry. I had an urgent—'

'We're here,' she said.

'Right. Good. I had to leave Brent Cross urgently, but I'll get—'

'No, here, Jason. Watching you.'

'What?' He started crossing the road.

'Mind that bike.'

A cyclist splashed across in front of him. Jason jumped out of the way and stared around. There was a large Irish pub on the corner with Euston Road and through one of the windows he could just make out two shadowy faces. One was on the phone, the other was aiming a camera in his direction. The tentative rays of sunshine retreated once more behind the clouds.

'I just love rushing around London,' she said, as he joined them at their alcove table.

'Am I glad you found me,' Jason said, bringing out his best smile. 'I had to chase up a lead at the town hall. I tried to phone you, but the network was down.'

The staffer seemed to be around his own age, strikingly blonde and intense, the intensity of a person who lived for her byline and little else. She sat bolt upright and tapped an electronic cigarette compulsively on the table in front of her. Next to her, a large man introduced himself briefly as Dudley Snipe and went back to paying close attention to a bottle of HoneyBrew and a collection of cameras with long lenses.

Jason slid into a seat opposite them. 'While we're at it, how did you find me?'

'You use a mobile,' said Zoe.

'You tracked my mobile? Is that legal?'

'I didn't ask.' She drained a glass of white wine and banged it back down onto the table with such force, Jason was surprised she didn't snap the stem. 'So, we've found each other. Let's get down to it. What have you got so far? Who's the father?'

Jason stared around the dark interior of the pub. How long could he stall? He checked his watch, even though he was perfectly aware what the time was. It was an hour and a half since he'd last heard from Potts. Had he run out of possible fathers? The man had his limits, after all.

'I want a six-month freelance contract, signed by Lyle.'

'I don't know anything about a contract.'

Jason stood up. 'It's been nice knowing you.'

'Wow,' she said. 'Hey, it's all cool.'

'It'll be cool when I get a contract from the Post. And an agreement that Liam Glass will get money for medical help, and a commitment to start a national campaign against knife crime.' He was amazed how he felt. He'd never bluffed like this before. He was agonisingly scared yet somehow mindlessly brave at the same time.

He started to walk off and the staff reporter shouted, 'No, wait.'

Jason waited and she said, 'Lyle has to know the name of the footballer and you need to give us some kind of proof.'

'That's good. When I see the contract, we can talk about the name and the proof. Right now, I'm off to talk to my exclusive interview subjects, my local contacts, the Mail, the Sun, the Mirror, the Star...'

She slapped the table. 'That's crap, Jason. We can't plan tomorrow's paper on the basis of hot air. Do you know how many people phone up with bullshit stories every day? How do we even know there is a fucking footballer?'

Dudley Snipe laughed to himself as if at a private joke, many chains jiggling up and down on his stomach.

'Do you want to give us a moment, Dudley?' said Zoe.

'I'll be outside as usual.' The photographer pushed himself to his feet, jangling. He picked up his cameras, still clutching his beer. 'It don't feel right anyway, being in the warm and not standing in the cold getting pissed on.'

Jason sat again. Zoe clicked open her handbag and took out a notebook. But Jason had run out of stalling ideas. For the second time in a few hours he decided honesty might be the best policy.

'I can't tell you who it is yet,' he started, and as he did so his mobile buzzed with a third footballer. Potts was still working on it after all.

'Lyle said you were still in negotiations.'

'Exactly.' Jason kept the screen away from her. 'I'm in discussions. Talks. Transactions.'

'Transactions with who?'

Two more profiles arrived, looking marginally suitable, at a stretch. Were there really so many men who wanted to be known as having fathered an illegitimate boy? Where did Potts find them?

Jason took a deep breath. 'Tony Potts.'

He saw her eyes flicker, working out the angles. He knew her type. She'd be on a rolling six-month staff contract herself and desperate to keep her job. She needed good bylines as much as he did. That was all that kept you in work. The Post was not a sentimental place. You were trained to deliver the story. Or die.

She paused for a moment, snatched up her phone and tapped a number.

'Tony?' she said.

Jason's heart gave a sharp jump. Zoe Sharpleside had a direct line through to Tony Potts. What would the man say? How much could he trust him? He listened to her start her preamble and then pause. She remained silent for about thirty seconds, twenty-five seconds longer than he'd known her manage so far. And then she handed her phone over to Jason.

'He says everything goes through you.'

'That's our agreement,' said Jason, trying hard not to show his relief. He confirmed to Potts that he'd received his emails, then returned Zoe's mobile.

'What emails?' she said, ringing off.

'Terms and conditions of the deal.'

'Let me see.'

'No.' He thrust his mobile into a jacket pocket for safety, where it continued to buzz with newly arriving messages.

Zoe tapped her electronic cigarette again. It seemed to be more a neurotic worry-prop than anything useful. In her handbag he spotted two half-smoked packets of real cigarettes, different brands. 'We have to approve any agreement you make before we come on board.'

'No,' Jason said quickly.

Her own phone rang.

'Lyle?' she called, as if no conversation for her was private. 'I've got Crowthorne. Yes, he's being difficult. No, I can handle him. No, we don't have the name. He's talking to Potts.'

She rang off without taking her eyes off him. Jason wondered how long his bluff could hold out. He didn't like being called difficult, but he urgently needed to examine those emails alone. Outside the window, Dudley Snipe was keeping his hand in, snapping pictures of passers-by, mostly young, female and wearing too little for the time of year.

'Look.' She took a puff of electronic nicotine. The end of the stick glowed weirdly green. 'I know what it's like not being on staff. You think everyone's going to rip you off. It's not like that. We have ethics. We don't rip off journalists. We rip off the public. We need you. If we ripped off people like you, who'd be left to help us rip off everyone else? And anyway, at some point you're going to have to stick out your neck and share with us or this isn't going to work.'

She reached out a hand stiffly and touched his arm in an attempt at reassurance. He could tell she wasn't used to physical contact. 'You've got to show us something.'

'I've got the CCTV of the attack,' he ventured with some trepidation. 'Lyle told you?'

She nodded.

'You want to see it?'

'You sure? I wouldn't want to push my luck. I mean, you want to show me something, finally?'

Jason didn't feel irony was her natural style. He pulled the cassette out of his jacket pocket and placed it on the table. He hoped desperately there was something on it after all. 'I don't suppose you know anyone who can play a VHS?'

27

Pictures Don't Lie

At almost the same moment, DC Rockham's home phone rang loudly and he slept through it. Then his mobile trilled, joining in the electronic fun, but still he slept on. He turned over, oblivious to the grey late-morning light that trickled through the thin curtains with a groundless optimism. His mobile rang once more. And then his landline and his mobile went at the same time and the baby woke and screamed, unusually loud and close, and even then Andy might not have woken, but he threw out his hand and encountered something warm and damp and slimy. He jerked away and looked over and Duane was lying there in Cheryl's place. The baby had stopped yelling, to his own surprise, and was staring at his father, gasping for breath and considering his options.

'Bollocks,' said Andy. He examined his hand and the nappy that he had found himself fondling, and he didn't like it.

Duane decided it was time to cry again, and Andy said, 'No, no, don't do that.'

But he did. Andy didn't know what the fuck to do. He could interrogate thieves, chase muggers, break into crack houses. But Duane he couldn't deal with. Duane didn't agree to go quietly or respect his warrant card or even his status as his father. Duane was like a wild animal and he didn't trust himself to tame him. He pulled himself out of bed and yelled Cheryl's name, but there was no reply.

The mobile rang again on the bedside table next to his alarm clock. He grabbed it and saw that Dog was calling and it wasn't yet noon.

'Where's the CCTV?' Dog said.

'What CCTV?' Andy struggled to hear him over the noise of his son.

'Did you pick up the tape?' Dog sounded far too vigorous, whatever time of day it was. 'From the newsagent's. There's no sign of it being logged in and no paperwork. We've gone and talked to the bloke and he says he gave it to one of us and if it was you we can't find what you did with it and if it wasn't you why not? The boss needs you in here now.'

'I can't come now. I'm here with the baby and there's no-one else.'

'Did you pick up the bloody tape?' Dog asked again.

Andy sat on the side of the bed, put his fingers in his ears and tried to remember what he'd done about the security footage.

'Fuck me,' said Dog. 'Is that kid all right? Are you water-boarding him? Is he confessing?'

'It wasn't me who picked up the CCTV,' said Andy.

'Well, come in and find out who did.'

Cheryl was nowhere to be seen. Andy tried to clean Duane and change his Pampers on the plastic-covered table in the boy's room and for a moment Duane stopped crying. All was calm. Then, as Andy unfolded the new nappy, Duane decided it was a good time to pee. His little spigot turned on and the jet rose triumphantly towards the ceiling. Andy ducked, but Duane turned his head at the movement and to his horror Andy saw the jet of triumph begin to curve round towards him. There was no cover. The pale liquid raked down and sideways like a machine-gun, following him round the room with murderous intent, until Andy dived for safety behind an IKEA toy chest.

'Duane!' he called. And poked his head up, which proved to be a major mistake.

Finally, Duane's supply of liquid ammunition ran out. Andy re-emerged to find the baby lying calmly on the mat, without an apparent care in the world.

He felt guilty and incompetent and he hated himself.

Cheryl came back half an hour later carrying Tesco bags.

'Where were you?' he said, louder than he intended.

She held up the bags as a clue.

'You left the kid alone.'

'Andy, you were here.'

'I was asleep.'

He could see that Cheryl was close to crying and he said, 'Look, sorry.' He tried to take her hand, but she pushed him away.

'I've got to get into work,' he said.

'You're on nights this week.'

'They need me to sort out some mess.'

'Well, I need you.' She turned to face him now. 'Don't they have any other coppers there?'

'Cheryl, you know how it goes.'

'I know that it's always work first.'

Her face was red like Duane's and there was nothing he could do about it. There never was. It wasn't her fault, but it wasn't his either.

The few customers in the basement of J Powney's Adult Videos generally entered quietly, added placidly to J Powney's profits and left without fuss. They certainly showed little interest in the group huddled around the video recorder in the corner, between *Swedish Handymen* and *Thai Lady-Boy Classics.*

Jason handed the CCTV cassette to the manager, a slim young Indian called Raj who seemed to be well known to Snipe. No sooner had Raj inserted the tape than he was called upstairs to deal with a retail issue concerning a video of two ladies and a red setter, and so Jason was delegated to take charge of the machine. He stepped forward apprehensively and pressed play. Black and white patterns whipped across the screen: attractive zigzags, energetic herring-bones and hypnotic rolling lines. Nothing made sense. Jason felt a cold dread.

'Somewhat art-house,' said Snipe.

A customer glanced up from the cover of *German Girls' Bootcamp 3D.*

Jason pushed a few more buttons. After some more esoteric shimmering, the picture managed to form itself into a blurry grey image. A row of numbers appeared at the top, changing fast. Vague shapes fizzed across the screen like ghosts on speed.

'You have checked this over, haven't you?' said the byline, puffing nervously on her electronic cigarette. The green tip shone intermittently.

'No sweat.' Jason tentatively pressed pause.

The picture froze and came clear. He felt a small flutter of triumph. You could see a distorted corner of the cash machine very close, with the square shrunk into the distance behind. The square was empty.

'Go on,' said Zoe, impatiently.

Jason pressed all the buttons at random and thereby discovered by complete accident that the camera recorded four still frames a minute. The right combination of buttons made it possible to inch the tape forwards a few stills at a time. But now the time on the tape was showing 6 am. Blotchy policemen flickered round the donotcross tape.

'Go back,' said Snipe astutely.

Time rewound in leaps. Dawn faded back to night and Jason saw himself, a distant shape engaging in conversation with a dull blur that was one of the constables before reversing jerkily back to his car, which reversed away in turn... The police un-appeared... He rewound further and suddenly ambulance men ran in backwards to crouch over something on the ground.

And there it was. A grey huddle. Despite herself, Zoe gave a sharp intake of breath. Snipe stayed silent. Jason inched back further. The time read 20:31:30. Liam Glass's body lay on the edge of the screen. Then Liam jumped up. He looked thin, misshapen in the distorted picture. A blur of something around him. And next he was gone. Or rather had not yet arrived.

Raj came back down to check everything was OK, the red setter problem apparently solved. Snipe gave him a tentative thumbs-up.

Muttering under her breath, the staffer reached awkwardly past Jason and put the machine into a slow forward of single frames. They showed the empty square. Nothing. Nothing. Nothing... Then came the teenager as he walked to the cashpoint. Now he was glancing to one side. Now he had moved away for some reason. Now there was an arm on the edge of the picture. Just an arm. The arm became a body, wearing a hood, and Jason could see the gleam of something. A knife. Then there were two figures. Blurred and hooded, their faces oval shadows. The moment of the attack. Not the most brilliant pictures in the world. You could just make out three people and a light blob that might or might not have been a blade.

He peered closer.

'Printable? Can you see the knife?' said Zoe to Snipe. The two nearest customers raised their eyes from a shelf of Bulgarian Snuff Movie classics.

'Splash,' said Snipe. 'For sure. Next to a shot of Dad scoring a world-famous goal. "While Millions Cheered..."'

'"Premiership Love-Rat Abandoned Son To Life Of Violence",' added Zoe with more relish than Jason felt was necessary.

'We don't want to be too hard on the father,' he offered with a tremor of concern. 'What about "Top Player's Pain Over Stabbed Son"?'

'"Love-Child Booted Into Touch",' said Snipe. '"Cast-Off Son Pays Ultimate Penalty".'

'"Secret Grief Of England Star"?' suggested Jason hopefully.

Zoe glared at her mobile. 'There's no signal down here.'

She trotted stiffly up the narrow, grease-stained stairs. Jason removed the tape and followed her at speed, leaving the three customers looking slightly bereft.

By the time Jason reached the street, Zoe was already on her phone to Lyle, discussing a front-page spread. The forsaken son. Blood on the streets. This could have been your boy. A choice quote from the victim's missing father, despicable role model for today's youth, full interview inside. No, she didn't have the name yet. Lyle seemed to be growing agitated at the other end.

Jason needed to look at Potts' emails as soon as he could. He moved nonchalantly away from the shop entrance, sheltered his phone from view and quietly flicked through the messages he'd received. There were ten from the Herald, a rather desperate spam mailshot from All Roads Lead to Royland offering discounted membership, and a total of six applicants for the job of Liam's father: two strikers, three midfielders and a goalkeeper. They seemed remarkably eager to be smeared. He clicked on the last of the six, and then noticed Zoe and Snipe had stopped talking.

'Is that him?' said Snipe. He reached out for the phone. Jason panicked and tried to snatch it away. Snipe restrained him with one large hand.

'It's nothing.'

Snipe peered over his shoulder and read aloud, 'All Roads Lead to Royland?'

'It's just a local gym,' Jason said lightly. The other two looked at him suspiciously. 'I pick up good gossip there.'

'Are you keeping something from us? Is this where we'll find the father?'

'Absolutely not.' They didn't seem convinced, but then it occurred to Jason that the gym wasn't such a bad idea. Maybe he'd be able to find some privacy while they snooped around. And in any case, Zoe seemed sure he was lying, so he might as well go with the flow. He shrugged. 'But if you really want to go there...'

Zoe snapped her notebook shut and stuck out a hand. A taxi stopped. Jason was impressed: she'd never even looked round. 'Give the driver the address,' she said, opening the nearside door.

'I think this will be a waste of time.'

'Now.' She climbed in. Snipe was still watching him warily.

Jason slipped his phone carefully into an inside pocket and joined them.

28

All Roads Lead to Royland

Royland Boyde Luther Pinkersleigh had already passed a frustrating morning on the phone to eight different council officials, trying to find out why they'd cancelled the youth contract, breaking off at intervals to advise the gym's patrons on such issues as why an exercise bike squeaked and how to retune the TV to *The World's Strongest Woman*. To add to his unhappiness, Sadé was in a mood. When she'd arrived at ten-thirty he'd looked up from the reception desk and waved, but she'd simply shaken the drizzle off her umbrella, walked into the office and slammed the door. He considered this a bad sign.

The council's head of sport and culture had always insisted he held young people's fitness as a high priority. Which was precisely why (he'd informed the Camden Herald) it was crucial to sell off playing fields and cut youth groups, to ensure they could balance their books. When Royland had suggested to Sadé that parts of the statement contradicted other parts and that he should write to the council and point out their mistake, she muttered something he didn't quite catch and returned to the office at speed, slamming the door again. For the last two hours, the council departments had had enormous fun passing Royland around from one to another like an inconvenient visitor from a foreign country who didn't understand the way things were done. Starting with Leisure and Sports, each agreed that cancelling the youth club contract was unfortunately timed, so close to an election. Each explained that times were hard but he should look on the positive side. That funding cuts would liberate companies such as Royland's to do even better work in a free market... And then they sent him on to another department which might be able to help. He'd now travelled in a circle through the town hall's phone system and finally found himself back with Leisure and Sports. Who listened sympathetically and agreed that cancelling the contract was unfortunately timed...

Outside the front entrance, Kingston could be heard mewling and grunting, breaking off to amuse himself by peeing against the bikes. Ben, Kingston's owner, was inside, struggling to lift some ten-kilo dumbbells. He'd been laid off by the council six months ago and he and Kingston were among the few regulars, though Kingston seemed to be the fitter of the two.

This time Kingston gave a different bark. Royland glanced up to see three new people entering, a man and a woman who looked smart but not too smart, followed by a larger man who looked decidedly unsmart. Police, Royland instinctively thought. He hardly dared look at them. Had they found the knife? Then he realised he should try to appear more relaxed, so he tried that, without great success. He took a deep breath, stepped from behind the reception desk and introduced himself with a firm shake of the hand, aiming at a confidence he didn't feel.

'I'm Royland Pinkersleigh,' he said to the three visitors. 'Fitness is my business, innit.'

A damp, patchy-haired dog barked at them as they pushed their way through the grimy glass doors of All Roads Lead to Royland and into the little reception area with its posters advertising Lycra compression shorts. Royland himself seemed nervous. Jason tried to reassure him, but the big man rubbed his hands compulsively and nodded and jiggled and hesitated and havered.

'Man, OK. Journalist, innit. Of course. Jason Crowthorne. Didn't recognise you at first. I thought you were police. I don't know why. No reason to think about police.'

Jason wondered if this police thing was getting to be a habit. Twice in one day. He glanced casually towards one of the full-length mirrors to see how he might have brought it on. Nothing was noticeable.

'Police?' asked Zoe.

'No reason,' repeated Royland, rubbing his hands even faster and looking with concern at Dudley Snipe, who had removed a large camera from his bag and was wandering into the exercise studio. 'Where's he going?'

'Don't mind Dudley,' said Zoe, trotting after the photographer with her stiff little walk. 'He's just looking for pictures.'

'Pictures of what?' Royland shifted heavily after them.

'Pictures,' said Dudley.

'That's OK, isn't it, Mr Pinkersleigh?' Jason remained in the doorway and searched around for somewhere secluded, where he could read Potts' emails. 'Like we did last time.' He slid his mobile from his pocket and tried to move to the far end of the room.

'Good publicity,' said Zoe with a fierce smile. She left Snipe and caught up with Jason by a glass-fronted chiller selling high-energy drinks. She contemplated the brightly coloured bottles. Jason slipped his phone away again.

'Aren't you supposed to be finalising negotiations?' she said quietly.

'Publicity...' mused Royland, absently tapping his hand on a Swiss ball. 'Yes, good. That's fine, innit, but...' The big man seemed to be flailing around for some reason that Jason couldn't understand.

'You know what you have here?' Jason returned and tried to place an arm round the man's shoulders but found this a stretch. So he turned the move into a pat on the arm instead and became suddenly aware of the size of the man's triceps.

'What do I have here?'

'You have an oasis of peace.' He gestured vaguely. 'A place where the races can mingle. A rare opportunity to get away from the cares and dangers of the world. A haven of fitness not just physical but also social.'

'Yes,' said Royland. 'You wrote that in the paper.'

Jason brought his hand back down.

'I did,' he said somewhat defensively. 'And I remember you told me your membership doubled.'

The woman in the office had finally noticed the newcomers and turned round to look through the glass door. She stared a moment, took off her glasses and came out.

'Everything's OK, Sadé,' said Royland as she looked them up and down.

Everything he was, Sadé wasn't. She was rake-thin, sharp-faced and stared right through them.

'Journalists? What's up?'

'Yeah, what's up?' said Royland, standing his ground more firmly now that they were two.

'There's been a stabbing,' said Jason, tapping an anxious foot, waiting for the next opportunity to slide away again. Snipe was fully occupied climbing a stretch of wall bars above a young woman on a rowing machine, in the hope of locating the angle that would reveal as much cleavage as technically possible.

'Really?' said Royland.

'Didn't you hear about it?' Zoe kept her eyes on Jason. 'Three hundred metres away.'

'Yes, didn't you hear about it, Royland?' Sadé broke in sharply. 'I got told by three people just on the way here.'

'Yes, that stabbing,' said Royland.

'Were there many stabbings last night?' said Zoe, taking out her notebook.

'No, just the one,' said Royland. 'As far as I know.'

'Maybe,' said Sadé. 'We see a lot of different things go on round here.'

'What other things have you seen?'

'Not much,' said Royland.

'None,' said Sadé.

'Nothing,' said Royland and was immediately blinded by Dudley's flash.

'Sorry,' said Dudley from above the cleavage. 'Good shot, though.'

'We see less than you'd think.' Sadé was shooting looks at Royland but he didn't seem able to stop. 'Me and Sadé, we just run this gym, like you say, an oasis of peace, and keep our noses clean, and even when we go for walks at night, it's like you just don't necessarily look. I mean, if I'd seen it, I'd have gone to help whoever it was. If I'd spotted it happen, innit, bro, or seen evidence. Or anything. If it wasn't too late. Whatever it was. Whoever it was. Who was it?' He ended with a certain abruptness. Sadé was doing a chewing thing with her jaw.

'It was a local white teenager who was stabbed,' said Jason. 'Liam Glass. Do you know him?'

'No,' said Royland with an appearance of relief.

Jason showed him a curled snap of the kid in a Chelsea shirt and he shook his head emphatically. Then he took the picture back again and peered more closely.

'Shit, yes,' he said. He seemed to shrink. 'He's been here. His mum works at Tesco's. Fuck, I saw him last night, too. He walked right past.'

While all eyes were on Royland, Jason saw his chance and eased his way quietly past the treadmills to the far end.

'Poor kid,' said Sadé warmly. 'But we got work to do.' She gave Royland a sharp tug.

He ignored her. 'Is he OK?'

'In a coma,' said Jason from the back.

'What was he like?' said Zoe, writing notes.

'Just a boy. He broke a window once with a ball. Kicking it around with a friend. But don't use that. I wouldn't feel good saying that about him.'

'Of course not,' said Zoe, not crossing anything out.

'They know who did it?'

'That's what we want to find out.' Zoe perched herself on the spin bike and twirled a fashionably expensive shoe. 'You said something about walking at night. Was that when you saw him?'

'We have to talk over the quarter's bank accounts, don't we, Royland?' said Sadé. 'Like, right now.'

But Zoe had scented blood. She smiled sweetly but didn't close her notebook. Snipe was also watching Royland from high above the rower. With their eyes off him, Jason slowly brought out his phone once more.

'Did we go for a walk last night?' Royland asked Sadé.

Sadé gave him a menacing look that would have cowed a lesser man. 'You don't remember? We walked home and neither of us saw nothing, did we, Royland.'

Royland shook his big head rapidly.

Jason quietly turned his back and opened the first email.

'Jaime Barea!' shouted Dudley Snipe. 'Fucking hell. Is that who it is?'

Jason whipped round. Snipe had trained his camera on him, with its long telephoto lens, and was reading over his shoulder.

Zoe jumped off her bike. 'Jaime Barea?'

'Hymie, who?' said Royland.

'Not necessarily,' said Jason, stuffing his mobile into his pocket, too late. He felt sick.

'What do you mean, "not necessarily"?'

'I mean we're talking.' Jason struggled to breathe.

'There's more,' said Dudley Snipe, dangling from the wall bars. 'I saw four names at least.'

There was something imperious about the way Zoe held out her hand. A sense of total entitlement. Royland, Sadé and the gym regulars were staring at Jason, knowing something serious was going on but not really understanding what. He felt like a schoolboy who'd been caught cribbing in an exam. He was a fraud. A pretend journalist. He wanted to pee.

He handed over his mobile.

'Outside,' Zoe said.

Outside, rain was dribbling once more from clouds that had grown heavy with melancholy. Jason shivered miserably in the spring wind. The game was up. As games went, this one was as up as it could be. Only Kingston seemed to be happy, welcoming the intrusion of these huddled humans into his territory with a friendly yowl, before attempting to water Jason's shoes.

Zoe stiffly sought shelter from the rain under a roof overhang and flicked through the emails from Potts.

'You're casting!' she said after a time. 'I don't believe this. You're holding auditions for the role of errant father.'

Jason shrugged and moved carefully away from the bike rack and Kingston's urinary forays.

Zoe raised her eyes from the little screen. 'Please tell me there isn't a casting couch.'

He shook his head unhappily. He tried to make an excuse but lost heart and his words trailed off, lost in the steady hiss of the rainfall. She handed the mobile to Snipe, who contemplated the six footballers in silence and then passed it back.

'Quite brilliant,' Zoe said.

Not for the first time in the past twelve hours Jason's brain jammed in neutral and refused to move.

'I wish I'd thought of that,' she continued.

'Fucking amazing,' added Dudley, smiling broadly.

'Whose idea was it?'

Jason swallowed. Was this for real? Were they playing him? Kingston yapped and jumped with excitement that his three new friends wanted to linger in his dank little street. Jason's knees felt weak, but there were only the bikes to sit on and they gave off a distinct farmyard odour.

'Yours or Potts'?'

Jason managed a shrug of self-deprecation. 'Well, I—'

'No matter.' She peered at the display. 'So, who have we got?'

Jason reached out a hand, but she kept the phone to herself.

'Jaime Barea,' she said. 'Why would he want to be a father?'

'Alcohol and girls,' said Snipe, removing his camera bag from the vicinity of Kingston.

Jason remembered having heard a number of rumours about the Spanish goalkeeper's clubbing and drinking habits, though Potts had managed to keep the stories out of the papers so far. A footnote from Potts suggested that fathering a child would be good for his soul, his liver and future sponsorship deals.

'Good one. We'd make page five at least,' said Zoe, flipping to the next.

'Allie Nabokov,' said the photographer, looking over her shoulder. 'Certainly needs to work on how he relates to kids.'

This was an understatement. The mercurial Russian playmaker had alienated his public by delivering genital expletives at a highly priced football camp for eight-year-olds. Unfortunately for him, one of the juniors had proved more adept with his smartphone's video camera than he had with a ball. Fatherhood and grief might provide more positive home movies.

'Page three.'

'Doesn't look right,' said Jason, recovering his voice slowly, along with his nerve.

Zoe looked at him.

'Red hair.'

'Who cares about fucking hair? We're talking headlines, not hairdressing.' She looked down to find Kingston poised to empty his bladder on her Jimmy Choos and delivered a penalty kick worthy of the great Nabo himself. The mangy schnauzer yelped and withdrew an optimistic distance to await further opportunities.

The third, Paul Griffiths, multi-medal-winning defensive midfielder for England, had a reputation for physical violence on and off the field, having been twice suspended for mixed martial arts in the centre circle and once placed on remand for breaking a driver's nose during an argument over a red light.

'He's got potential,' said Zoe.

'"A-Paulling! Scandal Of Coma Love-Child",' mused Snipe cheerfully.

'"Griff-Struck!"'

'"Gri-m For Pazza's Secret Son".'

'I feel—' started Jason.

But as he spoke, Zoe clicked on the next contender and began to smile. The smile turned into a laugh. She performed a small ungainly dance while the other two watched in suspense, and then immediately dialled a number.

'Who is it?' asked Jason, but she waved him away.

'Lyle?' she said.

There came some words from the other end, displaying a very audible level of fraughtness and urgency.

'Weaverall,' she said.

'Damballs?' could be heard from the phone.

Damon Weaverall, one of England's highest-scoring midfielders. Mr Squeaky-Clean, he'd never been booked or even suspected of foul play. Blonde, muscular, intelligent, with a six-pack to die for, his only image problem came from the conviction of every newsroom in the country that he was committed to a full-time male partner – this in a sport which had been homophobic since the first medieval pig's bladder met the first boot.

Vague rumours about the couple having been seen in gay nightclubs regularly drifted across the news desks, while Damon's sexual orientation was called into even greater doubt by the fact that he occasionally read books with long words in them. Somehow, through a combination of threats and bribery, Tony Potts had managed to keep the gossip from being printed. His agency supplied so much material that no tabloid editor could contemplate the possibility of Potts turning off the tap. However, he couldn't control the internet and there the rumours maintained a subterranean life. Damballs being a father would be massive celebrity news. Mr Clean with a secret sin they could talk about. And heterosexual, too.

From the squawks emerging through the phone, it appeared that Lyle agreed. Zoe nodded a few times, grunted a few more, said yes twice and no three times and then Jason's mobile rang. It was Lyle, on both phones at once.

'Have you got proof?'

Jason hesitated.

'I want rock-solid support within the hour.' Lyle was simultaneously yelling commands at Jason, shouting at Zoe and calling across the newsroom that he had to see the editor right now, along with the managing editor, the sports editor, the picture editor and sundry other lesser editors. 'This stays locked down, watertight. No leaks. You need to talk to Potts. We'll want signed documentation, exclusive contract, affidavit, photo call with Weaverall, personal interview. Ask if he can come to the hospital. No, don't ask, just get him there. Helicopter from wherever he's training today. Potts can afford it. If not, the Post can pay. I'm going to get Paddy to clear six pages. As soon as she's back from coffee with the police commissioner. Wow, Jason! This is your day.'

'I think he likes it,' said Zoe, dropping her phone into her bag with glee.

A new shaft of sunlight broke joyously through the

dark clouds above the gym and glittered on the rancid puddles and gutters.

Colour returned to the world.

29

Euphoria

Zoe Sharpleside, the walking, talking byline, held out her hand and manifested another black taxi from nowhere. As they raced back to the Camden General, Jason called Potts with the good news that he'd chosen Damon Weaverall for the starring role. He decided to use the singular and claim all credit for the choice. Zoe seemed not to hear or not to mind and busied herself googling Dazza's CV on her phone, while Snipe reviewed his cleavage shots on the screen of his Nikon.

Jason glowed with triumph. Calls, texts and emails flowed copiously in all directions. Damballs' signed affidavit shot across from Potts' office with impressive speed, not unlike one of Dazza's own free kicks. At the Post, Lyle Marchmont was freeing up pages one to five. He could be heard, when Jason phoned to confirm, firing orders across the newsroom, calling for a biography, comment pieces and action photos. He was commissioning expert opinions on paternity among footballers, violent crime among the lower classes and the effects of grief on the ability to score goals. It seemed half the Post's staff were working on the story. Furthermore, as luck would have it, Damballs was right now travelling to London for a midweek match at Tottenham and a fellow player had offered to drive him to the hospital once they'd arrived.

Next, Potts called Jason and told him proudly that he was hiring the best medical staff for the boy. He was owed a few favours and the country's specialists in coma and trauma would be arriving at Liam's bedside momentarily.

'You can never have too much medical expertise,' said Potts. 'Dazza would want nothing less for his son. That's the kind of dad he is.'

Jason rang off with a warm feeling. Everything he'd promised Katrina was coming true. He noticed Zoe and Snipe both looking at him.

'Yes?' He grabbed a door handle as the taxi took a particularly fast corner.

'Have you started renegotiating with Lyle?' she said.

He hadn't thought of it, so he nodded wisely. 'Absolutely. Renegotiating. Totally.'

'How much do you think he could get now?' Snipe asked the walking byline.

'Anything he wants.'

'The sky's the limit.'

'We're talking about weeks of headlines here. Damballs' secret son? We're into six figures, easily. Half a mill? Six hundred k.'

'Maybe seven-fifty.'

'Perhaps more. No need to get greedy, though.'

Jason nodded again, as if such figures came and went in his brain on a regular basis.

'Then there's Potts,' said Zoe. 'How much is he paying you? A hundred and fifty thou? Two hundred? Don't worry,' she said. 'We're not going to tell anyone.'

'Not a soul,' agreed Snipe, swinging round suddenly and catching a fast shot of someone who looked vaguely like Noel Gallagher coming out of a health-food shop. 'Probably not,' he muttered to himself and deleted it. It wouldn't fit the newspaper's line anyway.

Zoe said, 'I'll take thirty-five per cent. And twenty for Dudley here. We're your partners now.'

*

As the taxi continued its journey, slaloming across the borough, Jason was happy to be generous with the money he hadn't yet received. Even after deducting large sums for Zoe and Snipe and allocating an acceptable amount for Katrina, he felt rich. Sadly, though, his happiness was not total. Sometime soon he would have to tell Katrina about Liam's newly acquired family tree. He rather hoped that her footballer hatred was directed solely towards the actual father rather than the entire Premiership. And maybe her share of the money would distract her. It was possible.

Lyle and Potts must have been working hard. The new medical team had not yet arrived, but the NHS nurses, who were clearly itching to eject the three journalists, had nonetheless received executive orders from high up in the hospital trust. Unhappy but powerless, they let the three of them into ICU and took their revenge by insisting they strip down and cover themselves thoroughly in plastic overalls, gowns, gloves, hats, masks and copious applications of antibacterial gel.

After all this, Jason had forgotten what state Liam was in. Re-entering the room and seeing the teenager again came as a profound shock: a pale lump of meat with a pulse. He lay as if dead under his oxygen mask. Katrina was asleep, slumped sideways in her chair. Christine looked up at him, white-faced.

'What did the hospital consultants say?'

She shrugged.

Jason suddenly felt ashamed, his own concerns dwindling by comparison with the enormity of the boy's fate. What was landing a job compared to facing brain-death or a life of permanent disability?

But then he got a grip. He told himself firmly that

publicising Liam's story was bringing the boy the help he needed, would protect other lives – and by-the-by save a great footballer from a future ruined by homophobes.

His conscience thus fortified, he started to speak, but Christine put her finger to her lips. She pointed a maroon nail at Liam and whispered that Kat was exhausted. All these doctors coming to and fro.

Zoe avoiding looking at the boy. She had turned rather green in the face and was uncharacteristically quiet. After a short time, she announced she had vital emails to attend to and would do so in the canteen downstairs; while Dudley Snipe was happy to pull off his scrubs and patrol the corridors, camera in hand.

Jason contemplated Liam. He told himself it was important to discuss Damballs with the family before the superstar arrived in person. He was sure he could put his case strongly. He simply needed to be honest. However you did that.

He took a deep breath.

At that moment, Potts' medical team arrived to take over Liam's care. Jason was called out to meet them and couldn't pretend he wasn't relieved at the interruption. There was a short pause while the department baulked at the introduction of outsiders. The local staff vehemently rejected any suggestion that they were not up to the job. Jason called Potts. Potts phoned Lyle. Lyle contemplated for a moment, googled the board of the hospital trust and discovered a friend of a friend from uni. Gradually, through this shared contact and the promise of front-page publicity for their new MRI scanner appeal, the trust came to believe that their interests were in tune with those of the national press.

The new team exuded an unmistakable air of professional competence. They brought out their instruments, prodded, examined, inhaled and exhaled, called for new tests and nodded with intense concern. They woke Katrina and interviewed her at length, discussing all the worst-case possible outcomes. Having thoroughly alarmed her, they then offered her some Valium to calm her down.

Meanwhile, the ward's NHS staff had gathered morosely around the nurses' desk, their expertise ignored, their achievements in keeping Liam alive given no credit. They protested at the gross intrusion, but to no effect. Katrina, however, was impressed at the new activity and thanked Jason. He started to tell her about the magnificent generosity of the Post, to find she'd fallen asleep again.

'What was it you wanted to tell us?' said Christine, contemplating a split end.

'Another time,' he said. And excused himself quickly from the room.

V

Wednesday 1 pm

'There's no such thing as a nice story or a nice reporter.'
Gareth Whelpower, 'Off-Stone – Memories of a Newspaper Man'

30

Lunchtime

News was not much of a newspaper thing for the Gordon Road Estates, indeed it wasn't much of a television thing either. Some residents caught news every which way and some didn't catch it at all, not in the official manner of things. Some news was glimpsed on TV before a person reached for the remote or was half-seen in headlines on free papers handed out on the way to work. Most was brought by friends, exchanged in the walkways and alleys. Or on phones and bedroom computers: a business of texts, tweets, updates and pokes. The residents knew what they thought and believed and didn't need announcers and journalists to tell them, thank you.

But today they could see news being made before their eyes. Below George III House, young Nidhi Chatterjee spotted a cameraman setting up a tripod. Climbing onto the edge of the Chatterjees' balcony, balancing dangerously with the help of her brother's rusty bicycle, she observed a sound assistant fixing that strange grey furry animal on a pole and a reporter in a blue tie standing as close as he could to the donotcross tape that still stretched around the little square beneath. In fact, so Will Unthank had heard, the tape should have been torn down hours before, when the police gave up searching for knives and things. But news of the Liam Glass stabbing had started to spread. Two tabloid photographers arrived with two reporters and the paps asked the police to leave the tape while they took their shots. Then other paps drove up and the tape kept staying and it was still there.

More people pushed onto their balconies and walkways: Mrs West elbow to elbow with Mr Baines, Will Unthank waving blearily to Nidhi, still leaning precariously out over the six-storey drop.

Excitement mounted. A little van could be seen manoeuvring with a dish on its roof pointing up to the sky. A fourth TV person, a young black woman, flourished a clipboard and was seen in conversation with a fifth, who some recognised as one of their ward councillors, swathed in a coat and scarf. The word went around that this was BBC Local News. TV sets were tuned to the BBC. Laptops were logged on to. People made tea, opened a beer, lit a spliff, called a friend or just did nothing. Their rumours had become news. Their news was going to be everyone's news.

The Estates were going to be on TV.

Outside the newsagent's, next to the police tape, Jamila had been alternating between hot and cold as the sun dodged in and out. She'd been standing for a full twenty minutes waiting to record her interview and now that the clouds were back, she was cooling again. There seemed no obvious reason for the delay. Police community support officers wanted to remove the blue and white tape and leave, but a teenager with a clipboard and black and white dungarees was begging them to keep it in place 'for the shot'.

Jamila phoned her local party leader to tell him she was going to be on the local news, but he was busy campaigning in a pub on Primrose Hill, so she sent messages to the deputy leader and anyone else who might be interested. Nobody was. She zipped up her coat, wrapped her scarf tight and paced round the little square. She tried to rehearse the key points she wanted to make but found herself distracted by the growing crowd. She'd taught hundreds of businesspeople how to do this kind of interview, but somehow it felt different today. She tried to remember what Jason Crowthorne had advised about the security cameras. He believed it would be a mistake to talk about them, but she couldn't remember why.

The teenager rushed over, talking it seemed to thin air, until Jamila realised she had a shocking-pink Bluetooth headset jammed into her left ear.

'Emma's decided we're going on live – at one-thirty,' she announced breathlessly before spiralling off on some urgent new errand. Emma, it would seem, lived in some distant studio at the other end of the mobile connection.

'They're interviewing me live,' Jamila relayed to the assembled voters on the other side of the tape, who seemed surprisingly underwhelmed. She moved down the line, shaking hands, asking a few questions of her electorate and urging them to vote in four weeks' time, and as she did so she heard a woman's voice.

'Who is she then?'

A man answered. 'Search me. I thought she was the one pushed off *Big Brother*.'

'No way,' said a third. 'She got beaten up on *EastEnders*. The pregnant one.'

Andy had finally arrived back at the station, to be met by Dog, who was in a foul mood and wanted to know where the CCTV had gone. He'd phoned the newsagent, Naik, who'd irritably informed him that he'd handed the cassette to a policeman in a cheap suit... and did they want to totally ruin his business with the TV people now blocking the road too? Because he didn't mind, as long as he knew who to blame on his suicide note, if that was all right with him.

So Andy read through the logs for the night and woke up all the junior CID who'd been on duty and still got nowhere.

But then Dana Bookman rushed into the CID office. He was surprised to see her. Perhaps more pleased than he should have been. Her shift had ended with his at six, but she'd stayed on to rack up a few hours' overtime. She brushed aside his greetings and said they should watch the telly in the coffee room. She'd just seen a preview of a piece coming up on the local news.

Jason was currently walking up and down outside one of the Care for the Elderly wards, deep in thought. He'd tried to call Weaverall to find out when he was expecting to arrive, but his phone had been turned off. Every bed in the ward had a rental TV module attached and as Jason passed the door for the third time, Jamila's face appeared mutely if briefly on half the screens at once.

He texted Zoe, approached the nearest three beds and asked to appropriate three sets of headphones for a matter of national importance. However, the patients rather liked having sound with their television. Jason insisted. Great issues were at stake. A nurse was drawn into the negotiations. Zoe arrived with Snipe and together they compromised, finding a side room that belonged to a half-conscious man in his eighties – who watched in woozy surprise as Nurse Ramirez marched in with three strangers and turned on his TV.

Lyle caught the preview at the Post on one of the forty-inch LED screens hanging from the ceiling of the newsroom.

Tam logged on at the Herald to watch the interview on her office computer.

In the gym, Royland also spotted the trailer on the TV: a shot of the little square with its police tape. But the sound was too low. He liked to fill the exercise area with pumping music to create 'A Mood for Success' (Chapter Two of *Great Is Not a Four-Letter Word*).

He disappeared into the cupboard at the back of the cardio area and fiddled urgently with switches. The stations flipped merrily between MTV, Sky Sports and the Shopping Channel, while Sadé stood by the loudspeakers and called out that he was doing totally the wrong thing.

At the last moment, Royland located BBC One again, first vision without sound and then sound minus vision, and finally both together. By which time the local news anchor was already dropping her voice to an appropriately serious level.

'Last night...' she began.

31

Three and Three Quarter Minutes of Fame

After all the waiting, everything became a rush. Jamila was manoeuvred into place facing the pallid young reporter, whose hands, she could see – small consolation – were shaking too. The camera was focused on her. The black beetle of a microphone on her lapel readjusted at speed. The teenager in dungarees made obscure hand signals.

Jamila had just enough time to wonder if anyone was bothering to watch and then the reporter was asking the first question and Jamila felt the familiar pressure. It was like ten miles of sky were pushing down, flattening her into the glistening, damp pavement. She braced herself, pushed her chin up, realised that she had no idea what he'd asked or what she was going to say but drew breath and said it anyway.

But the reporter wasn't even listening. He was gazing at his notes, fiddling absently with his tie and scratching his left ear. This was horrific. If she couldn't even hold the attention of the person who was interviewing her, how much less would she hold the viewers at home, one eye on their texts and tweets, boiling their kettles and eating their sandwiches and fry-ups.

Think! No, too late... The reporter was already lifting pale eyes from his notepad. He asked earnestly for the facts. What facts did Jamila in fact possess? She needed a fact. But she was a politician, never knowingly lost for words – and so she talked on, wishing silently that the police had bothered to return her calls, trying to remember what Golam Kamal had advised her over the photocopying machine at the Sylheti Centre. Trying to recall what Jason Crowthorne had warned her about. What had he wanted her to mention and not mention? But no! Who was she to be in the pocket of the establishment and the press anyway? This was her domain. She was in her element. In front of the cameras. Her own woman. She scattered the seed corn of her fragmentary knowledge on the willing furrows of the midday news: not enough police, tragic child, rumours of Bengali attackers totally without foundation, police silence about CCTV.

Unfortunately, the sun had come out from behind the granite-grey clouds, straight into her eyes. She squinted, then decided this made her look shifty, so opened her eyes wide. This brought into focus the strange collection of onlookers: young hoodies of every ethnicity, old ladies clutching bright orange bags from Sainsbury Local, a man in a torn duffel coat and gym shorts, tugging a mangy schnauzer on a string... But she really had to avoid distraction.

The reporter had latched eagerly onto the twin issues of race and CCTV. He seemed to think she'd broken important news. Had she?

At least she'd woken him up. She fixed the interviewer with a steely gaze. 'So, tell me, why aren't the police releasing the pictures? These voters here have a right—'

'Is this about votes, then?'

False step. She backtracked rapidly. 'No, no, no. This is about yet another boy in a coma. A bright student. A gifted footballer with a glorious future in front of him. A community rallying round a grieving family.'

Little Miss Clipboard was waving to the reporter and pointing to her watch, but Jamila was in the zone. She threw out a hand. She grew Churchillian – with a pinch of Nelson Mandela, a hint of Barack Obama and a dash of Martin Luther King.

'This is a time for listening,' she continued, her voice deepening and slowing with rhetorical conviction. 'A time for healing, a time for truth and reconciliation.' There was no stopping her now. 'This is not the beginning of the end. Where there is community conflict, let there be peace. I have a dream...' The sun went in. Somehow she lost her thread. Everyone was waiting for her to finish.

The reporter started to speak. But inspiration struck.

'... of the entire ward joining together. I am calling a meeting...' she said with determination. Jamila was not normally given to internal analysis, but it did in truth feel as if she'd found her clarion call. The coming together of the races – under one leader. '... this very evening.' Her voice dropped yet further and she spoke straight to the camera, eye to eye, councillor to voter. 'To talk about CCTV... And other matters. For local people. Who deserve to be heard. Who want the best for poor Liam Glass. Because we can.' She'd reached her climax. Like all the memorable speeches she'd studied over the years. The crowd was hushed. Expectant. She smiled sweetly at the lens. 'Tonight. At the Evelyn Street Sylheti Social Centre. Eight o'clock.'

It was all over. A crammed and breathless three minutes forty-five seconds. She listened to the reporter return his viewers to the studio. Miss Clipboard congratulated Jamila on her excellent interview. Jamila tried to remember what actually happened. She was about to reply when she realised that the clipboard had already sashayed off to give the crew directions to their next story. A minute later, the satellite dish descended and the BBC van disappeared round the corner.

The onlookers found better things to do with their lives. Soon there was no-one left in the tiny square on Gordon Street except for the two police community support officers, who busied themselves ripping off the blue and white striped tape, or at least most of it, leaving a few souvenirs fluttering from the lampposts like forgotten banners of a miniature army.

And then Jamila was completely alone.

She waited for a call from the party leaders, but her iPhone remained silent. She sat on the droppings-splattered bench and contemplated the tragic isolation of a committed life. All her heroes and heroines had had to stand alone: Churchill, Blair, Dot Cotton...

Her mobile rang and she snatched it up. It was Golam Kamal from the Evelyn Street Sylheti Social Centre.

'Tonight!' he screeched. 'How on earth can we organise a meeting for tonight?'

32

Action and Reaction

While the square around her remained deceptively peaceful, Jamila's call for community healing had had an immediate effect elsewhere on the Estates. From Rhodes Gate to Melbourne House, doors had been flung open and residents had poured out in response. Bengalis emerged to heal BNP supporters. BNP supporters emerged to heal Bengalis. Small gangs of residents were beginning to form in the squares and alleys, threatening to heal their neighbours so effectively that they would never need healing again.

Andy had barely finished watching the broadcast in the coffee room of Kentish Town police station when his phone rang. At the same time, a dozen texts arrived. According to Andy's contacts, people were angry. Though no-one, including the angry people, was entirely clear what they were angry about. Andy passed the information on to Dog, who rushed off to speak to his next-in-command, and asked Dana to contact the operations room to see what other information was coming in.

Andy looked out of the coffee-room window. After a wet start, the clouds were now dwindling, leaving a glorious spring day. More than sixteen hours since Liam Glass had been stabbed and left bleeding in the gutter and the sun was drenching the low- and high-rise blocks, reflecting through the walkways, beckoning to all with promises of summer soon to come. Weather was always good at irony, Andy thought, especially in Britain.

When you were happy, it provided a cold drizzle that seeped through your skin and froze your heart; and when you wanted to cry, the sky turned blue, little fluffy white clouds floated above like candyfloss and the flowers sang with renewed warmth.

Over in the Post's newsroom, in Broad Street, Lyle was pleased with Jamila's TV interview. It prepared the way for the Damballs story without betraying any hint of the real scoop.

He scrolled through the blurred images that the picture editor had downloaded from Jason's tape. There was a tall mugger and a short mugger. You couldn't see their faces, but maybe someone would recognise them. He wondered languidly why the police were taking so long to release the footage themselves but didn't pursue the question any further.

Royland said nothing after the interview was over. He switched channels to catch the end of *Home and Away*, quietly helped a new client select her dumbbells, and began repairing an overhead press.

Katrina was woken by her mum, who'd been in the hospital canteen trying to make her mind up about a latte from the franchise counter when she heard these two customers going on about something on the telly. So she'd helped Katrina find a recording of the item on the BBC website. Maybe it was the tiny size of the picture on her phone or the fact that she was still half asleep, but Katrina felt she was floating around the room like she was in space. Nothing that was said had anything to do with the agony she was going through or the body of her son beating and breathing by machine next to her. She

wanted desperately to do something. At least when she'd
been talking to him, she'd felt she was making a
difference, but there'd been no change in him and she'd
lost heart. She told her mother to play Jamila's interview
to Liam. At least people were talking about him, there
on that little screen. Surely that would make something
happen. Surely.

Watching in the side room, Jason, Zoe, Dudley Snipe
and ward nurse Isabella Ramirez agreed that the
councillor had put on a good show. The elderly patient
whose room it was mumbled a few words but was
ignored. He didn't mind. These were the first proper
visitors he'd had for three days, and in some woozy
manner he assumed they were part of the treatment.

Jason was secretly concerned at Jamila having made
so much of the CCTV but reassured himself it was all
under control. Soon he'd speak to Lyle about sending it
on to the local CID: 'Journalist Brings Justice'. 'Mystery
Source Finds Missing Tape'. 'New Post Correspondent
Saves Police Blushes'.

Nurse Ramirez turned off the TV and suggested that
her patient needed rest. The patient actually looked more
lively than ever, but medical advice was medical advice;
they left him staring mutely at a blank screen and
reconvened in the corridor outside the ward.

'You've spoken to the boy's mother?' said Zoe.

'Spoken? We speak all the time.' He caught her eye.
'I'm just waiting for the right moment.'

'We do need her onside for this.' Her mobile buzzed
with a message. She read it quickly. 'Damballs has passed
Birmingham. Lyle's sending a video crew to interview
him and Katrina for the online edition.'

Jason stared up and down the corridor, hoping for a

way to postpone the inevitable. A man passed wearing a dark blue anorak. He seemed vaguely recognisable, but Jason couldn't quite place him and found this irritating. He prided himself on his ability to remember faces.

'Jason?' Zoe was saying.

'Yes, yes. She's asleep.'

'So wake her up.'

'She's had a tough night.'

Zoe glared at him.

'Right, I'm going for a smoke.' This from Snipe, who promptly did.

Zoe inspected her Jimmy Choos. 'It's OK, Jason. I understand some people don't have the balls. That's how it is.'

'Some people have sensitivity.' A trolley of hot drinks veered past with a middle-aged volunteer on the end of it. Jason waited for it to disappear into the ward. 'The sensitivity to know that certain subjects need to be broached with care and circumspection. You don't just barge in on someone who's suffering and grieving, Zoe. You don't trample over a person's feelings just to file a story.'

'Why not?' Zoe seemed genuinely puzzled.

'I mean...' He ran out of arguments.

Potts' new team were elsewhere, doubtless analysing their latest failed tests. Katrina looked at Jason blearily as he entered the room and then closed her eyes again. Christine was wrestling with the Post's spot-the-difference cartoon. Liam's machines bleeped gently. Jason could hear the soft whoosh of the oxygen, in and out like waves on a distant shore. It was now or never – and much as he wanted it to be never, it had to be now. He cleared his throat, which had become strangely dry.

'Come down to the canteen,' he said quietly to Christine.

'I just came back from there.'

'We still need to talk.'

Christine shrugged and put down the puzzle pages.

'I'm going spare in here anyway,' she said. 'You can get me an Americano.'

He'd gathered up his courage by the time they reached the ground floor. He prepared his words, led Christine out of the lift, pushed through the busy reception area towards the Costa kiosk... and stopped dead. Something was wrong. It took a moment for him to register what.

There were many more people in reception than usual. And they seemed different, as if they didn't belong. It wasn't that they appeared healthier than the usual crowd of patients and visitors. In fact, they appeared, on average, considerably less healthy. But they huddled in small groups and gazed about in a more deliberately unintentional manner. Some checked out the passers-by while others nursed coffees or tapped away vigorously on laptops and mobile phones.

Journalists.

33

Gentlemen of the Press

Jason pulled Christine urgently down a pale blue corridor towards the Medical School.

'The Costa's over there,' she said in alarm, seeing her chances of a free coffee disappear into the distance.

'I don't have time to explain.'

Keeping a reluctant Christine in tow, he trotted up to the next floor and back to the lifts to see if anyone had recognised him and was following. Nobody was. He felt rather let down.

Nevertheless, this was not good. He turned to Christine and informed her there were rival journalists about. She and Katrina had to stay out of sight. At which point she grew resistant and reminded him that he'd promised her an Americano. He swore he'd bring her one if she returned to the ward. Detecting a weakness, she negotiated an almond croissant rider, which he reluctantly agreed to before inserting her into the lift and launching her back to ICU on the fifth floor.

He took a moment to consider the situation. Journalists did not appear without a reason. Like flies to rotting meat, they were attracted to stories. Of course, it could be different rotting meat that had brought them, but he doubted it. A whiff of well-hung story had escaped. He had to tell Lyle, Zoe and Snipe, but he couldn't face telling them just yet. In any case, maybe he was wrong. Maybe it was another carcass they'd sniffed after all.

So Jason returned to the main reception, where the

reporters slouched with their paparazzi, talking to each other with the tired camaraderie of all journalists in the field. He knew the form. It was a careful dance. They would make small talk and share just enough information to see if the competition knew anything they didn't. Sometimes they'd share a lead if they felt that there was an advantage in attacking as a group. More often, they would misdirect, mislead and misappropriate. The big question was, what did they know?

On the far side, Jason recognised Simon O'Shea, a thin-faced young graduate from the Mirror, constantly sent, like him, on hapless missions to celebrity doorsteps. O'Shea was standing with a small group from the Mail, Express and Sun, clutching their lattes and discussing the latest rumours that one of the tabloids was laying off sub-editors and sending its copy to be subbed online in Scunthorpe. Jason walked rapidly through the crowd towards the main entrance – then stopped short and looked enormously amazed.

'Hey,' he said, shaking O'Shea energetically by the hand. He introduced himself to the others as the crime editor from the Camden Herald and expressed his surprise at seeing them all there on his patch.

'What's the big story, then?' he asked.

'Usual bollocks,' said O'Shea with a familiar mix of weary insouciance and suspicion. 'Everybody's talking, nobody knows.'

'What are they saying?'

'Something about a footballer. Could be cobblers, could have legs. Probably chasing shadows. Like always.'

The journalists variously shrugged, shook their heads and agreed without actually agreeing. Jason managed to keep smiling. However, he felt weak with dismay.

'You heard anything?' O'Shea asked without

appearing to care much.

Jason agonised. If he said he knew nothing, they'd immediately suspect he was lying. A reporter who really knew nothing would pretend to know it all.

'Of course,' he said airily. He made not to notice as other groups of reporters and photographers sidled nonchalantly closer. 'You know how it goes. I have my contacts here in the hospital. You'll be sure to tell me when you find out more, won't you. And I'll do the same.'

O'Shea nodded generously. The others smiled, said yes, no, waggled their heads and committed to as little as possible while appearing helpful. None of them trusted anyone.

'Jason...' O'Shea led him to one side and slipped him a business card. 'I've always liked your work. If you hear anything from your local contacts... I can look into some tip money for you. Get you a few gigs. Friends always help friends.'

'Totally, Simon. Friends help friends.' Jason made a point of admiring the card's remarkably attractive design, bid a friendly farewell to the group and wandered carelessly towards the hospital's grim multilevel car park. He found his Renault where he'd left it in the early morning, paid the cost of a flight to Brazil into the machine and drove off in the direction of the next hospital down the road. As he left, he looked in his rear-view mirror and noticed a number of cars pulling out of parking spaces behind him. Indeed, most of the journalists who'd been in reception appeared to be tailing him. He drove unusually slowly, indicated every turn with exceptional care and parked in a side street near the second hospital.

Here he bought a pay-and-display ticket for the

maximum time allowed. Marched into reception. Veered rapidly out of sight through the Friends' Shop. Detoured at speed down a back corridor. Hurtled unseen out of the hospital side exit and jogged back to his car to discover the other reporters' cars jammed into every available space, with maximum pay-and-display tickets in their windscreens. And the reporters nowhere to be seen, doubtless looking for him.

Jason drove rapidly back towards the Camden General, alone, and pulled out his Nokia.

Lyle answered immediately. 'What have you got for me from the mother?'

'The mother?'

'The boy's mother. The Glass woman. Wake up, Jason. Her feelings about Damballs. Her grief for her son. What the great role model was like in bed. He shoots, he scores. Eight hundred words. There's no problem, is there?'

'No. She's fully on board. Totally. No problem. Trust me.'

In Lyle's model of the universe there were only two reasons for making a phone call: a fresh angle or a problem. He decided to think negative. 'So what's wrong?' he said.

'Nothing to panic over.'

'Now I'm panicking.'

'I'm dealing with it.'

'Dealing with what, for fuck's sake?'

'We've got a leak.'

'Shit.'

Jason hurtled down a narrow street, overtaking four cars, and informed the news editor that he'd just found thirty rival shits in the hospital reception asking about footballers.

'Who've you been speaking to?' Lyle's voice had lost its gracious sheen. 'Who the fuck have you told about the story? If you've blown this, I'll personally ram your mobile phone up your jacksy.'

'Me? Not me, Lyle. No-one. I've not spoken to anyone.'

'Is it Potts? I'll kill him. I'll stab him myself. Better, I'll cut off his balls, toast them and feed them to him on kebab skewers with dog-shit sauce.'

'I don't think it's Potts. They didn't seem to know enough about what was going on. Potts would have briefed them better.'

Lyle fell silent. He knew the only other likely possibility was his own newsroom.

'They were all over the hospital, but I've diverted them up the road.'

'How long before they realise you conned them?'

Jason hazarded half an hour or so at best. 'Damballs can't show his face here.'

'He's not safe there, Jason.'

'That's what I'm saying.'

'No, the boy. We have to move him.'

Jason swerved past a truck.

'Move Liam? Isn't that dangerous?'

'No prob. He'll be absolutely fine. We've got private clinics nobody knows about. There's the one out in Norfolk where we stuck Amy Winehouse while we haggled over an exclusive. No – reverse-ferret. That one's too far for Dazza to get to tonight.'

'I mean, medically? In Liam's condition?' The lights ahead were turning red. Jason sped through, missing a courier bike by a foot.

'Of course it is, Jason. Absolutely. We do this all the time. Believe me. Two years ago we helicoptered that have-a-go hero from Walthamstow to Scotland with two broken legs and a smashed pelvis to keep him away from the Sun. And we nicked that runaway earl who'd scarpered with the au pair and the firm's pension fund. Flew him back by air ambulance when he got into a car smash in São Paulo. Unconscious. Woke up in St Mary's on a drip, facing his wife, her lawyers and the accountants and promptly went into cardiac arrest. Great photos and video. Liam will be better for it. We'll get him the best specialists in the country.'

'I thought Potts had already brought in the best.'

'Them? That was for show. No, don't get me wrong. They're good. I'd trust them with my wife. Well, maybe... I've got a good life policy on her. Jason, I'm joking. I really would trust them with my wife. But we can do better. Trust me. I'm talking about the real best. World-beaters.'

He rang off. Jason overtook a bus on the wrong side and turned into the Camden General again. He felt reassured. Of course Lyle knew what he was doing. He must have faced this kind of situation hundreds of times. Only then did he remember he needed to speak to him about getting the CCTV pictures back to the police. No matter, he could do it later. No rush.

34

Human Rights

'Tell me we have the bastard CCTV tape, for God's sake.'

'We have the story under control, sir.'

'Which means we don't fucking have it.'

No sooner had the TV interview finished than Dog's detective chief inspector was at his desk shouting at Dog on one phone while simultaneously being yelled at himself on another by the borough commander, who was sitting in his office upstairs getting earache from the council, local white groups and local Bengalis, all of whom wanted to know if he was going to be at this meeting that nobody knew about and nobody had authorised and now needed policing, while he in turn had been slagging off the borough press officer at the far end of the corridor, who (in turn) was demanding to be told who the hell was leaking what to the press, because she'd been fielding all this crap from newspapers and now radio and TV newsrooms, and to cap it all Area Press Office was on her back from Hendon, and Area was being given grief by the Commissioner's Office in Scotland Yard because it was all over the Internet that the police had lost the tape and what with conspiracy theories and cock-up theories and fucking paranoid-schizophrenic theories, they didn't need this, and nobody had released a statement yet, but it better bloody be put together fast. And where exactly was the bastard CCTV?

Where was the CCTV? This was a question that was

most definitely exercising Andy. To the point that he decided it would be politic to absent himself from the station. So, after Dana turned off the TV, he suggested to Dog that he (Andy) might go and investigate the mystery of the missing tape at ground zero. Dog ran his hand through his hair and agreed it would be useful. Andy asked Dana to come with him as his investigation team and she agreed, even though she was getting to the end of her second shift on the trot. But, she added with a warm smile, that didn't matter a bit.

Andy and Dana stood over his desk and made a rapid reassessment of the evidence list, which confirmed what everyone already knew – that surveillance pictures from other sources, such as local parking cameras, were of no use whatsoever, and that no police records, logs or contemporaneous notes mentioned receiving any kind of tape from the newsagent, Mr Naik. If Andy didn't locate it soon, his career future would rapidly become a career past. He'd seen people demoted for less. No, fuck it, he'd seen people sacked for less. And Dana knew this, because she didn't make any jokes about it. In fact, she didn't make any jokes at all.

Instead, she booked out an unmarked general-purpose car, a bright pink Astra. As she drove, Andy tried to shake off his lack of sleep and at the same time ignore her perfume, which was inspiring thoughts that were not appropriate to the situation. She was a good driver, fast and efficient, and he tried to think less about her scent and focus instead on her driving skills, the rhythmic movement of her legs, her flair for inserting the car through tight gaps, but for some reason this seemed to distract him even more. And as her hand came to rest softly on the knob of the gear stick, he found himself wondering again about the coppers who called her the

Station Bike and what evidence they might have.

'It may never happen,' said Dana, glancing over to him.

'I hope not,' he said heavily.

'Tapes don't just disappear.'

'Yeah, and the tape too.'

'Home trouble? I know a lot about that,' she said. And he remembered that she'd been shacked up with a civilian, an auditor who turned out to be married and had told his wife he was travelling a lot.

'Babies,' he said now as she turned into the narrow streets behind Euston station. 'Or rather, baby.'

'No, I don't know a lot about that,' she said, with a brief smile. 'Chance would be a fine thing.'

'Don't rush into it.'

Naik greeted Andy and Dana affably from behind his counter.

'I have given statements to a hundred and thirty-four policemen, haven't I?' he announced. 'And I am happy to give a statement to a hundred and thirty-five, anything to help.'

He appeared in a better mood now that the police barrier had gone, growing nostalgic for it and the extra crowds it had attracted. He'd even managed to cater for them by setting up ice creams and snacks on his trestle outside.

'This is a dreadful thing, surely, yes, of course,' he said, slapping the till in front of him with vigour. 'And justice must be upheld, the villains must be arrested and punished, and yes, I have handed over the CCTV tape at dawn. It was right here.'

He pointed down below the counter, then disappeared below said counter and after some sounds of scurrying and much moving of boxes reappeared clutching what (momentary joy) Andy thought might be a copy.

Naik waved the cassette importantly and said, 'This is precisely what it looked like, sir. This is the new tape that I have replaced the old tape with when I handed it over to the detective at five-one-five in the morning, precisely, when I was very busy preparing the newspaper round but still gave of my time, willingly and without hesitation.'

And when Andy asked him to describe this officer, Mr Naik also did this willingly and without hesitation.

'The man, yes, he was short, though not all that short, maybe on the taller side, taller than me, perhaps, and he had fair, tousled hair, or maybe dark, and indeed not that tousled, with piercing blue eyes, which could have been brown or hazel, and gentle rather than piercing, I am sure, yes, but not that gentle, and he wore a suit.'

Of that Naik was certain, yes.

'Definitely a suit, probably, and a tie, maybe, which if it existed could have been red or blue or green and he had an air of confidence, but not too confident, young, old, yes, well, perhaps in his twenties, maybe more and maybe not, and his voice was sharp,' he was convinced, 'but not that sharp, you could say soft, pleasant, but perhaps not that pleasant.'

Of that he was positive. Oh, yes.

Andy asked again about the hair, and the little newsagent screwed up his eyes as if seeing the man right in front of him, and said most definitely it was on the dark side of light, or the light side of dark, perhaps, and ruffled, or should he say curled, or wavy, or straight, absolutely.

'And he was tall or short?'

'Yes, more or less, a bit.'

Andy then left the shop abruptly, saying nothing more, and Dana hurriedly thanked the man for his help before following.

'That was a load of use,' she said.

Andy told her to get in the car and dialled a number on his mobile.

'I know you're fucking there. I need to speak to you now, before I kill you,' Andy said to the voicemail at the other end.

'Where are we going?' Dana asked.

Andy told her. She looked momentarily surprised. When they reached the hospital, she parked close to the entrance and they marched rapidly through the reception. There was an unusually large crowd round the lifts, so Andy headed for the stairs, dialling Jason again, and again reaching his voicemail. And then, as they were running up, Andy's phone rang.

'You've got my fucking CCTV tape,' he said.

'Not at all.' Jason's voice sounded strangely confident. 'I'm busy with Liam and his mother just at the moment, but if you tell me what you need, I'm sure I can try to help.'

'Don't try to snow me. I've just talked to Naik, who says he handed the VHS to a detective. And, you know, that aforementioned detective sounds like no-one I know at the nick, but he sounds very much like a sodding journalist I do know and whose neck I'm going to break, but only after I've made his face look like he's had a bad meeting with a pair of Doc Martens.'

'Innocent,' replied Jason with impressive calm. 'I would never pretend I was a police officer, that's against

the law. I did hear rumours that you'd mislaid the
security footage. And I'm very sorry for you, you must
be under an awful strain, in fact you sound totally out of
breath. Are you OK? You're not having a heart attack,
are you?'

At this point, Andy was jogging laboriously up the
fourth flight of stairs. Behind Jason, he could hear a
nurse talking to Katrina, and he urged himself faster.
'Are you... are you telling me you didn't go into Naik's
and skip off... with the CCTV shots... of the boy getting
stabbed? Do you swear?'

And Jason told Andy he would never lie to a good
friend, that he didn't skip anywhere, that he definitely
didn't tell anyone he was a detective. 'But if you like, I
can put the word out that you can't find the tape and I'm
sure there'll be some journalists who'd be pleased to help
you look for it.'

'You won't do anything of the sort, you bastard. And
you haven't actually said you didn't take it.'

But Jason's voice was starting to cut out.

'I can't hear you,' he said.

Andy checked his phone. He had a solid signal.
Jason's voice came back to him in gobbets of
unintelligible sound, half-words, chopped and distorted.

'You don't...' Andy said, panting the last metres to
the door into Intensive Care. 'I know you... I know
where you are.'

'Speak up,' came faintly and then the call cut out.

Dana pressed the intercom and called, 'Police.'

The security lock clicked open. Andy pushed past,
ignoring the nurses' protests, ran straight to Liam's room
– and flung open the door.

To discover no-one: no Jason, no Katrina, no Liam
Glass.

'How,' he said to Dana, the empty, stripped-down bed and the unplugged machinery, 'does he fucking do it?'

35

Writer's Block

At the very moment that Andy Rockham and Dana Bookman burst into ICU B, five floors below them Jason, Katrina, paramedics and orderlies were completing the long and delicate process of transferring Liam and all his connections into a gleaming new private ambulance.

Jason climbed in with Katrina and a consultant anaesthetist but was stopped by the staff as not being Liam's parent. He explained that if it wasn't for him, the ambulance wouldn't even be there. After a short discussion, he was waved inside and Christine was left on the ground as neither being Liam's parent nor working for the tabloid that was paying for the trip.

Jason felt temporarily bad that the boy's grandmother had to be sent under separate cover but reminded himself that there were other, higher issues to be aware of. He was the family's representative to the world. He was telling their story.

'It's good of the Post to be doing this,' he declared grandly to Katrina and the crew. They didn't seem as impressed as they ought to be. 'It's one of the pillars of our society. A free press. Free to help victims in their time of need.'

The ambulance turned out of the emergency bay and sped past reception, blue lights flashing. Jason could see eight of the journos who'd made it back from his detour, standing outside in the sunshine puffing on cigarettes. He slid back in his seat, making himself invisible until the hospital was out of sight. It felt good to get moving. The

Post was looking after Liam's best interests and Jason was heading towards his goal. It was strange, though, that the nearer Jason got to his goal, the less certain he felt.

He twisted around and looked at Liam, his round face and blonde hair visible through the gently waving tangle of wires and drips. He seemed even paler than before.

'This will be OK, won't it?' he said privately to the driver. 'Moving him.'

The driver shrugged. He was a rectangular Welshman called Wystan, with a goatee that looked like an insect had crawled onto his chin. 'Who knows? Some seem like they're at death's door and you meet them two weeks later running for a bus. Others look ready to jump off the gurney and dance and they go and die on the way. That's life.'

Jason stared for a moment at the winding road ahead and then enquired about the clinic. 'Is it far?'

'So-so.'

'And they're good there? They know their stuff, yes?'

'Don't ask me, boyo. We just pick them up and try to deliver them alive.' Wystan saw Jason's look of suppressed anxiety. 'Don't worry. I'm sure they're good. It's market economics, isn't it? They wouldn't be able to charge such high fees if their patients kept dying, would they?'

He leant forwards and flipped a button. The ambulance siren wailed and cars scattered in front of them.

Jason felt less than reassured, but rather than worry he tried phoning Damballs again. Once more the call went to voicemail. He pulled his laptop out of his bag. At least he could make use of the time by starting to write. Lyle would need copy very soon. However, the words wouldn't come. Struggling to write about painted hippos, he'd been sure all he needed was a good story for the words to flow. Now he had the best story in his career and he had writer's block.

An alarm started to trill in the back. Katrina stared numbly ahead, hardly responding. Jason wondered if she'd been given more tranquillisers.

'No problem,' said the anaesthetist quickly, turning off the alarm and inspecting Liam's vital signs.

Wystan glanced over his shoulder. The siren whooped once, louder than Jason expected. The ambulance sped up and then lurched as he braked hard.

'Strange. We don't usually get traffic jams here at this time of day,' Jason said. They were, as it happened, passing close to where Liam had been stabbed. A narrow canyon of a street between seven-storey blocks of flats on one side and the empty London Temperance Hospital on the other.

'You've got one now. Lousy time to transfer a patient, isn't it? Lunchtime.'

'It's past lunchtime.'

'Afternoon school-run, then.'

'It's too early for the afternoon run.'

The ambulance accelerated and promptly braked again as a man sprinted from the abandoned hospital and almost disappeared under their front wheels. Wystan flipped him the bird.

Jason's phone rang. He snatched it out of his jacket. 'Yes!'

'Is that Jason Crowthorne?' The voice sounded guarded and had a Midlands accent.

'It depends who you are,' said Jason carefully. Another two pedestrians ran past, they seemed to be shouting something. Others approached along the street, chanting in their turn.

'I'm Joey Swinson.' The name was familiar, but for the moment Jason couldn't place it. 'I play with Damon Weaverall, don't I? I'm driving him over from the team hotel.'

Jason felt a surge of panic. Damballs was in London.

The chanting grew louder as the men approached and now Jason could hear more clearly. They were chanting, 'CCTV.' His heart chilled.

'What are they shouting?' said the driver.

'No idea,' said Jason emphatically.

'Is everything all right there?' asked Joey.

'Yes. Totally fine.' Jason dropped his voice and turned the phone away from Katrina. 'Take a shortcut,' he said to Wystan.

'No way, boyo. Ambulances don't do shortcuts.' Wystan turned the siren on full and accelerated round two huddles of people in the middle of the road who seemed to be acting rather aggressively towards each other.

'Dazza wants to know what condition the kid's in. In fact he's very concerned. He's heard worrying things. Coma and that. He cares very much about the kid.'

'The boy is... good. Liam is... being well cared for.' Jason spoke as quietly as he could. 'We're just transporting him to the clinic right now.'

'CCTV... CCTV...' floated in from the outside.

'Sounds a bit noisy.'

'Does it really?' Jason laughed merrily. 'I suppose we get used to it.'

Joey was still chattering away in his ear. 'He'll make a great dad. He's a very caring person. He's already decided to set up the Weaverall Charity for Stabbed Children of Single Mothers. We often talk about charity work and such. When we are not on the football field, of course.'

'You do?' Jason tried to keep the surprise out of his voice.

'Yeah. Dazza sent money to a Kosovan orphanage last year. Didn't you see the photos?'

'Must have missed those ones.'

'No sweat. You know, Dazza's really looking forward to meeting the boy – and the mum too, of course.'

Jason asked gently what time Joey thought that might be.

'About an hour. Give or take. We've got to pick up one of his cars from one of his London houses. He says he's grateful for this opportunity to do some good in the world and help someone who's not had the chances he had. He's working on a speech. Nothing too long. He hopes that's OK with you.'

Not long was OK with Jason. He rang off. An hour. They were closer than he'd thought.

Liam's monitor alarm sounded again. Jason glanced over. There seemed to be fresh blood on Liam's bandages and the anaesthetist was urgently pressing down on an artery.

'Nothing to look at here,' he said. 'How long till we get there?' he asked Wystan.

'Seven minutes, I guess.'

'Just wondering.' The consultant anaesthetist seemed to be sweating. Katrina stared everywhere but at her son.

Jason shut his laptop without writing another word. Time enough later to find the right opening for the biggest story of his career.

36

Unrest

It is said: a wise general makes his plans knowing nothing can be planned for.

As soon as he heard about the growing anger among the residents of the Gordon Road Estates, Andy phoned the head teacher at Euston Comprehensive ('Our Future is in Our Hands'). Alarmed, she promptly cancelled lunchbreak and asked Andy to come to talk to her children. So while Dana stayed at the Camden General, trying to find out where Liam had been taken to, Andy dropped in on the school. The head teacher had assembled her children in the main hall. As he waited to speak, she informed them of the tragic stabbing of their fellow student.

'Let me use this opportunity,' she continued, 'to remind you of the dangers of sharp objects of any kinds. Stabbing people can cause serious injury, permanent disability, blindness, brain damage and death, among other possibilities.' Andy coughed, in the hope of stepping in with something a little more reassuring, but she was not one to be interrupted. 'No child is to venture beyond the school gates this afternoon at any point before it's time to go home,' she announced. 'Not that there is any reason to be scared, of course. But remember, children, if you have any fears arising from these very frightening incidents, the school counsellor's door is always open.'

Following her little talk, the smaller children, who hadn't been scared up to this moment, were now terrified, while the larger children made it clear that they were not scared of anything and were determined to prove it. To which end, they ran to the gates and shouted to those on the other side, describing what they were going to do to them as soon as they had suitable opportunity.

The only people on the other side, at that time, were three uniformed policemen and two surprised passers-by, on their way to Sainsbury's Local.

Tensions, Andy soon discovered, were rising even more rapidly elsewhere.

Nasir Uddin Meshu, one of the local community leaders, of whom none of the residents had heard, went public on Sunrise Radio, accusing the police of deliberately hiding the CCTV pictures of Liam Glass's attackers. 'They are clearly doing this,' he added, 'to increase suspicion of Bengalis. Look at those inflammatory tweets from early this morning – from @newsshouldbefree and @bestukjournalist. Now they have gone viral!'

Another community leader who nobody knew phoned LBC. 'Quite the opposite,' he replied. 'The cops can't wait to blame it on us whites.'

Heated discussion took place on Twitter, Facebook and local radio. Some said, 'We're not racist, but look how they treat us. Our grandfathers came from Kent and Essex and Ireland to build the railways. We had large families, strong religious beliefs and community values. We passed our council flats on from generation to generation. But then the money and the flats were given to the disabled and the special needs and the Pakis, weren't they? And our family ties are breaking. And those that are left are joining gangs.'

Others said, 'We're not racists, but look how they treat us. Our grandfathers helped build the British Empire. We came from Sylhet in Bangladesh. We had large families, strong religious beliefs and community values. We served in restaurants, laundries or the rag trade. We passed on our low-paid jobs from generation to generation. We got council flats and were grateful. But now the money and the flats are given to the disabled and the special needs and the Somalis, aren't they? And our family ties are breaking. And those who are left are joining gangs.'

As Andy sat in his car outside the school, the spring sunshine sparkling off the parked cars, he noticed more non-racists on the streets. He was about to call Dana to see if she'd managed to locate Jason and the tape, when his phone rang. It was Dog. The borough commander wanted to see him urgently. Dog sounded happy it wasn't him. A summons to meet the boss was rarely a good thing.

Andy entered Chief Superintendent Slocombe's office with some nervousness, sure that he was going to be cut to pieces over the CCTV tape, but to his surprise he discovered a larger meeting in progress, involving senior officers. The borough commander nodded briefly to Andy from behind his desk. Superintendents, detective chief inspectors, chief inspectors and inspectors variously sat and stood around the room. There was no space left for Andy, so he stayed facing the desk, feeling very exposed, while Slocombe finished off what he'd been in the middle of saying.

He had, it seemed, decided it was time to make his own stand on community values. He'd read through the paperwork, including the original statement Andy had taken from Katrina Glass with its reference to two Paki kids.

'You know the Estates well, do you?' he said, turning to Andy.

'Pretty well, sir,' Andy began to say, then realised he was expected to inject a measure of certainty and changed it to, 'Absolutely.'

'You can give us a list of the known Bengali thugs? Yes?'

'Well...'

'Good,' continued Slocombe. And ordered one of his senior officers to take the list of Bengalis from Andy, track them down and arrest any that could possibly be guilty of the attack on Liam Glass, or at least were not noticeably innocent.

Andy hesitated. The senior officers promptly informed Borough Commander Slocombe that this would overwhelm their resources. That most, if not all, the arrested Bengalis would be given bail the next day for lack of evidence. And if by chance any of them were guilty, they would immediately take an extended holiday with their grandparents in Bangladesh – like last time.

'And it could be seen as racist,' said his deputy, from the corner of the room.

'Bollocks to that,' said the borough commander irritably, leaning back in his chair. He was a tall man with a bullet head and a soft Leeds accent that sometimes fooled people into thinking he was a socialist or worse. 'We must be seen to have taken action. And if they run, then we'll know they're guilty and, better still, they'll be off our patch. Furthermore, I've got this fucking meeting that this idiot councillor has called this evening, and I want as many awkward, law-breaking troublemakers out of the way as possible, so we can concentrate on the awkward, law-abiding troublemakers who remain.'

He glared at Andy. 'And what are you doing about that fucking tape?'

'I'm tracking it down, sir.'

'Well, get on with it, man. What's stopping you?'

37

A Room with a View

Liam-baby, Liam-baby, Liam-baby, everything's going to be all right, it's all going to be OK. Look at this nice place we've come to, all glass and shiny metal and environmentally friendly Scandinavian wood. Even the automatic sliding doors look more classy than the ones at Camden General – you can't even hear a hiss when they open. That's top dollar, baby. This is real money here, real medicine, like the rich people get, like you deserve, like the celebs, and I'm here with you. It's going to be OK.

In the clinic's ambulance entrance, Katrina was greeted by two clinic doctors. White coats over nice suits to prove their medical credentials and two clinic nurses to assist them, two clinic porters in neat blue uniforms, even a Russian woman from accounts with an embossed blue folder, overseeing it all. Katrina could see they knew what they were about. There was this other journalist and her photographer, who should lose a few pounds if he knew what was good for him. They were from the Post, so presumably they were all right with Jason Crowthorne. In any case, he seemed a bit distracted.

And there was no hanging about, not once the clinic's medical staff had looked at Liam on the trolley. They went quiet and talked rapidly among themselves, though they waited until Jason had signed two forms, and then a third, then a fax from the Post and a few more pieces of paper, and then for the photographer to take his snaps of Liam. Then they made a little huddle round him.

Liam, if only you knew how careful they're being and how much they're checking things and shaking their heads.

One doctor led Katrina to one side and went, 'Mrs Glass, your son is in good hands now.' And she corrected him to Ms Glass, Mrs Glass was her mum, wasn't she? He nodded like he was almost listening and explained all the new tests they were going to conduct right now, and she could imagine Kate Moss there for something, or Prince Harry or someone. Of course, people like that didn't get stabbed going to the cash machine, but they'd come there if they wanted something done, like Botox or piles.

Jason looked at the huddle round the trolley and then saw Katrina watching him. He said, 'He'll be all right now.' Then, 'He'll be OK.'

Liam-baby, everyone's saying you'll be all right.

Then Liam was wheeled off and the clump of medical people hurried after him. Jason stayed. He looked a bit hyper, she thought, had been since they arrived, jumping about, even when he was signing the papers. Now he was peering behind the plants and nodding and saying, 'Good.'

Katrina said, 'Good, what?'

'No journalists. No paps.'

'But you're a journalist,' she said.

He laughed loudly. 'Apart from me. And the other two. I meant rivals. No rivals. We can't have rivals here.'

'I thought you wanted Liam's story everywhere, you told me. That's what you promised.'

He parted the fronds of a line of yuccas and looked into the street beyond. 'You don't understand how journalism works, do you? First we have to tell the story ourselves and it's only because nobody else has it that everyone else wants it. If everyone had it, then nobody would care about it, would they?'

Liam's new room was on the sixth floor, with a view to kill for over London, but of course his neatly made bed was empty right now while they did their tests. Though he'd be with them soon, very soon. Christine finally turned up and rapidly worked out how to turn on the TV. The blonde reporter was going on to the photographer about Damon Weaverall. It seemed he was even coming here to the clinic, for some reason, but they didn't say why and Katrina didn't like to ask. Footballers got things, she supposed, like torn ligaments. She remembered Liam coming back from a match one Sunday afternoon, legs covered in bruises. She'd rubbed embrocation on his legs and he'd liked that. He told her she was as good as a real club physio and it made her proud to feel she could do something to help his career. He said, 'Mum, Damballs wouldn't get better treatment.'

The reporter and photographer seemed very excited and were making plans. Zoe and Snipe, they were called. They introduced themselves to her and kept glancing at her as well, but she ignored them and then they left.

Oh, Liam, you'd love to know Damballs is coming here to the very same clinic as you. You'd nag at me to ask for his autograph. Like those you got when you were at Chelsea. I'll see if I can find out where he's going to be and maybe I'll try to get it for you. Something for when you wake up.

All this time, Christine was sat watching a daytime repeat of *Gossip Girl* on the room's flat-screen TV. After the others went, Jason came over to Katrina and asked if she was OK. She nodded silently, but in fact she felt exhausted.

'Have you eaten anything?' he said. 'I can get the clinic to bring you some food.'

She was grateful to be asked, but she simply shook

her head and sat down on a Scandinavian-style chair next to the bed. Not for the first time, she felt like she was nothing. In the way, even. Liam was being tested and operated on and she couldn't even give him a hug and tell him to be brave. She wanted to cry, but she made an effort and stopped herself. Crying wouldn't help. Nobody wanted a wet mess of a mother getting in the way.

Zoe and Snipe came back into the room and Zoe gave Jason a meaningful look.

Snipe said, 'He should be here very soon.'

He meant Dazza, it seemed, though Katrina didn't know why he cared so much. Except everyone liked to see famous people.

'Very soon,' Zoe said.

This time, when she did that thing with her eyes again, Jason responded. 'Mrs Glass,' he said, and he was talking to her mum. He had to repeat her name, because there was important things happening in the soap on the TV, weren't there? More important than her own grandson, it would appear. Finally Christine tore herself away. 'Can I have a word, Mrs Glass. What I started talking about before.'

Katrina was expecting her to tell him to piss off, she was watching telly, which was what Christine would totally say to her, but she gave him a brilliant smile and fluttered a hand girlishly and said, 'Absolutely. Right with you, kid. Just get me that Americano you promised.' And she went out of the room with him like they were old friends.

The reporter and photographer left again just as fast. Now it was just Katrina and the bed.

She looked at the view. She could see St Paul's far off through a gap between a bank and a half-built tower block. She could see the sunshine flickering on it, going in and out of the clouds, flickering on her. Flickering on the empty bed.

She sat in silence. And tried not to think.

38

Pubic Wig

Jason drew himself up tall, ready to live up to his highest journalistic standards. He placed his journalistic left hand on Christine's shoulder.

'We need to talk,' he said once more.

'I got that message. I need my Americano.'

'Follow me.' He led her to the lifts, desperately wondering how to broach the embarrassing question of Damon Weaverall. It seemed so simple, until he tried to put it into words. And, like most people who decide not to beat around the bush, he promptly began to circle the bush, beating enthusiastically.

He began a story about a young actress he'd once interviewed, interrupted himself, interrupted himself interrupting, detoured around the young diva's ego, reversed past her complete lack of ability and settled on her refusal to film a sex scene in the nude. By this time, he and Christine had stepped into the lift, joined by two nurses, a Filipina cleaner and a porter.

Christine waited quietly for Jason to get to the point, while he tried to ignore the presence of his motley audience. He was surprised, he'd told the actress, at her reluctance to do the nude scene, as he had just watched a romantic interlude in her latest movie in which she was visible in every respect, right down to her Brazilian.

The doors opened again and a sedated patient was pushed into the crowd on a gurney. The inhabitants of the lift were now jammed against each other in rapt silence. The doors slid shut.

'"No, I wasn't," the actress says to me.

'"But I saw it," I reply. "Your love triangle. Your forest of desire."'

The patient opened his eyes.

'"No, you didn't," she says triumphantly. "I wore a wig."

'"What's a wig got to do with it?" I say.

'"Down there," she says. "A merkin. A pubic wig."'

Their fellow travellers stared studiously at the floor indicator. The lift stopped again and a chaplain squeezed in with a shy apology.

'I didn't know such things existed,' Jason said. 'Matched precisely to... That wasn't her personal glory I'd been looking at between her thighs. It was the best woven yak-belly hair the producer could buy.' The chaplain found it necessary to check the time on his watch.

'Yak-belly hair?' Christine asked.

'Apparently that's the best match for pubic hair.'

'I'll bear it in mind.'

The lift reached the ground floor. The others departed with a certain reluctance. Jason steered Christine to one side.

'And your point is?'

'We need a merkin.'

'Do what?'

He didn't feel he'd expressed the plan quite as tastefully as he'd have liked, but time was pressing. 'Listen, Katrina doesn't want us to name Liam's father.'

'You can say that again.'

'So we don't. With a merkin you think you're looking at the real thing, but you're looking at yak's hair.'

'You're buying Liam a pubic wig?'

A passing nurse glanced briefly over her shoulder but kept walking. Christine was clearly trying very hard to understand.

'No...' Jason swallowed. He needed all his courage now. 'We're getting Damon Weaverall.'

'Damon Weaverall the footballer...'

'Yes.'

'... wears a pubic wig?' She twiddled her bracelet uncertainly.

Jason felt his courage retreating again. 'I don't think you've quite got the point, Christine. It's a metaphor. A figure of speech. Dazza is prepared to put himself forward – at great sacrifice, I might say – to be a figurehead. To tell the public he's Liam's father. This will get your grandson much more newspaper and TV coverage, better medical attention, police support... He'll be a human merkin.'

'Damon Weaverall.' She seemed stuck.

'Yes.'

'He's Liam's father?'

'No.'

'Damon Weaverall is not Liam's father?'

'I think it's highly unlikely.'

'Shame.'

'It's pretend. To help Liam. You'll be photographed together. We'll do a big interview. He'll speak out in support of the family.' There, it was out. No going back now.

'Dazza here!'

'Not so loud!' Jason looked round on a reflex. They were standing dangerously close to the clinic's coffee bar. But Christine had turned very pale. She waved purple nails in the air as she gathered her thoughts.

'There'll be money,' he said, pushing home his point

anxiously. 'A fee from Weaverall's agent. A fee from the Post. Money that will help create Liam's future. According to my calculations, she could get somewhere around seventy-five k.'

'Shit,' said Christine. She was shaking slightly. 'That's a lot of future.'

'We just need Katrina to agree. To the—'

'Pubic wig.'

'You got it.'

He reached nervously into his jacket and slid out a biro and a legal agreement he'd amended as appropriate for the acceptance of a footballing merkin. Christine folded them into her handbag.

'You'll speak to her? There's not much time. Deadlines. All of that.'

'He'll be a pretend father?'

'Precisely.'

'Leave it to me.' With the mention of the money, she seemed suddenly to have conquered the complexities of the issue. 'Let me talk to her. She's not stupid. She knows where her interests lie.'

Now Jason felt a wave of relaxation flow over him, like a swimmer in a warm Mediterranean sea. He wasn't personally so certain about Katrina's intelligence, self-interest-wise, but surely Christine knew her daughter better than he did.

Christine drew back her shoulders and set herself in the direction of the coffee franchise. 'Liam'll be chuffed when he finds out, won't he, eh?'

'Totally chuffed. As chuffed as could be. Beyond chuffed.'

'Damballs, the kid's father,' Christine said with a faint smile as she located a wall-mounted menu that said Americano. 'I wish.'

Jason wanted to punch the air in triumph. He wanted to dance. He felt an enormous glow of positive anticipation. He was almost there.

It was a glow that lasted precisely as long as it took him to leave Katrina's mother to her sustainably sourced coffee experience and stroll happily back towards the entrance...

... in time to see three taxis deposit three rival reporters and three rival photographers on the environmentally friendly York-stone pavement outside.

39

The Gathering Clouds of War

Jamila sat squarely on the guano-spattered stone bench at the side of the blood-stained square, feeling unexpectedly calm in the warm spring breeze. This was her ward. Shared with two other councillors, she admitted reluctantly to herself. But she was here and they weren't.

She noticed a little Chinese woman watching her from across the square, holding two empty Dragon Mart shopping bags. Jamila nodded to her with a smile and the other woman nodded and bowed. Jamila bowed and the other woman bowed deeper.

'Thank you,' the woman called in a high voice, bowing again.

Jamila bowed a third time.

'You save our tree. Very good. Very good councillor. I vote for you. Don't believe everything people say about you. Mostly. Very good tree.'

Jamila smiled and bowed a fourth time and thanked the woman as she tottered off, clutching her bags. Invigorated by this, she phoned her borough party leader again and still he was busy, so she left a second message and phoned his deputy, who promised she would watch the interview, whenever it was. Jamila asked the deputy for more support in ward canvassing.

'Support?' The deputy opposition leader was one of those tough, bluff people that local politics hammers out in every age and every country. She sat bolt upright at the desk in her party office every day, surrounded by ward maps and focus-group reports, planning town-hall coups with special-ops precision. 'I wish I could, Jamila. Support? If only. If I give you extra resources, I take away from others. Tell me whose resources I should take away in order to benefit you?'

'Have you seen the polls here?' said Jamila.

'Work to your strengths,' said the deputy opposition leader, sounding distracted. 'We trust you. Totally. You're a trooper. Go out and drag those votes in. When was that interview again?'

'Half an hour ago.'

'Will it be on iPlayer, do you think?'

Jamila sat in the blowy intermittent sunshine and meditated on the ups and downs of politics. Her phone rang.

'You were very good.'

'You think so, Mum?'

'I turned on and they said you would be on. Sometimes they say you're going to be on and you're not.'

'Sometimes a bigger story comes up.'

'I told everyone. We all watched.'

'Thank you, Mum.'

'You looked just like a real politician.'

'Thank you, Mum. I'll see you usual time Sunday.'

There were people moving slowly up the street in the distance. They tended, she noticed, to manifest themselves in small groups, carrying items she couldn't quite identify. Vaguely like bricks and lengths of wood with nails sticking out. She was not very up on the building trade.

Nevertheless, being in the area, she thought she really ought to knock on a few doors, canvass her constituents. The evening's meeting would also take some thinking about. But for some reason neither of these were at the forefront of her mind. The warm April day was just too nice. As she sat on the stone seat an unfamiliar feeling came over her. She might have called it pleasure or even joy, if such feelings had been common to her. But Jamila rarely had the time to feel joy.

Sirens wailed in the distance. Four police vans raced past and disappeared. Two police cars stopped at the far end of the road, a flat was entered and a clutch of youths were bundled into the cars before they raced away. Jamila sat through it all, eyes half closed, softly breathing the delicate spring air. The street grew still once more.

After fifteen minutes she opened her eyes fully again. She'd had enough peace and quiet, she had work to do. She stood up bravely and trotted round the corner towards Chamberlain, one of the medium-sized tower blocks.

Canvassing was the part of the job she liked least. Politics would be so much easier without voters. Today's voters were a disappointment. They never kept their promises. They said what they thought you wanted to hear. They told lies and shied away from the difficult decisions. Voters were only in it for themselves.

Ahead, on a low brick wall, sat five white teenagers watching her approach. On the other side of the road, eyeing them both, a gaggle of six Bengalis. She turned to the left, but both gangs followed, each slouching along its own side of the street, casting a sideways eye on the other, like duelling gunmen in the Wild West.

Jamila ignored them, dug her party rosette out of her handbag, brushed off a few cake crumbs left from a recent coffee evening and pinned it onto a lapel. The council blocks ahead of her grew even less welcoming as the sun disappeared behind dark, silver-rimmed clouds. A police siren passed in a nearby street before fading away. The thin birdsong fell silent and she began to notice a palpable sense of aggression on the estate. She wasn't used to actual violence. Like many politicians, she'd not grown up on mean streets – rather pleasant and tree-lined streets actually, in Edgware. When she talked of violence, of social deprivation, she was speaking with the firm authority of one who had read many books. But she had strong nerves, born of ambition, and she honestly wanted to help people, if only she knew how. Also, she had her canvassing timetable and she wouldn't be deterred from meeting her voters by a few youths. Clutching her briefcase under her arm, she targeted what was now the nearest block, Kinnock, a low-rise of council-military design. Approaching, she pulled out a sheaf of leaflets and pressed the first of the six entryphone buttons. There was no answer.

The two little groups stopped fifty metres away to weigh up their options.

Jamila pressed all five remaining buttons at once.

'They won't answer.' A frizzled grey head emerged from a ground-floor window, nodding like a pigeon. 'They won't answer, dear. Nobody's answering today. Give me the post and I'll pass it on.'

'It's not post,' said Jamila with due weight. 'I'm one of your local councillors and I like to hear the opinions of voters. We're having a meeting this—'

'No, thank you,' said the woman, still nodding.

'You're not voting?' Jamila thrust out a leaflet hopefully as the woman retreated.

'I don't talk to politicians.'

'I'll take one.'

Jamila turned in relief. A man was watching her from his patio next door.

'Do you know many people?'

'Nobody at all,' said the man pleasantly. He was squat with a merry smile, a bulbous nose and bright eyes. 'Crime,' he added, scanning the text. 'It's time they did something about it.'

'We're having a—'

'I'm not racist, but you know what the problem is? I had four Pakistanis move in beneath me and I was nice to them, wasn't I? And then they went and complained to the council about my motorbike. And them, they cook their food and shout their language outside in the street all day and night, don't they? Do I complain? But it's always my fault not theirs, isn't it?'

His nose seemed to have a life of its own, jerking towards her as he spoke, adding its own counterpoint to his words. He wasn't racist. Not him. Not even his nose. His nose would allow equality to all the noses of the earth, as long as they didn't live in his town.

Jamila waved her leaflets. 'We're having a meeting—'

'Next time I'm voting BNP,' he said with a happy chuckle. 'No offence. Everyone should support their own.'

'I'm not sure that's the answer,' said Jamila, sure that it wasn't. His jolly certainty had taken her quite off-guard. It was like finding out Father Christmas rather liked Hitler.

The man gazed about and scratched his nose and said, 'A bit tense round here, isn't it?'

And disappeared back into his flat.

Jamila steeled herself to look behind, but the road was now empty of everything except discarded food packaging. The two little gangs of youngsters appeared to have sloped off. She took a breath and leant against a wall next to an alley.

The white teenagers emerged from the alley. They

lined up in front of her.

'Don't we even get one?' said the tallest, moving towards her leaflets. His voice struck a hollow echo in the bare street.

'They're for a meeting,' she said, hugging them to her and moving rapidly in the opposite direction. She didn't dare look back as she trotted round the corner of the block.

The tall teenager caught up. 'So, we can't come to a meeting?'

Jamila doubled back, but the teenagers followed with ease.

'We're not good enough?' A tattoo poked up from below his collar – a hooded cobra and Gothic letters that began: Never k...

She stopped. She could smell his sweat. Her Mini Cooper was in sight, a hundred metres away, but the gang had surrounded her and each of them reached out and took a leaflet from her bundle.

'Thank you,' the youngster said with exaggerated politeness.

She went to leave, but he held out a large hand to halt her and started to read. She could feel her own hands trembling as his lips moved silently. He wasn't a fast reader.

'Are dey being a problem?' said a voice from the other side. It was the Bengalis. They were the same age, wore the same clothes and had the same mix of swagger and nervousness.

'No, no, not at all,' said Jamila.

'It's OK, sista,' said the lead Bengali, in full Bengali-Rasta, airily tossing a large brick in his hand. He was shorter than the white leader but punchier, and met him with a hard stare.

Jamila wasn't sure she wanted to be his sista. Her legs were shaking now to match her hands. One of the Bengali gang snatched a leaflet from one of the whites and for a second they all hunched and stuck their chins out at each other and did all those things hard men do when they are trying to make a point. As far as Jamila was concerned, the point had already been made.

'What's dis you give dem?'

Jamila rapidly handed each of the Bengalis their own copy.

'Crime?' the lead Bengali said, reading the first line. 'Is you behind all dem police arresting all my mates today?'

'No, no, no,' she said. 'Are they? Who's being arrested? I'll make sure to look into it.'

'Good, because we're getting angry. Very angry.' He gesticulated with the leaflet, jabbing towards the white leader.

'I'm not fucking police,' said the white boy vehemently. 'But they must have a reason, eh?'

'I value your opinions,' Jamila said quickly. 'It's good that we're all talking. Talk is an excellent way to avoid violence, which nobody wants.'

Silence fell. She had the distinct feeling that violence was, in fact, what all of them wanted. She felt oddly like a party pooper.

'Well, that's OK.' She tentatively eyed a gap between the gangs.

'So what's this even about, then?' The tall white kid pushed his face close to hers.

Jamila wondered if he was actually able to read. Trying to control her tremulous body parts, she fell back on what she knew best. She gave a speech. She expounded on her crime manifesto. She detailed her campaign for more community support and more youth clubs. Even as she spoke, she became despondently aware that these were the last things they cared about. In any case, she realised her chances of achieving any of her manifesto aims were almost nil. Even her own party didn't believe in her. Embryonic tears of self-pity began to well up. She sniffed them back and kept her voice strong. She was damned if she was going to let these thugs see her cry.

But she began to realise that political speeches had one significant drawback: they were rarely as exciting to the listener as they were to the speaker. For all her studies of Martin Luther King and Winston Churchill, Jamila's impact on her young listeners was less rousing than she'd hoped. Point by party-political point, their energy waned. Jamila felt crestfallen... and came to an abrupt finish that took them all by surprise. But her oratory had had one useful effect, shifting the youngsters from overtly threating behaviour to sullen grouchiness. This was her chance. She bade them a warm and rapid farewell, returned to her car with as much dignity as she could muster and got in, feeling their eyes on her the whole way.

Starting the engine nervously, she accelerated away, skidded round a corner out of sight of the two gangs, veered over to the kerb, stopped and burst into great sobs. Such great hopes of being of use to her constituents. At least none of them could see her now.

And then something made her raise her head. She'd inadvertently driven back to the crime scene. And ten metres ahead, focusing his camera straight at her, stood a photographer from the Camden Herald.

VI

Wednesday 3.30 pm

'Give me a good headline and I'll move the world.'

Gareth Whelpower, 'Off-Stone – Memories of a Newspaper Man'

40

Intruders

As Jason stood guard behind an expensive leaf-display, more taxis drove up and more cars parked in the street beyond. Screened by Mother-in-Law's Tongue and Variegated Fig, he watched journalists and photographers spread through the clinic's reception rather as the inhabitant of a small country might watch the arrival of newly invading troops. The army grew rapidly. Like mice tracking the smell of their fellows' urine, newspapermen and women could detect a story from the faintest of odours – and as new journalists joined the path, so each extra dribble made it more exciting.

Jason gloomily contemplated his rivals as they set up camp, rushing to the most comfortable chairs and finding charging points for their laptops. Was there nothing he could do to keep his story safe? Every time he thought he'd taken a step forward, he was pulled back.

The lift doors pinged and to Jason's horror Zoe and Snipe stepped out. He leapt from behind his Variegated Fig and bundled them back in, somewhat to their surprise.

'What the fuck?' said Zoe.

'Intruders,' said Jason, stabbing at the lift button.

'I wanted a fag,' said Dudley Snipe.

'They've found us again. This is a mess. Weaverall will be here in a few minutes.'

'Don't panic,' said Zoe. 'We'll get it under control.'

'I'm not panicking. I'll meet you upstairs.'

Snipe looked rather more concerned at losing a cigarette break than gaining three dozen rivals, but Jason couldn't stop to discuss the matter. He jumped out as the doors closed, caught sight of another two commando squads landing from the Mail and Star, and went in search of Christine.

They all convened five minutes later at the empty bedside, where Katrina sat staring at the unconnected leads that still dangled from blank medical monitors. The clinic's doctors had decided to operate on Liam as a matter of urgency. The nurses in the ward were now avoiding eye contact with Katrina. It seemed they had exhausted their day's supply of reassurances.

Someone had to take charge and it fell to Jason. In truth, for all the stress, he finally felt he was in the right place, doing the right thing. This was real journalism. This was what it was like on the front line. He even felt taller. Not much taller, it was true, but it gave him a certain sense of newly acquired authority. First he stood over Katrina, who looked up at him strangely, and he told her Christine had something to tell her. Next, ignoring Christine's look of concern, he gathered Zoe and Dudley Snipe and firmly ushered them out into the corridor. Here Zoe confirmed Weaverall's estimated arrival in fifteen minutes, Snipe adjusted one of his cameras in anticipation of a passing celebrity in rehab and Jason chaired a short meeting concerning the need to slip Damballs into the building unobserved.

'No problem,' said Zoe. 'We've done it a hundred times.' She looked at Snipe. 'You remember the cabinet minister's wife?'

'The one we got into the Post's offices inside a laundry basket?'

'No, that was the mother of the D-list rap artist.'

'Not her. She walked into the sexual-health clinic disguised as a Santa Claus strippergram.'

'It was Christmas,' said Zoe to Jason, by way of detailed explanation.

'I don't see Dazza putting up with a laundry basket or a Santa corset and suspenders,' said Jason. The other two could only agree.

'It would have been nice though,' said Snipe wistfully. 'Add something special to the story.'

Zoe suggested they should see if there was a back entrance in any case.

'The others will have thought of that,' said Jason.

'Depends on what they know. We don't know what they know. Or what they don't know. Or when they first didn't know it.'

'Or how they found us again,' Jason added. 'Maybe Lyle didn't stop the leak. Maybe someone hacked into one of our phones.'

'Phone hacking?' They both looked at him.

'There were those stories last year...'

'No way,' said Zoe quickly. 'That was just the once.'

'Rogue reporter,' said Snipe.

'Just the one. For sure.'

Zoe seemed very definite about it. Still, Jason was worried about the amount of information that seemed to be leaking out. He was worrying about it when Zoe and Snipe went to investigate alternative means of entry, and he was pacing up and down still worried when they returned to report there was indeed a back entrance and it was being watched by half a dozen of the more experienced members of the profession.

'So, we're screwed,' said Jason.

'No,' said Zoe.

Snipe had discovered a hospice linked to the main building. It was used mainly by patients who, despite the clinic's finest efforts, were determined to die. And so far no-one else had spotted it.

'No problem,' said Jason. 'Don't tell anyone. Not even the office. Not even Lyle.' He walked to a window and rang Joey Swinson.

'Problem,' said Joey Swinson, who said he was just ten minutes away, driving Weaverall at speed through King's Cross. Jason could hear cars hooting.

'Problem? What's the problem?' Jason's heart hit a higher gear.

'Dazza can't come through a hospice.'

'What? Why on earth not? Is it too demeaning for him?'

Joey dropped his voice as if he didn't want his prize cargo to overhear. 'He has this thing about death, doesn't he.'

'He has a thing about death,' Jason relayed to the others in the corridor.

'It's a very nice hospice,' said Snipe, scratching his stomach. 'A very classy way to die. Some of the best people are dying there.'

'Doesn't help any,' said Joey, overhearing. 'Anything to do with death spooks him. Graveyards. Obituaries. Sad films. Meat.'

'Meat?'

'He's strictly vegan. I thought this was well known.'

'I'll avoid offering him a steak sandwich. Can't he hear you saying this?'

'No, he's on his iPod, isn't he?'

'Life-affirming music, I hope. Look, it's only a place to walk through. He doesn't have to attend a postmortem.'

'Don't matter.' Joey could be heard accelerating hard. There was a squeal of tyres and a few choice words.

Zoe and Snipe were watching Jason's face carefully.

'Let me get this straight. This is one of England's best-paid footballers, steely cold under pressure, penalties in front of a hundred thousand...'

'That's Damballs.'

'I'll sort something out,' said Jason finally.

Joey sounded uncertain about any sorting out that could be achieved and added that the traffic was worse than he'd expected. Jason put away his phone and felt a surge of panic. Weaverall was almost there. Now he needed to see how Christine was getting on with Katrina. But at that moment Christine burst out of the room.

'She's fucking impossible,' she shouted, waving her hands in all directions.

'What pills have you been taking? They've done something to your head,' shouted Katrina through the doorway.

'It's a fucking story!' Christine yelled back. 'A bloody story to explain something.'

'Actresses without their knickers on?'

It seemed a useful idea to separate mother and daughter. Zoe led Christine to one side, while Jason went into the empty room with Katrina.

'Where's Liam?' she asked. 'I want my son. Why aren't they telling me anything?'

He put his arms round her and could feel her shivering uncontrollably. He tried to comfort her – to reassure her that no news was good news. The medical team were working against the clock, pulling out all the stops, going for broke. Not for the first time he wondered if it was possible to talk about illness without resorting to the newspaper lexicon of medical cliché. He knew he had to speak about Damon Weaverall, but he couldn't. He still had some drops of humanity left in him. At the same time, Weaverall would be arriving very soon.

'He stopped talking to me,' she said, her voice muffled against his chest.

'Who?' He was still thinking about Damballs.

'Liam.'

'Liam spoke?' This was unexpected. He had to tell Lyle. 'When?'

'Twice. Last night, Jason, he came when I was smoking outside the Camden General. Then this morning by the fire extinguisher.'

'Oh.' He mentally cancelled the call.

'He was walking and fine and everything. He said "Mum".'

'I see.'

'He told me he was going to be all right.'

'Yes, I'm sure.'

'But when I went back in the room, he was lying there just the same. And now he's stopped coming to me. He's trying to punish me.

'You do know that wasn't him, don't you?'

'Of course I do. I'm not stupid.'

Jason detached himself from her, slowly, as he glanced at his watch.

'But it was him, too,' she said, blowing her nose on a hospital paper towel. 'Everything about him. He was there. He knew.'

Jason caught sight of Zoe through the door. She seemed to be succeeding in calming Christine, although the purple nails were still spinning patterns in the air.

'You know...' he said, sensing an opportunity and hating himself for it at the same time. He ran his hand along the unused bed. 'I think maybe Liam was indeed trying to tell you something.'

'You do?' She looked at him uncertainly, crumpling the paper towel in her hand.

'I'm starting to believe that.'

'You're just making fun of me.'

'What if he needed your help? No, let me finish. That for him to be cured you needed to do something, say something. Agree to something that you might not normally do.' She was staring blankly at him now. Jason ran his hands through his hair. 'Like making a statement. Not exactly telling the truth but saying something in a way kind of like hiding a truth that you didn't want anyone to know. A sort of white lie.'

'I've always taught Liam that lying is bad.'

'And it is – mostly.' He glanced out of the window. Buses, cyclists and pedestrians passed in the street below and the London Eye could be made out in the distance, twinkling in the spring afternoon. He truly wanted Liam to live and see such sights again. 'And sometimes, you have to lie,' he said, 'to make someone happy, to get a job, to save a life. Don't you? Did you take him to see Father Christmas when he was little?'

She sat slowly on one of the Scandinavian designer chairs.

Jason looked at his watch again. Five minutes to go and this was the point on which his entire career might turn. On such tiny moments, world events swivelled. An assassin's bullet, a torpedoed ship, an office break-in. And yet, and yet, even as he was speaking, Jason's own words were starting to stick in his throat. Was it a journalist who said a writer needed a sliver of ice in his heart? Jason wanted desperately to keep that sliver of ice. But looking at Katrina's dulled eyes and her limp hands, which had flopped into her lap, he found himself caring more. He fought back against the feeling. Like a surgeon, it was his job to stay detached.

'Did you...' He took a chance now. '... always tell Liam the total truth about his father?' She started to speak and he raised his hand. 'You read newspapers. Do you imagine everything they print is the truth? Do you think Madonna always tells the truth to Hello! Magazine?'

He mentioned the amount of money the Post were paying in clinic fees, and then added the seventy-five thousand pounds she stood to receive in person if she gave them what they wanted. He told her the Post was going to tell a story anyway and that he already knew what tomorrow's headlines were going to be. As Katrina paled, he described those headlines. He explained that she could let the Post go ahead without her and not have her say, or with her and have control over the story and get the money she deserved. Money she could use to help her son have a good life.

'All you have to do is tell the papers something about Liam's father that's not true. A name. Just two words. You still tell the truth to Liam, or whatever you want to tell him, when he wakes up. Nothing changes. But you tell something different to the world. Think about it. You haven't told anyone who Liam's real father is and you still won't. You'll be just like Madonna, when she tells everyone how wonderful her next album's going to be. You say one name and Liam continues to get the top medical treatment he needs. And the reality stays untouched. Your secret.'

41

Fear of Death

There were no rival paps or journos around the hospice entrance, as Zoe and Dudley had reported. There was also, Jason noted with relief, no sign of the words Hospice, Terminal Illness or Palliative Care. The establishment was clearly in deep denial. The name inscribed in curlicues above the door was Rose Dell House, and although there was no visible dell in the very flat urban mews, there were plenty of roses – real ones, in flower beds and pots, and painted ones next to the name. The artwork in reception displayed a similar refusal to face reality, featuring cricket matches on sunlit village greens, children's crayon drawings of happy families, photographs of the Queen cutting a tape outside the hospice entrance – and yet more roses. There was nothing that Damon Weaverall could possibly object to, unless he was allergic to flowers.

Dudley had taken up his position by the front steps, shifted his angle three times, squinted through both of his cameras, tried standing on a low wall and finally settled peaceably on a bench with a Benson and Hedges. Zoe had remained upstairs in the clinic with Katrina and Christine. Jason was apprehensive about leaving the staffer alone with his two subjects. Like leaving a piranha in a pond with two prize carp. He wouldn't have put it past her to interview both and upload the stories to Lyle under her own name. But, as she said, someone had to prep them for the big meeting, now that Katrina had agreed and signed (in triplicate). Sometimes, she'd added, guessing his thoughts, you had to learn to trust even journalists.

Meanwhile the mews remained stubbornly empty, not only of rivals but also of cars bearing footballers. Impatient at the best of times, Jason found the tension almost unbearable. He dreaded the thought that a stray paparazzo might wander past and spot them, like an erratic fly in search of rotting fruit. So he told Snipe to hide inside.

'Fuck off,' said Snipe affably and stayed put.

Suddenly a taxi swept into the cul-de-sac and sped towards them. Jason leapt to his feet. Snipe stood ready. The taxi stopped and Lyle Marchmont jumped out with a video cameraman.

'I couldn't miss this. Paddy unlocked my handcuffs for an hour. She's off to have tea with the prime minister. Tom Dalgleish has come in early and has already shouted at most of the subs. Half the newsroom is working like shit just on your story, young Crowthorne. You'd better deliver. No pressure there, then. Where is he?'

Jason informed the news editor that the celebrity father had not yet arrived.

'He's late.' Lyle paid off the taxi and proceeded to rattle off directions to his cameraman, telling him how to get the best Damballs shots for the Post's website. All of which the cameraman politely listened to and clearly planned to ignore. Lyle turned back to Jason. In his moderately expensive coat, suit and pink-striped shirt he looked as much a banker as ever, but today he seemed more energised than Jason had ever seen him. He took a deep breath of rank London air, brushed a smudge of dirt from his moderately expensive collar and looked almost happy.

A thought occurred to Jason. 'How did you know we were here? We made sure not to tell anyone.'

Lyle shrugged noncommittally. 'Traffic's getting worse and worse,' he said, changing the subject. 'Especially round Regent's Park and Euston. Some kind of protest. The police are busy arresting people all over the place, but they say it'll be sorted soon.' He pondered a second. 'Isn't that where this kid comes from?'

Jason agreed that it was. His nerves had grown considerably more jangled on having Lyle appear in person. He suggested huskily that Lyle and the cameraman might like to go inside in case they were seen by rivals.

'Fuck off,' said Lyle.

So Jason went inside himself, checked his watch, nodded to the smart-suited Serbian receptionist and phoned Joey in some concern.

'How far are you?'

'We're parked nearby.'

'What? What do you mean, you're parked nearby?'

'I was telling you. Dazza doesn't do death.'

To Jason's consternation, Lyle had taken his advice and followed him into reception. So he shifted away towards a large photo of an extraordinarily smug benefactor in an Alexander Price suit and lowered his voice.

'There's nothing visible here. It doesn't even say it's a hospice. He need never know.'

There was a long pause on the other end. So near, yet so far. Lyle inspected a vase of pink tea roses. The Serbian receptionist concentrated on a textbook for trainee accountants. Jason came to a realisation.

'It's not him who's afraid, is it? It's you.'

'Can't we just enter the normal way?' said Joey.

'Hospitals are bad enough. All that sickness. I really don't think I can be doing with this hospice place.'

'You don't have to enter at all,' Jason hissed in frustration. 'All we need is Damon.'

'No, no, I have to be with him. He says he can't do this alone.'

Jason wasn't used to pushing celebrities around, but Swinson and Weaverall were pissing him off.

'Does he want this article? We can cancel it now. That's fine. I'm happy to tell Potts whose fault it was.' Lyle was watching him. Jason even scared himself with his own brinkmanship.

'Don't be doing this to me,' said Joey.

'I'm waiting.'

One minute later, an electric blue Lamborghini grumbled round the corner of the little mews and eased to a stop at the door. Snipe flicked his cigarette into a rose bush, grabbed the nearest camera and starting firing shots as the swan-wing doors lifted. The video cameraman almost prostrated himself on the ground to get an angle. Even Lyle held his breath. Damballs emerged looking precisely like he did on a thousand match reports, except taller. He was also surprisingly slim, though the thick muscles in his legs, arms and chest couldn't be disguised.

Joey stayed in the car, looking pale. He sported similar if fractionally less expensive sunglasses, similar if fractionally less blonde hair, a rounder face and a less sober casual shirt. Weaverall stared at the entrance through shades that probably cost more than Jason's laptop and thumped the roof of the car with the flat of his hand.

'Eh up, lad!' (Joey didn't move.) 'It's only where people go t'pop their clogs. We'll get a showing round the morgue if you like, Jozza.'

'Visit your own morgue.'

Jason introduced Lyle to both footballers while keeping an eye on the far end of the cul-de-sac. So far there was no sign of rival paps, but surely it was only a matter of time. He suggested a little nervously that they should be moving inside. Joey remained in his seat.

'What about the double yellow lines, eh?'

Dazza slapped the roof again. 'And what do you care if I get a ticket, fuck-face? This man's in a hurry. Just get out the car.'

Jason reassured them on a nod from Lyle that the Post would cover any parking fines and Joey emerged as if the walking dead might steal his soul at any moment. He was still hesitating when Jason spotted a rusted Fiat passing the far end of the mews.

'Inside,' he said sharply. They gave him a different kind of look and followed immediately. Jason felt relieved when the electric door hissed shut behind them. His nerves were jazzing now.

'The kid, yeah?' asked Joey in hushed tones. 'How is he?'

Weaverall was staring at the children's drawings on the wall.

'We don't know. I think he's still in the operating theatre. He's been unconscious since he was found.'

'Right dreadful.' Weaverall didn't look round. 'I knew a lad, keeled over in the park when I were thirteen. In a wheelchair and drooling when he came out six months later. Still is.'

Joey went paler and fiddled with his iPhone. The receptionist sat up at the sight of the two stars, his textbook forgotten. Snipe and the video cameraman danced round, covering all sides, while Jason made sure that at least a few pictures would show him proudly shaking hands, pointing and generally being an important part of the proceedings.

'Isn't Potts here?' said Weaverall, seeming slightly lost without his adviser.

'Stuck in traffic,' said Lyle. He looked pointedly to Jason. 'Where do we go?'

'It's a short walk.' Jason gesticulated in a manner intended to show authority.

Leading them past rooms with horticultural names such as Multiflora and Roundup, he couldn't help noticing that, once indoors, Damballs slowly dropped the bluff northern act. His accent was less obvious, his whole manner more nervous, and he glanced erratically from side to side. He was not particularly bright, but he wasn't thick either. He was street-wise, or was that media-wise? Joey Swinson walked anxiously behind them, almost as if he wanted to hide, although this was difficult as he was in fact slightly taller than Weaverall. He was also more diffident and thoughtful, although that might have been down to the proximity of the dying.

'Jozza's gran died in front of him when he were eight,' Weaverall was saying.

'No, she didn't.'

'You fucking told me. After your dad were mangled in that bus crash. He's a right bag of phobias,' Damballs confided to Jason. 'Aren't you, Jozza?'

'Yeah, and you've got your black underwear with each day written on the arse, and touching the pitch when you run on, and your mantra beads.'

'That's superstitions. S'not the same. And the pants look cool. I'm launching them as a brand next year, what do you think? Here, look.'

For a moment, Jason thought one of Britain's finest

footballers was about to drop his trousers, but Weaverall merely spoke to his phone and it obediently displayed a short movie of him modelling a new line of Y-fronts with his name across the fly.

'Great phone, eh, Jason? Voice recognition. It shows them in 3D too, if you like. I got the glasses.'

Jason imagined eyeballing the Weaverall lunchbox in three dimensions and politely declined. Dazza looked mildly disappointed.

The corridor to the main building seemed longer than Jason remembered it. Nobody spoke for a time, and the rooms they passed were silent, except for the occasional groan or muffled TV. Jason could hardly bear to think of the meeting that lay ahead. Weaverall started to talk to Lyle about a possible column on celebrity underwear and Jason grew nervous that Dazza might not realise Lyle wasn't in on the scam and let something slip. He dropped back and whispered a warning to Joey.

'It's OK,' said Joey with a thin smile. 'He knows and he can act better than you'd think. Don't look at me like that. He can con any ref in the country. Potts has him sorted to be in a movie next year. Believe it. He's got lines to learn and all.'

A shift from botanical to medical signage marked their transition from hospice to clinic. One more turn led to the lifts. This was the most dangerous part of the journey, as they were now visible to the enemy. All the lifts were in transit, while in the main waiting area beyond, a muddle of newspaper people argued noisily with four security guards over their presence in the clinic. Phrases such as 'the right to know' and 'public interest' floated past the yuccas. Jason pushed the button, told everyone to turn their backs and hoped the journalists were too busy defending press freedom to look in their direction.

A flash went off right next to him.

'Dudley!' he hissed. One lift arrived, empty, and he pushed them all in at speed.

'Sorry.' Snipe hid his cameras behind his back. 'It was a good one, though.'

The lift rose smoothly towards the sixth floor.

Lyle prepared himself for arrival. 'I've spoken to Tony, Dazza. We thought we'd give you a few minutes alone with the mother and then an interview. Tasteful of course. Pictures with the boy if he comes... I mean, when he comes out of surgery. And a full press conference tomorrow, once we've run the exclusive. Sound OK?'

'Whatever Tony Potts says is right by me.'

'In the car, Daz wanted to ask, is Katrina a good mother to her son?' said Joey Swinson, jigging up and down like he wanted to go and kick a ball. 'How is she? Does she care properly for him?'

'Right,' said Dazza. 'Mothers are important.'

'She's done a good job,' said Jason, more in hope than in confidence.

'Great.' Damballs cleaned his designer shades on a designer sleeve.

'And it's been a long time since you last saw her,' prompted Jason, trying not to look at Lyle. The ascent seemed to be taking an age.

Damballs nodded nervously.

'Great,' said Joey. 'Dazza is very keen on his planned charity too.' He practised a series of stepovers. 'We'll call it something catchy. Like Knife Out, or Sharp End.'

'Yeah.' Damballs replaced his sunglasses, straightened a lapel and smoothed down the brilliant white T-shirt underneath. 'A man has to give summat back. But it were Jozza's idea. Weren't it, Jozza? Credit where it's due.'

The lift pinged open. Damballs stepped out, ready for a reception committee and looked disconcerted to find only a parked tea trolley.

'Are they here?'

Jason reassured him that his hitherto unsuspected family was close by and led the small party into the ward. He was aware of a small giggling of excitement from the nurses' desk as they passed. But, more than this, he was conscious of a growing tightness in his chest. Katrina had agreed to the theory, but theory wouldn't be the same as seeing the man for real. And at the same time he couldn't forget those disloyal doubts, the feeling he'd noticed when he'd been persuading her of the benefits of lying. They were all looking at him now. This was his moment. Snipe positioned himself on one side of the door to the room which now bore Liam Glass's name. The video cameraman focused. Lyle gave Jason a nod.

He went to knock, but before he could, the door banged open and Katrina shot out, clutching a packet of cigarettes and saying, 'I'm not fucking waiting any longer, I'm gasping. My kid's being cut up on the operating table right now, and I need—'

And she stopped short. Damon Weaverall stood before her, resplendent in the finest smart-casual clothes and accessories that tap-in goals could buy.

'Katrina,' he said.

Snipe's camera went off in a fireworks display of flashes. Jason noticed Zoe was also taking pictures with a compact camera and the nurses had all produced phones and were snapping away. Weaverall didn't seem to notice this at all; it was presumably his normal life.

Christine came out after Katrina and said, 'Shit!'

At which point the ward door was flung open. Jason leapt round, sure that a rival journalist had found them. But it was Tony Potts who rushed in, preceded by a cloud of expensive aftershave and complaining about congestion on the roads.

He stopped at the little huddle round the door and rubbed his hands.

'We're all here then?'

Jason swallowed and said, 'I believe so.' Words somehow felt inadequate.

Damballs took off his shades and held out his hand to Katrina. 'It's been a long time, lass,' he said.

Jason couldn't help admiring his acting prowess. He was almost convinced himself.

Katrina stared at the hand for a long moment. Snipes was holding his camera at the ready. The video cameraman shifted closer. Zoe seemed not to be breathing. Jason could hear a hacking cough from one of the other rooms.

And then Katrina took Damon Weaverall's hand and shook it.

Warm relief spread through Jason's veins. It was going to be all right. She was smiling. The kind of embarrassed, awkward smile that everyone smiles when they first meet someone really famous. As if their brains have been reset to zero and all thought is blocked.

Thank God for celebrity, thought Jason. The exclusive was on the boil. Liam's treatment could continue. The knife-crime campaign was alive. The money was on its way. After everything Jason had been through on this long day, he felt he deserved this moment of triumph.

Snipe was orbiting the sacred pair, filling his memory

card with images destined for the front page and a thousand websites. Potts was clapping his hands. Weaverall prepared himself to embrace his newly minted baby-mother. Even the nurses were grinning like they were on nitrous oxide.

Then something changed. The handshaking stopped.

He heard Katrina say, 'No.' Softly at first, and then louder. Then she yelled it. 'No!'

Jason's blood ceased circulating. He looked at her face and it was frozen in hate. She was staring at him.

'NO! What have you done? No!'

What had he done? He didn't understand. He felt hot and cold. Sick and confused.

Then he realised she wasn't staring at him at all but over his shoulder. He turned.

Katrina was looking straight at Joey Swinson who had gone very red in the face and seemed to be sweating in the heavy warmth of the clinic's central heating. A door banged in the distance.

'Kat,' was all he said, but it was all he needed to say.

42

Martial Arts Spirit

Sadé had hardly looked up from the accounts when Royland wandered into the office and told her he was taking a very late lunch out. He said it nonchalantly, easily, as if this was not at all unusual. Sadé must have been very occupied with VAT and bank-balance reconciliation and the kinds of lists that gave Royland a headache just to think about, because she just grunted and said, 'You don't need to send a memo.'

The fact was that Royland's lunches were never either late or out. Every morning he prepared a nutritious meal of protein smoothie, vitamin pills and skinned breast of chicken. And at one-fifteen precisely he sat and ate it in a corner of the studio, watching the decreasing numbers of regulars puff through circuits on the resistance machines. But this morning it seemed he'd completely forgotten to make lunch and had only realised well into the afternoon.

Now that he walked through the glass doors, smelled the first spring blossoms on the breeze and felt the warmth of the sun on his skin, the big man discovered a surprising lightness in his step. He was nervous, certainly. He knew that Sadé would most definitely disagree with what he planned to do. But he knew he was Right. (He emphasised the thought with a nod.) Sadé was not always right. Sadé was sometimes most definitely wrong. He was sure of that, even though he could not at that precise moment remember any times that she'd actually been wrong. But that was probably because she was always the judge. And judges didn't convict themselves, did they?

He looked back automatically, half expecting Sadé to run after him, but there was no-one. Royland wished he hadn't thought of a judge convicting someone, not just at this moment. Not when he was about to take a large risk and do something which could look rather bad in the harsh light of a court of law.

He scratched his head as he walked towards Attlee Gardens, where he'd dropped the knife the night before, and as he grew closer the lightness in his step grew heavier. Royland Pinkersleigh was not a man who often thought of himself as heroic. But sometimes there were things that had to be done. His problem was he watched too many DVDs. There was always a scene in *Kung Fu Blood War* or *Warrior of Fear* where the hero drew inspiration from a wise man in a tastefully dilapidated hut, or stared into a crackling wood fire and saw his true path ahead. However, the pictures in the fire, so clear in a movie, seemed rather foggier in real life. He knew Sadé would not be so convinced as to his true path ahead.

He mulled over such thoughts in no particular order but with a certain characteristic circularity that tended to drive Sadé mad, until he found himself at the park gate, on the opposite side to where he'd dropped the knife the night before. The iron gate stood open and young kids were careering around like escaped animals. He'd heard their squawks and shrieks from afar and now saw them swinging off the double bars and fighting for the slide. He hadn't reckoned on there being so many children and adults about. Stupidly he'd kept an image of the little park as he'd last seen it in the early-morning mist.

Royland hesitated. He loved kids, but right now they were a distraction. A Martial Artist of Life made a commitment (see *The Kung Fu of Commerce*). Commitment was the martial arts spirit in action. However, his martial arts spirit was wavering. Indeed, it was preparing to turn tail and slink away. To march over to where he'd dropped the knife, under those scrubby bushes on the far side of the gardens, and to do it in plain view... All he could see was that judge sitting on the bench looming over him in scarlet robes. So he continued to hover nervously by the playground, watching the children play. And then he caught the eye of one of the mothers and realised that being observed watching young children was not a good career move either.

His martial arts spirit donned its armour once more. There might be risk, but there was also a child lying in hospital who deserved justice. He crossed the patched area of thin, muddy grass, working hard on his nonchalance, and approached the tulips. Here he drew breath and made some general stretching movements, in a manner he decided wouldn't appear at all suspicious. Then he pulled out a weight-lifting glove. And Sadé thought he wasn't able to plan ahead! The glove would ensure he left no prints or DNA. It was a stylish number in black and gold, though, unfortunately, like all weights gloves, the fingers had been cut away, so he'd have to be careful. Nevertheless, it was a glove.

The mother who'd been watching him was now engrossed in conversation with the others. Royland stooped over, making like he was working through a rather unusual circuit of exercises, and glanced down at the rotting leaves by the railings. Nothing could be seen. He reached tentatively into the leaves with his one gloved hand. Still nothing. Just the sweet, pungent smell of damp compost. It had gone! He had failed in his mission. He scrabbled around...

... and then there it was. He could feel the rusty knife against his palm through the synthetic rubber. His hand closed around the hilt and he slipped the knife into the pocket of his Lakers jacket. His pulse was thumping like he was running the treadmill at full speed. The birds sang strenuously above his head and the children still screamed at each other in the playground.

He retraced his steps of the night before, down the alleyway and past the row of shops, the Pot Luck Chinese takeaway and a mini supermarket. It was here he'd first spotted the knife at the side of the pavement. Things looked very different this afternoon. The light was fading as rain clouds spread across the sky once more. People were gathering on corners, looking like they wanted to give trouble to someone but weren't sure who. The whites and the Asians eyed each other. Royland stood waiting to drop the knife until everyone was looking the other way. For the first time he began to think it was going to be OK, and as he thought that he started to feel hungry. In fact he started to feel very hungry.

He ought to buy himself something. Sadé would want to see evidence of eating. She was probably already suspicious. He got a vision of a takeaway pasta with beans and a packet of crisps, which he shouldn't ought to, but it would be a reward for his bravery. 'Rewards make champions' (from *Be a Ninja for Success*).

With that vision in his head, and the higher purpose of training his ninja mind, Royland took some steps towards the mini supermarket and then remembered he hadn't actually replaced the knife yet. So he walked back and wiped the knife clean of fingerprints and dropped it next to the street dandelions, precisely where he'd first found it. But forgot to look around again first.

Immediately, he realised his mistake.

A Chinese woman was eyeing him from across the street. She shouted, 'What you do?'

'Nothing,' he said, trying to keep quiet. Wanting desperately to run.

She ran over clutching two bulging Dragon Mart shopping bags. 'You have knife.'

'No,' he said. 'I found a knife, innit.'

'You drop knife. I call police.'

This was fucked up. 'No, I found that knife, there. I'm phoning the police, look.'

And he took out his phone and the little woman nodded and bowed and shouted, 'What you do with knife?'

'I do nothing with knife.' He could hardly manage to press 999 with his fingers, they felt like sausages on the ends of his hands. He was still wearing that stupid weight-lifting glove too.

'Listen, police?' He pointed to the phone so she could see him talking to it. 'I found a knife, innit. You know where the stabbing was? I found a knife that someone's gone and thrown away. Someone who's not here, who's run away.'

Now the stupid woman was pointing her shopping bags at him and people started to gather, including some older white men, looking for someone to hit. Royland was sweating. She shouted, 'He man with knife.'

It was like all he could hear was the word knife repeated. It was his worst nightmare, only worse. He thrust his phone at her and said, '999, police, OK?' And he felt like stabbing her himself. She didn't stop with the 'Knife, knife.' There were even more people coming up now, the white kids in their gangs and the Asian kids in theirs.

'Whassee saying?'

'He's with the feds, isn't he?'

'Dey arrest my mate, Jared.'

'Nah, he killed that poor white kid. Stabbed him in the back.'

He got Sadé's face in his mind now, saying, I told you fucking so, didn't I, man? Didn't I tell you to leave well alone?

He appealed haplessly to the growing crowd. 'I only found this knife, here, didn't I? I was just passing and looking down, and I saw it. Didn't I?'

They surrounded him. They were angry, posturing at him and at each other. Some were furiously accusing Royland of being with the police, making arrests; others insisted he knifed the white boy in self-defence. Insults were being thrown. A siren was heard approaching.

He felt sick. His arms and legs went weak, and he had that feeling he remembered – that feeling when a school teacher nabbed you bunking off, and you wanted to giggle despite yourself. And you wanted to hide in the toilet. And you knew you were in trouble and you wanted to roll back time and pretend it never happened, press reload on the computer game, start a new game, but this is for real, Royland. This is no computer game, man. This is reality. You've been caught.

43

A Moral Stand

Katrina was still staring at Joey. She had developed a distinct twitch and her hands had stalled aimlessly in mid-air.

'What's he doing here?'

Jason's brain was still trying to convert the new data into certainty and wishing that the certainty wasn't so certain. But he only had to look at Joey's height, round face and blonde hair to see what he should have seen many minutes before, had he not spent the whole time staring at Weaverall.

'Oh, shit!' he said.

'You said—'

'I didn't know.' Jason launched himself towards her.

The others clearly had no idea what was going on. Snipe was still taking pictures – his tabloid brain telling him any story was a good story. Christine stood bemused, asking what the fuck was happening. Lyle had become dangerously still. Potts examined Damballs' expression in case this was something he had to spin. Weaverall himself was still braced, arms wide, for the photogenic hug that would now never come. Only Zoe, bright byline that she was, slowly groped towards the horrible reality.

'What's his name?' she asked, but nobody told her at first.

'Whose name?' said Weaverall, looking round.

'Get him out!' shouted Katrina.

The nurses rallied, trying to keep the tone of the

ward under control, but their calming words went unheard.

'Jozza?' said Weaverall, still struggling.

'You said... You said there wouldn't be nothing about his real father. You told me. You promised. That was the deal. You said this fucker wouldn't come anywhere near, not be mentioned. You said Liam would never... I agreed and you...' Katrina's voice rose higher and higher and Jason was her target now.

'Kat? Is that him?' Christine put her arms out to her daughter and Katrina pushed her away.

'You're all in this.'

'We didn't know.' Jason felt numb.

'I never even gave you his name. How did you...? You know, it don't matter. I don't care. Just get him away from here.'

'Liam doesn't have to know,' said Jason, flailing around for an escape. 'He need never know.'

Katrina was trembling dreadfully, pacing to and fro. 'I don't believe this.'

Joey now took this as his cue to hold out his hands in a gesture of contrition. 'I didn't tell them, Kati—' he said reasonably, but wasn't allowed to continue.

'I don't believe you. I don't fucking believe any of you.'

'I just wanted to see my son, Kati. When Dazza mentioned your name—'

'Get out. Get out. Get the fuck out.'

Joey hesitated then left, slamming the double doors.

Katrina turned on Jason. 'Screw your story.'

'This doesn't change anything, Katrina.'

'Really?' Her eyes were on fire.

He began to see what lay ahead and the premonition was not a good one. He hoped desperately he was wrong.

She was more animated that he'd ever seen her.

'Really? You fucking lie in your teeth and it doesn't change anything?'

A doctor came into the ward, a short Indian man with a neat moustache and a handful of medical notes. 'Mrs Glass?'

'It's Ms Glass! Fucking Ms Glass! Can't any of you get it right?'

She stormed out of the door.

'No,' called Jason, dashing after her, suddenly fearful.

'No,' shouted Zoe, sprinting behind.

'No?' repeated Snipe, clutching his cameras as he followed.

'No, no,' said Tony Potts, making up as much ground as he could in his heavy coat.

'Shit, no,' yelled Lyle, dialling the newsroom as he ran.

'No, Kat-baby,' yelled Christine, trying to catch up.

'What the fuck?' said Damballs, looking for where he'd put his shades.

Katrina having taken the lift, everyone made for the stairs at speed, but not speedily enough. Downstairs, the reporters and photographers had bought off the clinic's security staff. Some had their feet up on the expensive Scandinavian armchairs or were tapping away at laptops. Others huddled by the windows or stood in the entrance blowing cigarette smoke out through the doors. They were concentrating so much on exchanging gossip, filling in their expenses forms and checking their iPhones that they didn't initially notice Katrina striding into the middle of them.

She came to a halt, breathing heavily.

Jason managed to catch up with her and grasped an arm. 'This is not a good idea,' he whispered. He could feel her trembling.

She shook him off. A few of the journalists were starting to examine them.

Christine caught up. 'Babe...'

Katrina stared around, her eyes blurred, as if she'd been sleepwalking and had suddenly woken up.

'Come back upstairs.' Jason reached towards her again. He admired her moral stand, but he was growing scared. You could go too far with moral stands.

'Think of Liam,' he said, touching her on the shoulder, but it was totally the wrong thing to say. He meant it one way, but she heard it another. She stiffened and he wanted desperately to take the words back, but they were out and not to be erased or qualified.

Some of the nearer journalists starting asking who she was. Katrina gazed at them without speaking.

'Come back,' he said to her one last time, but there was no coming back.

She looked very vulnerable in her day-glo orange T-shirt and pink denim jacket. Now they all turned. They saw Lyle Marchmont, news editor of the Post, and Damon Weaverall, England legend, and the flashes started going off. Photographers called to Dazza to look in their direction and journalists shouted random questions. Jason glanced at Potts and the PR man drew breath, but Katrina trumped them all.

'It's my boy who's been stabbed,' she said.

Jason slumped into one of the comfortable seats as Katrina stood in the middle of the clinic's plush reception and blew away the exclusive.

Lyle dragged Jason out of his chair and into the gents. 'I can't stand there in front of all those hacks. I'll be a laughing stock.'

'I don't think they're looking at you, Lyle.'

'What game is she playing? What does she want from us?' Lyle paced up and down by the urinals.

'I don't know,' said Jason in deep depression, keeping the door open a crack.

Katrina was hitting her stride.

'I'm Katrina Glass. My kid Liam was attacked last night. He did nothing to hurt anyone, I just gave him my card, getting money for pizza. I told them. I told the police. I told that reporter. I just want my son to live. You want to know about him, I'll tell you. He just wanted to play football. That's all he ever wanted out of life.'

She did a good job. She could have been in PR. Seized control of the agenda. Pressed all the emotional buttons. Started to lose her voice with the stress. Wiped away tears at the right time. Then she turned to Dazza and denied he had any connection to her son. She didn't know why he was there. Despite everything, Jason found himself admiring her courage.

'Fuck her,' said Lyle. 'We're turning off the money hose as of now. And you can forget about the knife-crime campaign, too.'

'Don't do that, Lyle.'

'Where do you get off, telling me what to do, Jason?' Lyle stopped by a closed cubicle. 'As of the present, you don't have a story. Or a contract. Get Zoe in here.'

'I've got a contract for this story, Lyle. With your signature on it.'

'Do you?' Lyle's voice grew smoother than ever. 'That's very interesting. Try reading the small print.' He banged on the locked cubicle door. 'Whoever's in there, you use anything you just heard and I'll sue your balls and then come personally and cut them off and push them right up your anus.' There was no reply.

Jason went to fetch Zoe. By this time Damballs had taken over from Katrina and – after a brief whispered exchange with Potts – was expounding in fluent Humberside about the new charity he was setting up in Liam's name. He was standing on an armchair. He'd found his shades and was twirling them with a perfect mix of shy diffidence and pride. He was a true professional. He took care to address the journalists in every direction and ensure that all the paparazzi surrounding him had a chance to catch his best side.

'I've been lucky in my life,' he said. 'I heard about this poor lad and I thought, sometimes a man has to give summat back.'

44

Settling Accounts

'Sign here... and here... and date it here... and sign here...'

The walking-talking byline sat on the bed, kicking her heels, trying to be upbeat and currently staring at the clipboard and pen that had been handed to her by a woman from the clinic's accounts department. She was not the high-ranking Russian executive who had welcomed them in. This one was Spanish – thinner, older and harder, though her slim-cut suit was no less up-to-date. She dealt not with high-net-worth arrivals but low-net-worth departures.

Jason had retired with Zoe to Liam's empty room to consider their alternatives. He slouched in a soft chair, contemplating his complete lack of them. Suicide was the only one that sprang to mind. Lyle had left with hardly another word. Snipe had stayed downstairs taking photographs while Katrina and Weaverall blurted the story of Liam's stabbing to every rival newspaper, broadcast news and online facility they could find. Damballs had rapidly recast himself as Charityballs. Joey was nowhere to be seen.

'And now there are just three more signatures: here and over the page here...'

'What am I signing?' Zoe flapped uncertainly through a thick wad of papers.

Outside, in the corridor, Jason could hear nurses bustling up and down. Life was simple for them. They made their patients comfortable, administered pills and injections, served food and cleaned the body parts that couldn't otherwise be reached. Not always pleasant but rarely complicated. There were no important moral issues to face.

'... and your credit card number here, with expiry date.'

'My credit card?'

'To take over the treatment. Mr Lyle Marchmont made all the necessary arrangements five minutes ago to cancel his coverage of your bills.'

'He's so slow,' said Jason, meditating on the carpet pattern. It was deep russet and black, with swirls and dark vortices. He wondered if it was a way of disguising unthinkable stains. Or an abstract representation of the nine circles of hell.

The woman seemed puzzled at their reaction, but nothing fazed her for long. 'This is no problem. The outstanding debt as from Liam's arrival has been transferred to your account with us, all itemised on pages eleven to thirteen. Ambulance transfer, room booking, welcome flowers, fruit basket, meals eaten and not eaten, scans, urology, neurology, haematology, operation on your son. Do you have a pen?'

'It's not her son.'

'Not your son?' Signora Clipboard was still holding out the pen, a stylish gold number with the clinic's name embossed in black.

Zoe gave the woman a withering stare. 'Not my son. Not my credit card.'

'The patient's mother is currently downstairs, throwing away her future and ours.'

'So if you kindly have Ms Glass's credit card number...'

Jason informed her that they didn't hold such

information, nor could they forge her signature. The woman looked rather surprised at this restraint and checked her clipboard. He added that he doubted Ms Glass's credit limit would pay for much more than the rustic fruit bowl.

'This is also not a problem,' said the woman from accounts brightly, picking up the internal phone. 'We have appropriate procedures for all eventualities. The operation is just successfully finished anyway and the boy can be easily sent for recuperation to the nearest NHS hospital where there is a bed. Currently we expect this to be Oxford or Nuneaton. You will see from the small printing on page twenty-five that we cannot guarantee him to be returned to the hospital he came from.'

'You can't do that,' said Jason.

'It's no problem. There is no danger.'

'No danger?'

'Absolutely. We are not heartless. And we will ensure he is sent with all his medical notes.' She spoke comfortably on the phone and turned back to them. 'That's all arranged. Thank you for bringing your custom here and we hope you consider our clinic for any future medical needs.'

She gave them each a personalised business card and a dazzling smile and swept out.

A short silence followed.

'He'll be better off under the NHS,' said Jason.

'For sure.'

'And Lyle's giving up on the Weaverall story?'

'No, not at all.'

Jason lifted his eyes from the diabolical carpet in surprise.

'He's running it tomorrow as an exclusive. "Stab Boy

Mum In Dazza Dad Lies". She can't agree to stuff and then back out. That's just not ethical. Lying to the Post, making false allegations against an England star! Then the day after, he'll tell the nation about Joey being the real father. Lyle's got the best of both worlds. He runs his story and he doesn't have to pay. He'll keep this story going for weeks.'

'But what if she sues?'

'He'd be over the moon. Experts will discuss her unsavoury past, her obvious mental instability – why did she sign that second contract with you when she knew it wasn't true? What kind of mother does that? Maybe even campaign to have the boy taken away from her. If he lives. It's her own fault. If you don't lie to the newspapers, you have nothing to fear.'

'But you told her to. So did I.'

'That was when she was on our side.' Zoe kicked off her shoes and examined a small tear in her tights. 'She should have just told us the truth in the first place. Joey Swinson would have been almost as good a story. Not an international, but still Premiership. We'd have been happy with that. These people. If they don't want their private details published, they shouldn't use the media for their own ends. She lost her right to privacy when she first talked to you.'

'I first talked to her.'

'Same difference.'

Jason stood and wandered over to the window. Journalists were arriving and leaving six floors below like ants around a dead animal.

'What about me? Lyle still needs me.' He was sounding plaintive, but there was nothing he could do about it. He felt as if he'd been hit in the stomach with a brick.

'Nah,' said Zoe, complacently slipping her shoes back on and jumping off the bed. 'He doesn't need you, Jason. Nobody needs you.' She found a mirror and tidied her hair. 'Though we will mention you. We'll be saying how you lied to us too,' she said, unpicking a tangle. 'Sorry.'

'But he needs my interviews with Katrina and Christine. My background piece on Liam.'

'He can cope.' Zoe was avoiding his gaze, scrabbling around in her handbag.

The truth dawned on him with an even more sinking feeling – as if he'd eaten something bad. 'You hijacked them. You nicked their stories while I wasn't around.'

'I spoke to the two women and filed some pieces during the day. What do you think I get paid for?'

Jason now had no job, no income, and was about to be named as a fraud on the front page of a national newspaper. He couldn't imagine how he could face his daughter and ex-wife after this. He could see no way out. He'd ruined his career. He'd be a household name tomorrow for all the wrong reasons. A byword for deceit. He contemplated Zoe in despair.

'So what are you still doing here? Why aren't you out shafting some other poor reporter?'

'Oh, I got a text that the newsroom's biking something over.'

At that very moment there was a quiet knock at the door. Jason didn't move. Instead he stared out at the view with unseeing eyes as Zoe answered it. Then he heard her say, 'Ah.' The door closed. 'It's for you.'

He turned round and she tossed a thick padded envelope on the bed, picked up her bag and said goodbye, hoping there were no hard feelings.

Jason didn't reply, since there were indeed hard feelings, so she left with a shrug. He wondered what he'd have done in her position, desperate to hold onto her job, circulation down everywhere, staffers like her getting sacked every month. Once, he'd have had no doubt about doing the same as she had, whatever it took to file the story, but now he wasn't so sure.

He tore open the envelope. Every journalist needs luck, he said to himself. And he looked inside.

45

Comeback Kid

As Jason stepped out of the lift, he could see the clinic's security personnel breaking up the groups of journalists and escorting them to the exit in a determined manner. He caught the glint of a pair of shades in the crowd. Weaverall was still expounding as they left.

Jason chose the other direction, striding down the connecting corridor, his optimism fully revived. The vivid blue Lamborghini was still parked at an angle by the hospice entrance on the double yellow lines, unticketed. Some people are just lucky, he thought, or treated differently. The early-afternoon sunshine had long gone and a cold wind whipped up discarded colourful leaflets about health-insurance schemes and sexually transmitted diseases, but this didn't spoil Jason's new sense of purpose. At the far end of the cul-de-sac he caught a passing black cab and asked for Kentish Town police station. The driver nodded as if he took people there every day. Maybe he did.

Jason flopped back in the seat, clutching the padded envelope. He squashed it superstitiously in his hand, to check the contents hadn't fallen out. Then he felt inside. And just to make sure he wasn't deluded, pulled out the CCTV tape once more and looked it over. On the label someone at the Post had printed the date and a filing reference. He dialled Andy and was greeted by his I'm-not-here-but-I-care message.

'I've got what you want,' he said and rang off.

Just then the taxi turned the corner to pass in front of

the clinic and slowed to a stop. Jason grabbed a handle to keep from tipping forward. Two security guards were holding up the traffic. Flashguns fired as Katrina climbed shakily into the back of an ambulance, looking neither to right nor left. Jason caught a glimpse of Liam lying inside, surrounded by a spider's web of drip-feeds and monitor wires, before the doors slammed shut. Signora Clipboard hadn't wasted any time. She herself stood in attendance, to make sure the mother didn't surreptitiously slip her son back into one of the operating theatres unseen and unbilled.

The ambulance accelerated into the main road, blue lights flashing and with Jason's taxi following in its slipstream.

'Another unlucky sod,' said the taxi driver over his shoulder.

Jason tried another number. 'You're running my CCTV pictures?'

'You're not on the story now, Jason,' said Lyle. 'Your exclusive blew up. Sorry. That's showbiz. Zoe warned you we'll have to name and shame the lies you told us, did she? Do you have any comment to make? Put your side of the story?'

'No.'

'Pity. I sent you back the tape, as you asked.'

'Having downloaded the pictures to use.'

'That's our concern.'

'Not if I hand the tape back to the police.'

'Do what you like. Excuse me, I've got deadlines coming up. Much as I'd love to talk...'

'And if tomorrow morning you open the papers and see pictures of me handing the tape over and headlines that go something like "The Mail Tracks Missing CCTV", or "It's The Sun Wot Found It" or even "Post

Obstructed Police Search"? They're all interested. Very.'

The taxi sped along towards Euston. Jason could still see the ambulance's blue lights flickering in the distance.

'What are you asking?'

Jason slapped the door of the taxi. His career was back.

'Same as before, Lyle. A byline and a six-month contract, emailed to my phone now, in exchange for a picture of me handing over the tape on behalf of the generous, altruistic, popular Post. And drop the bit about the lies. Zoe and Snipe were in on it the whole time. As was Potts. And nobody's going to believe that you weren't.'

'You can't prove any of that.'

'No, but it'll look like you're trying to smear a rival.'

Lyle went quiet. Jason silently counted down from ten. He reached four.

'OK, you win, Jason. Tell me where you're going to be and I'll send people to cover it.'

'Ah, no, Lyle. Not this time. Need-to-know basis. Radio silence. I'd hate there to be some mix-up over whose story it is. You know how easily that can happen.'

'You're already past the deadline. I'm going into late-afternoon conference with Paddy in five minutes. She's due at the Tate for a private viewing with the head of the CBI. I don't know if I can hold the space.'

Jason smiled to himself. 'Both the Mirror and Star said they could cope.'

Somehow Lyle found he could hold the space. 'You've got half an hour. No longer.'

Jason started to speak, but Lyle had already rung off. So be it. Jason felt different. Tougher. He felt ready for Fleet Street. No more being pushed around by Tam, no more feeling second-rate in front of his daughter and ex-wife. He watched the ambulance turn off Euston Road, close to the Gordon Road Estates. The taxi followed.

'What's the traffic like at the moment?' he asked.

'There was some bother earlier,' said the taxi driver, his terseness warming to self-importance as he realised he had information Jason didn't. 'But it's over now. The radio said.' He glanced in his mirror and sped towards a red light as Jason looked at his watch. 'In a hurry to get to the nick?'

'Well, I wouldn't—'

The driver accelerated through the red, narrowly missing a motorbike and a lorry. 'I always help a cop, me.'

'I'm not—'

'My dad was a traffic warden and my cousin got nabbed five times for possession, so the justice system is in my blood, one way or another.' The driver swung his taxi round the one-way system.

The streets here were worryingly empty. Not a single person to be seen. The ambulance's siren could be heard echoing ahead. It was eerie. Then they turned the corner into Mafeking Street and saw what looked at first like a large welcoming party – fifty people spread across the road. The ambulance stopped as it reached them.

'What are they holding?' said the taxi driver, wiping steel-rimmed glasses and peering at the groups of men and women who seemed to be forming and reforming in clumps and waving placards about racist policing and mass arrests. Like an impromptu morris dance in grubby jeans and Muse T-shirts.

Jason took out his camera and grabbed some pictures. Then he texted Lyle about the traffic delay.

Bad traffic? Deal with it, came the reply.

The ambulance stood motionless, lights flashing.

'Not good for the poor bugger inside that,' offered the driver. He pointed a querulous finger towards the Estates. 'Dunno why he doesn't cut through.'

'Ambulances don't do shortcuts,' said Jason with authority. 'A driver told me today.'

Immediately, there was a loud whoop from the ambulance and it turned right at speed.

'There you go,' said the driver and followed.

'I wouldn't—'

The road was narrow, hemmed in by tall blocks, and people were running urgently to and fro, although it was not totally clear what they wanted. There was, however, an unmistakable feeling of menace. The ambulance had stopped again some distance ahead.

'What's this?' said the driver with less confidence.

'I told you not to—'

As Jason spoke, the first brick landed on the roof of the taxi with a bang like a gunshot.

'Shit!' The taxi driver twisted round to see if he could reverse, but now an angry line of locals had spread across the road behind and more were joining them. On all sides, protesters – white and Bengali – shouted at each other and also at the two trapped vehicles, which clearly represented something they had decided not to like.

Jason felt elated and sick at the same time. His first thought was that this would be a great story. His second thought was one of total fear. Hands shaking, he dialled 999. A man answered immediately, listened patiently, and asked him to stay calm.

'Calm?' said Jason, but the line had dropped.

A lump of metal smacked against the back window and he dived to the floor. 'Get the fuck out of here,' he called to the driver. From his kneeling position, he phoned Andy, who answered immediately this time.

'Where's the bloody police?' he shouted.

'Are you in the Estates?'

'Too true. I'm coming to give you the CCTV tape. I've got it here.'

'You know, we're a bit overstretched. We've got a load of kids here we arrested earlier and they all have to be processed.'

'Overstretched? I'm being mobbed. Send some vans. About a dozen should sort it.'

'No problem,' said Andy evenly. 'I believe they're calling in the Territorial Support Group. Should be with you in an hour or so, depending on traffic. Now, tell me about this CCTV. Did you take it in the first place?'

A stone ricocheted off the taxi's bonnet and cracked the windscreen. Jason flattened himself as low as he could on the taxi's floor, aware that he wasn't quite showing the war-correspondent dignity he would have liked.

'An hour? There'll be deaths in an hour.'

'It's out of my hands. What was that about taking the tape?'

'I'm trying to bring it to you.'

'I can't hear you. How did you get it?'

'I can't reveal my sources. Just get here and—'

'Sorry, your voice is breaking up.'

'Look, I play that game too. I know you can hear me. We can't wait—'

'Can't hear a thing.'

The phone went dead.

Another brick bounced off the cab. Jason poked his head up over the edge of the window. He could see stones hitting the ambulance in front. He dropped down and his phone rang.

'Andy?'

'That traffic delay...' Lyle said.

'I've found out.'

'It seems there's a riot going on. Are you inside the Estates?'

'Funny you should say that.'

'Apparently the police did some kind of mass arrest and it didn't go down too well. No problem. "Estates Scum Hold Up Lying-Mum Escape Run". "Benefits Thugs Stop Dying Boy Mercy Dash". They're bound to be on benefits, don't you think? This is almost as big as the Weaverall story. Find out how the boy's doing.'

Jason stuck his head up again. A small van had made the mistake of turning into the road between the taxi and the ambulance and was now trying to reverse out. He could just make it out, half hidden between the white and Bengali gangs. The ambulance itself tried to move forward but stopped again under the barrage of missiles. It gave a plaintive whelp on its siren.

'I'm guessing he's still alive.'

'You're our man on the ground now,' said Lyle, in friendly manner. 'Have they hurt you yet?'

'No.'

'Shame. Get some pictures. We can always make it look worse at this end.' He rang off.

Jason mustered a few shreds of courage and pointed his pocket camera over the partition in front. A group of white men were now attacking the van ahead, rocking it from side to side. One pulled open a door and dragged the driver out onto the road. To Jason's shock, he recognised the newsagent, Naik. The Indian was immediately surrounded. He waved a small card as the attackers kicked him.

'This is dreadful. We've got to do something,' said

Jason, taking more photographs.

'Like what?' said the taxi driver. He was looking considerably more nervous now.

The ambulance gave another wail. The crowd turned and now both whites and Bengalis threw stones and bricks at it, united in their fury against anything official. Jason heard shouts of 'Pigs' and 'Babylon'. Naik saw his chance and tried to run.

A journalist's job was to stay out of the story. Jason knew this. A reporter reported. He didn't get involved. He watched the dead pile up on the battlefield and filed his reports to a shocked world. But for once Jason forgot. He saw a lone man being attacked by a mob and made a moral choice. He stopped taking photos and flung open the taxi's side door.

'Over here!' he yelled, still on his knees. The locals obliged by throwing stones at him instead.

'Stop! This is a private taxi hired by the Post!' he cried.

To his surprise, the rain of stones intensified. Naik tried to duck and weave across the pavement towards him, but the way was cut off.

'Closer,' Jason said to the cab driver.

The ambulance gave another whoop and moved forwards. The taxi accelerated to join it, open door flapping. The little newsagent leapt over a low metal railing with a surprising burst of athleticism.

Jason jumped out onto the pavement to encourage him, still clutching the padded envelope. He felt scared and vulnerable on the cold, damp tarmac.

'I'm a journalist!' he shouted manfully. The missiles redoubled once more. Perhaps they'd misheard. He turned to jump back into the taxi, but it started reversing away, door still open.

'Hey,' he called. But the taxi driver was fully occupied in saving his skin. He found a gap in the mob, swerved a U-turn and accelerated into the distance. Jason shouted after him to no avail. The locals of all ethnic backgrounds focused on this unexpected gift, soft and unprotected.

'Press!' he yelled, but the stones continued to fall. This was clearly not a crowd that respected journalism. He sprinted for the ambulance, desperately holding on to the CCTV tape... and the mob sprinted after him.

Naik reached the ambulance first. The passenger door opened, he jumped in and Jason tumbled in on top of him, gasping for breath. He slammed the door shut moments before the rioters arrived. Fists and sticks clattered angrily against the sides.

'Go, go, go!' yelled Jason.

'Where?' yelled the ambulance driver.

'Anywhere.' He waved his press card urgently through the window.

'I don't think they're your readers, boyo,' said the ambulance driver, a Welshman with a goatee like an insect on his chin. He broke into a broad smile. 'Hey, Jason!'

They slapped hands. 'Wystan! I thought you were private not NHS.'

'I work for anyone, man. Wherever the agency sends me.'

The friendly anaesthetist was the same friendly anaesthetist. Katrina sat as before, strapped into her seat at the back, her face terrifyingly pale. Liam lay in his cocoon of state-of-the-art equipment, stiller and greyer than ever.

Naik shook hands politely all round and then squeezed into the only remaining space at the front between Wystan and Jason. He gave Jason a puzzled look as if he recognised him from somewhere but couldn't be sure. Jason pulled up his jacket collar.

Katrina said, 'What the fuck are you doing here, Jason?'

It was a good question. Jason could think of many answers, but none of the replies that sprang to mind seemed entirely adequate to the situation. The ambulance was rocking worryingly now. Wystan turned off the siren in an attempt to pacify the crowd – without much effect. Jason watched the men and women outside pushing the ambulance, banging the sides, their faces contorted with fury at the lackeys of the state. Somehow he'd become the enemy and he didn't understand why. Couldn't they understand he was on their side? He wasn't on the side of the Man. He was with them, fighting the Man.

A brick splintered half the windscreen into a fine sunburst of lines. He flinched and then suddenly lost his patience with them all. He'd unearthed a national scoop, fought to publicise their issues and save a life. Incensed, he pulled out his camera and photographed their angry faces.

'I've got your pictures!' he yelled through the closed window. 'You're all going to be in the paper tomorrow. Hall of Shame.' He fired off more shots. 'You can't threaten the press! Who stands up for your right to demonstrate? Think about that! Where would you be without us?'

If the protestors had been prompted into becoming more thoughtful by his speech, assuming they could even hear him, it wasn't immediately noticeable. However, whether by luck or good karma, a small space did open up for a moment in front. Wystan was alert to it. He accelerated, but the locals were quicker in running to block it again.

'Run the bastards over,' shouted Jason and reached across Naik to grab the steering wheel. Wystan fought him off and the vehicle veered left and right. People scattered.

'Go for it!' he yelled.

'Get off,' shouted the ambulance driver, punching him in the face.

'Jason!' cried Katrina.

'Don't hang around!' bellowed the anaesthetist from the back, starting to pummel Liam's chest.

Jason looked round, his nose throbbing. A monitor alarm was bleeping frantically. The boy's face had gone horribly blue at the edges.

The anaesthetist reached urgently for the defibrillator pads. 'Stand back!' he called.

A new gap appeared on the pavement. The driver accelerated for it, bumping up the kerb. Liam swung in his trolley. Katrina screamed. She looked very strange, but to Jason everything now looked strange. His heart beat faster than it ever had before.

'Press freedom!' he yelled with increased fervour. 'Knock them down!'

Luckily they didn't need to resort to wholesale manslaughter. Whether it was Jason's demonically transformed face through the windscreen or a renewed sense of urgency in the driver, a passage briefly cleared. The ambulance raced through. Beyond the lines, the demonstrators were fewer and less inclined to direct action. With lights and siren playing full, Wystan skidded round the groups of teenagers and abandoned cars and reached the main road on the other side of the Estates.

Jason gave a victory cry and thumped the roof above him. His heart was drumming a drum'n'bass breakbeat. For once in his life he was on the winning side. He felt dramatically off-balance and wired. Time seemed to have leapt into fifth gear. The anaesthetist stopped pummelling and wiped his face with his sleeve. Ordinary cars and buses sped along as if they were toys on journeys with no meaning. Police cars and vans raced down Hampstead Road towards the Estates, blue lights flashing and sirens singing their unworldly siren song. Liam was breathing energetically and his face was pink once more. They were all alive and nothing else mattered. Life was beautiful. Everything was connected and yet empty.

Jason wondered briefly if this was true Buddhist enlightenment. Years of dreary yoga classes with Josette and all it needed was a homicidal mob and a punch on the nose. He hugged the driver, then hugged the surprised newsagent and squeezed through between the seats to hug the helpful anaesthetist. Katrina was staring mutely ahead. He grabbed her and gave her a kiss on the mouth. Then another. For a long time.

He withdrew in order to breathe. Katrina seemed foggy and detached still. It was like she was in another world. He felt muzzily embarrassed. The others muttered in a restrained manner about the luck of their escape. Jason just wanted to do it all over again.

The ambulance rushed on, siren blaring. Squashed again into the passenger seat with Naik, Jason eagerly watched the cyclists float towards them and considered how their pedalling revealed the ultimate meaning of life.

'Are you happy with the service I've provided?'

'What?'

Wystan leant across and handed Jason and Naik each

a feedback form and a pen. He smoothed a fat hand over his goatee with slight embarrassment. 'Annual appraisal coming up, isn't it? I need good assessment marks from clients.'

'You've been brilliant,' said Jason, enthusiastically ticking all the most positive boxes.

'Really?'

'Everyone was brilliant. Life is brilliant.' He handed the form back in the spirit of the warm friendship he now felt towards his comrades in battle.

The newsagent looked at Jason closely now and suddenly he said, 'You took my tape! You pretended to be a policeman, yes, surely. Now you say you are gentleman of the press.' He reached for the VHS in Jason's hand and Jason pushed him away – gently, given his new spirit of enlightenment.

'My tape,' Naik repeated.

'This is going to the police now.'

'That's what you said before.'

Jason slid the tape back into his jacket pocket. 'I'm not arguing,' he said, calmly.

'I report you to the police. False identity.' Naik took out his mobile and inspected it with some concern. 'As soon as my phone is charged.'

By luck, a new Intensive Care bed had come free at Camden General, so the ambulance was able to return them all to the hospital Liam had left just a few hours earlier. The NHS staff took one look and went quiet. His trolley was rushed inside with considerable urgency. Various members of staff insisted they had everything under control. Katrina followed close behind, still looking dazed.

Naik stepped down and was directed towards the nearest Tube station. He shook his head as if he couldn't fully understand what had happened. 'Ironic, is it not?' he said, standing next to the ambulance in the ambulance bay and preparing to leave.

'Ironic?' said Jason, smiling ecstatically.

'There's not many of us Indians in the party.' He waved the membership card he'd been trying to show the white men who'd attacked his van.

'BNP?' said Jason.

'I tried to tell them I was a member, definitely, yes. But they weren't listening. This must be it. Or they were liberal-multiculturalists. That must be it. Though liberal-multiculturalists... Do you think... do they generally do rioting?'

46

Scoop

Jason was reunited with his car in the hospital's brutalist multi-storey car park. He could have done without the new parking charge, which was enough to bail out the Greek state, but he kept reminding himself of the money he was going to be earning at the Post once he'd delivered the CCTV. Maybe not as much cash as Potts had been promising, but that had always felt like a fantasy anyway. One side of the parking receipt thanked him for helping the finances of the hospital trust. The other offered him a discount latte in the canteen.

He drove out of the car park in high spirits. He even forgot for the moment that he hated the little red Renault with its controls that never did what he expected because they were different from all the other cars he'd ever driven and still confused him even though he'd had the thing now for five angry years.

He was in high enough spirits to let another car cut in front of him, giving it a merry flick on his windscreen wipers when he'd intended to flash the lights. He cheerily parked near Kentish Town police station, laughed as he bought a ticket from the machine to cover at least three times as long as he needed – and then reality hit. Not slowly but suddenly. The reality of what he'd been through in the last hours. His hands started shaking. Then his whole body. He leant his head against the steering wheel, unable to move, unable to do anything except replay the pictures. He saw Liam struggling for his life, turning greyer and limper, getting closer and closer to death, no matter how much he tried to help. He saw Katrina looking at him in horror. He saw the fury in the faces of the mob, heard the crack of the stones. He'd never felt so personally hated, and yet what did they know of him to hate him so?

Slowly, the shaking subsided. He felt as limp as a sheet of newsprint. He reminded himself why he was there. He was a reporter. It was his job to report. He had a career to create. One last chance to help Liam and campaign against violence on the streets. One last chance to get into the Post. The energy began to flow again. So near, yet so far. His purpose returned. You were as good as your last byline.

He phoned Andy and Andy's phone was on voicemail again, so he phoned the police station. They wouldn't confirm or deny that Andy was there, which meant he was.

Inside the glass cubicle around the station desk stood a woman with a sharp face and sallow skin reporting her fears about the man next door. She looked set for the rest of the day.

'Could I jump in front for a moment?' Jason asked most politely when she paused for breath.

'No,' she said. Politeness was clearly not her way. She felt it was her turn and amazingly the desk sergeant agreed with her.

'You do realise,' suggested Jason, 'that if your Albanian money-launderer neighbour really does want to set fire to your flat, as you say, he'll probably be doing it right now and you'd probably be better off at home, standing guard with a fire extinguisher.'

The desk sergeant was a thin, dry woman with the terse tone and heavy-lidded eyes of one who clearly felt she deserved more important tasks. 'Everyone has to wait their turn, sir,' she said. 'And could you kindly speak less loudly.' She also asked what meds was he on.

'I'm not being loud and I'm not on any meds. Just find DC Rockham. He'll thank you for it. I guarantee.'

So the desk sergeant grudgingly disappeared to make a call and Jason asked the other woman to keep her personal opinions to herself. He was about to reply to her unjust response when the desk sergeant returned, sooner than expected, and asked Jason to wait the other side of the glass door. Quietly.

An elderly black man was already sitting in the waiting area, wrapped against the elements in a tweed coat and tartan scarf. Jason flung himself down onto the seat next to him, elicited his name, held his arm and said, 'Marcus, you are about to take part in an important news event.'

Marcus looked faintly concerned at this. Jason leant in closer and gave him detailed instructions.

Andy walked in two minutes later and said, 'You're in a hurry.'

Jason stood with great forbearance. 'I survived the riot, thank you for asking. And I have a deadline.'

'Well, I'm not sure I'm surviving this day, and you don't look good. You should get that nose looked at. How's the boy?'

'Not doing well. You wanted the CCTV tape?'

Andy set his jaw. 'Too bloody true. And I'm prepared to do personal damage to get it.'

'A polite thank you will be sufficient. I've found it for you.'

'I thought so,' said Andy. 'You had it all the fucking time.'

'You can think that,' said Jason, knowing they were both thinking that. He took the VHS out of its padded bag. 'I'm just doing you a favour.'

'Some favour. You took it. Don't even bother to shake your head.'

'Furthermore, I'll make sure you come out of it looking good.'

With this magnanimous introduction, he passed it over. Only he held onto it longer than Andy was expecting. There was a flash and Andy realised the elderly black man in the corner had taken a picture with Jason's pocket camera.

'Widening your staff intake?' he said.

'You don't know how much you have helped me, Andy. We may be heroes, you and me.'

His success gave him a warming glow that spread to generosity. He knew he'd caused Andy trouble, though of course Andy had partly caused the problem by forgetting to get the tape from the newsagent in the first place. But it had all turned out well in the end. Now Jason had two new stories, the CCTV and the riot. He was truly grateful to Andy and truly meant it when he said he'd make sure his friend came out looking a hero.

Andy introduced himself to Jason's new photographer and Marcus smiled politely if a little nervously, graciously accepted Andy's offer to shake hands and apologised if he'd caused any offence.

Andy waved the apology away. 'I've got another photograph for you to take,' he said.

The old man nodded and got himself into position, hunched down, holding the camera out in front of him, ready for action.

Andy clutched the precious security tape in one hand

and beckoned Jason closer with the other.

'Jason James Crowthorne,' he said, putting a friendly hand on his shoulder. 'You're under arrest.'

VII

Wednesday 6 pm

'There's nothing in this world worth solving that can't be set right with a good front-page splash.'

Gareth Whelpower, 'Off-Stone – Memories of a Newspaper Man'

47

Health and Safety

Early in the evening, the ever-darkening clouds opened once more over the Gordon Road Estates. The rain streamed down, drenching the pavements and swirling through the gutters, washing down mud, dead leaves, cigarette butts, blood, plastic bags, empty beer cans, discarded crisp packets, all the merry ornamentation of urban life. The rioters kept rioting of course, at least the younger of them. Andy sat in the CID office, watching the reports come in. Men and women of all colours were now united in fighting the Man, setting fire to waste bins, smashing parking meters and chasing anyone who looked at them the wrong way. A spot of wet never stopped people breaking heads. They fought police. They broke the windows of Va-Va Video and Boutique Bling in the name of anti-capitalism, and they acquired useful designer goods.

But when the rain failed to ease off, their revived community spirit began to pall. Drier, warmer situations grew more attractive. Making war in damp hoodies and cargo pants felt less and less heroic. Trainers squelched and gouts of water ran down necks. More and more residents slunk into pubs and coffee shops or retreated to their flats to console themselves and compare scorecards. The older of them would be reminiscing over the fights they'd seen in their youth. And the younger starting to plan for when their clothes had dried.

We Brits, Andy thought to himself, are not so easily distracted from ruining our neighbourhoods, whatever the colour of our skin.

Jamila had planned to spend just ten minutes with Golam Kamal preparing for the evening's meeting but was still trapped in his office an hour and a half later watching him shuffle papers from one side of his desk to the other. Initially, there had been fearful shouting outside the Evelyn Street Sylheti Centre and the sounds of breakages. Now rain pounded against the windows.

The Estates had been starved of money when the council had any and now that the council had no money, it was cutting more. The Dunkirk Road library was to be closed, the Rorke's Drift Street football project slashed, the staff of the Gallipoli House nursery cut by half. It would take so little to make things better and for a brief moment on the panel at the meeting that evening Jamila might have a chance to show what she was worth and fight for it. But to do that she'd need to go face to face with a senior Tory from the council cabinet and, despite ninety minutes of phone calls, there was still no confirmation that a senior Tory would be present. She thought of asking Jason Crowthorne to mount a flank attack from the press, but he wasn't answering his messages. She tried to persuade herself that the meeting didn't need a governing member after all – she could still make a strong speech. She was warming to this idea when her own party finally replied.

'Well done,' said the deputy council opposition leader on the phone from her bunker. 'You've managed to build great media interest in the meeting tonight.'

'Thank you, Deputy Opposition Leader. And I—'

'Luckily, I've managed to clear a space in my diary. I'll be on the panel.'

'That would be wonderful, but—'

'Of course, Jamila, there won't be room for two Labour councillors on one platform, so we'll be asking you to step back a little, but we all want to congratulate you for creating this opportunity. I'm sure you understand and will be happy to put the stronger woman into bat.' She gave a modest cough. 'Hey, personally, I'd prefer this to be a simple local meeting. I find all those TV cameras and journalists rather wearing. They tend to get in the way of a good honest political debate, but we have to put our own preferences to one side. You understand.'

Meanwhile, Golam was clearly not happy about the meeting – even less happy than he had been with his photocopier. He faced Jamila over his neatly tidied desk, with his glowering manner and his pointed elbows. And for the tenth time he explained to her how this meeting was too soon, too unplanned, too wrong – in short too much not his own idea.

Jamila's phone rang once more. The borough commander had issued a general decree – health and safety. Too much unrest. Threat of arson. Damage to persons. Intimidation, racial and otherwise. Curfew ordered. All meetings cancelled. No gatherings allowed of any kind. She flung down her mobile with a shriek of annoyance, making Golam jump.

'I told you this meeting was risky,' he said irritably. 'Now the council will delay and delay.'

'Then we must stop them.'

'We can't stop them. They have a thousand ways to delay.'

'They're running scared, Golam.'

Golam Kamal addressed himself to a cup of tea and a slice of Sainsbury's lemon-drizzle cake. 'Even the borough commander says it's dangerous.'

'Everything is now health and safety. What's safe? You might scald yourself on your Earl Grey. No, he just doesn't want to face my questions.'

'He says that riots are not healthy or safe. He has a point.'

Jamila waved a hand. 'There is trouble happening out there,' she said.

Golam had noticed.

'We can't just let it continue,' said Jamila. 'I was personally attacked. Yet I survived. There is your health and safety, yes?'

Golam's latest slice of cake paused on the verge of entrance. 'You were attacked yourself?'

'A gang of youths. Vicious and racist. I am still shaking. Look.'

She held out a tremulous hand. And then described the incident with great eloquence. The shock and the fear were totally real. Though the size of the gang, the degree of the danger, her bravery, and the expert oratorical skills with which she brought peace and understanding might have been slightly inflated.

In the process of describing the moment, something strange happened – a new realisation. By the time she had finished, Jamila's speech to the two gangs had become a turning point. Canvassing was one thing – direct engagement with the people on the streets was quite another. Politicians mattered. She could bring peace through talking.

Golam was not convinced, although he took care to show this with no more than a gentle nod of his pointed beard.

'You see,' said Jamila, jumping up regardless, 'only talking will solve this rioting. I talked... I solved. Only people with courage can face the problems and speak honestly. Now do you see how important this meeting is?'

His beard nodded again and he inspected his tea cup, which was empty.

'We mustn't give up,' she said. 'Now, if you don't mind, I must go get my car from where it has doubtless been burnt to a potato crisp.'

48

Fruit of the Poisoned Tree

In the cells at Kentish Town police station, chaos had settled in and Andy was busy trying to deal with it. Following his meeting with the borough commander, three raids had been conducted on the Gordon Road Estates. First, teams had been sent out under senior officers to round up every youngster with a brown face and a suspicious record who might have been involved with the attack. Then a matching set with white faces, for balance. This helped set off the riots, so the Territorial Support Group joined in to arrest as many rioters as they could, sharing them generously around the police cells of the five neighbouring boroughs.

As had been eagerly predicted, the facilities were overwhelmed. But the borough commander could now issue a statement, announcing that fast, serious and concerted action had been taken. That it was fast was more important than whether it would lead anywhere. Fast, serious and concerted action rarely did, in Andy's experience, but it read well in the press. And right now the borough commander needed good press.

There was little room for Jason Crowthorne in the custody suite, which was already crammed with people of all colours and ages being processed into the cells. He found his ribs jammed against the counter of the custody desk alongside Andy, while the custody sergeant shouted for silence. As the noise lessened, Jason made his stand, stood tall, ignored the pain in his side and informed

Andy loudly that he couldn't arrest him. He mentioned freedom of the press, freedom of association, freedom of assembly, freedom of information, freedom of movement and a number of other freedoms that came to mind.

'Watch me,' said Andy Rockham and lightly touched on such matters as obstruction of justice, impersonating a police officer, theft, criminal trespass, perjury and numerous other interferences, misdemeanours and full-blown crimes. The words book and throw at came up a few times. He pointed to Jason's rucksack and told him he was going to appropriate that too, along with the notes, the voice recorder and the laptop inside.

'This is personal,' said Jason in desperation. 'You're pissed off at me and you're taking out your frustrations on me.'

'I never said that,' said Andy. 'But, since you mention it, yes, it is personal.'

The assembled gang members, rioters and innocent teenagers watched this new development with interest. Jason turned from the counter and raised an arm like a lawyer making an appeal or a politician addressing his public.

'I have a deadline. I've got to file my story. I need time to do that.'

The onlookers looked to Andy.

'No way,' said Andy, unimpressed. 'You are a suspect in a criminal enquiry. You may apply for bail in the morning.'

'The morning! I can't wait till the morning. I've got to file now.'

'You should have thought of that before.'

With that response, the response of the official since officials became officials, Andy dropped his shoulders, folded his arms and waited. Andy was generally a good guy, but he hated being taken advantage of.

Having clarified that there was no way out of this, Jason left his public to their own devices and asked to make his one phone call

'Oh, dear,' said Lyle.

Jason could hear excited shouting behind him in the newsroom. 'But the Post will stand by me, won't you? You'll get me a lawyer.'

'A national newspaper can't defend a journalist who has broken the law. Or employ him. You understand that?'

'I haven't broken the law! The man handed me that tape of his own free will. I've got a signature.'

'That's not what the borough commander is saying now. It's on the wires already. We'll be reporting your arrest, of course. And the trial. Can you send us the date when you know it? And a recent photo. The picture desk have been asking.'

'What happened to being innocent until found guilty?'

'We'll print that too.'

'Lyle!'

The sergeant behind the custody-suite desk gestured at him to talk quieter. Jason was disturbing the teenagers, thugs and vigilantes.

He subsided. 'Lyle, I don't know what to do.'

'Just tell the truth. If you're innocent, you have nothing to fear.'

Jason had heard that line before. He'd not believed it then and didn't believe it now.

'Don't worry,' continued Lyle. 'You know, Zoe's come up better than I ever expected. Front-page splash and single byline. You have to feel proud for her.'

Jason felt under no such obligation. 'I was in the middle of the riots. An eye-witness. I saw it all.'

'Sorry. Fruit of the poisoned tree.'

'What?'

'Don't you watch American legal dramas? Can't touch you. Anyway, we've got eye-witness accounts coming out of our ears. Tweets, photos, videos shot on phones. It's the new journalism, Jason. Everyone's a reporter now. Embrace the future. Is there anything else I can do for you? I'm in a bit of a rush, you can imagine. Paddy's out playing squash with Prince Harry.'

The custody sergeant took pity on Jason and with some careful juggling managed to put him in a cell on his own. He sat on the hard grey bed and stared at the hard grey walls. There was a small sink in one corner, a toilet in the other. He could hear shouting and complaining from the other cells. He'd never felt so depressed. White lettering was stencilled onto the ceiling. It told him if he'd committed other crimes, he should confess now. He felt strangely compelled to search his mind. Maybe even invent a few. It would be easier to fess up to some imaginary shoplifting than face the reality. He remembered telling his daughter stories of persecuted journalists in China, Bolivia and Iran and how they both used to admire their stoical strength, locked up for writing the truth. He tried to emulate them now. To sit up straight, a master of his emotions, proud of his calling – to imagine Bea reading about his imprisonment with pride.

He couldn't do it. He flopped back on the bed and stared up at the words overhead. *Confess now!*

Bea wouldn't feel pride – she'd feel ashamed. Ashamed to have him as her father. What had he been thinking of? His career, of course. But that wasn't really the answer, was it? He'd somehow been sucked in. He wanted to confess to caring too much. To being ambitious. If Andy had sent him here to sweat, he was already sweating. He felt sick to his gut and his thoughts skittered from guilt to anger and back again. He thought of Zoe the walking byline, credited for what should have been his story. He hated her and the splash that the Post would be designing on the back bench even now. He imagined how they'd lay out the CCTV pictures. Lyle would be able to exploit them to the full, stripping them across two pages, moment by moment, following the narrative Jason had outlined only that morning: from cashpoint to pool of blood... from Liam in his Chelsea kit to Liam's fight for life. Then he wondered how the boy was doing, whether he was even still alive, and the guilt returned. Everything he'd tried to do for the boy had made him worse. Maybe if he'd never got involved, Liam would be recovering even now. His guilt grew deeper.

For a moment, he'd forget where he was and his pulse would beat fast again as he found the compelling opening to the story, the pungent turn of phrase, and then he'd remember, like a punch to his chest, that it was no longer his to write. He lay on the hard grey bed and waited for the end.

49

Interrogation

After an hour going on a week, the door to the waiting room banged open and Royland jumped up. A uniformed copper told him brusquely to follow and led him down a series of winding grey-green corridors that went on and on, like hell designed by a civil servant. And with every step Royland's thoughts grew darker.

He'd never been in a police station before. He'd never had reason to. He'd always had a friendly, helpful attitude that helped him sidestep the temptation to do anything wrong. Of course, being black and big made him visible. Police would stop him and check him over and ask him to turn out his pockets. But being the kind of person he was, he simply did what he was told. Now he was here and it scared him.

Earlier, following an inner struggle of five minutes, he'd phoned Sadé.

'I'm caught up with something,' he said.

'What that mean, you caught up with something? You went out for your lunch and now it's almost six and you don't answer your phone. I didn't know what to think, did I? There's that Packer woman who's come for a training session with you, and you not even here. Get over here, wherever you are, whatever whore you're with.'

He told her where he was and why. He waited for the explosion and it didn't arrive, which made him more scared. If Sadé didn't shout, it was serious. Instead, Sadé said she'd come right over and he said there was no point. He needed her to train the Packer woman. It was their only booking of the afternoon.

'I've never done a training,' said Sadé anxiously. 'I'm not a trainer. I never learnt.'

'She don't know that,' said Royland. 'Show her some of the exercises I showed you last week. That'll keep her busy. Get her sweaty. They like to think of the calories coming off.'

'What if she spots I've done something wrong?'

'Tell her it's the new way. Give it a name. A name's always good, innit? Sadé's Muscle Rip – something like that.'

Royland had done his best to sound on top of it all, but when she rang off he'd felt even more down than before. He really wished she could rush over and tell him everything was going to be all right.

He arrived finally at an interview room and was joined by a detective constable, who introduced himself as Andy Rockham. He looked serious – indeed, grim. DC Rockham indicated a chair at a table. Royland's legs had become as weak as some new kid in the gym, he could hardly sit down under his own control. The room was bare and ugly, with six notices on the wall about how you could get legal help if you needed it. He thought, do I need it? He felt like he needed it, but then if he started calling for a lawyer, would that make him look even more guilty? And who would pay? He couldn't afford no lawyer.

The detective sat down facing him. There was a woman too, in uniform. She informed him her name was Dana Bookman. She looked just as serious. They said something or other about rights and Royland could scarcely listen for fear. He did notice them turn on a tape recorder and he asked if he was being charged with something and the detective said, should he be?

Royland said all he'd done was find a knife. He was walking this afternoon and he saw this knife, that was it. Nothing more. He was innocent.

'Innocent of what?' asked Andy Rockham.

'Innocent of everything, innit. I didn't do anything except help the police. That's sure.'

'Let's take it in order,' said the detective heavily.

Royland squinted to help himself think clearly, then closed his eyes to help think some more, then he wondered if that also looked guilty, so he opened them. But when he opened them he saw he was in a police station and closed them again in fright. And all the time those two was staring at him, wondering why he wasn't saying nothing. He could tell them the truth, and they'd want to know why he moved the knife. He could stick to his story, but then what if they found out he was lying? He wasn't good at lying.

'Mr Pinkersleigh?' said the woman.

'Just a minute,' said Royland.

'Just tell us what happened.'

'That's what I want to do. It's difficult.' Royland gritted his teeth and tried to think what Sadé would tell him to do. 'I just want to get my facts straight.'

'What's difficult about that, Royland?'

So... he drew himself upright and he told his story in some kind of logical order, or at least as much of it as he dared. And the order turned out to be less logical than it had seemed in his brain before he told it.

'I phoned 999,' he said, 'because I thought... well, evidence... And was it? I was hungry, maybe... Lunchtime. Just walking. There it was... And I realised the knife... Saw it, didn't I? Because I saw the news, innit? Evidence is important, yes? So, it could be the one, do you think? I wasn't sure. Yeah.'

Royland slapped his thigh, having put it as clearly as he felt possible, his heart beating faster than he ever knew it. Andy Rockham puffed his cheeks a little and Dana confided that she wasn't entirely sure she understood. Perhaps if he started again – at the beginning.

Royland didn't precisely start at the beginning. For some reason beyond his control, he found himself starting near the end. Then he jumped to earlier, missed out the middle and if he didn't quite end at the start, then he only missed by a few inches.

Andy suggested they abandon today's events, for the time being. They asked him about the night before. Where was he? And his heart beat even faster still.

'Last night?'

'If you don't mind.'

'I found the knife this afternoon.'

'It could be useful.'

Royland nodded in serious agreement and they waited.

'In your own time.'

'I was working at the gym till late, then I walked home with my partner Sadé Brougham and we didn't see nothing, well, I saw the boy what got stabbed, before, when I was cleaning the outside of the gym, innit, he was just walking past and I thought didn't he once come to the gym, long time ago...'

'What time was it you saw him?'

'Eight, just about, a bit after, but like I said, no stabbing, nothing, nobody, not at any time—'

'Mr Pinkersleigh...' Andy cut him off with a certain impatience. Dana got him to spell Sadé's name, both parts, and asked if she'd witnessed Liam walking past.

'No, she was in the office.'

'And did you see anyone else at the time?'

'No. No-one. Not that I noticed. But I was busy swabbing down, wasn't I?'

'And after, when you were walking home, you said you didn't see anything then?'

Royland felt the shades of the jail-house closing in. He said no, they walked by Attlee Gardens, and she asked why they were there, when it didn't look like it was on their route home. He got himself tangled because he couldn't think of a reason that made sense, and the two of them listened and the tape whirred and he felt worse and worse. In the end he said lamely that they just wanted a walk. Even his voice sounded thin and weedy, like it didn't believe him any more than they did.

They said nothing and stared at him. Here was his chance to open up his heart, to avoid making things worse. It was so heavy holding onto lies, so difficult to remember which fitted with what. He could hear doors banging outside the room and voices raised for a second. Andy Rockham slowly tapped his notepad with a blue biro.

Finally Royland gave a deep sigh and resolved to tell the truth. But at that moment the detective switched off the recorder and said, 'That's it.'

'That's it?'

'Yes. Isn't it? Is there any more?'

'No,' said Royland hopefully. 'No, that's all, innit. That's everything, like I told you.'

'You're sure?' said the policewoman, Dana.

'Yeah, I'm sure,' said Royland.

Then they asked him to wait a moment and went. He waited much longer than a moment, then they came back with a form to sign. He signed, his hand so wobbly that his signature looked like a piece of knotted spaghetti, and he hoped they wouldn't compare it with any other signature he'd ever made. The moment he'd signed, he saw the trap. They'd got him to lie. Now they were going to arrest him.

They said he could go.

He almost cocked it up by looking surprised and then he tried to look like this was what he'd expected all along. Innocent people always got let free. He talked too much at that point and Andy Rockham was giving him strange looks so he had the good sense for once to shut up.

In the outer reception area he phoned Sadé and she said, 'Is everything OK?' and he said, 'Everything's fine.' She said she'd pick him up, the gym was empty, everyone was either on the streets or hiding at home or somewhere. Not exercising, any case. He didn't know at first what she was talking about. He'd been in the police station during the main part of the rioting. He didn't believe what had been going on while he was sitting waiting.

She arrived in ten minutes – she must have driven fast. Royland was all ready for a bollocking, but she kissed him and said let's get back to work.

He knew there'd be trouble later, but for the moment he resolved to take peace where he could.

50

A Martyr for Press Freedom

From time to time, Jason could hear heavy doors being slammed. Young gang members were audible, accusing the police of a variety of biases, some truer than others. For fifteen minutes a drunk screamed abuse at the government, then either lost interest or fell asleep. After a while, Jason's deep depression turned into profound resignation; there was no further to fall. It was such a cliché of a police cell. He lay on the bed in his crumpled suit without tie and shoelaces and, when not forgetting himself and trying to rewrite the Glass story, he remembered himself and waited to be charged.

As the minutes inched past, he took to contemplating his career. Like a sick patient's chart in a cartoon, the line zigzagged up and (too often) down. He didn't understand why or where he'd gone wrong. He could see through the facades of others – and yet he had no insight into himself. Maybe he'd just been lied to all these years. All those people who had told him that talent would win in the end. They'd misled him or they'd themselves been misled. It was like his marriage. All the right ingredients had been there. Everyone agreed. Yet somehow it hadn't worked and he'd never understood why.

Maybe he needed therapy. But no, that wasn't it. He wasn't about to blame his failures on his upbringing in Melun Road, Basingstoke, his mother's neurotic obsession with yoga, or his father's ten-year affair with a hairdresser from Birmingham, embarrassingly tabloid as it was (a hairdresser!). Maybe it was, after all, just the way the world was. All fucking unfair from beginning to end. You stood up and tried your best and other people got the rewards – neurotic but pushy staffers like Zoe Sharpleside. And the remainder got knocked down. For every great prophet whose chariot rose into the heavens there were a thousand little people who got crushed under the wheels. That was it. He'd thought he was one of the prophets, but it turned out he was simply a squashed pedestrian. His lot was to suffer and never be known. His talents snuffed out like millions of common people who came from places like Melun Road, Basingstoke (and would probably never have the courage to show their face in Melun Road, Basingstoke again). He wasn't the rising star his daughter could boast about to her friends. He was on his way to being just another convict, receiving awkward, embarrassed, irregular visits from Bea, his parents and his few remaining friends. He was an ordinary person, and it hurt.

After a considerable length of time (afterwards Jason was unable to say exactly how long), a constable led him up to an interview room. Andy came in alone and sat down across the table. He placed the CCTV cassette in front of him, now in a transparent evidence bag. Next to it he put the plastic bag of weed Jason had found in Liam's bedroom. And he said nothing. Jason's heart had sunk many times already that day, to the point that he'd thought it could sink no further. He was wrong.

'How's Cheryl?' he said, if only to break the awful silence. 'And Duane?'

Andy stared at him. 'They're fine.'

'That's not my weed.'

'I thought it seemed a bit low-grade for you. Whose is it?'

'It's... no matter.' Jason ran his fingers through his hair. He felt grubby. 'OK, tell me, what am I facing?'

'Obstructing justice, impersonating a police officer—'

Jason held up his hand. 'I don't need the list. As a friend. How long?'

Andy laughed quietly to himself and Jason didn't like that laugh. However, he drew himself straight with the paltry spirit he had left and waited.

'I did think you were a friend. That's what I really believed, Jason. From back when you started and I was just out of police college and we used to have a laugh and a few drinks. I dug you out of a few holes. You made me look good in your reports. Sometimes. We went down the Lane once or twice, when one of us could snaffle a pair of freebie tickets. Of course, journalists don't have friends, do they? They just have sources.'

That hurt. 'Is it so different for detective constables?' Jason said, with a certain edge in his voice.

Andy thought. 'Three years,' he said, 'maybe four, depending on who's on the bench on the day.'

'Open prison? Somewhere nice?'

'You'll be fucking lucky. This is national news. The kid could still die. He's being operated on again.' Andy dropped his head and hunched his shoulders as if he was the one about to be charged. 'Just tell me the truth,' he said, talking to the tabletop. 'Do me that honour. Show me that respect.'

'The truth?' said Jason.

'Not a story. Not what you'd like to think happened. Just what did happen.'

'You've spoken to Naik?'

'I spoke to Naik.'

'He told you what he saw, what he said?'

'Jason!' Andy stared at him. 'I don't give a shit what

he said, I want to know what you say.'

'OK, OK.' Jason said nothing for a long moment. 'Should I have a lawyer?'

'I don't know. Do you want a lawyer?'

He sat back in his wooden chair and thought about this, and he simply didn't have the energy. He just wanted it all to be over, to be led down to the cells again.

'This is the truth,' he said. Was that so unusual? He'd believed he was dedicated to telling the truth. Perhaps the truth he normally told was a different kind of truth – a truth that had been carefully shaped to fit the specific newspaper he'd been working for. It should have been a shocking thought, shouldn't it?

He told Andy Rockham precisely, or as precisely as he remembered it, how he'd walked into the newsagent's and spoken to Mr Naik and how Naik had looked up from the trestle table and seen him in his suit. And the newsagent, unasked, had handed him the CCTV tape with the security pictures on it, and Jason had not pretended to be a policeman at any point or said anything that might have made Naik think he was a policeman.

'You didn't flash your press pass quickly, with your thumb over the bit that reads press, and say, "Police"?'

'Not once.'

'You've done that before, though.'

Jason hesitated. But he was committed to the truth this evening. 'Yes. I've done it before.'

'And you knew I was supposed to collect this VHS?'

Jason took a deep breath. He had to admit it. Yes. 'But you hadn't.'

He knew it sounded limp, but then, he thought to himself, maybe the truth often does. How many times had he dug out the true story behind a story, taken one look at it, in its full lameness, and then dug it back in again? Like a good magic trick, the glittering illusion was usually more interesting than the dull reality.

'You could have phoned me. You could have brought it to the station.'

'Yes,' said Jason, and then he got a whiff of his old fight back and banged the table. 'But that wasn't my fucking job, Andy, was it? I'd been given the tape in good faith. I'm a bloody journalist, it's my job to get stories into papers. I'm not hired to collect evidence for you lot.'

'And you're not hired to keep it from us either.'

'No,' said Jason and subsided again.

Andy was enjoying this. He was clenching and unclenching his fists like he wanted to punch Jason more than once. Jason would have preferred that. He was now talking about how Jason had warned off the culprits and made it impossible to catch the real villains.

Jason interrupted. 'Have you seen those pictures?'

'Yes.'

'You do know you can't see a fucking thing. The muggers' faces are covered by their hoodies. The attack is half off the edge of the frame. They make a great newspaper story, but they're not evidence. What about the other cameras you've got?'

Andy didn't answer.

'Oh, shit!' Jason almost laughed. 'They're all pointing the wrong way, aren't they? Jamila was right, they're all filming the parking spaces. All those fucking cameras and all they do is collect parking fines.'

'That's nothing to do with it,' said Andy.

'And all those kids here who've been arrested? Do any of them look remotely like anyone Katrina saw?'

Andy said nothing.

'I thought not. Usual police fuck-up. Your lot couldn't nick a bank robber at a bank robbers' convention. What is it with you? Have you got an allergy against arresting the right guys?'

'I've arrested you.'

'Oh yes. Point proven. Well done, Inspector Clouseau. You've arrested someone whose job it is to report your cock-ups.' Jason grew increasingly sarcastic. It was perhaps not his best move, but he couldn't stop himself. 'So charge me. I can see the headlines. "CCTV Points the Wrong Way While Youngster Is Stabbed". "Muggers Escape but Car Drivers Don't". Great coverage.' Once voiced, he started to warm to the idea.

'Maybe,' said Andy. 'But not for you, it won't be. I reckon you've pissed off the Herald once too often.'

Jason took a long breath. 'True,' he said. 'I fucked that up.'

Andy looked at his watch. 'And it's more or less past the Post's deadline,' he said. 'So I reckon that job's screwed as well.'

Jason drew himself up in his seat and stuck out his chin. If he was going to be a martyr for press freedom, then he was going to be taken down with dignity. In fact, martyrdom was starting to appeal. It gave meaning to his arrest. He wasn't alone, he was part of the everlasting fight between journalism and the powers of darkness. He was being sacrificed because the police wanted a scapegoat. He began to realise that jail might be the best thing that could happen to him. He'd see prison from the inside, be able to write about the criminal-justice system with personal insight. He'd spend an appropriate time inside (not too short but not too painful either). He'd sell a series of anonymous and eye-opening features written from jail. He'd use a pen name at first and reveal his true identity at the perfect moment. Then he'd emerge with his stature enhanced. There'd be a blog, a book deal, a prestigious column in a daily broadsheet, maybe even in one of the Sundays, a TV dramatisation to be discussed (but he wouldn't sell out for money or try to make jail look any less grim than it was).

'OK,' he said, holding his hands out to be cuffed. 'Do your worst.'

'My worst?'

Andy clenched his jaw, then stood up. He went out of the room, leaving the door open, and came back carrying Jason's bag with his tie and shoelaces and said, 'Take them.'

Jason didn't totally understand.

'Get out,' said Andy.

'What do you mean?'

'I mean go. Leave.'

Jason processed this information. 'You can't not charge me after all this, Andy.'

'Yes, I fucking can. Sod off.'

'You were never going to charge me!' Jason said. 'You just wanted to get your own back by putting the frighteners on and screwing up my deal with the Post. Well, you succeeded in doing that. This isn't about justice. This is about revenge.'

Andy gave a kind of ticking sound with his tongue like he was a bomb about to explode, then said, 'We can charge you and prosecute. It's the newsagent against you. You don't come out of it looking good, but we look like prats too and I end up looking the biggest prat of all.'

'You have to charge me. You have to. I've got to go to jail for what I've done.'

'You really want to?' said Andy. 'You really want to

do that?'

Jason thought about it for a moment. He could still have his chance to be a press hero, to find out what prison was really like.

Then he saw the red flush across Andy Rockham's forehead. And he thought about three or four years of incarceration, long days and nights surrounded by men of violent disposition and unimaginable desires, somewhere miles away from Bea.

'Sod off,' said Andy. 'Before I change my mind.'

51

A Good Father

Ouaiiouauoauoauoauoghrggrrraouaoughhghhrtttaouaou
aou… The Mini's engine sounded rough. Jamila changed
gear. Iaiuaouauoauoauoauoghrggrrraouaou… Something
had happened to her car while she was with Golam.

'Ouaouangngngngggrrraoubxxbxxbxxaouayxxxxx…'
came from the radio as she drove east, past broken shop
windows and smashed cars. 'Brxxbrxxbrxx. Respec' for
the hood. Brnggnbrxxbrxx. Respec' for the brothas and
sistas that fight the cause. Dis am Gian'killa Mo
broadcastin' from Free Sout' Camden.
Ouabrxxngbrngbrgbrnngnggngghr.' For months Jamila
had listened to Gian'killa Mo, broadcasting illegally from
the Estates. It had made her feel in-with-the-hood, until
one day she visited a small flat above Sainsbury's Local,
where Gian'killa Mo turned out to be a fifty-three-year-
old white primary-school teacher with a degree in Greek
drama and a room full of old valve radios.

Ouaobuauobauoauoabuoghrggrrraouaoughhghhrtttao
uaouaou… Car and radio wailed in unison. Her meeting
was slipping away from her, and with it her chance to
help the people of the Estates and grab a small amount of
council money to make their lives better, when everyone
else seemed to want to make their lives worse. She
dialled Jason Crowthorne for the fifteenth time. She
needed support from the press. But for the fifteenth time
her call went to voicemail. Right when she needed his
help most, he'd disappeared. So she called the borough
commander.

'I can't allow it. And you wouldn't thank me for it, lass.' The chief superintendent's Leeds accent sounded more pronounced. This was always a bad sign. 'I'm paid to make the tough decisions. Is your car all right or are you strangling a cat in there?'

Jamila suggested that tough decisions didn't necessarily mean right decisions, but he wouldn't be moved. It wasn't safe to go out on the streets, to meetings, even if they might bring about more safety, and even though those very streets were now very wet and very empty and Jamila was driving through them as she spoke.

'Talking is safer than not talking,' she said.

'Not according to the council,' he said evenly. 'Ask the cabinet member for community safety. Even your very own local Labour leaders have accepted it. You really should get that big end fixed.'

She dialled the council cabinet member for community safety.

'Jamila!' he said. 'It's great you phoned. We've got to make this meeting happen.' Nigel Ponting was a deceptively frail man in his late thirties, a one-nation Tory with a lower-middle-class twang that went down well in meetings, while fronting policies no-one could object to. In fact that was the problem. Because the policies were like marshmallow: sweet, fluffy and entirely devoid of nutritional value.

'So you agree!' she said with some surprise, braking suddenly and narrowly missing the only pedestrians still on the streets. A pair of Bengali youths in hoodies, one tall, one short, they scowled at her and continued nonchalantly across the road, each hooked to one ear-bud of a shared iPod.

'Oh yes, I do. But unfortunately the police won't let

us arrange a thing. I'm out of ideas. I'm so sorry.' Ponting had a clever way of sucking the life out of any situation.

Jamila accelerated towards King's Cross. 'So you'll come then? If I get the meeting back on for tonight. I can tell the borough commander you want it to happen?'

'Tonight? I wish I could, but it's not possible. Totally not possible.'

Jamila felt a rising anger. 'Why on earth not, Nigel? This is your remit. For God's sake. You can put on the pressure.' She reversed into a small parking place.

'In the normal way of things I'd love to be there. You'd have to chain me to my desk to stop me being there. As it happens, I'm out of town right now on council business. But...' He flannelled on.

Jamila walked in the town-hall entrance and headed up the wide marble stairs. 'That's a shame. But you appreciate the importance?'

'Totally, totally. As we said in our own recent press release...'

'Good,' she said, turning left at the top and entering his office.

Nigel Ponting looked up in surprise from his desk. Unchained. There were two other councillors with him, a man and a woman.

'Did we have a meeting?' he said, rising.

'Yes. Tonight.'

'I just said—'

'Is that what you're going to say to the residents of the Gordon Road Estates? "As we said in our recent press release..."'

'We care deeply about community safety, and after the election—'

'Good,' she said. 'So you'll be coming tonight. Now

that you're back in town.'

'The police—'

Jamila was angry or she probably wouldn't have said what she said next. Not to a politician as clever as Ponting. 'Is this because it's only Bengalis, Nigel? Just Pakis that are getting beaten up and arrested? I'm talking to Jason Crowthorne, who's writing it up for the Herald. He'd be happy to hear a quote from you on this.'

She looked around the office, daring them to answer back. A secretary had come in behind her, to see if she could help throw Jamila out. The two other council members were watching carefully. How ambiguous could they possibly be? They were members of Ponting's party and on his side as long as it was safe to be.

Nigel sat down again and tapped a bony finger on his desk. 'Jason Crowthorne's been arrested.'

Jamila wasn't often lost for words. 'I don't believe you,' she said finally. 'What for? I'd have heard.'

'Why are you doing this anyway, Jamila? I heard you were being pushed off the panel.'

'Don't believe rumours, Nigel.'

'Oh, fine. Good. I was just worried for you. Look, I'm delighted that you've found a cause after four years, even if your party doesn't appreciate you...'

Jamila thanked him.

'... but you overvalue the efficacy of talk. It does less good than you think and a lot more harm. Those whom the gods would destroy, they first get them to attend meetings. I've seen sensible people talked into doing stupid things just because there's a room full of passionate idiots. Your meeting will be a disaster for you.'

'I still—'

'No matter. It won't happen.'

He turned back to the briefing document he'd been discussing when she came in. Jamila stood for a moment, speechless with frustration and then realised there was no more she could do. She left the office, slamming the door behind her.

She'd been humiliated and there was nothing she could do about it. She stopped in the hallway, flushing hot and cold, and leant against an elegant marble wall to regain her breath. After a moment, she took out her phone and tried Jason one more time, without luck. Nobody on the Herald knew where he was either. Maybe Ponting was right about him having been arrested. She'd put nothing past the police in their attempt to suppress free speech. And then, just as she thought it couldn't get any worse, she heard the confident click of high heels and saw the deputy opposition leader striding purposefully along the landing towards her.

'Hey, Jamila,' hailed the deputy opposition leader with the bonhomie of one who knew she was always on the side of the righteous. 'I need to reschedule that little local meeting you announced. Email my assistant about dates for next week, once everything's cooled down. I'll try to see that you're called to speak from the floor, but I can't promise. But, hey, the party is very grateful for all you've done. Do remember that.'

And the deputy opposition leader strode off, her heels tapping with self-satisfaction all the way down the marble stairs.

A parking ticket had been slipped under the Renault's wipers outside the police station, but at least the car hadn't been clamped. Jason stuffed the ticket into the glove compartment, where it joined a number of others. Maybe prosecution for accumulated parking offences would be martyrdom enough.

The weather had turned a little warmer as dusk approached. Pink and white blossoms nodded in the shadows for those who felt like looking. At the traffic lights he observed people crossing as if nothing mattered aside from their own preoccupations. He felt like a condemned man, watching the world through the barred windows of a prison van. He'd had a future once, he mused to himself. His phone rang.

'Dad? Where are you?'

'Bea?'

'When are you collecting me?'

He checked his mobile: there were three messages from her and sixteen from Jamila. 'Shit. What time is it? Was I collecting you from school? It's a bit late for school. It's a bit late for after-school.'

'It's not after-school. You knew that.'

'Of course I knew. After-after-school – musical maths and yoga. I'll be right there.'

'No, that's Tuesdays. And anyway, after after-after-school I went home with Brent, didn't I? I'm with her now.'

Brent? He didn't remember a Brent ever being mentioned.

He duly collected Bea from the address she gave him. His daughter seemed entirely cured of whatever severe illness she'd had earlier. On the way back to Josette, she asked him about his special story about the boy and he didn't have the heart to tell her the truth. 'It's going to be brilliant,' he said, with all the false passion he could muster. 'All over tomorrow's papers.'

'On Twitter they said you'd been arrested by the

police. Brent said you were a criminal and deserved it. I punched her.'

Jason tried to concentrate on the road ahead. 'You shouldn't fight with fists, only with words.'

'Was it like Gandhi and Nelson Mandela? Did they try to force you to betray your friends?'

'Well, I wouldn't exactly say...'

He reminded Bea that she'd mentioned Josette and Arthur having arguments and suggested she might tell him more. But she was more interested in discussing the pros and cons of non-violent action and Brent's cousin who was beaten by police at the G20 protests.

'Brent's been bragging about him for a year. I can't wait till she reads all the papers tomorrow. I'm going to send her the links. Read that, girl.'

Jason drove on in silence.

Josette was sporting her white towelling dressing gown again. She'd just washed her hair and had tied it up in a band. Arthur had apparently also been partially cured, or was at least germily occupied in important meetings on the other side of town, so after Bea bounced off to check her Facebook page, Josette offered Jason a drink. As she moved around the kitchen, the dressing gown slipped slightly from one of her shoulders. Her voice was warm.

'Thank you for picking her up.'

'It's nothing. I'm her father. Don't open a good red.'

'I was going to open it anyway.'

They clinked glasses and the wine was a very good one indeed. Velvety and soft, it warmed all the way down. Josette leant up against a half-wall by the breakfast bar, and once again the dressing gown slipped, this time a V-cut that revealed her legs. She'd always had good legs.

'How's the story going? You said it was a big one. You were OK picking Bea up tonight?'

'Nothing to worry about. Nothing to stop me spending quality time with my little girl.'

'You have such a hard life. If you ever give up, I have friends in PR. I could make a few phone calls.'

Jason wondered about sharing his despair with her but hesitated. It didn't seem the appropriate moment to disclose his failed career. Instead he suggested possible times for Bea to come over and stay the weekend.

'Despite everything. I mean, you can be a bit of a shit, but your heart is in the right place,' she said, sipping thoughtfully. 'There's nothing wrong with working hard. Maybe not everything went well with us before, but you've always been ambitious. And you do your best for Bea. You're a good father.'

'You said. This morning. But I don't know. She's getting older so quickly. I don't know what to say to her half the time.'

'You worry too much. She loves you and admires everything you do.'

He could smell a musky perfume and wondered how far away Arthur was, and for how long. And then told himself not to be stupid. This was his ex. 'This morning you said I should have more children.'

'I did.' She gave a sigh and contemplated the rich red in her glass. 'I think I make a good mother too.' She twirled a loose damp strand of hair around her forefinger.

'You do. You make a very good mother.'

'We did well with Bea. Though we were very young.'

Jason was curious as to whether this conversation was really going where he thought it was. 'Why did we stop, Josette?'

'I don't know. We could do it again.'

Jason swallowed more of the wine. 'We could?'

'I'm ovulating right now. I've been counting.'

Jason put his glass down on the pine table. Maybe his life was not lost. Maybe with Josette behind him again, he could find the strength to resurrect his career. He stood up slowly and moved closer to her.

'I understand,' he said. 'Bea mentioned you and Arthur had been having arguments...'

'She did?'

He felt it was time to be magnanimous. 'I'm sorry, really sorry. I didn't mean to pry, but she just said. You know, you two seemed so right...'

She was laughing. 'Oh, no, we're fine.'

'You're fine?' He didn't get it.

'We shout a bit, but that's life. You should have shouted at me more. It would have been good for you.'

He sat down again and she sipped at her wine with a smile.

'No, Jason, we've been trying for a child for years now, but Arthur's had tests and he can't. We discussed it and thought you could help. I mean, you're so good at it.'

'And Arthur...?'

'Arthur loves the idea. He'd be father too, just like with Bea. Father one and father two. No problem. He's totally open to it. There's lots of ways. If you don't want to have sex with me, there's always a turkey baster. Arthur keeps some dirty mags in the downstairs loo. He made a point of staying away this evening. Let me fill up your glass. Where are you going?'

Jason was pulling on his jacket. 'Thank you for the wine.'

'You're not angry? Look, I'm sorry I rather jumped

this on you. I thought you were more open-minded.'

'No, no, no. I'm flattered. I've always wanted to be valued for my prick.'

'Your semen, Jason. Don't do yourself down like you always do. Your DNA. Your intelligence and your kindness. And you were always pretty good in bed. I really am ovulating now.'

'I'm delighted for you and I'm sorry Arthur's been having spermatozoal problems. I really do have a big meeting to go to. I told you, I've got this big story to follow up. It's going to be all over the papers tomorrow. Just tell me when you need me to pick Bea up again.'

'You are angry.'

'No. I'm not angry, Josette. I'm just really busy right now.'

Jason didn't mean to slam the door quite so hard on his way out. He sat in the Renault for a minute and he tried to cool down and breathe deeply. The street was growing dark. Then he realised she could see him out of their front bay window if she looked, so he drove off, slightly erratically, though he'd not had all that much wine.

He wondered how hard it would be to get a job in PR.

52

The Community Speaks

From the start, there'd been mixed feelings on the Estates about Jamila's meeting, particularly among the older ones. After she'd announced it live on lunchtime TV, they progressed through many stages. Who was she to poke her nose in, they said to each other. Meetings never solved anything. A load of talk. We're busy with a hundred other things, they tweeted. Staying in our flats to watch *Corrie* or *EastEnders*.

But then people started to have second thoughts. Maybe it wasn't such a bad idea, emailed Mrs Chowdhury. We have issues to address, texted Hugh West. Grievances to air, said Medhi Shah when he met Chantelle Cissé on the stairs. And mightn't it be good to turn up at the Sylheti Centre to watch Them making a mess of it. Many residents weren't sure until They called off the meeting and then people grew angry. It was our choice if we wanted to stay at home and be apathetic, not theirs, tweeted Hugh West. All the time, the community leaders gathered their forces, took the temperature, felt the pulse, listened to the way the wind blew.

It occurred to some of the residents that a community acquired leaders in proportion to its problems. Solid, upstanding suburbs worried only about parking zones and dropped litter, and sported few leaders. The Estates, on the other hand, spawned dozens, scores, hundreds. They boasted elected leaders and appointed leaders, self-styled leaders and would-be leaders. They acquired a couple of reluctant leaders (usually the best and always in short supply). They developed voluble leaders and argumentative leaders, attractive leaders, inspirational leaders and scary leaders. There were even a few leaders who knew what they were talking about.

Soon it would be the moment for the leaders to stand up and be counted. Leaders liked that. Standing up seemed to be the preferred position for a community leader, and being counted added to the gloss – although most leaders preferred the counting to stop at them. Their time had not come yet, but it was on its way. Soon. Soon.

As the sun re-emerged from behind the rain clouds then dropped red and flaring beyond the blocks of flats on the Estates, more and more of the residents set their video recorders, pulled on their coats, gathered their wits, bandaged their wounds and came to feel that Evelyn Street outside the Sylheti Social Centre was the only place to be.

'Hello? I'm sorry to bother you. You're probably soaking in a hot bath or having a well-earned drink. It's Suzen. From this morning... the breakfast thing... I delivered the leaflets. Anyway, I saw you on TV at lunchtime. You were very good. I'm sorry I've been too busy at work to phone before. Look, I don't know if you've been checking Twitter or Facebook, but there seems to be something going on with your meeting this evening. They say all kinds of people are turning up demanding to be let in. Hey, it's on YouTube now. There's this tall man from the centre standing by the front door waving his arms, trying to stop them and saying things about health and safety. And there's a crowd of people all round him arguing. Listen, I wouldn't have bothered you, but I thought you might not know. Anyway, I'm going along, to see what it's all about. It's only round the corner from work and it looks fun.'

'Golam?'

'Yes, yes? What? Who? You'll have to speak up, please. I can't hear myself shout.'

'It's Jamila, Golam. What's happening there? I'm at home reading and I start getting these messages.'

'It's terrible. Terrible. All these people outside say they want to come in. They're shouting about choice and who makes all the decisions. Banging on the doors and yelling about democracy. There are community leaders and everything. They say you called the meeting and they want it.'

'So, let them.'

'The police said no, and I had the chairs put away again, and I cancelled the refreshments—'

'Forget the police, forget the refreshments, get out the chairs. I'll be there as soon as I can.'

'But—'

'I'm sorry to disturb you, Deputy Opposition Leader...'

'Hey, Jamila? I thought that meeting was cancelled. Now I'm hearing—'

'Me too. Threats of violence. Vigilantes. The police are cordoning the whole area off. I'm driving there now.'

'Is it safe?'

'We need you there, Carol. We need someone of your stature and depth of experience to face the danger, to stand in front of the crowd with their sticks and things –

with the bravery to calm them down.'

'Of course. Normally I would be the first to be there, Jamila—'

'Great. I knew you'd want to, violence or no violence—'

'— and at the same time, I honestly feel that this is your ward, you have the local knowledge—'

'But, Deputy Opposition Leader, surely you don't—'

'— and you know the party is behind you all the way—'

'Are you behind this, Jamila? I'm standing watching half the fucking neighbourhood push their way into the Sylheti Centre. It's chaos. I can't guarantee anyone's safety now.'

'This is the grassroots, Chief Superintendent. Popular opinion.'

'Fuck popular opinion. What do you expect me to do now?'

'How about joining me on the stage here inside?'

'Nigel—'

'What's that shouting?'

'You'll have to speak up, there's quite a lot of shouting.'

'I said—'

'It looks like there's a meeting taking place after all, Nigel. There's about a hundred people here in the hall with me who would appreciate the point of view of the council cabinet member for community safety. Plus a few TV cameras, of course.'

'TV cameras?'

'There's a seat right next to me on the platform, Nigel, waiting just for you.'

*

Royland locked the gym early and sellotaped a sign to the door saying: Exercises Off Tonight Due To Local Issues. Sadé had not originally intended to join him, but now she agreed to come along for the first few minutes. To show willing.

At first, Andy Rockham had no intention of attending the meeting either. He'd been working in what should have been his time off since shortly after midday and in a few hours it would be his scheduled shift again.

He sat at his desk in the CID main office and took out a folder of photos of the knife Royland had found. Shots had been taken from all sides, but there were no fingerprints anywhere. It seemed to have been wiped fairly thoroughly. Brown stains on the blade had tested positive for blood, but that was all. He'd sent the knife to be checked over for DNA but didn't expect to find much aside from Liam's, assuming it was indeed the right knife. Next, he pulled out a sheaf of blow-up prints that had been made from the CCTV and inspected the grey blurs for any recognisable human features. But Jason was right. There was nothing visible inside the hoods. One of the muggers was taller than the other, but that was it. In each of the images, at least one hoodie was partly cut off by the frame.

He turned back to his computer, where he'd loaded up all the stills from the original tape, and inched through the frames a step at a time. He stopped at one. There was a glint from the right wrist of one of the muggers. Was it a watch, meaning that he was left-handed? Or just a bracelet?

He sat back in his seat and stretched. His neck crunched in worrying fashion. The fact was that muggers almost never got caught. The publicity with this one might help. But the Estates were not often police-friendly. Or rather, they were mixed. The police-friendly residents never knew anything worth hearing, while the ones who might know something were never friendly. The press department had put out selected pictures edited from the CCTV – more to ruin the Post's scoop than in the hope of eliciting any worthwhile public response. To prove his point, they'd received forty-seven phone calls, none of them any use at all.

Dana came in and offered to help, but he sent her away brusquely and then immediately hated himself for it. He took out his phone to call Cheryl. He always tried to speak to her early evening, to see what her day had been like. But recently she'd sounded preoccupied, either busy with Duane or making her own supper or something. He put his phone back again.

Once more he began to feel all the excitement was happening elsewhere. To other people, not him. He reasoned he could be more use at the Sylheti Centre than in the station. He might be able to talk to people on the quiet. Pick up some intel. There'd be witnesses who might slip him some information in the confusion of a big crowd. He'd need someone to assist him.

He went looking for Dana to apologise.

53

Thai Green Curry

It was one of those annoying evenings when it couldn't decide whether to stay fine, turn cold, rain or stop raining. So it did everything. As Jason drove home, the gaps in the darkening clouds suddenly turned red but then disappeared as a thin drizzle returned.

He didn't feel ready to go back to his empty flat. He couldn't yet resign himself to an evening spent reviewing his wasted life, reading through the eight years of newspaper cuttings that lay yellowing in box files under the bed. From now on he would be a nonentity. So be it. In a way, it was a relief – as if an enormous weight of expectation had been lifted off his back. It was a strange sensation: he felt listless yet surprisingly peaceful. He was a has-been who never was. Many billions of people never were. He'd gone straight from up and coming to past it. In fact, he'd done more than many. And now he could stop.

He found himself parking at the Camden General. He wanted to see Katrina one last time, to find out how Liam was doing and to apologise to her. He locked the Renault, the click echoing chillingly off the concrete of the multi-storey car park. A clutch of reporters and photographers still littered the forecourt of the hospital, waiting optimistically for Weaverall or Katrina – or a doctor to tell them that Liam was dead, a vegetable or awake and break-dancing on the floor of his room. As long as it could be expressed in a photo, a caption and three hundred words.

He slipped in via the side entrance. At the lifts, the doors slid open to reveal Tam standing there with Tyronne. For a moment, none of them spoke.

'Jason,' Tam said finally. She looked smaller than normal, or maybe it was the effect of being out of the office. Her mouse-coloured hair seemed more tangled. He asked himself how she'd felt so intimidating, ball-breaking.

'Tam.' He nodded to her and to the Herald's new crime correspondent, who nodded back sheepishly. 'How's the promotion going?'

Tyronne shrugged.

'You'll be OK. Listen, it couldn't have happened to a nicer guy.'

'It was good of you to come,' said Tam, stepping out of the lift with Tyronne to let three student doctors in. 'He'll be pleased to see you. He's not in a bad way at all, considering.'

Jason stared at her for a few seconds, wondering if Liam had suddenly woken up.

'I emailed you three times. Gareth Whelpower has had a stroke. He was found in his office last night, face down in a foil dish of Thai green curry holding a cutting about the miners' strike from the Yorkshire Post.'

Jason felt strangely wrong-footed. He recalled the odd wording she'd used on the phone when she'd fired him for the second time – phrases like 'at a time like this' and 'respect' which he'd simply dismissed as typical Tam-like overreaction – and now they made awful sense. 'Where is he?'

'It's in the last email. Eighth floor. Stroke Ward.'

Jason nodded automatically. They were both looking at him, waiting for him to say more. But he wasn't going to share how he felt about his mentor. 'You've been to see the Glass family?'

The deputy editor shook her head. 'Security lockdown. Nobody can get in.' She seemed rather cool about it all. Jason had to remind himself it wasn't his story anymore. 'We've got to go,' she added with a crooked smile. 'How's your new job?'

He decided to be truthful. 'It's not.'

'Oh, sorry.' She didn't immediately offer to take him back and he hadn't said it for that reason. He was just sick of keeping up a front.

'I'm sorry, too,' said Tyronne. And then a text jingled on his phone. 'Look I've got to race off to this—'

A look from Tam stopped him.

'To this what?' Jason looked from one to the other. He felt the prickling of his journalistic nose once more. 'This meeting? Is it on again?'

'This nothing. Just… nothing.'

'It's OK.' Jason patted Tyronne warmly on the shoulder. 'I'm not a journalist anymore.' And when he said the words, he felt a strange sense of resolution.

He found Gareth Whelpower in a single room, staring at the ceiling, his right hand lying limply on the pink blanket. He took a tissue from a box by the bed and gently wiped his mentor's mouth. The editor glared up at him and tried to say something, but it came out as a cross between a groan and a sigh.

'I just came to pay my respects,' Jason said.

Whelpower said nothing, because he couldn't.

'You don't look good. In fact you look like crap. I'd put in a complaint about it, if I were you. You always liked complaining.'

He wiped him again, tenderly. This was the man who'd taught Jason most of what he knew. Who had done it all: locals, tabloids, broadsheets, dailies and

Sundays. Who had pursued the vilest and publicised the best. Or was it the other way around? Whelpower looked three decades older than his years. His eyes were dull like a cornered reptile.

'I blew it,' Jason said. 'What do I do now?'

His mentor dribbled some more.

'There's money in PR,' Jason continued. 'Good money. Less pressure. Job security. Proper pension plan. I've got a friend who works for an oil firm. All he has to do is deny global warming. He wears a nice suit, works with a very sexy assistant, probably screws her too, and gets evenings and weekends off – as long as someone hasn't spilled gallons of crude all over some baby seagulls, of course.' He saw Whelpower's eyes shift to look over his shoulder. 'And he probably won't end his career face down in a bowl of Asian takeaway.'

Jason glanced round. A TV screen hung on the wall behind him, the sound muted, showing some *Big Brother* rip-off, with half-clad teenagers sitting on bean-bags.

'You want to watch that? You want something else?'

Jason searched for the remote and discovered it under a plate of rich tea biscuits. On Channel 4, he found a big-name reporter standing in a bombed-out city delivering a big-name report. Even with the sound off, Jason could tell it was important. An important man talking to important people about important things.

'You want that?'

Whelpower stared at it suspiciously.

'You taught me everything you knew,' Jason said to the editor. The eyes didn't move from the TV. 'Fuck it,' Jason said.

He wanted to look in on Liam on the way down, but the door to Intensive Care was now guarded by hospital security and none of his hospital contacts were answering the phone. At reception, he tried to find out how Liam was doing, but even when he explained he was a friend of the family the receptionist refused to phone through to the ward.

Instead, he stood in reception and called up his PR friend Mike. Yes, he was well. And so was Mike. Yes, Jason's work was going great too. And he remembered what Mike had said once about jobs in his company...

'What about meeting up, say, tomorrow? Friday?' It seemed Mike needed to check his diary and get back to him.

'That's OK. No rush. I'm pretty booked up myself.'

Jason was just fifty metres from the car park when Katrina came out of the main entrance of the Camden General, clutching a packet of Lambert and Butler's and pursued by a crowd of unfit journalists. She made the mistake of stopping to light her cigarette and the crowd caught up.

'Katrina, here.'

'Mrs Glass!'

'Look this way.'

'Over here, Kati.'

'Give us a smile.'

They were still surrounding her when Jason drove out of the car park a minute later.

'How's Liam?'

'How much were they paying you, Kat?'

'Who's the father?'

'Who's he play for?'

'Kati, Kati!'

'Did he wear away kit in bed?'

Katrina gazed blankly at each in turn, as if she'd discovered some alien species. Jason started to turn left, changed his mind and swung the car round to stop a short distance away. Leaning over, he opened the passenger door and called her name.

'Has Liam spoken?'

'Does the kid know?'

He called her name again and hit the horn and then she was pushing her way through the journalists, her fag held aloft for safety.

'Come on, Kat!'

'Tell us your side.'

'We just want to hear your side of the story.'

'We just want the truth.'

She scrambled in, flashguns flickering. Jason started off with a jerk, straight at the crowd. Sundry reporters and photographers leapt aside with unexpected skill.

'It's OK. They're insured,' he said.

She stared ahead and he wondered if she was going to hit him, scream at him or laugh. Instead she simply said, 'Can I like smoke in here?' He never usually allowed smoking in his car, but he nodded. She sucked on her Lambert. 'I was going mental wanting this. I thought I could maybe get out for a minute without getting spotted.'

'Have you thought of disguising yourself as a Santa Claus strippergram? I'm told it's very effective.'

She said nothing for a long minute. Jason turned into the main road and thought of different ways to apologise for the behaviour of the press, tried them out in his head, rewrote them, abandoned them, thought of some more. Before he could finish the draft, she spoke again.

'Anyway, Liam's going to be all right.'

'They've told you? Great. That's enormously... an enormous relief. What did they say?'

'No, I just know.'

'Oh, right.'

She waved her cigarette in a circle. 'He's been going on at me to chuck these. Especially now, in hospital and all.'

'He's still talking to you?' Jason sped past a group of cyclists in bright yellow.

'They're doing another operation at the moment. But even when he's in the operating theatre, he visits me. He's a good kid. You should put that in the article.'

'Well, I—'

'He wants justice, don't he?' Katrina jabbed the fag-end hard on the door frame and lit another.

Jason wanted to reassure her that everything would indeed be all right. He wanted to believe that he could help. Once he would have believed that. Was he foolish to have ever thought a headline could make a difference?

'Where are we going?' she said suddenly. 'Where are you taking me?'

'I don't know. Where would you like to go? I don't have any plans for this evening. A meal out. Go to a film...'

She smiled briefly. He didn't remember seeing her smile before. She had a nice smile.

'You know about this meeting they're having? They asked me to go, didn't they? Then they told me it wasn't happening anymore.'

'It's happening again.'

She tipped ash out of the window. 'You sure?'

Jason glanced at her. 'It's none of my business anymore, but maybe you should go. They'll be talking about Liam. There's a load of nonsense being said. You might be able to help calm things down.'

'It'll be like back there only worse. Liam doesn't know if it's right for me. I asked him. I saw him outside the ward.'

Jason was growing fed up with humouring people, whether news editors or grieving mothers. 'Liam's in a coma on the operating table,' he said, perhaps more sharply than he intended.

'He says there's no point in me hanging around everyone like a spare part.'

'Katrina.' Jason braked hard and looked her in the eye. 'Liam isn't talking to anyone. He didn't tell you to go to the meeting. He didn't beam himself down. It wasn't him.'

'I know that. I told you, I'm not, like, mad.'

'Good.'

She contemplated the tip of her cigarette.

'He says, if I go, he wants you to go too.'

54

The Meeting

And so it was that between ninety and a hundred and ten residents of the Gordon Road Estates jammed into the Sylheti Centre's downstairs meeting hall, which had been carefully approved by the London Fire Brigade for a maximum of sixty-five. They were excited and afraid. They felt exposed and eager. They were there. They were going to listen. They were going to fix things at last, although they didn't exactly agree about which things and how. And many believed in their hearts that meetings never changed anything. But maybe this time would be different. And if it wasn't, many were ready to smash windows and break heads.

They crowded in through the doors and sat on the window ledges and in the gangways, and leant against the wall at the back, and stood on the stairs outside, peering past those in front towards the stage. They saw Golam Kamal rub his head in concern as the numbers grew and more blue plastic seats were carried in from the youth centre upstairs and the offices below. Then there were no more seats to bring.

Local and national TV news set up cameras at the back, each surveying the assembled masses with their single stern eye. Journalists more used to having special areas set aside found themselves fighting for seats, waving notebooks, voice recorders and press passes in a vain attempt to pull rank. Press and residents photographed everyone who sat down or stood up, in the hope that someone might turn out to be famous.

*

Meanwhile, on the platform, Golam Kamal bent over his chairman, Mr Shahanuddin Shah, to share his concerns that the meeting would not be covered by the centre's insurance, and they would all be liable, and that this violated every kind of by-law. Mr Shah was a self-made man, a local solicitor, proud of his legal qualifications, the first in his family. But he was a shorter, stouter man than the social centre's administrator and he felt that Golam never failed to arrange things so that he was reminded of this. They rarely seemed to be standing except that Golam would find a reason to loom over him, rarely seated except that Golam would jump up to point something out.

So Mr Shahanuddin Shah looked up at the other man, pressed his stubby fingers together and said drily that he was not unaware of the law. Nevertheless, he would prefer to take a chance with legality than remove twenty to thirty upstanding citizens from the premises – and in any case, wasn't it exciting?

But Golam was not excited, rather he was anxious. Being anxious was usual with him. Being excited was usual with his chairman, who in Golam's view had no conception of the many and varied calamities that could lie ahead in the next hour and a half.

Royland and Sadé arrived early and planted themselves in the middle of the middle row, where Royland sat straight-backed, gazing around him with a kind of fascinated glee, as if he was waiting for the start of a top new movie. Sadé seemed less impressed, more depressed. She gloomily surveyed all the people who could visit their gym but didn't, even though, judging by the various belt sizes and wobbling jowls, they clearly should.

Worse, she had not yet told Royland about the latest accounts. Financially, All Roads Lead to Royland was no longer on its last legs. The cancelled youth club *was* its last leg. She had a mad urge to stand up and shout about the heart attacks everyone faced, the strokes they would all would succumb to if they didn't start working out. Specifically at All Roads Lead to Royland. But what was the point? Now the gym was disappearing and it was too late.

Under her desk she'd found their last remaining box of glossy leaflets. Glamorous sleek young women trod the treadmills (as glamorous and sleek as she'd been able to hire for the shoot). Muscular if dim young men (including Royland in a variety of Lycra outfits) sweated away at the barbells and resistance machines. She'd brought them but now realised she hadn't the courage to hand them out. Or the heart. Any more than she had the heart to call Royland a pillock for getting picked up by the police. What good were leaflets or pillock-calling? The gym was gone. His dream was over. All that remained was to teach him the final lesson of the accounts book and be the person who destroyed his hopes forever.

She looked at him, as he inspected the crowd, so childishly pumped up and ignorant of all reality, and she bit her tongue and let him live his dream a little longer.

Tyronne pushed through the crowd a short time later. He felt awkward. It should have been Jason Crowthorne covering this story, but Jason had resigned or been sacked – he wasn't sure which. And he'd looked very strange at the Camden General just before. The Herald's former chief correspondent had appeared grey in the face, haggard, unkempt and weighed down. So the Herald's new crime correspondent swallowed his uncertainties and squeezed in between two large white women with short hair and treble chins. The pair talked across him while they waited, mainly about how the Pakis and Blacks took all the housing. They seemed not to notice him there. Or the colour of his skin.

While Tyronne fidgeted nervously and jotted a few hopeful notes, Jamila was already seated on the platform. Nobody was going to budge her now. She didn't care if the council deputy opposition leader, the council opposition leader or even the prime minister turned up – she was staying. For the first time, she was at the centre of things. She was going to have a chance to stand up to Nigel Ponting. She was going to make life better for the people who'd voted her in, just four years ago. And might be about to vote her out again. She wished she'd had more time to plan what she was wearing – a bright lime-green sari, the first item she'd found that didn't need extensive ironing. She wished she'd had more time to plan what she had to say. She wished she'd gone to the toilet. She wished many things, but she didn't for one moment wish she wasn't there.

The borough commander had joined her shortly after their phone call. He shook her by the hand, and even then she didn't stand up from her blue plastic stacking-chair, in case someone snatched it away before she could sit down again.

'You got your way,' he said, leaning down confidentially towards her in his impressively ironed uniform. 'So far.'

'Not my way,' she said. 'The people's way.'

'So long as you are happy with what the people say, Councillor Hasan. Democracy can be a very ungrateful child. It can turn on you when you least expect.'

And then Jamila spotted Suzen, the woman from the printer's. The morning meeting seemed such a long time ago. She'd found a place at the very front. Jamila smiled nervously down at her and the woman from the printer's waved merrily back.

But one chair remained worryingly empty. The one she most needed to be occupied. The chair that should have belonged to Nigel Ponting, cabinet member for community safety.

The hall filled with expectant noise. Mr Shahanuddin Shah (solicitor) sat up and prepared to speak.

He cleared his throat, unheard in the din of ongoing conversations, felt a little dry around the mouth. On the long table in front of them had been set four pens, four pads of paper, four upturned glasses and four bottles of Fenland Well to demonstrate the Sylheti Centre's devotion to its adopted land. He poured himself a glass of patriotic water, sipped and called the meeting to order. Which, as the noise now rivalled a small football match, didn't happen.

He tried clapping his hands. He tried going shhhhhhhhhhhhh. He tried entreating the assembly to listen, and finally decided to proceed as if people were listening, then maybe in a few minutes they would be.

So Mr Shah stood up and spoke into the hubbub. He introduced himself and the panel. And indeed a few at the front did realise something was happening, and then the rows behind, followed by the rows behind them. By the time the chairperson had reached the middle of his speech, a relative silence had been obtained, although at the expense of most people knowing who anyone was. And this uncertainty led to a low-level hum of enquiry that circulated the room like a grumbling basso continuo under a baroque tune.

Jamila grew increasingly anxious as he wittered away. Where was Nigel Ponting? Had he bottled out after all? Ponting was a tough fighter, and she was nervous of opposing him, but the opportunity would not last long. In a few days, a few hours even, she knew, the momentum would shift. The council would close ranks. Her party leaders would push her aside again. And the voters would go back to watching *Britain's Got Talent*.

The assembled crowd, meanwhile, listened attentively, in the optimistic hope that some interesting disaster would strike. It didn't take long.

As Mr Shah's opening speech rose towards its climax, by way of reciting the Sylheti Centre's evening-class programme, he was interrupted by a growing muttering from the crowd by the entrance. The muttering was followed by a grumbling, the grumbling by a chattering and then a more specific complaining: Nigel Ponting was attempting to arrive.

A frail man, he pushed with the little force at his disposal. The crowd pushed back. He resorted to elbows and briefcase corners. The crowd resisted manfully. Finally, the pressure broke and the council cabinet member for community safety was impelled into the hall like a pallid cork out of a bottle of particularly gassy wine.

He took his time squeezing through to the stage, then apologised for being late. 'I'm sure,' he added with a self-deprecatory wringing of his hands, 'Mr Shah has said many interesting things and I'd appreciate a brief summary of them.'

Mr Shah fixed Nigel Ponting with his most critical

expression, then reprised his words in just five short sentences. Ponting nodded and smiled thinly at Jamila. It was a particularly snake-like smile and it seemed to say: this is where your troubles start.

She tried – and failed – to smile confidently back.

The same force that had injected Ponting into the meeting also launched Jason and Katrina into the crowd behind him, and separated them. As he bumped and rebounded, Jason had the weird feeling that he'd somehow been sucked into the pages of the Post and the Herald, and that the people who were now elbowing, propelling and rebuffing him were their articles come to life. Not merely articles, but the whole mad confusion of headlines, colour pieces, letters, adverts, cartoons, classifieds, photos, faces he recognised, faces he didn't recognise, pushing and swearing. Finally, he landed against a side wall. Standing upright here was made impossible by TV cameras and lights. But he could lean at a sharp angle, while giving the impression that this was precisely how he preferred to be at important meetings. His odd position, he reasoned blearily, would at least keep him awake.

Jason felt strangely passive, bent like a paper clip under the cameras. This was his world. He should be scribbling in his own rarely legible shorthand, pondering his intro, planning the article, considering side issues that might go best into a breakout and listening for quotes. Building the campaign against knife crime under his byline. But there was no article, no intro, no breakout, no quotes, no campaign and no byline. Above, below and around him were crammed the members of the press. But where once he might have felt fellowship or even jealousy, now he looked at them – gossiping among themselves, whispering, texting, googling, chuckling at some private joke – and felt only revulsion. They weren't interested in truth, they just wanted a story.

Meanwhile, raucous attempts at questions from the floor were ignored by the chairperson, who bowed towards his microphone and called on the borough commander to speak. The hall grew quiet. Chief Superintendent Slocombe drew himself up in his stackable seat and surveyed the room, its mass of variously coloured faces looking like hopeful pebbles on a beach. He'd had a hard day. He was criticised if he sat back and let thugs get away with violence, but if he went into the Estates and made a few arrests, he was criticised for overreacting. Some people were never happy. His coppers had screwed up by losing the CCTV tape, but then, when they'd got their hands on it, they'd found little more usable than two ink blots. He'd wanted to throw the journalist who'd nicked it into jail but was advised it would be difficult to make the charge stick. No matter, he'd find something to catch the bugger on. Now he knew that Jamila Hasan was waiting to tell him to double his patrols and open police stations that he'd closed so he could keep his budget balanced – and himself in a job. But he was more than her match when it came to taking the moral high ground.

He began in a quiet voice, which meant people had to stop talking and lean forward. He radiated common sense and Yorkshire grit. He had the advantage of piercing grey eyes, wide shoulders and a uniform with epaulettes. He had also been well trained. For many decades, the Police Staff College at Bramshill had taken senior police officers who loved to speak their minds and taught them not to.

He clenched his jaw, nodded firmly to Jamila and reminded everyone that a teenager lay gravely injured. A mother grieved beside his hospital bed, their pictures splashed heartlessly all over the Internet. As voices challenged him from the packed hall, he reassured everyone that the police took such incidents very seriously indeed. So seriously that the word serious came up many more times in the following few minutes. Indeed, the Serious Crime Squad had been notified, and serious note had been made of serious community interest. He ploughed on, ignoring heckles. He couldn't comment on the current investigation except to say that a serious number of people had been questioned and an equally serious number were being held overnight. The situation being as serious as it was.

This comment led to a greater muttering among the crowd. Jamila, growing more frustrated by the minute, tapped her pen, made notes on her Sylheti Centre headed notepaper, poured glasses of water and did all she could to stop herself shouting out.

Then a voice called from the mass below, asking if all the arrested young thugs were going to be released next morning, like happened last time, innit.

The borough commander squared his shoulders and said that it was not for him to comment on the decisions of the judiciary, past or future.

Interruptions grew louder. He raised his voice. He stated that his streets were safe, though they needed more police, but he couldn't afford them. He was one hundred per cent dedicated to ensuring his streets were even safer in the future, even though they already were. In short, David Slocombe committed himself to as little as possible, did his teachers proud and sat back with an appropriately pensive steeliness to await general approval.

Jamila leant forward once more and once more was sent to the back of the queue by Mr Shahanuddin Shah, who beckoned to Nigel Ponting. How could she be Churchillian and statesmanlike if she never had a chance to speak? He was probably acting in what he thought were her interests by giving her the last speech, but the assembled locals were growing restive. Ponting would talk as long as possible in the hope that they'd lose patience and Jamila would be drowned out. She tried to remain calm and statesmanlike, which lasted twenty seconds. Succumbing, she scribbled the chairman a note to hurry things along, then a second to let her make challenges, then a third to tell him to agree to the first two. Each note he read slowly and carefully, then he gave her a gentle wink and a small smile and proceeded to do nothing.

By now Nigel Ponting was easing his way into his own statement. Following the brave example of his borough commander, the council cabinet member had started by saying as little as possible, continued by saying less and now finished by saying nothing at all. However, he did it with style and élan. Jamila had to admire him. The body language was superb. Ponting frowned, smiled gently, nodded and shook his soft head with the precision and elegance of a ballet dancer.

Years ago, Nigel Ponting had discovered the danger of verbs. Verbs forced a well-meaning politician to take a stand and create a sentence that risked meaning something. Much safer to avoid them. Nouns were his best friends and he clung to them as a fencer to his épée.

The people wanted Commitment – they should

become volunteers. Volunteers were the way forward. They wanted Money – they should stop complaining and find more creative ways to raise finance. Creativity was the way forward. Look to the example of their own council, which hadn't whined but had creatively abolished unnecessary nurseries and libraries and creatively set out their plans for a £38 million state-of-the-art civic centre that would centralise all the services they hadn't already outsourced to India. This was the future. His voice rose on his last lines and died away, like a lounge singer who knew how to make a showstopper milk the applause.

Jason's eyes went to Jamila. He willed her on, but she was looking unsure of herself. Ponting was a star.

However, there were some in the meeting who remained unswayed. Once more the groundswell of would-be questions was waved into the future by Mr Shah, who praised the council cabinet member for his honesty and determination to do what he could for the community, and almost sounded as if he meant it.

Now the chairperson turned to Jamila, ward councillor.

The meeting grew quieter and more expectant. Jamila shuffled her notes. She rearranged her thoughts. She squinted into the TV lights. She reconsidered the best order in which to embark on what she wanted to say.

The residents waited. Jamila was supposed to be one of them, although some had their doubts. She was a politician and they had no high regard for politicians. True, they'd heard no rumours of her claiming thousands of pounds for a moat around her West Hampstead flat, but then council expenses limits were rather limited. To some of the crowd, such as Fiona

O'Malley and Bill Baines, her career was a matter of
admiration: a sister, whatever her colour, who had
achieved. To others, such as Salma Chowdhury and
Medhi Shah, it was less admirable: a sista, no matter her
colour, who had sold out.

She cleared her throat and started to introduce
herself, but her voice sounded thin and raspy. She cleared
her throat again. She gazed down from the platform and
made out the expectant faces of people she wanted to
impress. She saw journalist Jason Crowthorne, leaning at
a rather strange angle against a side wall. In the middle,
she saw Royland Pinkersleigh and his partner Sadé, who
struggled on with their little gym. At the front, she saw
Suzen, from the printer's, waiting for some eloquence.
And she felt unworthy. She didn't know any clever
diplomatic tricks. She decided to tell the truth, and that
was her first big mistake.

She highlighted errors that had been made. She told
of the loss of the CCTV tape. The security cameras
trained onto parking spaces not pavements. The cuts in
services for the young. And promptly alienated potential
allies in the police and council.

Nigel Ponting interrupted and said this was exactly
what he'd feared from Jamililana Hashmi. He'd been
lured there as a cabinet member, but now Jaminini
Hosseni was indulging in electioneering. This was a low
tactic from Jalilah Hassen.

Jamila apologised and tried to regather her courage,
but, unused to thinking policies through for herself, her
passion sounded naive and unprepared, even to herself.
Dispirited, she lost her way again. Uncertainly, she
attempted to describe the gangs she'd faced personally
that afternoon. People shouted her down from all sides.
Mr Shah tried to regain control and give Jammana a

chance to complete her address. Thanks to Ponting, even he had grown confused over her name.

This was the disaster the deputy party leader had tried to save her from. She was just not experienced enough. Nobody wanted honesty. They wanted clever rhetoric. They wanted to be told everything would be all right.

She recognised Katrina Glass in the crush and in desperation she pointed to her.

'There's the mother of the victim who everyone talks about so easily.'

People looked round and saw Katrina and called to her to speak. Jason stood a few metres away and could see her turn pale. Despite what she'd done to him and his story, he felt for her. None of this was her fault. He wanted to push through, to protect her from the mob, and not least from the journalists. But he was pinned back by the TV equipment and the journalists themselves as they surged forwards.

'Come up here, Katrina,' Jamila called. 'Have your say. What do you want? Come up here on the platform.'

Katrina shook her head furiously, but still they shouted. Journalists fought to get a quote. TV reporters asked her to turn to them. Mr Shah tried again to call for order and said it was not for Jamila to say who should be on the panel, but Jamila kept pointing. 'This is the mother. Her son is in a coma. She is the one who is suffering.'

Katrina avoided their eyes. She turned and fought her way back along the side wall towards the exit, jabbing with her elbows. There was commotion in all parts of the hall. Katrina found herself facing Jason. The reporters waved microphones and voice recorders. For a moment she froze.

Jason felt awful for her. He said, 'I'm sorry.'

She said, 'Fuck off.'

She pushed her way out through the doors and people were crying out all around. Katrina disappeared beyond the landing and Jamila's opportunity was gone. She tried to make a new point about funding, but nobody was listening. Mr Shah stood and waved his arms a great deal and begged everyone to stay calm. Borough Commander Slocombe and Cabinet Member Ponting sat watching comfortably. Chaos worked in their favour. Jamila would have no chance to build a strong case against them now.

In the uproar Nigel Ponting leant over to Jamila with a pale smile, like a cat contemplating a half-dead mouse.

'Tough luck. That's how they go sometimes. You gave it a try.' He put a soft hand on her arm.

She couldn't utter a word.

55

That Is the Man

Outside the Sylheti Centre, fifty policemen in riot armour stood to one side under the bright street lights, looking up and down and waiting for someone to hit. Katrina pulled out another fag.

It was growing colder. A bunch of photographers and a couple of TV cameramen had followed her out, snapping and filming. But seeing she was doing nothing but stare into the distance, they soon drifted back inside. She brushed her hair out of her eyes. Even with fifty coppers the road felt empty and sad. The wind caught at some discarded leaflets and fluttered them in spirals before tossing them back in the gutter.

They landed at Liam's feet. From across the road he watched her, standing half in, half out of a pool of light. He was all in white, wearing his favourite white hoodie, white chinos and the trainers with the red flashes. He waved and she waved happily back. So she walked over and joined him. They stood together for a few minutes, not saying anything, not needing to.

After a time, Liam tapped her on the shoulder and loped off past a newsagent's and a mini supermarket.

'What do you want?' she called, but he didn't answer. 'What do I want to go down there for?'

He stopped and looked back at her, and then he lifted his arm slowly in the white hoodie and pointed down the road the way he was going. His arm was limp and yet the pointing seemed to mean something. Just she didn't know the fuck what.

She asked him what he was going on about, but he only went and stuck his hand out like he did before.

'What's this, a fucking quiz?'

He was pointing towards the place where he was stabbed. He was pointing past that towards their home.

She shook her head and went, 'You want to go home? Just say it, then.'

But he just stared at her – with no expression.

And then Katrina totally knew for certain what Liam was telling her, what would bring him back.

Inside the hall, things had grown even hotter and louder and a hard desire clutched at people's hearts. It was like the cynics always said. You couldn't trust anyone.

Some shouted. Some wondered if it was time to throw a few chairs around. Give Jamila the help she needed. Make a show of force. Or just have some fun breaking people...

Golam had compiled a list for Chairperson Shahanuddin Shah – a sheet of A4, naming the leaders of local organisations who had a right to speak from the floor. He'd spent much time arranging them in logical order according to status – but now everyone was trying to talk out of turn. Arms waved. Eyes flashed. Mr Shah was required to exert discipline and firm governance and wasn't doing it.

'Some of my friends are Pakis,' began a small middle-aged Irishman who nobody knew. He was clad in beige slacks, puce shirt, red pullover and apple-green jacket, no item of which matched any other.

'Wait your turn,' called numerous voices including Mr Shah's.

Two gentlemen recited urgently from tattered pro- and anti-immigration articles they'd clipped over the past thirty years. Those around them shouted variously to sit down and shut up, or stand up and tell the world how things were. There were those who wanted more locked gates for the Estates and those who wanted more litter bins. There were those who suggested the Bengalis would prefer to go home. There were Bengalis, born in Camden, who felt they *were* home. There were others who gave thanks for the chance to come and run English newsagents' and become English chartered accountants and *not* be back home... In this way the meeting struggled through the community leaders, from cooperative to association to self-appointed, with varying degrees of sense, acclaim and opprobrium.

Jamila despaired – despaired of humanity, of her people. Despaired of herself. The politician and the policeman smiled to each other, knowingly. This was how it always was.

Suddenly an Asian in his late twenties pushed to the front and seized the microphone. It was the Bengali-Rasta from the morning meeting, with his radically shaggy moustache and radical goatee, and he declared that he was sick of his people being attacked, punched, insulted, stabbed, shouted at and called Paki by people who couldn't read a map of the world.

'I were in a gang, innit,' he said. 'We stood up for ourselves.' His camouflage-green anorak flailed backwards and forwards, at risk of taking out a neighbour's eye with one of its many zips and buckles. 'We're innocent but we may as well be guilty. Dey think it were one of us what did it anyway. Well, let's give dem someting to call us guilty about,' he continued as some applauded and others shouted that he wasn't helping the cause.

Jamila snatched the microphone back from him. She

urgently reminded the floor that the police and council both insisted that the stabbing was not gang- or race-related. But the floor was not interested.

'Look at dem cops,' said the ex-gang member, pulling the microphone back with another extravagant sweep of an arm that narrowly avoided damaging the elderly white woman on his right. 'Lost dem CCTV pictures. Conven-i-ent. You believe dat?'

The borough commander, who'd been reading messages on his phone, murmured something and his eyes rested on Andy – in the middle, taking notes and suddenly feeling very exposed. Andy put up his hand to speak, but Dana touched him quickly on the arm and restrained him. People all around were muttering about police bias and lies and racism. The mood was growing ugly. Andy could see Naik the newsagent near the front of the stage. Now Naik locked eyes with him and pointed in his direction and the people either side of the little newsagent started looking the same way.

Then Andy turned towards Jason, still leaning obliquely against the side wall, and he wanted to do to him what he should have done before...

Jamila also noticed Jason. The place was getting impossible to control. An ocean swell of angry opinion and conviction, and every opinion and conviction different from every other. She glanced across at the borough commander, but Chief Superintendent Slocombe sat back, his arms crossed, calmly watching and waiting. It was no problem to him if people started hitting each other. In fact it would make things easier. His fingers moved slowly towards his police radio.

Nigel Ponting remonstrated loudly with a group of Asians who'd forced their way to the foot of the stage. Shahanuddin Shah shouted for order, to no effect.

This was what the borough commander had predicted. This was true democracy. Something that bit you back when you least expected it. A hall filled with people arguing, shouting and threatening each other. The inalienable British right of everyone to do the most stupid thing not in their own interests. What was the point of any of it?

Jason was watching Jamila from his position jammed against the side wall and saw her spirit fade. He tried to will her on, but it felt useless. He could hardly have felt lower. He'd always believed that she was irrepressible. For four years she'd supported anything that would get her onto the middle pages of the Camden Herald – from local allotments to cycle paths. And for the first time she seemed lost for words. She looked at him and he shrugged. She stared back at him. He gave a wry smile and a weak Black Power salute with his fist. And he saw Jamila smile faintly in return.

Suddenly, she stood up and snatched the microphone for one last time, surprising the self-appointed spokesperson currently holding it. Even with the microphone, it was almost impossible to be heard. Everyone was yelling at everyone else in English, Sylheti and a number of other languages. But she threw out a hand in her most Martin Luther King manner, pointed across the room to Jason Crowthorne and called, 'That is the man. That is the man. That is the man who knows about the missing tape.'

This was dreadful. Why was she doing this? What did she want from him? Was this her revenge? At first her words were lost in the din, so she repeated them and repeated them, and slowly people began to hear and turn and point to Jason. He flinched, and looked round anxiously for a way to escape, but there was none. He was surrounded.

Jamila waved her phone, showing an old message on it. 'He was the one who found the missing security tape. And the police arrested him for it...'

It took time for him to realise what she was actually saying. Like a beaten dog, he still tensed automatically, waiting for the next blow to fall, bent sideways under the cameras and lights. Jamila, however, was in full rhetorical flow.

'They tried to slur his name. But he was the one who wanted to help Liam. Jason Crowthorne. He wanted to make sure your voice was heard. He fought for the truth. He got your story into the newspapers and onto TV. There stands someone who decided to make something happen. There stands a hero. He's the one you should thank.'

More and more faces turned to Jason, hunched against the wall. Some wanted to shake him by the hand and some still wanted to throw chairs.

Jason, in turn, could see Andy Rockham starting to push his way through the crush but getting stuck, his face red with anger. Jason shook his head quickly, refused to allow himself to be praised and tried to slide away, but he was stuck there, forced to accept the plaudits.

Sadé and Royland watched from a short distance away. Royland stood up to go shake Jason's hand with the others. Now there was a thick crowd around the journalist, and Shahanuddin Shah was waving, trying to persuade everyone to sit down again – those who had chairs – but seats were being thrust aside in all directions. Royland started to push through and Sadé tried to pull him back. He brushed her hand away. 'How often do you know a hero, innit?'

She watched him shoulder his way into the crowd, and then she realised what she should do. She shouted, 'And that's the man who found the knife. He found the knife what stabbed the boy. Him.'

Suddenly everyone was looking at Royland. Royland stood still and Sadé said again, 'He's another local hero. Look at him. He went out and he found the knife and he could have said nothing. He could have just left it on the ground in the dark and walked on, but he didn't.'

Now everybody wanted to shake hands with Royland and Royland felt numb and confused, but if people wanted to shake him by the hand, that was OK by him. He saw the detective that interviewed him, Andy Rockham. He was staring suspiciously at him now and Royland tried not to look back.

Sadé pulled the last of the gym leaflets out of her rucksack. She held them up and said, 'This is the kind of person he is. People talk about working for the community. He goes and does it. With no help from no-one. No money from the council. This is your local gym.'

She started handing the leaflets round. She made sure she held them up in front of the TV cameras and she gave one to anyone who looked like they were a journalist.

Then she said, 'And we want to help, so we've got a special offer on for local kids right now.'

Royland looked at her in surprise and started to say something and she gave him a look like thunder and he shut up. He never knew what she was going to say next, and he'd never known anyone like her before. It was true love. He'd never love another...

Next, Jamila looked down, still clutching the microphone, and at the front was Suzen, watching her and waiting. This confused her. What was she waiting for?

Then she realised. She pulled her green sari around her and called for attention again. She said, 'All these heroes and what are the police doing? What's the council doing? Are they leaving it all to you? Or are they going to join you, and keep open the police stations, give us more CCTV cameras pointing where they can help us, more money for youth work and gyms like this man's?'

'And more litter bins,' shouted a woman from the crowd.

'If you want,' said Jamila, feeling inclusive. She turned to the borough commander and the council cabinet member.

'I don't know about the finances of all that,' said Nigel Ponting, hedging. His face was a furious white.

Jamila pulled her phone from her handbag once more and tapped the screen three times. 'OK, I have the personal number of the director of finance, let's ask him about the finances of that? Let's ask him now if you can't afford to protect the people of this borough from gangs, muggers and thugs?'

She held the phone aloft, hoping no-one would hear it connecting directly to Dim Sum To Go.

'And more litter bins,' called the voice hopefully.

David Slocombe cracked first. He had the wisdom to know when to look at how the wind was blowing, a wisdom that had blown him to chief superintendent and could yet blow him all the way to the commissioner's personal office in Scotland Yard. That wisdom didn't fail him now. He stood up tall, announced that he would personally fund an extra squad of constables and a sergeant just for this ward, and asked Ponting if the council would match that.

While the applause was still dying away, Nigel Ponting brushed aside the offer of Jamila's phone call to Dim Sum To Go and stood next to the borough commander. He was delighted to be happy to be pleased to confirm that he would find a way to ask the council ruling group to recommend whether to discuss whether to propose a feasibility study as to the possibility of seeing if they could perhaps vote extra money for the police for more officers and maybe keeping stations open, plus (he drew breath) new security cameras. And (he caught Jamila's eye) he would personally oversee the likelihood of potential aid to local community sports and arts initiatives including...

He faltered over the name, as he hated being specific... including... and then finally he spat it out as if he'd been forced to swallow something rather bitter... including All Roads Lead to Royland.

'And more litter bins!' floated up from below.

'And we'll certainly look into more litter bins too,' said Ponting.

'When?' asked Jamila.

'I can't put a precise time-frame—'

But Jamila knew that commitments without dates meant nothing and so did he. 'When?' she asked again.

Until he also finally cracked and committed to a ball-park rough maximum time for the CCTV of three to six months, subject to careful consideration and review depending on budgetary constraints and—

'And All Roads Lead to Royland? You can meet the owner to find out what he needs,' said Jamila.

'Of course.'

'First thing tomorrow.'

'First thing tomorrow,' said the committee member for community safety, detesting the words even as they emerged.

There, the commitment had been made and recorded in reporters' notebooks and by the TV cameras and radio microphones. Nigel Ponting did his best to smile warmly as if this was what he'd been intending all along and David Slocombe stood tall and broad-shouldered and exuded all the authority of one who was damn sure he wasn't going to reveal the extent of his defeat.

Jamila expressed her gratitude that these two men had listened to sense and to her constituents, and added that if she was re-elected she would make certain the council kept to all the agreed deadlines...

Royland kept shaking hands and being hailed a hero.

Sadé received fourteen new subscriptions for the gym and the names of three local groups who wanted to discuss bookings.

Jason shook so many hands himself that he forgot he was no longer a journalist. Moving closer to Royland, he misremembered sufficiently to ask if he was interested in giving an exclusive interview about his heroic act. He had, as it happened, a blank confidentiality form in his pocket.

Royland said thank you, but he didn't feel it right to exploit his position and anyway he didn't trust journalists.

And Sadé said thank you, but in the last five minutes she'd already received offers from five national papers that Royland was going to be considering very seriously indeed.

And somehow her heel came down, entirely accidentally, on Royland's big toe.

56

Anniversary

As the meeting broke up into fragments and huddles, Golam Kamal expected trouble from those who felt they'd lost. However, it appeared everyone had decided they'd won. They tweeted and emailed and texted and even talked to each other as they milled around. Those who'd wanted to have their say felt they'd made their point; while those who hadn't wanted the others to have their say felt they'd effectively impeded, deflected and rebutted them. And those who liked breaking heads felt that their afternoon's work in the streets had contributed importantly to the outcome. Everyone, from sixty-four-year-old Salma Chowdhury to twenty-something Neil Gunthorpe, regarded it as indisputably right and proper that the police and council had been forced to spend more money, whatever it was to be spent on. Everyone – black, white, brown and the other fifty-eight shades – welcomed the advent of more cameras that would show clearly what others were up to and stop them doing it.

They even celebrated the fact that there would be more money for gyms and other activities for kids – the enthusiasm being all the greater, it seemed to Golam, because relatively few actually visited gyms or were currently kids.

As they stood together surveying the emptying hall, tipped-over chairs, crumpled papers and snack wrappings, Shahanuddin Shah (solicitor) announced that he was pleased to have presided over a memorable meeting. Golam for his part was pleased that the centre was still standing, and that his chairperson hadn't said anything they'd all regret.

Chief Superintendent Slocombe shook hands with Cabinet Member Ponting. They wished each other well and then they shook hands with Jamila Hasan and wished her well. They were professionals. You won some, you lost some – and other phrases people used to pretend they were happy even though they'd been ambushed. They wished each other the good luck they'd have hated the other actually to have.

Jamila met up with Suzen and they agreed to go for a coffee to talk about Jamila's campaign future and other matters. On their way out of the hall, Jamila called the deputy opposition leader to tell her what had been achieved and was too high on the buzz of it all to even care about the way the deputy patronised her.

Andy Rockham checked his watch and looked at Dana Bookman. It was almost time for him to clock onto his regular shift. He'd stacked up sixteen hours of overtime, and he felt more like going to sleep, but instead he drove Dana to the crime scene. It was just over twenty-four hours after the stabbing – the anniversary, as he'd been taught to call it. It was one of those things he'd been trained to do: to check out the scene around the time the crime had taken place. At the anniversary, you never knew what you might learn.

So it was that, a little over an hour and a day after the boy was attacked, they sat in the unmarked car and stared at the little square under the implacable orange street lights. The latest showers had passed for the moment and the evening was turning chilly. Dana looked as good, on no sleep, as she had the night before and her perfume smelled as fresh. He wondered how she managed. How did she find time to wash and respray? Life was so different for women.

'You must be tired,' he said.

'Not very.'

'If I've been a bit weird, it's because I hardly got any sleep this morning. What with Duane, and then the phone call. And working non-stop since I got back in.'

'Don't worry about it,' she said after a moment of silence, during which she regarded the dashboard and then her nails. 'And you haven't been weird.'

'Thank you,' he said.

He looked at her and her perfume was all around him. The moment had come. He was just clearing his throat when the duty sergeant drove up. He joined them without fuss in the back seat of the general-purpose car along with one of the other DCs. Andy nodded silently to them and went back to watching the empty scene.

The duty sergeant picked at his fingernails. The other detective constable was a dumpy man with a hook nose and an unnaturally cheerful demeanour who hummed a tune without realising it. Dana Bookman stared straight ahead. An elderly couple crossed the road to examine the large damp pile of flowers that now surrounded the cashpoint, and a middle-aged white woman in a blue bobble-hat hung a bunch of home-grown primulas on a parking meter. She stood a minute, facing the square as if in prayer, and then wandered off.

'Two goals in the last three minutes,' said the other DC, checking his phone.

'Fucking typical,' said the duty sergeant. 'Every bloody time.'

'The refs hold on till they score. They always do for them. Seven minutes of injury time. Would you credit it?'

They lapsed into silence again.

'You think we've caught the scrotes that did this?' asked the duty sergeant suddenly, thinking of all the Bengali and white kids in the cells.

'Maybe. Maybe not.'

'There's talk that Area's going to take over the case. With all the publicity there's been. Throw everything they've got at it. There's a Gold Group meeting in the morning.'

'They'll arrest some more, then.'

Andy contemplated the pile of bouquets without speaking. The security pictures had shown two kids in hoodies, one tall, one short. No faces, no other distinguishing features, nothing. They took Katrina's card and Liam's phone and stuck a knife into him, maybe from panic and fear, maybe because Liam Glass tried to fight back. Also from fear. Fear, it was always fear. All that changed was what you were afraid of.

The other two climbed back into their car and drove off. Andy sat a few minutes longer with Dana and her perfume beside him. But the moment had gone.

He said he was going to check out something and dropped her back at the station to catch up on some paperwork. But then he drove all the way home.

He sat in the unmarked car outside his house in Pinner and rolled a joint from the weed he'd found in Jason's rucksack. He lit it and took a puff. It wasn't bad. He watched Cheryl through the front-room window. She walked in and turned the light on and tidied the chairs. Then he phoned her and said he was in the CID office, and he'd be on until the usual time in the morning. She was talking to him on the phone, not knowing he was outside watching. Duane was asleep, she said, dusting a table as she talked, and she'd been worried that the phone would wake him up, but it hadn't.

After he rang off, he sat and watched her tidy away her magazines and straighten the cushions. Then she turned the light off and the window went black. And he wondered what *he* was afraid of.

Then he turned the car round and drove back to work.

Like many an addict who has resolved fervently to change, by the end of the meeting Jason was tempted to slip back. He found himself pushing through the crowd to tap the panellists for an exclusive quote. Old instincts still twitched. The chicken still ran around, even though its head had been cut off. But cut off it had been.

It didn't help that some of the locals, as they passed him on their way out, praised him for having stood up for truth and justice. He nodded graciously and reminded himself of his new journalism-free future. He sidled up to Sadé again, standing outside in Evelyn Street next to the disgruntled line of riot police, and congratulated her on having gained the interest of the nationals.

'Stage time is wealth time,' said Sadé. 'A good businessman is a good publicist. Your network is your net-worth. Stuff like that.'

If frequent repetition was the way to transmit wisdom, Royland had been a good teacher.

'A word of warning,' said Jason generously. 'Don't get pegged to just one outlet. It's important to spread your message wide. I could help.'

'Which paper are you writing for now?' she asked. 'The Herald? The Post?'

'Oh, neither of those. I'm moving into PR. I'm looking forward to it. A new challenge.'

Sadé nodded as she waited for Royland, who was at that minute standing by the front steps, chin raised, waiting to see if anyone else wanted to meet and greet.

'You don't have any celebrity gym members, do you? Royland didn't once trial for a football team, did he? I could build something on that for you. It all helps.'

She shook her head.

Jason drove to the crime scene in time to see a police car speed off, followed shortly by an unmarked car driven by Andy Rockham. Andy turned as he reached Jason's Renault and seemed to look straight through him. The woman constable was in the passenger seat, staring grimly ahead. Jason thought Andy might have noticed him, but the detective accelerated noisily away.

He walked over to the square. He didn't know why he'd decided to come here. He had no deadlines to meet, no story to file. The car ticked quietly behind him as it cooled and the ground smelled damp. It was turning decidedly colder, so he zipped his coat up to his chin. His phone buzzed with a message from his PR friend, Mike, but he ignored it for the moment. Contemplating the bloodstains still faintly visible under the cashpoint and the piles of flowers in their sodden cellophane wraps, Jason had the strange vision that they were all – him, Andy, Liam – simply collections of cells, just like the clumps of weeds and the spindly tree on the other side. Growing and dividing, trying to protect themselves and procreate. It might have been a depressing thought, but to his surprise Jason didn't find it so. He found the idea real – and strangely warming. Instead of constant fear, he felt relaxed and... He searched for the precise words as he always did, as he'd been trained to do. He felt he was seeing the world clearly. Each part knew its place. He felt Right. At Ease... He felt... Rooted.

He had no job, no income, no partner, and yet he felt rooted. It was a delusion, no doubt, but as delusions went, it was at least temporarily pleasant.

He was starting to think about going home when another car stopped. A black Honda hatchback. Nobody got out. After a minute he walked over.

'Hello, Katrina,' he said.

She stared at him without moving.

'How's Liam?' he asked. 'How was the operation?'

'I had a call from the doctors, just now,' she said, winding down the side window. 'They've taken something out and repaired something else, but he's still not waking up, they said. They don't know why not.' She spoke very calmly, in a flat, muffled tone that worried Jason more than if she'd burst into tears.

'I'm sorry,' he said once more, with difficulty. Apologising was not something he'd been trained to do. Maybe it would be good practice for working in PR. 'I didn't want to hurt you or Liam. I don't know how it all went so wrong. I fucked up.'

He fumbled his way through some more words and Katrina listened patiently, as if it was a chore she'd been ordered to take on. Then when he started to repeat himself, she interrupted.

'I need your help.'

'I'll do anything...'

'Get in.'

Jason opened the passenger door uncertainly and she gestured him in with impatience and told him to fasten his seatbelt.

'What...?' he began. Hardly had he turned to look for the buckle than the car pulled out fast and he was jerked back in his seat. 'Where...?'

She talked over him again, but what she said didn't

make a lot of sense. She knew what she had to do. It was connected in some way to Liam. And Jason could help her do it. Whatever that was.

'I'm not going to be in newspapers anymore,' he said as the council blocks and shops zipped by. It was strange hearing the words again from his own mouth. Frightening, even, as if repeating the words made his decision more and more real. 'Public relations. Some people think it's selling out, but it's really just journalism by another name.' He didn't know why he felt the urge to justify himself to her. 'Is that speedometer saying what I think it is?'

The tyres were squealing now as she cornered.

'Katrina, I'd feel more comfortable if—'

'It's what I have to do.' She changed gear with a fearful grinding sound. 'Liam told me, didn't he? Shout out if you see them.'

It gradually dawned on Jason that they were driving in a pattern, turning left three times then right, criss-crossing the darkened area as if on a search.

'Katrina, Liam didn't say anything.'

'He told me. He told me it had to be done to make everything right.'

'It wasn't Liam,' Jason said with increasing urgency. 'Listen to me.'

She took another left turn, bumping over the kerb, and passed the square with the flowers once more. She missed out two roads and turned right at the third.

'Like, it's all about justice, isn't it?' she said suddenly. 'Justice and fairness. Balance. Making things right.'

'I don't understand,' said Jason. Then unexpectedly he found himself projected forwards into his seatbelt as the car skidded to a halt.

She was staring straight ahead, breathing heavily. He

followed her gaze: two teenagers at the far end of the road, larking around, throwing things at each other playfully, old crisp packets and crumpled cans. They were Bengalis as far as he could tell and wore hoodies. One was tall and round-shouldered and the other was shorter and more straight-backed and they shouted and whooped and then went quiet for a moment, then shouted again.

'If we make things right, he'll wake up,' Katrina said.

'How do you mean, make things right?'

'Balanced. I told you.' She was starting to sound annoyed at how slow he was. 'Justice.'

She'd stalled the engine, so started it again, over-revving the accelerator with a harsh roar.

'I saw them in the street when I was looking for Liam.'

'These two?' He squinted at them and tried to compare them to the grey/black blurs he remembered from the security camera. 'You think it's them?'

'Liam told me.'

Jason felt that old pulse beat again. If only he was still a journalist. He felt in his pocket for his digital camera.

But instead he took out his phone. 'We should call the police. It's not our job—'

She grabbed the phone out of his hand and tossed it out of the window.

'What the fuck?' he said.

'Make sure you put this in the paper.' She was revving the car again like she was about to start a Grand Prix.

The two teenagers were so out of it, they hadn't noticed. They'd moved a few metres further, to a shop parking bay. The tall one was pretending to play air guitar and laughing.

'You saw their pictures.'

'I can't tell. You can't be sure from the CCTV. It's all—'

Without warning, Katrina jammed the car into gear and accelerated. Jason was pushed back in his seat.

'No, Katrina!' he shouted.

The two boys turned and watched the Honda racing up the street towards them, staring gormlessly, as if they'd not seen anything like it before. They didn't move until it was almost on top of them. Then they leapt aside.

Jason looked back. They were laughing, flipping the bird and shouting, 'Losers.'

Katrina hit the brakes hard with a horrible scream of rubber. He could smell it, hot and burnt, like an incinerator. She flung the car round with determination.

The two teenagers mocked them and made ugly gestures, then turned their backs, dropped their jeans and mooned.

'You can't do this.'

'What do you fucking care? It'll make a great story.'

She was right. He instinctively lifted his camera to take a picture of the boys.

But then he realised that Katrina wasn't the only one who could make a moral stand. Jason finally discovered his conscience. He had reached the end of his ethical tether. He'd found a line he wouldn't cross. And he turned the camera off.

She looked across at him for the first time since they'd started driving round. Put the Honda into first gear and accelerated again.

'Stop this.' He grabbed the wheel and pulled it to the left.

She hit him on the ear with her elbow. It was

surprisingly painful. He let go in shock. She yanked the wheel back. He wrestled with her. The car hopped and swerved like a drunk duck, smashed into a bollard, bumped the kerb and stopped.

They were yelling at each other like an old married couple. Katrina started the engine once more. She jerked into reverse and Jason pulled on the handbrake. Katrina punched him in the eye. The car bounced across the road, hit a parked car, skidded back on the rebound and slammed into a post-box.

The boys jeered. Jason tried to snatch the keys and she beat him off.

In the last twenty-four hours, he'd been thrown into a wall, sacked, reinstated, sacked again, attacked with bricks, punched in the nose, thrown into jail, sacked once more, elbowed in the ear and hit in the eye. He'd gone without sleep, had hardly eaten and it all hurt...

He finally let go. Totally and utterly let go. Of his hopes and his fears, of everything he loved and hated. He opened the car door.

Katrina swore at him.

'You're mad,' he said. 'Totally fucking mad.'

'No,' she said. 'Everyone else is mad. You're mad. You don't think about the balance.'

He got out to find the two kids. They had to save themselves. Thankfully, they'd run off. He took a deep breath, then they reappeared at the far end of the street, next to a locked-up mini supermarket, laughing.

He yelled at them furiously to get the hell out of there, and they just gestured and laughed some more and invited him to come and make them if he felt big enough.

He ran towards them, waving them away, but they simply stood making obscene signs.

He heard Katrina's car start behind him.

He turned with his hands up. Blocking her way. Shouted, 'Stop.'

The front bumper hit him first – square on the legs. He went down with a crack to his forehead on the roadway. The Honda reversed and came at him again, lights blazing. He tried to crawl to the kerb. The car struck him on the left side and he felt an arm snap and a rib collapse with an unpleasant crunch.

It was like he was separate. Inside. Watching. Making notes. He braced himself, curled up on the ground like a baby, trying to protect himself with his unbroken arm. He didn't want to move. He just wanted it to stop. Katrina reversed again and accelerated at him and another rib smashed.

He could hear the car reversing and returning and hitting something else, as if it was a long way away. And then it left.

He had no strength to do anything anymore. He could smell the damp on the paving stones by his head. And taste grit in his mouth. He lay half in, half out of the gutter and it was hard and still wet from the earlier rain, or perhaps it was dew. It was cold. It felt like it might turn to frost later, but even that feeling seemed very distant and increasingly numb.

He looked down the street and all he could see was emptiness. There was no shouting. No-one came. So he turned his eyes, to gaze up at the stars.

Only there were no stars either, just the winking red lights of a plane, passing high overhead and disappearing, fading slowly into the darkness of the night.

57

Final Call

The returning rain spattered the high, wide windows of the newsroom, blurring the bright jewelled lights of the City below. Lyle should have left work almost four hours ago, but he'd stayed on. Partly to tidy up the mess. Partly because there were new stories to follow on his computer's PA feed. It was quiet now around Gordon Road, but rumours had been circulating of possible copycat riots in Bradford, Northampton and, for some strange reason, Weston-super-Mare. Sadly, however, the eagerly anticipated violence had so far culminated in little more than a fistfight between a part-time electrician and a parking attendant outside a mosque in Coventry. And that, he suspected, had been set up by the local freelancer.

Then there was Paddy. The editor had been in a foul mood since the whole Glass story blew up in their faces and had prowled the office looking for someone to blame before she flew to Russia to spend a day with the president in his dacha. Lyle was pretty sure he wasn't at fault. But he'd personally taken the decision to reallocate staff and had committed the Post's money, even though he'd reneged on most it. The owner wanted to know what the fuck was going on and had bent Paddy's ear for an hour on the phone from Dubai, where he was in a conference with arms dealers, oil tycoons and members of the World Bank. So Lyle thought it politic to show commitment with a touch of unpaid overtime. In turn, he made it clear to Zoe Sharpleside that she was expected to do the same.

Anyway, Paddy had come out of her office after the call looking like she was hungry for raw antelope. One suggestion was to hire a private firm to dig dirt on Katrina Glass. Lyle leant instead towards a front-page splash outing Weaverall as gay. But that would mean Tony Potts would cut them off from his celebrity clients for at least a year.

One chief constable and a senior politician from each of the main parties were kept on large retainers for ghost-written columns. So after Paddy left, Lyle put in calls to see if the police could find something to arrest Katrina for, or at least to have her smeared in the House. Meanwhile, he looked for something positive to distract himself with and found the previous night's story about a spillage from a nuclear power station. They'd spiked it because of a super-injunction, but he decided to print it anyway. Sod them all. Let them sue.

Now he wandered over to Zoe's workstation and looked over her shoulder. She'd been writing up a story that had come in from a local paper. Schoolchildren dressing as hippos for charity.

'Anything?' she said.

'Total peace. Apart from the traffic warden in Coventry. Apparently his nose can be fixed. Paddy's going for "The Lull Before the Storm".'

'"Local Communities Paralysed With Fear".'

'Something like that.' Lyle felt dreadfully tired. 'I like the hippos. A heart-warming symbol of humanity's charitable side.'

She nodded.

'What really happened?' He pushed a pile of day-old papers out of the way and perched next to her.

'The hippo kids?'

'No, the Glass woman. Why did she blow it like that? She's all set to take our cheque and then suddenly she confesses she's been lying all along. We'd have been just as happy with Swinson from the start. So what was all that about?'

'No idea.' Zoe turned quickly back to her computer and found something terribly important to concentrate on. 'Ordinary people are strange beings. I think they're a different species.'

'She'd have been rich, Zoe. A Lottery win.'

'People don't always do what's in their own interests.' She punched a few keys as if they owed her.

He walked across to Tom Dalgleish to hand over for the night. The night news editor was glaring at his screen as if it had personally insulted him.

'Quiet night after all, Tom.'

Dalgleish made an incomprehensible Scottish sound constructed from a collection of vowels with no noticeable consonants. Lyle informed him he was officially going home. However, he didn't move.

He scanned the wires, but none of the breaking stories filled him with hope. There were items about the election, but still nobody seemed to care for either side. The sports desk had been preparing an over-excited piece about how dreadful one of the top Premiership sides was, until they'd managed to win in the last minute of injury time. Now they were extolling their undying quality. It was all very uninspiring.

'Shame about the Glass story,' Tom said finally. 'I was looking forward tae a nice campaign about knife crime. That local guy was right. It's time we did something serious on those lines. We've had some strong campaigns in the past.'

He rested his foot on a revolving chair and they

reminisced for a few minutes about the good campaigns they'd run – obesity and body image, postcode health, MPs for sale, rip-off trains, graduates who couldn't spell.

'Good ones, aye,' said Tom.

'We should do some more.'

Then Tom said it was time for his cappuccino and Lyle went back to his own seat to get his all-weather coat. He stopped for a moment as he pulled it on, gazed at the quietly industrious office and mused for a moment on the future. Would Zoe Sharpleside have a job in ten years' time? Would he? People talked about the internet, but nobody knew. Sales dropped and yet somehow newspapers struggled on. There was talk of an enquiry about phone hacking, but he doubted it would come to anything. These things never did. In his experience, most things just went on as they were without dramatic visible change. Like a tree slowly rotting from the inside.

Katrina drove slowly back to the hospital, parked her car on a single yellow and wiped smears of blood from off of the front bumper and radiator grille.

Liam-baby. Soon, baby. Soon.

She'd done it, just what Liam had asked. And she knew he'd wake up now. Would probably have already woken. But she took a moment to enjoy the feeling before going up to the ward. Meanwhile, she looked around and remembered meeting Ruby outside so many hours ago. She felt sad for her new friend, so she went and asked the black man on reception to phone and ask how her biker boyfriend was.

Very soon, L-i-i-i-am.

There were no reporters, no visitors. It was as quiet as the night before. All the lights shining down on empty seats. The night receptionist put down the mobile he'd been writing a text on, and he didn't exactly rush. Then he looked up the number of the ward in a ring-file and muttered a few words into his desk phone. He handed her the receiver.

'Motorcyclist?' a voice went.

'The man who came in last night,' Katrina said, all patiently. 'With the girlfriend in leather gear. He got knocked down by a truck.' There was a long pause and Katrina felt bad.

'Is you a relation?'

'I'm like a close family friend of the girl. She's got a brother. Marko. With a k.'

The voice went and came back. 'He's woken up and is doing fine.'

She bought herself a cup of coffee from the machine to literally celebrate, and went outside and lit a cigarette and smoked it under the awning on the ramp where the cars and ambulances came in. She thought about what Liam would say when he saw her again in a few minutes.

Upstairs, Katrina smiled to the Filipina nurse on duty at the desk. She was surprised when the nurse looked nervous and said the doctor wanted to see her. She shrugged and went in to see Liam, still smiling.

He was lying just how he was before. There was a new crêpe bandage round his head. His eyes were gently closed like they might open any minute, but they didn't. The lights flickered and blinked, red and green. Katrina sat and parked her handbag and thought about it.

'Tell me,' she said to Liam. 'I did what you wanted. What else is there? Tell me what to do now.'

But this time Liam stayed silent. Footsteps paddled up to the door, then went past and away. She could smell the antiseptic, sharp and fresh, and hear the soft murmuring of voices.

She stared at her son and then she knew. Cause and effect. For every cause there was an effect. For every effect there was a cause. Everyone literally knew that. You just had to find out what was necessary. And now she knew.

She'd give up smoking. That would be it. That would be what Liam wanted. Once she gave up smoking, Liam would wake up. That's what she would do.

She sat and laid her hands comfortably in her lap, and as she did so, even as she confirmed her decision to herself, it happened. A flicker of an eye. Almost too small to be seen. Only a mother could have seen it.

But she had. She was certain. She'd sit there and keep watching before telling the nursing staff, just wait one more minute, just to be sure.

Jason stared into the darkness. He felt no pain for a few moments and then he did. It stabbed into his side, it tore his head apart, like it personally wanted to make him suffer. He'd never felt anything like it. He took a deep breath of night air and that hurt his chest even more.

Cold spits of rain fell on his face. Some metres away there was a mound of clothes that might have been one of the two Bengali hoodies. It wasn't moving. The second Bengali was nowhere to be seen. Jason lay with his head against the hard, damp edge of the kerb for five minutes, trying to pluck up the courage to face the pain, and then he called out as best he could. And immediately clutched his side in agony. He tried to shift his position but stopped and found himself coughing blood. It felt like a rib might have punctured a lung.

The street was still empty. The nearest buildings were shuttered shops and lock-ups. It could be hours before someone came down here.

He called again, more a croak than a call, and this time he heard the teenager groan. Jason lifted his head slightly.

'Are you OK?'

'Whad'ya think, man.'

The kid was lying on his side, one arm flung out like he was swimming. Bea used to sleep like that in her cot. Jason would stand over her, listening to her soft breathing, thinking there was nothing more wonderful in the world than to have someone who depended on you. Or more scary. Now, he wanted above all to live for her sake. To see her. Not to have to prove anything to her. Just to be with her. Life could really be so simple if you let it. All that time he'd wasted.

'I can' see my phone,' called the boy now. 'Can ya phone an ambulance, eh?'

'Where's your friend?'

'Dunno. He's not really a friend, eh.'

'Evidently.'

'He run away. Good on him, yeah. Every man for himself.'

The spitting rain was turning into a heavier drizzle. It fell like bars straight from the sky. Jason's own mobile lay at the far end of the road where Katrina had thrown it, but he could see something black, close by in the gutter. He couldn't move his legs anymore, so he used his arms to drag himself towards it, growing wetter. It was excruciatingly hard. Slowly he reached out and clutched the phone with numb fingers. He stared at the display. The phone's battery sign flashed red.

He found he'd been crying for some reason. He wiped the tears with his sleeve and they were mixed with blood. He touched the number nine and then stopped.

'Ambulance, man?' croaked the pile of clothes.

'Yeah,' said Jason, speaking with increasing difficulty. 'No worries. Trust me. I'm a journalist.'

After a long moment, he deleted the nine and painfully tapped in a different number. His ribs hurt, his head hurt, the night was growing colder and darker, and he could hardly see the mobile's screen anymore.

'Did you stab that kid?' he managed to say, finally.

'Jus' phone 999.'

'The headlines are written,' Jason said. 'Don't you want to tell your side of the story?'

The night news editor answered.

Jason gathered the last of his strength. 'Jason Crowthorne.'

He could just make out the gentle sound of the newsroom in the background, orderly and reassuring. There was a pause on the other end. 'Youse no supposed to be in shifting with us tonight?'

'Tom...' said Jason. It was like the pain vanished. 'I've got a new story for you.'

As he spoke, the rain stopped. And the moon came out, bright and silver, from behind the clouds high above. It was the most beautiful sight.

— O —

Acknowledgements

This novel would have been impossible without the help of many people and their insights from behind the scenes. Some put their jobs at risk sharing information and must therefore remain anonymous. Those I can name, with gratitude, include many at the Daily Mirror, The Daily Star, The Hampstead and Highgate Express and the Camden New Journal. In particular, I'd like to thank Nick Fullagar, Richard Wallace, Anthony Harwood, Barry Rabbetts, Jon Clements, Victoria Murphy, Kieron Saunders, Andy Wooding, Eric Gordon, Bridget Galton, Laura Evans, Lorraine King and Ben McPartland as well as Andy Gardner, Joshua Rozenberg, Danielle Wrate, Mukid Choudhury of the Bengali Workers Association, DCI Dave Little, DI Carol Andrews (CBE), Inspector Paddy O'Leary, ex-Camden Councillors Linda Chung, Adrian Oliver, Maya de Souza and James King; Judy Spector, Dr Stuart Wolfman, Mary Murphy, consultant neurosurgeon, and Peter Dalton of the London Ambulance Service.

Jan Woolf, Eve Richings and Charlie Hopkinson went, as ever, beyond the call of duty with their feedback on the manuscript. And I am enormously grateful to Lindsay Clarke for his unique combination of experience and inspiration, as well as Pam White and Linda MacFadyen, for their help with the publishing industry; and Bryony Hall of the Society of Authors and Richard Moxon for their legal advice.

Thank you to Lucy Ridout for her brilliant editing, to

John Goldsmith and to Mark Turner of Marble City for believing in this book and making it a physical and electronic reality.

And finally my wife, Elaine, who has lived through its creation and many other dramas.

The bits that I got right are largely thanks to the people above. The bits I got wrong, I managed to do all by myself.

If you enjoyed *The Breaking of Liam Glass* then please share your reflections by posting a review online. It really does make a difference. Marble City Publishing would be delighted to hear from you direct at admin@marblecitypublishing.com.

You can also read Charles' blog at www.charles-harris.co.uk and on the same site you can join his mailing list for articles about his writing, short stories, previews of his next novels and news of appearances and events.

Charles Harris is on Twitter at @chasharris and on Facebook at charlesharris008.

Thank you.

Marble City Publishing

Printed in Poland
by Amazon Fulfillment
Poland Sp. z o.o., Wrocław

57452355R00249